Hanging on to the tab... the other to Noah. She was a little bewildered when he just stared at it without taking it. Then shock waves pulsed through her when he took her hand and stood beside her.

Drawing her to his side, he tucked his arm around her waist, his big hand resting just below her breast. Samara leaned against him with a sigh of sheer, unadulterated, pleasure-filled relief. His body, hard, warm, and reassuringly masculine, felt delicious.

As he guided her between tables, she barely noticed the amused and curious faces they passed. If she'd been more sober and aware, she might have been embarrassed to be almost carried through the restaurant. Instead she felt only abject relief that they were leaving as the incredible anticipation for what was about to happen mounted.

Noah led her outside and a taxi appeared before them. He nudged her into the backseat and then slid in beside her. His arm came around her shoulders again. Groaning softly, Samara snuggled deeper under his arm and rubbed her face against his jacket. He smelled delicious . . . clean, masculine musk. A strong surge of heat flushed her body.

Closing her eyes, she was surprised to feel herself drifting off and blinked her heavy eyelids rapidly, not wanting to miss one second of this glorious feeling. Since staying awake was imperative, she decided that one of the best ways to do this was to kiss him. No way would she fall asleep with those delicious lips on hers. Cupping his cheek in her hand, she brought his head down to her level and pressed her mouth against his.

ALSO BY CHRISTY REECE

Rescue Me

RETURN TO ME

A NOVEL

CHRISTY REECE

BALLANTINE BOOKS • NEW YORK

Return to Me is a work of fiction. Names, characters, places, and incidents are the products of the author's imagination or are used fictitiously. Any resemblance to actual events, locales, or persons, living or dead, is entirely coincidental.

A Ballantine Books Mass Market Original

Copyright © 2009 by Christy Reece
Excerpt from *Run to Me* copyright © 2009 by Christy Reece

All rights reserved.

Published in the United States by Ballantine Books, an imprint of The Random House Publishing Group, a division of Random House, Inc., New York.

BALLANTINE and colophon are registered trademarks of Random House, Inc.

This book contains an excerpt from the forthcoming book *Run to Me* by Christy Reece. This excerpt has been set for this edition only and may not reflect the final content of the forthcoming edition.

ISBN 978-0-345-50543-9

Cover design and illustration: Tony Greco

Printed in the United States of America

www.ballantinebooks.com

OPM 9 8 7 6 5 4 3 2 1

To Jim, for believing in me and loving me

prologue

Lexington, Kentucky

"Hey, it's Manda," the voice whispered. "Did he call?"

"No . . . hold on." Ashley Mason padded to her bedroom door and eased it shut. Turning, she perched on the edge of the bed. "He just IM'd me. I'm meeting him tomorrow night."

"Ohmigosh, where?"

"The Night Owl. He says he knows a guy who can get us in."

"Are you excited?"

"Nervous and excited. I can't believe I'm going out with the quarterback from Nelson."

"What're you going to tell your mom?"

"What we talked about . . . that I'm coming over to your house to study. She won't care. She's working late again anyway."

"What're you going to wear?"

"That green skirt and top I bought Saturday."

"You think he'll believe you about your age?"

"People are always telling me I look older than I am."

"Yeah, but you told him you were sixteen. You won't even be fourteen till December."

"He won't notice. He—"

"Damn. Ashley, I gotta go. My dad's coming up the stairs and I'm supposed to be asleep."

"Okay, see you tomorrow in class."

Closing her cellphone, Ashley fell back onto the bed as excited shock tingled inside her. She had a date with a junior, but not just any junior. The star quarterback at Nelson High School. Everyone knew him. And he wanted to go out with her.

She'd found him on a fluke. Out of boredom a couple of weeks ago, she'd been browsing a teen chat room and started up a conversation with QB1201. After chatting a few minutes, she asked him what his handle meant and that's when she'd learned he was the quarterback at Nelson High. She had played it cool, all the time absolutely thrilled to be talking to one of the most popular boys in the city.

Ryan Davidson was written up in the newspaper every week as doing something spectacular on the field the Friday night before. She'd seen his picture numerous times. He was tall, with blond, curly hair and dimples in both cheeks. Last weekend, when her mom had thrown the paper away, she'd pulled it out of the garbage and cut his picture out. She now had the beginnings of a photo album she was going to devote fully to Ryan.

Every night, after her mom went to bed, Ashley went online and spent hours chatting with him. Last night, when he'd asked her to meet him, she'd panicked and shut the computer down. Tonight, she'd just gotten online when he'd IM'd her, asking if she was mad.

This might be her only chance to actually date a hunk like Ryan Davidson. Reluctantly she agreed to meet him, positive she could make herself look sixteen. What she'd told Manda was true. People were constantly telling her she looked a lot older. She'd have no trouble convincing Ryan. Last week, she'd emailed him a picture taken a few months back. After he got it, he'd told her how pretty she was and hadn't said a word about her age. She knew she could pull this off.

With a sigh of pure pleasure, Ashley closed her eyes and imagined how Ryan would grin at her when they met. Just wait till all the kids heard about it at school. They'd be talking about her all year.

Excitement curled in her stomach, giving her a warm, cozy glow. Tomorrow she was going to meet her dream man.

one

Birmingham, Alabama

"I found the man I want to marry."

This announcement received mixed reactions from the three women sitting at the table with Samara Lyons. Rachel just rolled her eyes, Allie ignored the comment because of the cute guy at the bar making eyes at her, and Julie, the newest member of their Thursday night margarita-fest, leaned toward her eagerly.

"Where'd you meet him? What's his name? Have you been dating—"

"Wait . . . hold up," Rachel interrupted as she raised her hand to signal their server. "Let's call for another round and then Samara will explain to you. With your psychologist degree, you can tell us the name of Samara's mental illness."

Samara grinned and stuck her tongue out at her best friend since the first grade. Rachel, the cynic, as she fondly called her, didn't believe in "happily ever afters." Samara, on the other hand, knew they existed. She'd seen them firsthand. Having parents who'd been happily married for over thirty-five years, not to mention five very happy brothers and sisters-in-law, reinforced her beliefs.

Rachel referred to Samara as Pollyanna for what she called her amazing belief in the goodness of humanity when all evidence showed the exact opposite. Samara never argued with that statement, because it was true. She did believe in the basic goodness of people and so far, with only a few exceptions, she'd never been proven wrong.

"Okay, girl." Rachel took a sip of her frozen concoction, licked the salt from her mouth, and leaned forward. "Who is it this week?"

Being humored didn't bother Samara in the least. "Did you see that new foaming bath commercial where the husband runs a hot bubble bath for his wife and then takes the kids to the park while she has the house to herself?"

"Yeah, so?"

"He's the one."

Only Julie looked startled by this statement. "Do you know the man in the commercial?"

Looking satisfied with how the conversation was going, Rachel settled back into her chair with an amused, knowing expression.

"No, I don't know him. He's just the guy I'd like to marry."

"But why?"

Ignoring Rachel's smug grin, Samara attempted to explain her philosophy. "I have the ideal man in my head. I've just never met him. But sometimes, I'll see a guy on television or read about him and I recognize a certain characteristic I want in my future Mr. Right."

Julie nodded. "Actually, that's a very healthy attitude."

Rachel stared at Julie. "You gotta be kiddin' me. Don't encourage her lunacy. Heal it!"

"No, really. It is healthy." Julie waved a hand at the crowded bar in Mama Maria's. "Look at all these people, searching for that one special person they think they want to spend their life with, and most of them have no clue what they're looking for. At least Samara has a good idea what she does and doesn't want."

Taking a long, icy swallow of her drink, Samara couldn't help but be glad that at least someone thought knowing what she was looking for was a good idea. She also knew what she didn't want, having learned that the hard way. She took another sip, refusing to give the humiliating memory any more thought.

The sound of sizzling fajitas headed their way caught her attention. Her stomach rumbled with a welcoming growl as the spicy aroma hit her senses. Samara looked around in anticipation. Behind the waiter, to her left, her gaze was caught and held by the tall, looming figure in the corner. A man she'd gladly walk barefoot across the country to avoid. Her stomach backflipped and spiraled downward. What was he doing here? And why did he have the expression of a hungry tiger on his too-perfect face? He sure as hell hadn't looked that way the last time she'd seen him.

Refusing to acknowledge him, Samara turned away. There were a thousand reasons he might be here, none of them to do with her. He'd made it painfully clear he wanted nothing to do with her and she had every intention of showing him she felt the same way. Now, if only her pounding heart and adrenaline-drenched bloodstream would cooperate. Despite herself, she dared another peek. *Dammit, he was still staring.*

Noah McCall hadn't been able to keep his eyes off Samara since he'd walked into the bar. Some people glowed with purity and light. Samara did that more than most. His jaw clenched at the reason he was here. She already hated him, and he doubted his request for help would make her like him any more.

The decision to come here hadn't been easy. Coming anywhere close to the South always set up a burning in his gut that would take him days to dispel. The air was different here. Thick and warm, it had character, life. Sucking at you, pulling you down. The warm, cloying sweetness made him want to gag.

Noah threw off his disquiet and shut down the memories. This wasn't about him. Never would be again. This was about doing the right thing, no matter the cost.

Straightening from his slouch against the wall, he sauntered slowly toward the beauty glowering at him. More than aware it would rile her even more, he plastered on his most cocky smile. And Samara had enough reason to be angry for a lifetime. A year ago, he turned down the sweet, sexy offer of her beautiful body. He knew enough about human nature to know that kind of slight wasn't something one quickly recovered from.

Fiery sparks shot from ice-blue eyes, making them appear even more glacial. A genuine smile kicked up his lips. Feisty, spirited, and sexy as hell . . . Samara Lyons was just what he was looking for. Perfect for the job in every way.

"Hello, Samara."

Myriad emotions flashed across her expressive face, none of them friendly. *Good.* She would need that anger to fuel what he was going to ask of her. He'd channel the anger in the right direction. Until then, he'd just enjoy the show.

She did what he expected. After giving him a glare of pure loathing hatred, she turned her back on him. Her spine so stiff, it looked as though it would crack at the slightest touch. Testing the theory, his index finger lightly brushed the nape of her neck . . . a tender, fragrant spot his mouth watered to taste.

Jerking around, the glare grew hotter and Noah couldn't hold back his laugh.

"What do you want?" Her tone indicated that whatever it was, he shouldn't plan on getting it.

"I need to talk to you. Let's go."

"Excuse me? Just who the hell do you think you are?"

Ignoring the wide-eyed gazes of the three women sitting at the table with her, Noah leaned down and whispered in her ear, "I need you."

Samara jerked away from him and, starting at his feet, gave him a scathing full-bodied once-over. Bringing her gaze back to his face, her voice dripped with disdain, "I've got nothing you want."

Something tugged at his heart . . . the one he knew he didn't have. He'd hurt and humiliated this woman and she still stung a year later. If he had a conscience, he'd leave and find someone else. Since that didn't exist and he needed her cooperation, he did the next best thing. Saluting her with a small wave of his hand, he retreated into the shadows. Having others around when he talked with her wasn't optimum anyway. He'd allow her this small reprieve.

Samara watched Noah back away and disappear out the door. Fury and hurt waltzed like dancing buffaloes throughout her body. Why should seeing him again bother her? He meant nothing to her other than a humiliating moment she'd sworn had been erased from her memories. How dare he come and stir them up again. Noah McCall, devil-handsome and arrogant as sin, could piss her off faster than anyone she'd ever met.

"Good heavens, Sam," Rachel said. "You going to just sit there and stare into space or are you going to tell us who 'Mr. Tall, Dark, and Please-Jump-My-Bones Sexy' was?"

Samara dragged herself back from the dark memory and looked at the stupefied faces of her friends. "Just someone I'd rather forget."

"Forget a man who looks like that? No way." This from Allie, who'd even stopped flirting with the cute guy at the bar to weigh in on the sexiness of Noah McCall.

Samara gave an emphatic shake of her head. "Looks aren't everything."

Allie flashed a wicked grin. "No, but they sure don't hurt."

While the girls continued chatting, Samara retreated back to her thoughts. What could Noah want to talk to her about? The last time she saw him, she'd been lying on the bed with the room whirling around her. Noah had just carried her to bed, kissed her on her forehead, and walked out the door.

Samara had wished more than once that she'd either had too much to drink so she wouldn't remember her humiliation, or that she hadn't had anything to drink at all. Unfortunately she'd been sober enough to remember Noah's refusal and just drunk enough to have issued the invitation in the first place.

In Paris for the wedding, she thought she had accepted and resigned herself to the fact that the man she planned to marry, Jordan Montgomery, was in love with another woman. She told herself she was happy for them. Jordan and Eden had suffered enough and deserved every happiness. But that was before Eden walked in the room for the ceremony and Samara saw Jordan's face. The tiny crack in her heart became a gaping crevice. Never had she seen a more honest, naked look of adoration.

After the wedding, they'd all gone to a small restaurant to celebrate. Since she, Noah, and a friend of Eden's were the only guests, the party broke up quickly.

The happy couple headed to their honeymoon and Dr. Arnot, Eden's friend, said goodbye and left. Barely saying a word, Noah had disappeared abruptly, leaving Samara alone at the table.

The first time she met Noah, she'd been instantly attracted to him . . . until he opened his mouth. Within seconds, the man had her fuming. He'd been arrogant, cocky, and evasive and those were just his good characteristics. She'd gone to him for help and he'd practically laughed in her face.

Samara was used to people, especially men, being nice to her. At just a little over five feet tall, with a slight build, creamy magnolia complexion, and large, ice-blue eyes, most men tended to treat her as a fragile doll. It wasn't something she encouraged or took advantage of, just something she was accustomed to having. With five older brothers, she'd been taught how to take care of herself, but that didn't stop men from feeling as though they needed to protect her.

Noah McCall hadn't even acted as though he knew she was a woman. He'd refused to give her information on Eden for Jordan, laughed at her temper, and then had practically thrown her out of his office.

So why had she found herself sitting alone at the table, fantasizing about him? Were those broad shoulders really as strong as they looked? Was his short ebony hair as soft and silky as it seemed? Did his deliciously sensuous mouth taste of the wine they'd had with dinner?

Physically, Noah McCall was the most perfect-looking man she'd ever seen. Tall, muscular, with a swarthy complexion and the deepest, darkest brown eyes she could ever imagine. The kind of eyes a woman could lose her soul in, lose herself.

What happened next was inevitable, but also one of

the most painful experiences of her life. Why couldn't she forget? And now, how could she, when the cause of that pain had stood in front of her only minutes ago?

Samara took a gulp of her slushy margarita. She remembered everything as if it were just yesterday . . . overwhelming need, consuming heat, and then cold, frozen reality.

A year earlier
Paris, France

"Would mademoiselle care for more wine?"

Samara blinked up at the waiter, a little surprised he'd had to ask. Couldn't he recognize when a woman wanted to get rip-snorting drunk? She nodded emphatically, wondering vaguely why her neck felt so loose on her head.

"No, mademoiselle would not care for more wine."

The masculine, somewhat harsh voice disturbed her pleasant fog. She glared hazily up at Noah McCall. Or Beautiful Jerk, as she'd come to call him in her mind. He merely shot her a condescending, knowing look that rattled her down to her four-inch stiletto heels. Just who did he think he was?

"Mademoiselle would most certainly like another drink. Who do you think—"

A large, male hand covered the top of her glass to prevent the waiter from carrying out her wishes. Samara stared at that hand. Swarthy dark skin, slightly raised veins, and a scattering of ink-black hair. All in all, a very nice hand. Why didn't it belong to a nice man?

He pulled a chair close to hers and sat down beside her. "Come on, sweetheart. I think it's time for a long summer's nap for you. As tiny as you are, one more drink and I'll be picking you up off the floor."

Samara gave him the glare she'd practiced on her brothers, a little disappointed when he just grinned at her . . . just as her brothers often had. Well hell, she'd just lost one man and now this handsome hunk was treating her like his kid sister. For a woman who'd always been fairly confident in her powers of attracting men, her ego had taken some major bruising lately.

Needing to reassert herself as a sexy, desirable woman, Samara took the hand that had covered her wineglass and held it between her hands. She turned it over and ran her finger in a soft, zigzag movement down the inside of his palm.

The hand closed on her finger. Samara gasped and looked up at him, losing all breath. Desire, hot and potent, promising her endless hours of pulse-pounding pleasure, burned in his eyes. Then, as if a wave of cold water had hit him, the heat disappeared and cool arrogance returned.

Samara snatched her hand back and stood. The room blurred, spun, and then settled into a surreal, fuzzy setting. She grasped the table with her fingers, refusing to acknowledge that if someone so much as pushed her with a fingertip, she'd keel over.

A loud sigh drew her gaze back to the table. Noah's too-perfect mouth lifted into one of the sexiest smiles she'd ever seen. Knowledge hit her, causing another wave of dizziness. She wanted him. It was as simple and unadorned as that. The thought sobered her quickly. Could she do this? Actually have sex with a man she didn't like, when she was quite certain that if she knew him more, she'd like him even less? Her entire body throbbed with the answer . . . an unequivocal yes.

Hanging on to the table with one hand, Samara held out the other to Noah. She was a little bewildered when he just stared at it without taking it. Then shock waves pulsed through her when he took her hand and stood beside her.

Drawing her to his side, he tucked his arm around her waist, his big hand resting just below her breast. Samara leaned against him with a sigh of sheer, unadulterated, pleasure-filled relief. His body, hard, warm, and reassuringly masculine, felt delicious.

As he guided her between tables, she barely noticed the amused and curious faces they passed. If she'd been more sober and aware, she might have been embarrassed to be almost carried through the restaurant. Instead she felt only abject relief that they were leaving as the incredible anticipation for what was about to happen mounted.

Noah led her outside and a taxi appeared before them. He nudged her into the backseat and then slid in beside her. His arm came around her shoulders again. Groaning softly, Samara snuggled deeper under his arm and rubbed her face against his jacket. He smelled delicious . . . clean, masculine musk. A strong surge of heat flushed her body.

Closing her eyes, she was surprised to feel herself drifting off and blinked her heavy eyelids rapidly, not wanting to miss one second of this glorious feeling. Since staying awake was imperative, she decided that one of the best ways to do this was to kiss him. No way would she fall asleep with those delicious lips on hers. Cupping his cheek in her hand, she brought his head down to her level and pressed her mouth against his.

His lips . . . soft but firm, and incredibly arousing, tasted of the dark chocolate mousse he'd had for dessert. He allowed her to press little kisses against his mouth and then with what sounded like a soft curse, he turned her body, pressed her against the seat, and set his mouth on hers. *Heaven.* His mouth ate at her, moving ravenously, he swallowed her groan of arousal as she sank deeper into his arms. When his tongue teased at her lips, asking for entrance, Samara obliged.

With the first plunge of his tongue, any semblance of grogginess disappeared. He made love to her mouth. His tongue plunged, retreated, licked at her lips, and then plunged once more. Over, then over again. Never . . . ever . . . had she thought she could become aroused and close to orgasm by a kiss alone. *Dear, sweet heavens. This man knew how to kiss!*

The kiss ended as abruptly as it had started. One minute she was rounding a curve, the sun hot, glowing, heating her skin, headed straight to paradise, and the next second everything came to an abrupt, screeching stop.

She blinked her eyes open. Noah's hard midnight gaze burned into her like a laser, but she was gratified to hear him panting slightly.

"What's wrong?" Her voice was low, thick with arousal.

He jerked his head at the window. "We're here. Get out." The words were like chunks of ice and ground from him as if he had to dig them out with an ice pick.

Reality and embarrassment slammed down on her. Before she could respond, he tilted her chin with his finger and brought her gaze up to his. "Samara Lyons, you are a dangerous woman."

Taking her hand, he helped her out of the taxi. Stumbling a little in her heels, she held tightly to his hand as he pulled her toward the heavy glass doors of the hotel entrance.

Samara didn't know what to think. First he'd acted disgusted with her, then as turned on as any man could be. Then he turned cold and unemotional. Now he was acting like the overprotective brother again.

At least now, after all that, she was much more sober. Hell of it was, she still wanted him. The alcohol had loosened her inhibitions, but they hadn't made her want this man. If she were honest with herself, she'd admit she had wanted him from the first time she saw him.

Noah led her into a crowded elevator, his arm once again draped over her shoulder as if he were concerned she'd collapse at his feet. He thought she was still tipsy and she took advantage of that to lean into him. Had a man ever felt this wonderful against her body before?

When the elevator stopped, Noah maneuvered her around the people in front of them and led her down the narrow hallway. A curious thought hit her when he stopped at her hotel room door. Not once had she told him where she was staying, what floor she was on, and certainly not her room number. How had he known that?

Once inside the room, he closed the door and released her.

Samara turned toward him, wanting more than anything to wrap herself in his arms again and relive the magic she'd experienced much too briefly moments ago.

Without warning, Noah scooped her into his arms and carried her across the room. Thinking he meant to settle her on the bed and follow her down, Samara giggled at such an amorous gesture. Though he hadn't seemed the type, she appreciated the romanticism.

In an unceremonious and undignified move, he dumped her on the bed. Her body had barely stopped bouncing before he kissed her forehead and growled, "Watch how much you drink next time."

Stunned, she watched as he strode across the room. Her lips finally unfroze just as he opened the door. "Where are you going?"

Without looking at her, he snapped, "Home."

"But . . . but . . . why? I thought you wanted . . ."

Finally, he turned toward her and her heart shriveled. The cold smirk was back in place. "Have a good flight home." He walked out, shutting the door quietly behind him.

"Sam, are you going to eat your fajitas or just absorb them through osmosis?"

Jerking her head up, she blinked at Rachel. "What?"

She gestured at her plate. "You've been staring at your food for five minutes. Something wrong with it?"

She shook her head. "I'm just not as hungry as I thought."

Rachel knew a lie when she heard it. Her hand touched Samara's wrist. "You okay? Did 'Mr. Too Sexy for My Heart' upset you?"

A smile tickled her lips. . . . Her best friend could always lighten her mood. "He's a friend of Jordan's. Seeing him reminded me of some things I'd rather forget." Rachel didn't need to know that it wasn't remembering Jordan's marriage to another woman that upset her, but rather the gorgeous man who'd had the nerve to turn her down.

She also knew not to mention his name. Few people knew who Noah McCall was or what he looked like. Jordan and Eden had explained that no matter what, his identity should always be kept private. She had no problem with that, since she didn't even want to think about the jerk.

With almost no appetite, Samara forced herself to eat at least one fajita. Two margaritas in her system meant slightly tipsy for her. She needed something to counteract the alcohol. Though seeing Noah had sobered her up quite well. Funny how he seemed to be able to do that.

After driving through the apartment complex twice, Samara blew out an exasperated curse. She was going to have to park quite a distance away from her apartment entrance. She'd only been in Birmingham a couple of months. Since she hadn't known if she'd like living in the South, she had moved into an apartment. Now, having decided she did like it, she would soon start looking for a small house. She was already tired of living like a sardine. Having grown up in an oversized, rambling house, with a giant yard, several dogs and cats and assorted other animals her brothers were always finding, she missed the comfort of a private home.

Grateful for the well-lit lot, Samara grabbed her purse in one hand and her keys in the other. Almost to her building, she stopped abruptly and bent to adjust the strap on her shoe that had rubbed a blister on her heel. She adjusted the strap and straightened.

Hard, muscular arms wrapped around her, trapping her. A big body pressed against her. A hand covered her mouth, stifling an automatic scream. Her heart and adrenaline raced. Samara screamed muffled curses against the hand as her feet were swept off the pavement.

Legs dangling, she kicked back at the brute, trying for a shin or an even more vulnerable spot. The arms squeezed tighter. A new panic ensued. Was he going to crush the breath from her? Her arms pinned at her side, her legs swung uselessly. She wiggled and squirmed harder, determined this bastard wouldn't win.

Warm breath teased her ear as a familiar masculine voice growled, "Easy now. I'm not going to hurt you."

Tsunami-force fury rushed through her. *How dare he!*

two

With renewed effort, Samara began to fight in earnest. Before she'd been merely terrified. Now she was furious. The arms tightened around her and Samara knew he would either squeeze the breath out of her until she passed out or she exhausted herself. Neither one would give her what she wanted, which was an opportunity to punch the jerk holding her. With that delicious thought in mind, she went limp in his arms.

"Good girl. Now, let's go talk."

Samara didn't move. As long as he held her like this, all he had to do was tighten his arms and she'd be helpless again. She stayed limp and forced her breathing to slow, soften.

"Samara . . . you okay?" He shook her slightly and Samara barely restrained from grinning, anticipating the moment when the tables would be turned.

"Shit," he muttered, "you're so tiny. . . . I didn't think . . ."

With lightning quickness, he hefted her over his shoulder like a sack of grain and started running. Indignation made her want to yell. She forced herself to wait. As she bounced against his shoulder, several thoughts flashed through her mind. First, how could a man run full force with an adult on his shoulder and not even breathe hard? Where the hell was he taking her? Why the hell was he doing this? And then a sudden urgent thought as her stomach roiled. What was he going to do when her two margaritas, chips, salsa, and fajita ended up on his ass when she started throwing up?

Within a minute, Noah had reached her apartment door and the bastard actually opened it as if he had a key. The door opened and shut quickly, with Samara still hanging upside down like a bat. Gritting her teeth, she prepared to move. This had gone on long enough.

She allowed him to pull her off his shoulder. Before he could set her feet on the floor, she sprang into action and struck. Her right fist slammed into his eye. A left fist headed toward his stomach. He didn't stop the punch to his face, but a hard, firm hand grabbed her wrist, preventing her from dealing the gut punch.

Still holding her arm, he pushed her away. "Now that, sweetheart, was impressive." He sounded amused . . . maybe even a little bit pleased. The nerve!

Samara pulled away from him sharply, backed up, and then, like a small bull, lowered her head and targeted his stomach.

Hands grabbed her shoulders before she took half a step. And he laughed. "That's really cute, but not too smart. You could break your neck, coming at me like that. Why don't you settle down and let's have a— *oof!*"

Her hands came up and broke his hold on her shoulders, then she half slapped, half punched his face. It was a puny effort by anyone's standards. Her brothers would be disgusted with her.

A long exasperated sigh, and then that tinge of amusement again. "Mara, you're going to get hurt if you don't stop."

Turning away from him, she grabbed the nearest weapon, a photograph of her entire family. She swung at him.

He easily grabbed her wrist and held it, grinning. "What are you trying to do, frame me?"

She was getting damned tired of his amusement and his one-liners. "You want to tell me what the hell you're up to?"

"Glad you're talking, instead of all that physical violence . . . but you might want to lower your voice."

She raised her voice higher. "Don't you dare tell me to lower my voice in my own home. You abduct me, manhandle me, break into my apartment and you have the nerve to—"

Expelling a huge sigh, he grabbed her, threw her over his shoulder again, and carried her into the kitchen. Dumping her in a chair at the kitchen table, he quickly and efficiently tied her hands behind her and then to the back of the chair. Shrieking with rage, she rose and tried to ram him. He laughed softly as he pushed her down. Going to his knees, he wrapped a length of rubber tubing around her ankles and then the legs of the chair.

"Noah McCall, untie me, you rat bastard!"

Piling on even more insult, Noah turned away and pulled dish towels from a drawer. She opened her mouth to scream. One towel was pressed on her mouth as he tied another around her head.

Tied up, mute, and more furious than she could ever imagine being, Samara had heard of a killing rage and now knew exactly what it felt like. When he let her go, she would not be responsible for her actions. The man was dead meat.

Though furious, it never occurred to her to be frightened. Once she knew who he was, the only emotion she'd felt was fury. She was one of the few people in the world who knew Noah McCall and was alive to tell about it . . . not that she ever would. He might be a jerk and a brute, but he also was the founder of Last

Chance Rescue, an organization whose sole purpose was to rescue and save victims, many of them children. She could still hate the man even while she admired what he did. Without a doubt, he wouldn't hurt her. Piss her off? Most definitely.

Noah couldn't help but be impressed with Samara's spirit and ingenuity. He could've sworn she was unconscious when he'd brought her inside. Had even felt a twinge of guilt for that. And she surprised him. Danged if she hadn't even gotten a good lick at him. Few people had ever been able to do that. His little tiger kitten had claws, making him like her even more. At that thought, he drew quickly back. There were only a handful of people he actually liked in this world. Samara Lyons didn't need to be one of them. He was here for her help, not friendship.

Noah pulled out another chair, turned it around, and straddled it. The grin kicked up his mouth again. It was hard to look at Samara and not smile. No, she wasn't at her best, trussed up like a Thanksgiving turkey, hostility gleaming from those remarkable eyes of hers. Her long, almost blue-black hair gleamed under the stark brightness of the kitchen's light fixture. Petite, delicate, and 100 percent pure femininity. The first time he'd seen her, that was what he had thought. She was like a small, fragile doll. Until she opened her mouth. *That mouth.* How many times had he woken up in the past year, with a raging hard-on, dreaming of that mouth?

A muffled sound of rage brought him back to the present. He needed to get back to the reason he was here. Tying her up hadn't been in his plan, but he rarely went anywhere without his ties.

"Listen Mara, I know you're pissed . . . and you're still angry about last year, but I need your help."

Those incredible eyes widened in disbelief. Yeah, he could understand that. She still held a grudge against him and instead of trying to talk sensibly to her, he'd abducted her, manhandled her, tied her up, and gagged her. *Not so big on the charm these days, McCall.*

"If I take the gag from your mouth, will you promise not to scream?"

Gratitude gleamed in her eyes as she nodded emphatically. There went that little tug where his heart should have been. Ignoring it, he stood, untied the knot, and pulled the cloth from her face.

Panting slightly, she stayed true to her word and didn't scream. In fact, said nothing at all. That kind of worried him. Samara not talking meant she was planning something. He best get to explaining his presence.

"Listen, Mara, I know I haven't gone about this the right way . . . not really sure what the right way is anymore, but that's another story. Bottom line . . . I need your help."

"Why do you keep calling me Mara?"

"Huh?"

"You keep calling me Mara. . . . Why?"

He lifted a shoulder. "It's just a nickname."

She studied him as though he were a newly discovered species of vermin. Disdain clouded her eyes. "Do I have to hear you out, tied up like this?"

No way was he falling for that. "Yeah, you do. I don't have time to tie you up again. I need to talk and I need you to listen. . . . Okay?"

Glaring, she closed her mouth.

"You know what I do. . . . Right?"

She nodded.

"LCR's been asked to find a missing girl. Her name's Ashley Mason. She's thirteen years old and disappeared three weeks ago from Lexington, Kentucky."

Despite herself, Samara leaned forward, caught not only by Noah's words, but also his eyes. Everything else about him seemed cold, controlled, even slightly amused ... except his eyes. They blazed with purpose and determination. Again, Noah McCall might be an A-number-one low-lying jerk, but he actually cared what happened to these kids.

"All leads have pretty much dried up.... That's why her mother contacted us."

A memory hit her. "Wait, I heard about this on the news. Her mother is running for some kind of political office. Didn't they decide her daughter's disappearance was tied to that?"

Noah nodded. "That's one theory, but not the one we believe. From what we've been able to get from her friends, Ashley was chatting with a guy she met online. They'd been chatting for a couple of weeks and had arranged to meet each other. She hasn't been seen since."

"An online predator?"

"Probably ... no, not probably, definitely." Noah stood and pulled an envelope from his back pocket. He opened it, took out a photograph, and slid it across the table. "That's Ashley. She disappeared October 5."

Samara looked down at the blond-haired, blue-eyed girl. Though innocence shined in her eyes, the makeup and hairstyle made her look at least three years older than her real age.

Another photograph flew into her vision. "Courtney Nixon, age thirteen, Asheville, North Carolina. She disappeared two days before Ashley." Another photograph appeared. "Joy Harding, age fourteen, Knoxville, Tennessee. Disappeared five days after Ashley."

As Noah slid photo after photo before her, tears pooled in her eyes. All these innocent children. Why? Who?

After the twelfth photograph, Samara turned away from them and looked up at Noah. If his eyes had been hard and determined before, they were even more so now. This was a man intent on saving Ashley and as many other girls as he could.

"How do you know the disappearances are related?"

Finally out of pictures, Noah slumped into his chair. "Every one of them was to meet with a boy they met on the Internet. All of the boys are high school jocks from another school in the city, different from the one the girls attend. The boys were checked out, and so far, none of them seem to know anything about the girls. They've not been ruled out by the police."

"But they have by you?"

"Same MO. Hundreds of miles apart. Within a one-month time frame. Girls about the same age." He nodded. "Yeah, they're connected."

"But how could the same person—" She stopped when he shook his head.

"Not the same person . . . the same organization."

Now that was even scarier. She jerked at her restraints, needing her arms and legs free. Samara was a woman who couldn't sit still long, especially when she needed to think something through. Being tethered like this was driving her crazy.

"Okay, you have my attention. Untie me and let's talk."

That slow, sexy smile she remembered too well spread across his face. He stood and within seconds had her completely free.

With a relieved sigh, Samara popped to her feet, needing movement. She halted abruptly when his hand grabbed her wrist.

"I bruised you." Regret and something else gleamed in his black eyes.

A thumb lightly caressed her forearm where a small bruise was beginning to form. Samara gritted her teeth to hold back a shiver of desire. No way in hell was she going to get drawn back into an attraction for this man again.

She pulled her arm away and walked to the refrigerator. "You want some water?" When he didn't answer she turned around to ask him again. The words froze on her lips. Noah stood beside the table, and for the first time ever, Samara actually saw an emotion other than amusement or arrogance on his face. Had he actually been disturbed he'd bruised her?

"Noah, I'm fine. Okay?" For some strange reason she was reassuring him. Shaking her head at her own stupid behavior, she turned back to the fridge, grabbed a couple of small water bottles, and slammed the door shut.

Returning to the table, she handed him a bottle and plopped into the chair across from him. "Okay, there's a reason you told me about all of this. I think I'm beginning to see why, but tell me anyway."

Noah took a long gulp of water and then blew out a sigh. "It's the same organization. I know it is. But we have almost nothing on where they are. Since all the abductions happened in a short time frame, I think they're gathering the girls together into one large shipment."

"Shipment? For what?"

"Last year, LCR helped shut down a well-run human trafficking ring. There were five houses, in different areas of the world, where people were held and sold for various reasons. We closed down four of them."

"And the fifth?"

Noah lifted a shoulder as if it were no matter. "We had a mole. One of our best operatives was killed. We apprehended the head of the operation. Unfortunately, his second in command got away, went underground.

My sources are telling me he's reemerged and is back in business. I believe this is his new business venture."

"So you're saying he finds young teen girls on the Internet. Posing as a star athlete from their area, he arranges for a meeting place, the girls show up, and they're nabbed."

"Yeah."

Samara nodded. It made sense. As a social worker, she'd done plenty of family and teen counseling. The bastards who'd put this together knew just how to prey on young girls going into or struggling with puberty. Their dream of popularity, acceptance, to be the prettiest, with the most popular boyfriend, made them easy prey. No, not all young girls felt that way, but she'd seen more than her share to know that these people had a huge cache to pull from.

"So, how are you going to stop them and how can I help?"

Appreciation glinted in his eyes. "I think the window of opportunity will be closing soon. They know they'll only be able to do this for so long until word gets out that there's an online predator organization and what the MO is. If we're going to find them and hopefully the girls they've abducted, we have a very short time frame to work within."

"Okay, but where do I come in?"

"I want to use you as bait."

Wow. You don't get much more blunt than that. Even though that's where she figured this was headed, the words still shocked her.

"It'll be completely controlled. First, we've got to attract him. Once we do, we'll play along. He'll suggest a meeting place. You'll be there, just in case he wants to see you before he comes in. Once he sees you and enters, I'll take over."

"You act as though this will be just one man. What if it's more?"

"No, it'll be more than one. I'll make sure we have enough to cover you."

"What happens once you nab him, or them?"

"I get information."

"How?"

"You really want to know?"

His voice was mild, his expression neutral, but for some reason she shivered. Noah McCall would do what he thought he had to do, no matter what that was. She shook her head, not wanting to go further into just how ruthless this man could be.

"So, will you do it?"

"Why me?"

"You're small, young looking, but smart and old enough to handle yourself."

She raised a surprised brow at that. Her size made him ask for her help? "LCR doesn't hire small women?"

"No, only tall, busty blondes."

Samara laughed. Who would have thought it? Noah actually had a sense of humor. And she knew they weren't all busty. Eden, Jordan's wife, was a little over average height, slender, and not heavily endowed at all. "No really, why me? There's got to be plenty of other—"

"Not at LCR . . . at least, none available this quickly. They're either involved in other cases or not able to carry it off."

"Why couldn't they carry it off?"

"You have an innocent air about you. You don't just look younger. Something in your eyes, the way you stand . . . I don't know, you just don't look twenty-seven."

Samara grimaced. The bane of her existence . . .
always looking ten years younger. "My mom told me
I'll appreciate it when I get older."

"Well, I appreciate it now. So, will you do it?"

Help save innocent young girls from probable rape,
possible murder? What other answer could she give
him other than "Hell, yeah"?

Noah cracked opened the door to his hotel room.
His gaze zoomed to the floor, at the edge of the door.
Yep, the tiny piece of thread was still there. A small
security precaution to make sure no one had entered
since he left.

Throwing his keys on the desk, he stripped off his
clothes and headed to the shower. Tonight had gone
better than he'd expected. Tying her to a chair had
been unexpected, but she was almost to the point of
getting hurt. Samara getting hurt in any way wasn't
something he was willing to chance.

Hot water beat down on him; Noah lowered his
head and closed his eyes. He'd bruised her skin. That
bothered him, more than he'd like to admit. He told
himself it was because she was an innocent young
woman, but he knew it was more than that. There was
something about Samara that brought out his protective instincts. It wasn't just her size, though she was a
tiny little thing. There was another reason. One he refused to give any credence to. Being attracted to a
woman like her would be suicide. She wasn't the type
to heat up the sheets and then wave goodbye without
a backward glance. That was the only kind of woman
who interested him.

He stepped out of the shower and dried off. Pulling
on a pair of shorts, T-shirt, and running shoes, he
headed out the door. It might be after midnight here,
but he was still on Paris time, which meant no sleep

until sometime tonight. He bypassed the elevators and ran down six flights of stairs. Exiting the back entrance, he started at a slow jog. Running through the parking lot filled with semis, SUVs, and the occasional rattletrap, he turned out of the lot and headed down the street. This time of night, there was little traffic, totally different from Paris, which never slept.

A good hour run, then he'd go back to the hotel and do a little more research. After that, he'd pack up his gear and head over to Samara's. After much discussion, they'd agreed to work out of her apartment. He'd basically have to move in, as most of the online chatter would take place late at night. It just made sense to stay close. True, he could try to attract this creep's attention on his own and just use her when the time came for a meeting. But it'd been years since he'd been around teenage girls. Samara would know a hell of a lot more about how they talked than he would. She hadn't been crazy about the idea of his moving in, but reluctantly agreed.

Once he had gotten her agreement to let him stay with her, he'd left. After she told him she would help, things had become a little awkward. Her thoughts, no doubt, on what happened in Paris. She needed some time to think about what she'd agreed to, and he'd needed to get away from her for a while. Focus was an important part of what he did. With Samara, he had a tendency to lose it . . . one of the reasons they'd almost had their own little tango in Paris. He'd lost both focus and control. That sweet mouth of hers called to mind all sorts of things he wanted to do with it. And when he'd tasted her . . .

Noah came to an abrupt halt and bent over, breathing out harsh breaths. Almost impossible to run with a hard-on. He needed to get his head on straight before he saw her again. Once this project was over, he'd go back to Paris, she'd go on with her life here. In the meantime, they had a job to do. Neither one of them needed the distraction of attraction.

Regaining his control, Noah made a quick turn through a deserted mall parking lot and headed back. Thick, humid air coated his skin. He used to love running in the southern heat, the way it fought back as you ran through its dense atmosphere. Not anymore. Anything that remotely reminded him of his past was something he'd gladly chew glass to get away from.

Noah let himself into the hotel room, once again checking the unmoved thread. The phone rang just as he grabbed a water bottle from the minibar.

He took a long swallow and answered on the third ring, already knowing who it was and what she wanted.

"Did you find her?"

"Yeah."

"And?" The husky, feminine voice held amused impatience.

"And she said yes."

"I never doubted she would."

"You tell him yet?"

"Oh yes." A little sultry laugh gave him a good idea of how she'd gone about it.

"What'd he have to say about it?"

"Before or after I plied him with wine and had my way with him?"

Noah grinned. Eden St. Claire Montgomery had a way with persuasion, especially with her husband, Jordan. Though this particular time, Eden probably had a little more trouble than usual. Convincing Jordan that his former girlfriend would be able to handle this job couldn't have been easy.

"Not so simple?"

"Hell, no. I'm exhausted. But I finally made him realize that no matter what was involved, you would protect her with your life."

"And I will. But she's not going to get close enough to danger for that to be a concern."

"How's she doing?"

The concern didn't surprise him. Eden's compassion for the young woman Jordan had almost married was one of the things that made her the woman she was. No one knew better than Eden how rejection from someone you loved could tear you apart.

"Still a little shaky, but overall I'd say good. Moving all the way across country was probably good for her. Getting away from everyone who knew her."

"Tell that to her family. Seems like my husband is on the phone to them every week reassuring them she's fine."

"Why don't they check for themselves? They're a heck of a lot closer."

"Seems little sister demanded they give her at least six months before they came down. So, long distance it may be, but they call here to ask."

"Can't blame her about that. Can't be easy having that much family around worrying about you."

"She's gutsy though, don't you think?"

The affection was evident in her voice. Just in the short time Eden and Samara were together, they had created an interesting bond. Though they both loved the same man, Noah never saw jealousy from either one of them. Which was one of the reasons he'd been convinced Samara could handle the task he asked of her.

"Yeah, gutsy and smart."

"You'll both be careful, won't you?"

Though Eden knew a lot about the operation, there were still certain things Noah hadn't shared with her.

Things Eden suspected but hadn't pressed him for. Not that it'd do any good. When the time was right, all would be revealed. Until then, total secrecy was paramount.

"Wouldn't have it any other way."

"We'll check back soon."

Clicking the phone off, he stripped his clothes and headed to the shower. Though Jordan was in charge of the Paris office until Noah returned, he wanted to check on a few things. Letting go of control hadn't been easy, but he'd had no choice. Noah was the only person who could conceivably get this job done to his full satisfaction.

Jordan Montgomery was capable and experienced, but that didn't stop Noah from wanting to know how all his operatives were doing. He'd recruited every one of them, knew their backgrounds, strengths, and most of all, their fears. At thirty-two years of age, Noah might look nothing like a Father Goose and none of his operatives would appreciate being referred to as his chicks, but sometimes that's the way he thought of them. Being responsible for over one hundred highly trained mercenaries might not be anyone else's idea of a dream job. For Noah, it was all he knew, all he wanted to know.

Pulling on another pair of shorts, Noah pulled his laptop from under the mattress. Not the most original place to hide one, but his choices were limited. Besides, there was nothing on the computer that could be tied to him or his organization, but it'd be damn inconvenient to break in a new one if this one was stolen.

Clicking on, Noah was soon immersed in emails, updating him on existing operations all over the world. No names were ever used, locations were never revealed, and no information disclosed. The first six months of training for all LCR operatives was the full understanding of a distinctive language known only to their organization. Though he could speak ten languages fluently, Noah knew this code better than he knew his own name. He should, since he'd devised it himself.

Three years in prison had given him ample thinking opportunity. Last Chance Rescue had been created inside his mind as he lay in bed night after night, unable to sleep. The dark, sometimes horrific sounds of suffering, crying, cursing, and the occasional gruff laugh only kept the flame burning brighter. Other men might have been dreaming of going the straight and narrow when they got out. Others might have planned to go back to the same kind of lifestyle. Noah wanted neither.

With an agonizing scald of guilt in his gut that nothing could extinguish, Noah had vowed to rescue innocents. Thanks to his arrogance and pride, he'd failed one person and she'd paid an immeasurable price. He'd vowed to heaven and hell that he would never fail again. No matter what the cost.

three

Samara woke the next morning with the overwhelming need to clean. Anyone who knew her and saw her with a bucket, sponges, disinfectants, and mop knew she had something major on her mind and they should get out of her way. Cleaning cleared out her mental cobwebs.

After Noah left last night, she'd been alternately excited about helping him catch this online predator and reeling with anger at how he'd approached her in the first place. What angered her more was that she'd let him get away with it. Once he told her his purpose for needing to talk with her, she'd forgotten everything else other than the need to assist him in any way she could. Though she fully intended to help him, at some point she hoped to be able to show him she wasn't a weak little mouse he could just sling over his shoulder when the mood hit him.

She couldn't deny that part of her was secretly thrilled that Noah actually thought she could help. With five brothers, an overprotective father, and various other concerned relatives, Samara had rarely been treated as anything other than a delicate creature who needed to be protected and shielded. Noah actually treated her as an intelligent woman who could take on an online predator and win. Oh, she knew full well that her size and youthful appearance was the biggest reason he'd asked her for help. But it didn't negate the fact that he had asked.

On her knees now, scrubbing her bathtub, she contemplated how it was going to feel to actually have him living with her. Her father and brothers would have Noah's head for asking for help. If they learned he was going to live with her while they tracked a predator, she was pretty sure parts other than his head would go missing.

The squeak of the paper towel against the mirror comforted her as she acknowledged that the attraction was still there. Too honest with herself to deny its existence, she was also fully aware that from all appearances, Noah still barely saw her as a female, much less an attractive one. Other than that brief passionate kiss in Paris, he seemed to see her only as a tool to be used.

As she made up the guest bed for him, she breathed in the fragrance of freshly laundered sheets as she contemplated Noah McCall. Eden and Jordan seemed to think highly of him. Eden called her at least once a week, just to chat. Though she rarely mentioned Noah, when she did her voice was always full of affection and respect.

The familiar whine of the vacuum barely penetrated her ears as she vacuumed over already pristine floors. Was it odd to have a friendship with the woman who'd married the man Samara had planned to marry herself? Though not normally a jealous person, it only made sense that she be somewhat resentful of Eden. But that wasn't how she felt. Once Jordan found Eden again after years of looking for her, Samara could only feel gratitude that they'd found each other.

She hadn't loved Jordan as much as she thought she had. A woman didn't just give up the man she loved without a fight. And she certainly didn't stand up as the maid of honor at the wedding.

Even so, she'd been a bit bruised from his rejection. Moving from Virginia to Alabama had been a wise move, though her family hadn't seen it that way. Once her relationship ended with Jordan, they'd wanted to do what they'd always done with the baby of the family, which was to protect and coddle her. Samara loved her family beyond measure, but their suffocating compassion had only made her heartache worse.

Rachel Enders, her friend since the first grade, had moved to Birmingham right after college. When Rachel had asked her for the zillionth time to try Birmingham, Samara finally took her up on her invitation.

Starting all over again in a new city with no job was both scary and exciting. She had enough money saved up to wait another month or so before she had to find a job. After this thing with Noah was over, she'd have to start looking in earnest.

Being a social worker was not only a challenging and enormously fulfilling profession, Samara also knew she was quite good at it. Her references were impeccable and she'd already put out several feelers around the city. When the time came for her to go back to work, she didn't anticipate too much of a problem finding a job.

She turned off the vacuum and surveyed her sparkling apartment. It wasn't fancy but comfortable enough. Other than furniture essentials and her more personal belongings such as photographs, she'd put most of her stuff in storage. The housing market was less expensive here and she'd sold her little house in Virginia for a decent profit. Looking for a house would have to be put on hold until this project was over.

A stomach rumble reminded her she'd had only

coffee this morning before she set to work. Returning her vacuum cleaner to the hall closest, she headed to the kitchen. Opening her refrigerator, she made a dismal discovery. . . . She needed to go to the grocery store. Not one to procrastinate, Samara grabbed a piece of cheese from the deli drawer, stopped at her kitchen table for an apple, and munched her way to the bedroom.

Tossing the apple core in the garbage can, she shimmied out of her shorts and top, turned the shower spray on high, and jumped in. As the water hit her face, she went over the things she needed to get at the store. She opened her eyes and then jumped back as the spray almost blinded her. What kind of food did Noah like? She knew so little about him other than he lived in France. Did he grow up there? His accent was normal, without a hint of Parisian to it. In fact, he didn't seem to have any kind of accent at all.

She shook her head and finished her shower. Heck of a time to remember she knew almost nothing about the man who would basically move in with her today. She pulled her long thick hair into a ponytail, put on a minimum of makeup, dressed in her usual jeans and T-shirt, and headed to her phone. There was one person who knew Noah better than anyone. . . . Why not ask her?

Eden answered on the first ring. "Don't blame me for the acts of my boss."

Settling into a chair beside her bed, Samara giggled. Eden never said hello like a normal person; she thought it was a waste of valuable time. She didn't bother asking how Eden knew Noah was here. More than likely, Eden and Jordan had been in this from the beginning. "I'm not complaining, just need to know what he likes to eat."

"Huh?" The überelegant Eden sounded inelegantly confused.

"I'm going to the grocery store. I thought you might know what he likes to eat."

"Now that, my sweet, is something I know nothing about. I've seen him eat, know he's not opposed to it, but other than that, I've no clue. We've never discussed our favorite dishes."

"You've known him for years."

"You'll soon learn that knowing him for years doesn't mean knowing him. The man created *mysterious*."

If anyone had asked her, she would have said that if Noah had created anything, it would have been *sexy, maddening,* or *arrogant*. Though *mysterious* suited him, too.

"Okay, so what can you tell me about him?"

"That he'd die before he let anything happen to you."

Something tugged at her heart. Noah was probably the most unemotional man she'd ever met, but Eden's words rang true. He might not react as a normal man to most things, but when it came to protecting her, she never doubted his abilities.

"I know he would, but he said it wouldn't be dangerous."

"It won't be, but stay alert. Be aware of your surroundings. The air around you. Sounds . . . insects not chirping . . . anything at all that feels off. You can feel danger if you're on your toes. There'll be several around to protect you, but remember to always be responsible for yourself."

Samara took the advice to heart. Eden was a trained LCR operative. If anyone knew how to protect herself, Eden did.

"Thanks, that's good advice. So, how's our man

doing?" She knew the other woman wouldn't take affront at this. Eden had Jordan's heart wrapped up tight.

"Marvelous, as always."

"Just remember I taught him everything he knows."

"I'll be eternally grateful," came the amused reply.

Samara could only smile at the confidence Eden exuded. The woman was impossible to offend.

"Give him a kiss for me."

"Will do and remember, be aware."

Samara hung the phone up and took a deep breath. She still didn't know what to buy at the grocery store. Well tough. He was in America now and could just adjust his eating habits accordingly.

Grabbing her purse and keys from her dresser, she checked her appearance one more time. Grimacing at her plain but tidy appearance, she scurried to the door. She'd worry about her looks after she filled her fridge. Opening the front door, she let out a little squeak. Noah McCall stood before her.

She looked better today. Not as shell-shocked. Fresh and innocent but with a sweet, unaware earthiness that he found sexy as hell. Noah slammed a mental door shut. Those kinds of thoughts would get him in a world of trouble and Samara in a world of hurt. The cold, moist bag in his hand reminded him of why he was here. He shoved the bag toward her. "Here. The ice cream's melting."

She looked somewhat dumbfounded as Noah nudged her back into her apartment. "I figured you might need a few things, so I went to the store."

A little crease appeared on her smooth forehead as she peeked inside the grocery bag. "I'll unload this." She disappeared into the kitchen.

Noah set another bag on the coffee table and took out the half-empty wrapper from his breakfast. He heard a gasp and turned, the chocolate Zinger hanging from his mouth like a fat cigar.

"Noah McCall, you're a junk food junkie!" She sounded both astounded and delighted.

Swallowing half the cake in one gulp, he mumbled, "Am not."

She grinned. "Are too." Then she turned and headed back to the kitchen.

Noah looked down at the bag holding all of his favorites. He'd been discovered. Eating junk food once a week was a habit he'd developed when he got out of prison. An "in your face" to the other six days where self-discipline and self-denial were all he knew. Seeing the Americanized version of many of his favorites at the grocery store, along with some things he remembered as a kid, had been an irresistible temptation.

Noah downed his Zinger, picked up the bag, and headed to the kitchen. A cold glass of milk was called for. He stopped when he saw Samara was holding not only his chocolate milk, but also his gallon of rocky road ice cream.

"Mara, put that ice cream away before it melts."

Beaming at him as if she knew something exciting, she deposited the ice cream in her freezer. Without his asking, she poured a large glass of chocolate milk and handed it to him.

"How'd you know?"

"It's what I would want."

Noah pulled out another Zinger and handed it to her. "I think we'll work well together."

Samara giggled and accepted her treat. Unwrapping it, she took a big bite and licked the white cream off her lips. A surge of lust slammed into his gut, surprising and irritating the hell out of him.

Noah turned and slumped into a chair at the kitchen table, ignoring the feeling. He might allow himself to forget self-denial once a week with food, but no way did that include having any kind of attraction for Samara. Allowing her any closer would be stupid. For him, stupid got left behind years ago.

"I still need to go to the store and get some real food," Samara said.

Noah shook his head. "No need. I'm having some stuff delivered."

She pulled out a package of Oreos and a bag of peanut M&Ms from the grocery bag and stored them in a cabinet. "Hopefully something that's not going to put us in a sugar coma?"

"Yep, all the vitamins and nutrients a growing boy and girl need. . . . Even your mother would approve."

"You know about my mother?"

"That's she a nutritionist? Yeah."

"Did you get this from Jordan or have me investigated?"

He lifted a shoulder. "I needed to know you before I asked you to do this."

"Just how much do you know?"

"Enough."

"Enough for what?"

"To know you can do this job."

"How did investigating my background tell you I could do it?"

"It didn't . . . just gave me an idea of who you were."

"So, don't I get to know something about you, since we'll be working together?"

He would share, up to a point. "Like what?"

Her eyes narrowing, she stared hard for a few seconds. For someone who was a master at reading people, Samara was one of the few who could surprise him. Though her expressive face revealed her thoughts most of the time, a couple of times last night she'd caught him off guard. He waited, surprisingly tense, to see what she wanted to know about him.

"What was the name of your dog when you were growing up?"

Of all the things she could have asked, this seemed to be the most innocuous. "Indy."

"You grow up in Indiana?"

"No, my mom liked Indiana Jones." He jerked at the information he'd just spilled.

Admiration gleamed in Noah's eyes and Samara had to repress a giggle. She knew she'd surprised him and gotten information he hadn't meant to share.

"Damn, you're good."

"Thanks. My brothers told me I could squeeze juice from a fake lemon."

"You mean Mark, Peter, Scott, Stewart, and John?"

"Wow, you even have them memorized."

"And I'm assuming 'Samara' was chosen because it's a mix of your mom's and dad's names . . . Sam and Mary?"

"Yep. I complained about it one time, because it's so unusual, but Mom told me I should just be grateful their names weren't something like Fred and Ethel, since they would have called me Freckle."

"That would have suited you, too."

"Why?"

"Because you have a tiny freckle on your left earlobe."

"How'd you know?"

"I noticed it in Paris."

Since this was a subject she most definitely didn't want to explore, Samara turned back to the refrigerator, staring blindly at the near empty shelves. "What time are the groceries being delivered?"

"Probably around noon. If you'll check out the bottom of that bag, you'll find a box of Krispy Kremes."

Okay, now that was a junk food she could get behind. Samara dug back into the sack and pulled out a box of her favorites. As she prepared another pot of coffee, she knew Noah's eyes watched her every move. What should have made her nervous seemed amazingly comfortable. She didn't ask herself why. The reason would be useless. Once this creep was caught and her job finished, Noah would be gone from her life. She ignored the curious wave of sadness at this thought. Having feelings for this man went beyond the boundaries of idiocy and into the realm of lunacy.

She turned from her coffeemaker, determined to put everything else out of her mind other than the reason he was here. "So, how do we get started?"

"I figured we'd start by exploring the chat rooms the girls frequented. There are about thirty of them, so it'll take most of the day to do that. Tonight, we'll start trolling. We'll introduce you, where you live, your age, things like that."

Samara poured each of them a cup of coffee and set the cups on the table, pushing the creamer and sugar his way. Noah shook his head, indicating he drank his coffee black. Another unimportant detail, but since she knew almost nothing, important to her.

Biting into a crème-filled doughnut, Samara closed her eyes and took a second to savor . . . *heaven*. She opened her eyes to find Noah's gaze on her mouth, a hungry, unguarded expression on his normally expressionless face. Warmth suffused her body, targeting a couple of spots where they set up a hot throb of awareness. How startling that with one look, Noah could make her more aware of her femininity and sexuality than any man she'd ever known.

As if aware he'd given a thought away, his face shut down and he took a long gulp of coffee.

Samara winced, even as she hid a smile. She'd just poured the coffee, it had to have scorched his mouth, but he gave no indication of pain.

"You said you'll recognize him when you see him answer. How will you know?"

Noah grabbed a doughnut, halved it with one bite, swallowed, and answered, "He'll be a star athlete, someone who's fairly well-known in the city."

"How do you know he's not finished? Taking twelve girls and getting out of Dodge before he can get caught. If the police are onto him and you're onto him, he's got to know his time's running out."

"I think he'll take fifteen before he quits."

"Why fifteen?"

"It's just a hunch, but it's the best shot we have."

His face showed nothing different, but Samara got the distinct impression he was holding back information. Wouldn't do any good to ask more questions. She knew almost nothing about this man but knew enough to know he wouldn't share information he felt she didn't need. She tried not to resent that, though it was hard. If it weren't for the fact that she actually thought she could help him track this creep, she'd tell him to leave. Being used wasn't one of her favorite pastimes. But she trusted Noah enough to know he would tell her anything that might help with this case. She told herself to be grateful for that and let everything else go.

"So, what kind of information do I share?"

"Basic stuff. You're sixteen, attend Pelham High School. He'll be from one of the larger schools in town, so you'll know his name and face, but not him. Then, based upon what questions he asks, we'll go from there."

"I still don't understand how you'll know it's him."

Another shrug. "Gut instinct. I'll know him when I see him. That's about the best answer I can give you. Now, before we get started, do you have a photograph of yourself, something you could send out to lure him in?"

"Yeah, I think so." A cold chill ran through her bloodstream. Before, when they'd talked about chatting with him, that seemed safe and distant. Sharing her picture with the predator made her uncomfortable.

"You won't get hurt, I promise."

She should have known he'd guess her thoughts. "I know. It just seems creepy, sending out your picture to people you don't know, like you're advertising yourself."

"Yep, that's pretty much the gist of it. Lots of people do it all the time, with no consequences. Unfortunately, you never know when it's safe and when it's not."

Standing, Samara began to tidy up the kitchen. After a Zinger and a doughnut, the sugar zooming through her system required movement. While she finished in the kitchen, Noah went back to the living room to set up his computer.

When she went to check on Noah, she was surprised to see he'd pulled the small desk from the guest room and was already online.

"What do I do?"

Noah went around her and retrieved one of the kitchen chairs. "Come on over here and let's see what we can find."

Samara settled beside him and for the next couple of hours sat in amazement. She'd never been one to sit in front of a computer for very long, so visiting chat rooms wasn't the norm for her. Though aware she kept shaking her head, she couldn't seem to stop.

People said some of the most incredible things to one another. Suggestive, raunchy, silly, and some downright mean. And didn't these people have spell-check? Her English-teacher father would have a stroke if he saw some of their garbled garbage.

When she gasped at one particularly disgusting comment, Noah glanced over at her. "You going to be able to do this?"

"I know I act shocked. . . . I am shocked. But this is nothing I haven't heard before. I'm a social worker, I've heard it all. . . . It's just . . ." She shook her head, unable to articulate her dismay. "Don't these people have anything better to do?"

Noah shrugged. "Probably not. And a lot of these people are legit. Just looking for some conversation, a connection." He clicked onto another chat room. "Here's one that three of the girls frequented the most. It draws a lot of younger teens. I tried sending out a few messages a week or so ago and got nothing . . . but I know he's still out there."

The doorbell rang; the groceries had arrived. Noah carried the boxes to the kitchen and Samara unpacked them, noting he'd been true to his word. Fresh veggies, lean meats, and whole-grain bread. Her mother would most definitely approve.

She threw together a salad and turkey sandwiches, making two sandwiches for Noah. When she'd finished, she called out, "Lunch."

He appeared at the door, looking surprised and uncomfortable. "You don't have to make meals for me. I can do that myself."

She grinned and bit into a carrot stick. "You can make dinner."

"Deal. Hope you like sloppy joes."

"What?"

"Hey, if I'm cooking, I'm making what I want."

Already her stomach rebelled at the thought, but she nodded. A deal was a deal.

They ate lunch quickly, each seeming lost in thought. Samara put the dishes in the dishwasher while Noah put away the food in the refrigerator. It was a surprisingly comfortable ease . . . until he spoke again.

"Samara, we need to talk about what happened in Paris."

Whirling around to him, Samara could only stare. He was bringing this up now? Why? It would serve no purpose other than to embarrass her.

She forced a cool smile. "I rather like the notion of, what happens in Paris, stays in Paris."

"But it didn't stay in Paris, did it?"

"What does that mean?"

"You're attracted to me."

There was arrogance and then there was *arrogance*. Forget *sexy* or *mysterious,* this man had mastered arrogance. Did he think she was going to just nod and simper like some kind of idiot? If so, he knew nothing about Samara Lyons. Perhaps it was time he learned.

Her brows raised, she shot him her most challenging look. "You're attracted to me, too."

"That's something I can overcome."

"Oh, and I can't?"

"Not what I'm saying at all. You just need to know that whatever attraction there is can't lead to anything."

"Thanks for the warning, but you might want to get your facts straight. I was drunk when I came on to you in Paris. You, however, weren't. And I remember enough about that night to know you were very turned on." When he opened his mouth to speak, she raised her hand to stop him. "No, you wait. You started this conversation, so let's finish it. You've given me several looks today and let me tell you, not one time did I want to throw myself against you and have my way with you." Okay, so the last part was a lie, but not any longer. If there was one thing that could make her lose attraction for a man, it was this kind of attitude.

He blew out an exasperated sigh. "You're taking this the wrong way. I was only—"

"Yeah, you were only trying to warn me off. There's no need to do that, Noah. You're an arrogant ass and I find that the least attractive kind of man. You're off the hook."

Grabbing her purse and keys, Samara stalked toward the door. "I'll be back in a little while. The air in here suddenly smells like a cloud of noxious gas." She slammed the door behind her.

Samara figured she was the second-stupidest person on earth. Noah McCall being the first. After stomping out of her own apartment like a teenage nitwit, she threw herself in her car and enjoyed a five-minute tear-fest. Good cry, but pointless in the end.

Allowing herself one last sniffle, she blew her nose, dried her eyes, and cranked up the car. In her state of mind, having no idea where she was headed was no reason not to drive. Getting away from Noah right now had to be her first priority. When she got to where she was going, then she'd know where she was headed.

She had to give him credit. He'd not only manipulated her into admitting she was attracted to him, but also ensured that she would do everything possible to avoid showing that attraction in the future. Damn, he was good. She had brothers. She knew all the male tricks, and she'd let this one almost get past her. If she weren't so pissed at him, she'd be applauding. Noah might be one of the best manipulators she'd ever seen.

Slamming on her brakes as the line of cars in front of her braked, Samara hissed a curse. Maybe driving around Birmingham on a Friday afternoon wasn't the best way to overcome anger. Now stuck on Highway 280, she had only herself to blame.

Taking her life in her hands, she turned on her blinker and swooped behind a pickup truck, ignoring the blast of a horn from behind her. Keeping her signal on, she turned into the Summit shopping center.

Finding a parking spot in the middle of the giant lot, Samara started to walk. Spending the next few hours window-shopping was a good way to work off the explosive emotions careening inside her. Samara wasn't one to buy frivolously. Not only did she not have a job, but spending money on anything other than absolute necessities went against her budget-minded conscience. So it was with complete dismay and not a little anger that she found herself the proud owner of a new rug for her kitchen, three scented candles, two refrigerator magnets, and a rolling pin. None of these things was a necessity, though if Noah continued to be such a jerk, the rolling pin might come in handy.

She threw her bags in the trunk of her car and got in. Her stomach took a nosedive when she thought about what waited for her at home. Sloppy joes for dinner? She had a good idea that greasy delicacy would be coming right back up if she attempted one. Whipping into a parking spot at one of her favorite restaurants, Samara grabbed her purse. She was on no certain time schedule. After a nice, relaxing dinner, she'd head home. She had plenty of time before they started looking for the creep in the chat rooms. She anticipated needing as much good nutrition and strength as she could possibly get. Not only to do this job, but also to handle Noah.

After allowing his manipulation earlier, what was she going to do about it? The man thought he could control what was happening between them but he'd yet to face Samara Lyons doing what she did best. Fighting with her own kind of manipulation . . . the God's honest truth.

As she headed to a table for one, soft, muted music floated above her, easing her tension. A smile sneaked up on her that she couldn't repress. Noah McCall might well have met his match.

four

Noah paced through the small apartment, waiting for Samara to return. He'd known his words would make her angry—that's why he'd said them. She was right, he was the one who'd been sending out signals, but she'd responded in kind. That couldn't happen again. They had a job to do and once it was over, he'd be gone. The last thing he needed was to have her pining after him.

He ignored the small bite of conscience for hurting her feelings. Better now than later. He also chose to ignore the voice inside him that whispered that it might not just be her who would get hurt. Those kinds of feelings had been beaten out of him in a hell no one left alive even knew about.

Had he gone too far with her? She'd looked, in equal parts, angry and hurt, when she'd stomped out the door. He was so used to hardened, thick-skinned LCR operatives, he'd forgotten that Samara wasn't used to the gruff, sometimes cruel ways of his world. Had he hurt her tender feelings irreparably and jeopardized this op to boot?

As he prowled through the apartment, he learned even more about Samara Lyons. He'd known she was close to her family, but he was surprised by the number of photographs, scattered on her walls and every available surface, of people she wasn't related to . . . or at least he didn't think they were related. She obviously had a lot of friends. The stark differences between him and Samara couldn't have been more apparent.

Her apartment was filled with memories of people she loved. His apartment had no personal pictures or mementos. He had expensive art on his walls, an extensive library filled with rare books and hundreds of DVDs and CDs. And if he never went back, he wouldn't miss a thing.

Samara's apartment felt like a home. Soft, colorful chenille pillows decorated her sofa and chairs. The furniture was comfortable and had a broken-in feeling to it, as if she might have bought it secondhand.

Celeste, his decorator and occasional lover, had done his apartment. He'd given her carte blanche to do what she wanted. Since it was just a place he slept, he barely paid attention to his surroundings.

Looking at what Samara had done to her apartment in the short amount of time she'd lived here, he couldn't help but be impressed. Social workers didn't make a lot of money. Her parents weren't wealthy and her background wasn't one of privilege. Samara had worked for everything she had. That, to Noah, spoke volumes about the kind of person she was. Strong, self-reliant, and determined. Admirable in every way.

A stomach growl reminded him it was time for dinner. With little enthusiasm for what he'd originally looked forward to, Noah browned the ground beef and prepared his sloppy joes. Piling three meat-filled buns onto his plate, he grabbed the potato chips from the cabinet and a soda from the fridge. Sitting at the kitchen table, he wolfed his meal down in grim silence.

His mother had made him sloppy joes every Friday night. She had known they were his favorite and Friday was the only night she could safely do something for him without inviting his father's wrath.

His father, Farrell Stoddard, had a weekend routine no one dared screw around with. On Friday, after a long day of fishing or hunting, he went carousing, bedded as many women as he could get it up for, and drank himself into a stupor. He'd come home after daybreak on Saturday and sleep all day. Saturday night he'd do what he called his "God-given right" and rape and beat his wife repeatedly. Come early Sunday morning, he'd stand in the pulpit in front of all of God's sinners and preach a fiery, mind-numbing sermon, demonizing everyone from the government, to other races, to women. Sunday nights, after church, he'd discipline his children in "the way the Lord advised him." Which, to Farrell, meant beating the shit out of them until they could no longer stand.

His mother left when he was ten and Noah had been glad. Not because he didn't love her, but because he knew she would finally be safe. He'd tried numerous times to protect her, but always ended up getting beaten instead and he greatly feared the beatings she received were much worse because of his interference.

One day, without a hint of warning, she hugged him and his brother, tears streaming down what used to be a pretty face, and whispered she would come back for them. He'd stood in their barren dirt yard and watched her walk down the black-tarred road. Thin, stooped, and old beyond her years. He had known he'd never see her again. Noah had never felt such loneliness as he had at that moment. Of course, she never returned. And by the time he'd found her, years later, it had been too late.

When Farrell discovered his wife had left him and he couldn't find her, he returned home and beat both boys until they bled. Then he'd left for three days. He and his brother, Mitchell, lay in separate beds, alternately crying and cursing. Mitchell did what he always had done. He blamed his mother for everything and defended his father.

Noah could barely move. His father always made sure he got the worst of the beatings. Mitchell was his favorite. He might beat the hell out of his brother, but he always made sure Noah got the brunt. Though he and Mitch were identical twins, nothing besides their looks was similar, including their father's feelings for them.

By the time Noah was thirteen, he was big enough to defend himself against his father. One night, after a drunken binge, his father attacked him while he was asleep. Noah opened his eyes just in time to see a meaty fist headed to his face. Noah sprang out of bed and then beat the literal shit out of his father.

After that, it became mostly verbal abuse. Noah usually ignored him. . . . His opinion mattered nothing. Sometimes, just for the fun of it, Noah would give him a look and Farrell would slam his mouth shut.

Mitchell continued to be Farrell's favorite. They would leave for days, hunting, fishing, and camping. Noah learned to fend for himself. He'd never seen the sport in killing an innocent animal. He understood it was an adventure for some, but it never appealed to him.

Mitchell, the favored, good son was the one who received gifts, special treatment, or leftover money. Noah took what was left or what he could steal.

The first time he stole, it had been out of hunger. Stupidly, he'd been caught. His father picked him up at the sheriff's office. Noah hadn't been scared of him. He knew he could whip his father. He hadn't counted on his brother helping out with his beating.

They'd tied him to bed and taken turns. He hadn't been surprised Mitchell had helped. The brother he once knew, had shared a womb with, was no more. He was mean, possibly meaner than his father.

They eventually let him go, but Noah had learned an important lesson. He could only count on himself. After that, when he stole, he was more careful. But he had a reputation now. A police record. Store owners were told to look out for him. Suspicion followed him and if something happened and no one was immediately caught, he was often hauled in to talk with the sheriff. He'd had few friends at school. Soon, he had none.

That had been fine with Noah. Depending only on himself felt right. But he continued to break the law and thumb his nose at any authority he chose. He hadn't cared what happened to him. He'd been wild, untamable, and angry as hell.

Farrell Stoddard somehow continued to maintain his reputation, despite his drunken ways and violent habits with women. Mitchell followed in his footsteps and hid his evil ways under a charming smile. He fooled everyone but Noah.

Noah tried to stay out of his way, his line of fire. Mitchell, for whatever reason, hated his brother. Before their mother left, anything Noah received, Mitchell had coveted. After she left, Noah had nothing, but the jealously continued.

His brother's envy had amused him for the most part. What the hell did he have that Mitchell could want? He stayed out of his way and did his own thing.

Until Rebecca. Rebecca Stanley had been the most beautiful, fresh, and innocent thing Noah had ever seen. She moved to Monarch, Mississippi, in the middle of the school year. Noah and all of his sixteen-year-old hormones had fallen instantly in love.

He'd never seen anything as pretty and delicate as Rebecca. With honey-blond hair, soft brown eyes, and a sweet personality, Rebecca had become instantly popular. She could have had any guy in the school as her boyfriend, so it was a complete shock that she actually flirted with and seemed to like Noah.

Before he knew it, he was doing all the stupid, idiotic things teen boys did to attract a girl's attention. He offered to carry her books if they looked even remotely heavy. He made sure he left a seat open at the lunch table in case she wanted to sit by him. He'd even gotten into a fistfight when one of the guys cursed in front of her. He had known she was too good for him, too pure, but that didn't stop his adoration.

It'd been stupid for him to show his fascination for her. He should have known what would happen. Should have known that Mitchell wouldn't allow someone as wonderful as Rebecca to show any attention to Noah.

Noah had been diligently working on his homework at the kitchen table when the sheriff showed up, gun in one hand, handcuffs in the other, and arrested him for the rape of Rebecca Stanley.

Sickened and outraged, Noah had proclaimed his innocence. No one believed him. Why would they? He was the bad Stoddard. The one who was always in trouble, always stealing, breaking the law, causing problems. The one destined to come to a bad end. Mitchell was the good son, the righteous one.

He tried not to think what Rebecca had gone through, but couldn't stop. What had once been pure, fresh, and innocent had been destroyed by his brother's hand and Noah felt responsible. He had known his brother coveted what Noah had and he hadn't thought to protect Rebecca.

After a while, Noah stopped asserting his innocence. He was responsible for what happened, if not by deed, then by sheer stupidity and carelessness. Noah was sentenced to two years—his lawyer told him that was the best he could hope for. Noah hadn't cared.

A young girl was brutalized, her innocence destroyed, and his brother, his identical twin, remained free. And there hadn't been a damned thing Noah could do.

Noah always wondered if he might have gotten out and gone on to lead a normal life if that had been all that had had happened to him.

Cursing himself for rehashing what couldn't be changed, he took his half-eaten meal and threw it into the garbage disposal. Quickly cleaning up the kitchen, he headed back to the living room. There was no point in going back in time. No use crying over spilled blood. That wasn't all that had happened and he and normal would never be acquainted again.

Normal to him would probably scare the shit out of most people.

At night, alone, angry, afraid, and then finally resigned, Noah had created in his mind an organization that did care. One that would do anything and everything, no matter what the cost, to protect innocents.

When he'd finally gotten out of prison, he only had one desire, and that was to see his dream fulfilled. With the help of the most decent man he'd ever known, along with much sweat and the occasional bloodletting, he'd created Last Chance Rescue. Rescuing innocents was his life, his reason for breathing. He hadn't saved his mother, because he was too weak. He hadn't saved Rebecca, because of his selfishness. Now he saved as many as he could.

And someday, very soon, he would finally repay a debt no one but Noah could pay.

The door clicking open alerted him that Samara was home. Sitting at the small desk in the living room, his body loosened from the tension he hadn't been aware he had. Eyeing her, he hid his concern under an expression of cold rationality.

She looked calm, no longer hurt. Her eyes sparkled clear, but the telltale swollen eyelids revealed she'd been crying. Something tugged in his chest. He hadn't come here to hurt her, but they'd been working together for one day and he'd already made her cry.

"You okay?"

Her animated face flickered with something, before she cocked her head slightly and said, "You're a jerk, Noah McCall, but I've seen worse. You need my help for this job, so in the future, I would recommend that you don't piss me off too much."

He clenched his jaw to keep from grinning at her. "Deal."

"Good. Now, I've been thinking." Dropping her shopping bags on the floor, she threw herself on the couch and slipped out of her shoes. Bending her toes back and forth as if they needed exercise, she continued, "Since you're going to be here working day and night, I need to let my friends think I'm out of town. The last thing I want to do is get them involved or hurt."

"No one is going to get hurt."

"It'll still be easier if they believe I'm headed to my parents' for a visit. I'll take care of that."

Noah nodded. He should have thought about that. Having her friends around would certainly put a wrench in their plans. "Samara, there's something else." Her *what now* expression had him biting back another smile. "You know not to mention my name or anything about me, right?"

"Yes, Jordan had this conversation with me when he was barely conscious in the hospital."

"Good. Now, do you want a sloppy joe?"

A delicate shudder. "No thanks. I stopped for something before coming home."

"I guess we're ready to get started."

Noah watched her pad barefoot into the kitchen, her enticing bottom twitching with a sexy femininity he swore he would ignore but didn't keep himself from appreciating. He might never have a normal kind of life, but it didn't mean he didn't have a normal male appreciation for a fine female form. Samara's form was most definitely in that category.

She returned with two bottles of water. Handing him one, she took a long swallow of hers and then sat down at the desk. "Okay, let's get started."

They began with going into each chat room and checking to see who might be there. After checking, Samara watched Noah type in a brief message.

Hi, my name is Carly. I live in Birmingham, Alabama. I'm sixteen. Like to swim, hang at the mall and write poetry. Anybody out there want to talk tonight?

After the fifth time without much more than a "Hi, nice to see you here," Samara started to see that this was going to take more time than she'd originally thought. Not that she thought they'd go online for the first day and find the predator, but trolling through all the chat rooms one by one was beginning to look like the "needle in a haystack" analogy she'd always hated . . . mostly because she'd never heard it applied to anything good.

She cut her eyes over to Noah. He looked exhausted. His normally swarthy darkness now paler, shadows made half-circle sweeps under his eyes. The lines around his mouth made him seem older, grimmer. It was seven hours later in Paris. "When's the last time you slept?"

Typing another message into yet another chat room, he grunted out an unintelligible sound.

"Excuse me, didn't quite get that."

Noah pulled his eyes from the screen, blinking rapidly as if to clear them. His too-perfect mouth lifted into a slight smile. "What day is it?"

Ignoring the heart flip his smile always evoked, she concentrated on his words. "So, basically days?"

He shrugged and returned his gazed to the screen. "At least two."

That did it. Samara stood and stretched. "Then let's call it a night."

His eyes back on the screen, he shook his head. "You go on. I can—"

"We're not getting anywhere." She squinted a look at her wall clock. "It's after two in the morning. If he were on tonight, he would've already replied."

Noah blew out a long sigh, his face grim. She knew he would have liked to make contact the first night, but making a hit the first time out wasn't reasonable . . . even she knew that. Noah was so determined though, he probably thought he could have made it happen by will alone.

For the first time since she'd seen him again, Samara's heart softened for this man. He might be a jerk of the first order and arrogant to boot, but what he did, saving victims all over the world, was phenomenal. What had brought him to create Last Chance Rescue?

As he shut down his computer, she suddenly found herself wishing there was something she could say or do to make him look less grim. Stupid? Absolutely. The man had done little since she'd seen him again but insult her and piss her off. Why the hell she should want to see him smile wasn't something she wanted to contemplate.

Samara showed him where the guest room was, the towels and other things he might need. Whispering good night, she closed the door to her bedroom, ignoring the dangerous notion of following him into the guest room and finding out exactly what those dark looks he'd flashed her today really meant. Noah had made it more than clear he wanted nothing to happen between them. Samara's mind was totally convinced and on board with that concept. Now she just needed to persuade the rest of her body to cooperate.

Darkness swirled around him. Like bubbling black tar, it coated his entire being, pulling him deeper into a thick black abyss. A small part of his subconscious knew he was dreaming, but refused to release him from the vicious claws. Helpless to escape, the nightmare flooded his senses, choking, smothering.

Farrell Stoddard stood before him. Belt in hand, he flicked it against his own leg and barely made a grimace each time it hit. The anticipatory gleam in his evil, dark eyes told Noah exactly what to expect. Noah tensed, his mind screaming for him to wake up, even as he heard the whoosh of the first strike.

Pain seared his skin. Squealing, excited giggles sounded beside him. Noah twisted his head. Mitchell stood on the other side of the bed, knife in one hand, his other hand covering his crotch. He wore Noah's clothes . . . the light blue shirt he'd worked for a month at the gas station to be able to afford. The shirt Noah wore the first time he'd flirted with Rebecca.

Another sound . . . a sob. Noah turned. His mother stood at the door. Her dress torn, hanging in shreds from her thin body, welt marks on her face, chest, and stomach. Her eyes were hollowed out, defeated, empty.

A young girl stood beside her. *Rebecca.* Long blond hair, dirty and tousled, hung down over her thin shoulders. Her sallow complexion made her look years older than fifteen. Her eyes accused, reproached, destroyed. She was nude; semen and blood dripped down her legs.

He had failed them. His mother and Rebecca. Failed to protect them, failed to keep them safe. Noah twisted the sheets, willing himself to wake up, telling himself it was all a dream.

Samara stood beside the bed. Her pretty face marred with tears and bruises. Her expression hurt, reproachful. "Why?" she whispered.

Noah woke on a stifled shout. He threw the sheet off and slammed his feet down on the solid, carpeted floor. Hell and damnation, he'd not had a dream like that in years. Why now? Because he was so close? Or for another reason? Was he putting Samara in jeopardy? No, she would be safe. He would make sure she was safe. She was his chance, perhaps his only chance, to catch these bastards. He was accustomed to using people, so why should this be any different?

Knowing he wouldn't sleep any more tonight, Noah pulled on a T-shirt and a pair of shorts and headed back to his laptop in the living room. He switched on the lamp and checked his watch. Five-thirty. He'd slept about three hours . . . enough to get him through another day.

He clicked on his laptop and signed on. His pulse kicked up. Three new messages waited. Had they gotten a nibble? The email addresses were innocuous enough. BS626@ramsey.com, mjj@Mozart.com, and bob@missionridge.com

Noah clicked on and read the first.

Hi Carly, I saw your post on teen things chat room. My name is Brian Sanders. I go to Madison High in Montgomery. I'm seventeen and play football. . . . I'm a running back. Email me back if you'd like to talk more.

The second email read like a typical lonely, horny teenager. The third one was an invitation to come to a church revival and repent. Since he was pretty sure the last one wouldn't attract a sixteen-year-old, he ignored that one. The lonely teen . . . he read again:

Carly, I'm John. U sound cut. R U?

Noah shook his head. No, too illiterate. He went back to Brian's message and read it again. Sounded like what he would expect from the bastard, but he'd have to wait and see. He didn't answer back. What sixteen-year-old would be answering this early on a Saturday morning? He'd wait a few hours, then see if that nibble turned into a full-fledged bite.

A slight sound drew his attention from the screen. A groggy fairy sprite shuffled into the living room and didn't glance his way as she continued her early-morning slide into the kitchen. Noah's mouth kicked up in a small smile. Evidently Ms. Samara Lyons was not a morning person.

It took barely a second to make this realization and then proceed to the next. Samara's sleepwear consisted of a cropped T-shirt with the picture of a frog on the front and the words *Kiss me and see what happens* on the back. The shorts covering her delectable bottom were brief and showed an enticing length of smooth, tanned legs. His cock rose to celebrate the occasion. Hell, was there any time this woman didn't turn him on?

He watched her disappear into the kitchen and resumed his mental lashing of how inappropriate it was to lust over a woman he was working with. It was a cardinal rule for him. No personal involvement with another operative . . . even if said operative was temporary.

Noah stared at the screen and reminded himself of the reasons nothing could happen between them. The mission was and always would be of top importance for him. Nothing else could matter.

The shuffling drew closer. Samara was returning from her trek into the kitchen, coffee cup in hand. She had yet to even acknowledge his existence and much to his surprise, that bothered him. Was he invisible?

"Good morning," Noah said.

In one simultaneous action, Samara's coffee cup went up in the air, she squealed a shriek high-pitched enough to excite a dolphin, and, turning, grabbed a vase filled with silk roses and threw it in his direction.

Noah jumped up, barely getting out of the way of the flying vase. His reaction time slowed by shock at her actions. "Hell, Samara, what's your problem?"

"Noah, dammit!" She glared at him. "Do you have to scare the crap out of me every time?"

"Scare you? I just said good morning. What's scary about that?"

Hands on hips, she continued to glare and Noah breathed in a curse. Hell, did she not realize her breasts jutted out even more? Nipples distended, Noah's mouth watered at the thought of tasting the sweet berries, of pulling up her shirt and taking her entire breast into his mouth. They weren't large, but beautifully shaped, rounded and firm. His palms tingled at the thought of pushing her breasts together and suckling them at the same time.

Slender arms wrapped around her chest, distorting his view. "Would you stop staring at my breasts and look at me?"

"I am looking at you. Go put on a bra if you don't want me staring at your breasts."

"I don't wear a bra to bed."

"I don't see a bed anywhere in this room." And thank God for that because if there was one, he greatly feared he'd already have her on it.

With one last glower, Samara turned back to the kitchen and returned with a dish towel. She kneeled and began to mop up the coffee spill.

Noah knew human nature enough to realize he had embarrassed her and that bothered him for some reason. He took her arm, and pulled her to her feet. "Go put on some clothes. I'll take care of the mess."

Not meeting his eyes, she nodded and practically ran into the bedroom, slamming the door shut.

Resisting the impulse to throw herself back on the bed and bury her head under the pillow, Samara instead pulled off her shirt and put on a bra. She pulled her T-shirt back on, cursing under her breath. Her breasts were small. What was the big deal? She often went without a bra and thought nothing of it, so why . . .

Good heavens, had it been so long that she hadn't even recognized the signs? He'd been staring at her breasts not from outrage that she wore no bra but from desire. She'd been slow before, but never this slow. The man wanted her. Despite his warnings, his attempts to put the blame on her, there had been desire on his face.

Drawing a brush through her hair, she smiled at her reflection. Her day was definitely looking up.

She returned to the living room to find the spilled coffee cleaned up and Noah in the kitchen. She eased in, wanting to gauge his mood before she said anything. The man was volatile, outrageous, and unpredictable. Definitely not an easy person to know or like. So why couldn't she stop smiling?

Noah stood at the stove, scrambling eggs. He shot a brief look over his shoulder. "Breakfast will be ready soon."

Samara poured two cups of coffee and sat them on the table. "Need any help?"

"No."

Okay, fine with her. Deciding he could wait on her and she wouldn't mind in the least, Samara sat at the table and waited for breakfast to be served.

Noah slid a plate filled with eggs, toast, and bacon in front of her. He sat across from her and attacked his food as if it could escape at any moment. His head bent to his meal, tense silence surrounded him.

Samara ate at a slower, contemplative pace. She was used to men and their vagaries. With five brothers, she could guess almost any mood of a man. Noah was harder to read. It was almost as if he had developed such a talent for subterfuge that showing anything real got locked up faster than lightning. Why couldn't the man have a real, honest-to-God emotion and show it?

"You need to learn some self-defense moves." The grumbling voice jerked her from her Noah analysis.

"I beg your pardon?"

"You fight like a girl."

Instead of addressing his insult, Samara leaned forward and seared him with her eyes. "Let me ask you a question. Do you even know how to relate to people?"

"What are you talking about?"

"You kidnap me, tie me up, insult me, accuse me of coming on to you and overexposing my body. Now you tell me I fight like a girl . . . which by the way, I am, and don't tell me you haven't noticed."

His expression revealed nothing but granite impassivity. "So what's your point?"

"My point is you work awfully damn hard on pissing me off just to keep me at arm's length. I'm wondering why."

Taking his empty plate and hers, he stood and walked to the sink. "You've got a vivid imagination." Noah turned and gave her what looked to be a genuine smile. "What I told you last night was the truth. You keep giving me the vibes and I don't want you to think that anything can happen between us. And as far as kidnapping you, if I'd thought you'd listen any other way, I would have done it differently. You're the one who turned down a talk, not me."

Standing, Samara nodded, realizing she would get nowhere with him. He was so far into denial, it probably wasn't even in his vocabulary.

"I'll clean up since you were kind enough to fix breakfast."

A small flicker touched his face. Surprise that she'd given in so easily? She hadn't given in, but had backed off. Having learned long ago that there was nothing wrong with retreat in order to go in a different direction, she'd wait awhile and find another way inside him. Her brothers hadn't nicknamed her Bulldozer for nothing.

"When you get through, come on into the living room. I got a couple of responses back. One of them may be our guy."

Samara nodded. She might be in a cat-and-mouse game with Noah, but she needed to keep her mind on the real purpose. Saving these girls' lives. It wasn't something she planned to forget. Teaching Noah a little lesson in humanity might be a small side benefit, but the most important thing was to rescue the girls and catch the creeps preying on them.

Since Noah left little to clean, she was seated in front of the computer within minutes of breakfast.

He clicked on the three messages and let her read through them.

"What do you think?"

"Mmm. Not the Mission Ridge guy, and probably not John, since he sounds either too young or maybe not so bright."

"Yeah, my thoughts, too. I did some research on Brian Sanders. He is who he says he is. Popular kid, plays football. Definitely a high school jock. Only question is, is this really Brian? I've sent some of my people to check him out. In the meantime, we'll play along." He clicked back onto Brian's message and slid the laptop toward her. "Want to answer him back?"

Samara nodded. Chewing her lip in concentration, she replied, *Hi Brian. I'm a sophomore at Pelham. I love football. Maybe I'll come and watch you sometime.* Before she could press send, Noah's hand stopped her.

"Wait—don't you think that's coming on a little strong?"

"Excuse me? When's the last time you were a sixteen-year-old girl or even around a sixteen-year-old girl?"

"I'll admit it's been a while. I just don't want him to think you're pushing a meeting. The last thing we want to do is scare him off."

Though she still didn't think it was too forward, Noah was right. They did need to play it safe until they had him hooked. "Okay, how about this?" She deleted what she'd typed, typed a few new sentences, and slid the screen toward him.

I like football . . . really all sports. It's just my mom and me here at home, and she's not into sports. Do you play anything else besides football?

"Better. Send it and see what happens."

Samara hit send and stared at the screen. Nothing

happened. Of course, he was probably doing other things. If he was the real Brian, he might be mowing the grass or doing whatever teen boys do on a Saturday morning. If he wasn't the real Brian, she hoped he took the bait so no other young girl got caught up in his wicked net.

"While we're waiting, do you want to learn a few self-defense moves?"

Samara blinked at him. He was offering to teach her? "Why?"

"Because you need to know how to protect yourself. There's nothing dangerous about this project, but you never know when something might happen. Like the other night. You should have been able to do some damage to me."

"I fooled you into thinking I was unconscious."

That beautiful smile lifted his perfect lips and Samara had to literally catch her breath before she expelled it on a sigh of sheer awe. Why did this man have to be so incredibly delectable and so frustratingly irritating?

"Yeah, you fooled me. But I was doing my damnedest not to hurt you. If someone hadn't cared about that, they could have taken you with no problem."

Samara stood. Pride told her to say no, she didn't need his help. Her brothers had taught her all she needed to know. Curiosity, along with an anticipation of being close to him, forced pride away and made her say, "Okay. Show me what I should have done the other night."

As he rose to stand beside her, a voice inside Noah's head cursed him for his stupidity. He'd done his dead level best to keep away from her and now he was about to get even closer? Just how masochistic could one man be?

"Okay, first of all. Always park as close as you can to your apartment."

"I would have except there weren't any spaces available." She shot him a narrowed-eye glare. "You probably got my spot."

"Second, always make sure you look around when you get out of the car. If you feel even the slightest apprehension, something seems off, whatever, get back in the car."

"That's kind of what Eden told me."

"You talked to Eden? When?"

"Yesterday."

"She gave you advice on keeping safe?"

"Just a little."

"Are you worried that something's going to happen to you? Because we can change—"

"No, I'm not worried and neither is Eden. She just wanted me to take responsibility for staying aware of my surroundings."

"Good advice. Now, I came at you from behind. Turn around."

Samara turned and Noah immediately grabbed her. Samara swung around and threw a punch at his head. He easily dodged it, but she'd surprised him. Her movements were graceful and quick. He grabbed the hand that swung at him and pulled it behind her back, careful not to hurt her.

"That was a nice move, but now I've got you in a lock and could easily break your arm."

Noah looked down at her head, which came to just the top of his chest. Silky black hair, pulled haphazardly back into a loose ponytail, tempted him. His nose twitched at the delightfully fresh scent that he'd bet his last dollar hadn't come from any bottle.

She struggled against his grip and he forced his mind back to where it was supposed to be. "If you were taller, you could just throw your head back and knock me in the nose. Since you're small, your best bet is to go limp like you did before."

Immediately she stopped struggling and collapsed in his arms.

"Good. Now, what I'd do is loosen my arms, just a bit. When I do, stomp on my foot, kick me in the shin, or slam your arm or fist into my crotch. But whatever you do, when I let go, run from me as fast as you can."

She twisted to look up at him. "Run?"

"Absolutely. You're not staying around to teach this guy a lesson. Your number-one priority is to stay alive."

"That's what my brothers always told me to do."

"Why'd you seem surprised, then?"

"Because I doubt that's how you trained Eden or any of the other female operatives you have."

"That's not true. I taught them to stay alive. If they're outnumbered or in danger, they run. They can always go back and fight later. Hard to do if you're dead."

Samara stomped lightly on his foot with her heel and whirled away from him. Wanting to teach her a lesson of moving quicker and hitting harder, he easily grabbed her arm and spun her around. Catching her against him, his forearm nestled her breasts, and her nipples peaked immediately, pressing against his skin.

His eyes closed, he gritted his teeth and fought the almost overwhelming need to turn his arm slightly and cup a breast in his hand. Why did her breasts fascinate him so much? They were just breasts, smaller than most, larger than some. Women everywhere had them. He'd seen and enjoyed his share, so why the hell did seeing and tasting hers seem like such a dire need?

"Noah?"

Her voice, soft, questioning, and tinged with desire, put a quick halt to his insanity. This could never happen. He released her quickly and stepped back. "Good job. Just be sure you move as fast as possible and leave them with so much pain, they'll think twice about coming after you."

Her back stiff, the nape of her neck turned a charming bright pink. Was she embarrassed by her arousal or by the more than obvious hard-on that'd pressed against her ass?

"Do you get turned on every time you train an operative?"

Noah sighed. He should have known she wouldn't let that pass. "It's a normal male response to a beautiful woman. Nothing more."

Turning, her mouth lifted up in a small smile. "Well, at least you think I'm beautiful. That's something." She headed toward her bedroom. "Thanks for the lesson. I think I'll take a shower."

Noah watched her walk away and, for the first time in a long time, resented his life and the restrictions he'd placed on himself. If ever there was a woman who could tempt him to forget his obligations, it was Samara Lyons. Another reason he needed to get this project finished and get back home. Having fantasies like these did nothing but stir up long-forgotten desires he was no longer human enough to handle. Samara deserved more than a cold-blooded, heartless bastard. Once she learned the full truth of this project, any and all attraction she had for him would be destroyed.

He told himself it was for the best and though he knew he was right, what was best felt like shit today.

five

Samara emerged from her bedroom to find an empty apartment. Having no idea where Noah had gone and being too irritated with him to care, she straightened up her already tidy apartment and then plopped onto the sofa.

Noah was seriously attracted to her. She'd been around enough men to recognize the signs. There was no denying the erection that had been digging into her butt. Normal response to an attractive woman? Maybe. But she had a feeling it was more than that. Question was, what was she going to do about it? It was pretty damned clear he intended to ignore what he felt. Which meant she could let him and nothing would come of it, or she could do her own pursuing.

She wasn't a shrinking violet or a wimp. Normally, when she wanted something, she went after it with every intention of winning. Did she want to win Noah? Billion-dollar question. The man was mysterious, arrogant, and worked in an area she had little knowledge of. If she did pursue something, she felt sure Noah would see it as only a temporary arrangement and everything would end when he returned to Paris. That should be what she wanted, too . . . if she wanted anything at all. So why did that thought leave her with such an empty feeling?

She wasn't one for indiscriminate affairs, having had only two serious relationships. One lasted three years during college and then Jordan, which had lasted almost a year.

Coming on to Noah after the wedding last year was totally out of character for her. But she admitted to herself, sober or intoxicated, she wanted Noah McCall. Something about him drew her to him more than any other man she'd ever met, including Jordan, the man she'd thought she would marry. What did that mean?

Before she could delve too deeply into this astonishing realization, her phone rang. Samara grabbed it, eager for a distraction from her insane thoughts.

"Hey Sam, we still on for racquetball tomorrow?"

Well, crap. She'd forgotten to call Rachel and explain she was going out of town. "I'm sorry, Rach. I should have told you the other night. I'm headed out of town for a few days."

"That's a surprise. Where're you going?"

"Home. Just a little homesick. You know me . . . need a family fix. If you need me, call on my cell, okay?" The last thing she needed was to have Rachel call her parents' home and tell them she was supposed to be visiting. If she didn't arrive, her entire family would be in Birmingham in a matter of hours.

"You sure everything's okay? You sound a little weird."

That's because she was a terrible liar. "Of course everything's fine."

"That guy that came to Mama Maria's the other night . . . he's not bothering you, is he?"

Yeah, bothering the hell out of her. "No, of course not. I just haven't seen my folks in a while. Mom's been after me to come back for a visit. Just thought I'd go ahead and do that before I started looking for a job."

"Okay." There was a world of doubt in that little

word, but thankfully Rachel didn't pursue it. "Want me to come over and water your plants?"

"No, one of my neighbors agreed to do it, so you don't have to worry with it."

"When are you coming back? The sooner you start looking for a job, the sooner you'll have one."

Samara smiled at the typical Rachel wisdom. She was always the sensible one. "I know. That'll be my first priority when I get back."

"Okay, well . . . give everyone a hug for me and I'll talk to you when you get back."

"Thanks, Rach. Talk to you soon." Samara hung up quickly before she had to lie anymore. She was scrupulously honest, and lying bit at her conscience like stinging little gnats. When this was over, she'd explain some of it to Rachel. That thought gave her little comfort. Lying was one of the few things Samara had always felt was close to unforgivable, and now here she was doing it to her best friend.

A key turning at her door gave her warning that Noah had returned. Samara took a deep breath, still not sure what she should do about this overwhelming attraction.

She should have known Noah had regrouped and would come at her with both barrels loaded.

His expression grim, he sat in the chair across from her. "I think we need to call this off."

"What?"

"This thing between us, it can't happen." He raised a hand before she could defend herself. "I know, it's not all you. But that's beside the point. If we don't have our focus totally on this, something could happen. That's the last thing I want."

"So you're saying unless we pretend there's no attraction at all, you're going to let the opportunity to catch this creep go?"

"Hell no, I'll find him. Just not this way."

There was her decision, made for her before she could make it on her own. If she pursued anything with him, he would walk out and she'd be left wondering if she could have helped.

"Fine. From now on, it's strictly professional. It's not as if you're so gorgeous I can't control myself." What was one more lie today, anyway?

The relief on his face caused a small pain in the region of her heart.

"Good. Now, let's see if we've got a response back yet." Noah stood and moved over to the small desk. He opened the laptop, then pulled out chairs for both of them and sat down.

Samara sat beside him, telling herself this was the decision she would have come up with on her own anyway. He'd just made it easier for her. So why did that pain in her chest hurt even more?

She was somewhat surprised to see that not only had Brian responded, there were ten more emails from others. They definitely had their work cut out for them, determining who the real predator was . . . if it was any of them. Noah was right, this should be their only focus.

Without looking up from his laptop, Noah listened as Samara counseled yet another family member. He'd been living with her for over a week and this had to be the tenth counseling session he'd heard. Not that she would call it a counseling session, but he couldn't think of it as anything else. After a little chitchat of finding out how she was doing, she "uh-uhhed" her way through each conversation, offering a soft murmur of advice from time to time, but for the most part just listening.

The more he knew Samara, the more he realized

something. People wanted to talk to her, tell her their problems. In his experience, most people who told you their problems only wanted to hear you say you agreed with them. From his vantage point, that wasn't what Samara did. He'd heard her, more than once, call someone out on what they'd said or done. Evidently it hadn't angered them because they'd continued to talk with her.

And she sat there and listened, as if talking to each person about their problems was the most important thing she had to do. That took patience and skill, but it also took something else . . . something he had suspected all along. Being with her the last few days had confirmed the belief. Samara Tyong had a good heart. She actually cared about people, wanted to help them.

He heard her say a soft goodbye and close her phone. He turned his thoughts back to the computer screen, irritated at his distraction. What Samara did on her own time was her own business. He had more than enough to occupy him.

A soft sigh caught his attention. Without will or purpose, Noah found himself glancing around at her. "Problems?"

The black silk of her hair swished around her shoulders as she shook her head. "No, just the opposite. Though John doesn't see it that way."

Telling himself he didn't need to get caught up in her family issues, he turned completely around to face her. "John, your brother?"

"Yeah. Monica, his wife, is pregnant again."

"He doesn't want it?"

"Of course he wants it."

Noah's mouth worked not to smile at her look of outrage. "So, what's the problem?"

"This is their third child in four years. They're both

still paying off student loans and Monica's wanting to quit work after this baby's born."

"Why'd he call you?"

"He just needed to talk."

"They all seem to need to talk."

"What's wrong with that?"

He found himself shrugging defensively. "Nothing, just an observation. Your family calls you a lot."

"Of course they do. . . . They're my family." Tilting her head slightly, she asked, "Don't you talk to yours a lot?"

Well shit. He should have known not to get caught up in this kind of conversation. He turned back to his computer. "No."

He could almost feel her stare boring a hole into his back. Daring a glance back, sure enough, her eyes were full of questions. No way did he plan to answer any of them.

"You don't look like any of your brothers."

A lame tactic to change the subject, but thankfully, she allowed it.

"Of course I don't."

"Why 'of course'?"

"I thought, in your investigation of me, you'd have discovered that my brothers are adopted."

Once again, he found himself turning back to her. "No, I didn't know that. How'd that happen?"

Propping her bare feet upon the coffee table in front of her, she settled in as if she were relating a favorite story. "My mom and dad had tried for years to get pregnant. After a while, they decided to adopt. They got put on the list for newborns. In the meantime, they volunteered to be foster parents. One day, they got a call about twin boys who had lost their parents."

"Twins?"

She grinned. "Yeah, Peter and Scott . . . not identical except in mannerisms and stubbornness."

"So how'd they end up with three more?"

"All five of them were brothers. Their parents had been killed in a car accident and there were no known relatives. When Mom and Dad heard they were going to have to separate the family, they said they'd take them all."

"That took a lot of guts."

"Yeah, especially since they could barely afford two of them. But my parents both came from big families with very little money, so it wasn't that big of a deal. They fostered them and then, eventually adopted."

"How'd you happen to come along?"

"They decided to try one more time . . . and finally got me."

"Tell me about them." The moment the words were out, he wanted to snatch them back. He didn't need to know anything else about her family.

She looked so delighted by the request, he decided it wouldn't hurt to listen to a couple of stories. An hour later, he was still listening and admittedly enthralled. She loved talking about the people she cared for. She shared not only stories about her immediate family, but also about her numerous aunts, uncles, and cousins.

What he really enjoyed was the way her face lit up as she related each event. Samara was rarely still. Her storytelling was no exception. She jumped up more than once to act out the behavior of a particular character. Despite himself, Noah felt both charmed and entertained. Not only by her obvious enjoyment of the telling, but by her deep affection for each family member.

Having a family like that, large and loving, was a mystery to Noah. He'd been on his own for so long, his life private and hidden from everyone, even the few people who knew him well. What would it be like to have such an enormous amount of people care about you? Know so much about you?

He shuddered at the thought. Privacy was of utmost importance to him. Having people in your life like that invited all sorts of problems. They'd want to know your business and probably have an opinion on everything. No, his solitary life was much better . . . quiet with no worry about what anyone else thought. He lived just the way he wanted.

Samara's devotion and love for her family was just another example of their extreme differences.

Samara eyed the man beside her. He seemed tense. Much more than usual. The past few days had settled into a surreal but interesting routine. She learned that Noah slept little and talked less, while on assignment.

Each morning she woke to find him hunched over his computer. She knew he wasn't only working on this case, but monitoring various other LCR activities. After breakfast, they reviewed the emails, responding to the ones they considered possibilities. During those times, Samara would sit in awe at how Noah determined those that were real people and those that were potentially the kidnappers' bait. She soon discovered that Noah's mind was as devious, possibly more so, than the creep they were targeting. Thank God, he was one of the good guys.

When she had decided this, she couldn't say. But seeing his dedication and determination to save these children inspired her. It also had another unfortunate effect. She had become even more attracted to him. Not that she would do anything about it.

After answering their emails, Noah would change into running clothes and disappear for hours. When he returned, his muscular body would be sleek with perspiration. The first time she'd seen him like that she'd actually had to excuse herself. Never had she looked at a man's body and literally wanted to jump his bones, sweat and all.

The self-defense lessons continued, but they avoided as much body contact as possible. Extremely hard to do, but neither of them wanted to tempt fate. Whenever she saw Noah's obvious arousal or the hot, sensual expression on his face, she pretended it didn't exist. And he did the same when her nipples peaked or her breathing turned to excited pants. So far, it had worked. Admittedly her dreams were much hotter than ever before, but at least dreams didn't leave a hole in your heart.

"Mara, you bored?"

Jerking, she almost spilled the soda she held in her hand. "What?"

"You've been staring out the window for half an hour. You didn't even read the last five responses I sent."

"Sorry, just a little stir-crazy."

"Why don't you go out for a while? I can finish up here."

Now was the time to tell him. Silly, but she dreaded it. "Well, I am actually going out this evening with a friend."

Dark brows loomed over his eyes. "I thought you told everyone you were visiting your family."

"I did, but I forgot about a date I made a few weeks ago. Brad's been out of town, on a camping trip, and I've not been able to reach him."

"So he's home now?"

"Yes."

"Call him and cancel now."

Huffing out a sigh, she got to her feet. "I'm not going to cancel this late. Besides, there's no real reason for me not to go. We don't usually get busy until after midnight anyway."

"Is this guy something to you?"

She shrugged, not caring to explain that she'd been somewhat attracted to him, but compared to Noah, Brad was nothing more than just a simple, nice guy. "I've been out with him a couple of times. Rachel set us up." She shrugged again, feeling defensive for some reason. "He's a nice guy and I enjoy his company."

"Will you bring him back to your apartment?"

She wouldn't, but she didn't like him questioning her like this. "I don't know. Maybe."

Noah slammed the top of the computer shut and got up. "Hell, Samara, if I'd known you were involved with someone, I never would've asked you to help."

"What does that have to do with anything?"

"You don't need the distraction. Call him and cancel."

Hands on her hips, Samara forgot all about any tender feelings she'd been having for him. "I most certainly will not. You're not my employer, my boyfriend, or my father. I don't owe you a damn thing and I'll not have you tell me what I can and can't do."

"Fine. Go fuck him for all I care."

Speechless, she watched as Noah grabbed his car keys and stalked out the door, slamming it behind him.

"Arrogant asshole." Grabbing a pillow from the sofa, she hurled it at the door.

What right did he have to say that to her? She'd done nothing for the last few days but work with him and this was the thanks she got?

She huffed and puffed through her shower, alternately cursing Noah for being such a jerk and herself for allowing him to get away with it. Wrapping a towel around her soaking hair, she glared at the woman in the mirror. One of Rachel's sayings came to mind. "Mad as a wet hen." That's exactly what she looked like.

Eyes closed, she took a deep breath, then exhaled slowly. After several breaths, calmness washed over her. Allowing herself to get angry over Noah's words and actions gave him a power over her she couldn't allow. After this was over, he would be gone and the very real possibility existed that she would never see him again. Having any emotions regarding this man, even anger, was pointless.

With that thought, Samara was able to get ready in her usual quick and efficient manner. Dressing up was actually a treat for her. In her job it was usually business casual. At home she went for comfort. Tonight she wanted to look especially nice. She told herself it had nothing to do with the infuriating man she was briefly sharing her home with. Brad was a nice guy . . . she wanted to look pretty for him.

Standing in front of her full-length mirror, Samara observed the way the turquoise wraparound dress enhanced her eyes and how the silky material hugged her curves in a silken embrace. Her eyes, almost the same color as the dress, sparkled. She'd emphasized them further with blue liner underneath and a hint of blue on her lids. Her long hair, which she usually either allowed to dry naturally or blew-dry and pulled up in a ponytail, she took extra pains with tonight. Naturally curly hair could be a curse when one was in a hurry or had no talent for hair design. Tonight she dried and then straightened it. The results were a long, silken fall of ink-black hair flowing down her back.

With a bite of her lip and a wince of an eye, she stepped into the four-inch stilettos. She might have only worn them once, but she still remembered the pinching pain. Glancing at her legs in the mirror, she decided the pain was well worth it. Her legs looked long, toned, and fabulous.

"Take that, Noah McCall."

Refusing to ask herself why those words sprang from her mouth, Samara grabbed her purse and keys just as her doorbell rang. She opened the door, her smile of welcome firmly in place for the tall blond man standing at the door. His eyes gleaming with male appreciation, Brad Fleming smiled down at her. Easy on the eye, successful, pleasant . . . what more could a woman want?

Closing the door behind her, Samara chatted easily with Brad as they headed toward his car, determined to put the arrogant, mysterious, and irritating as hell Noah McCall completely out of her mind.

six

Hours later, Noah let himself back into Samara's apartment, feeling like a first-class prick. So she had a date. Big damn deal. She had every right to a social life. She'd done nothing for almost two weeks except help him. And how had he repaid her? By belittling and insulting her.

Slumping down onto the sofa, he took a deep breath, inhaling the light fragrance Samara always wore. He hardened with an almost unbearable erection . . . his normal response to anything to do with Samara.

He needed to get laid, that was all. It had been almost six months since he'd been with a woman. Ever since he'd heard about Bennett's reemergence, his mind had been totally focused on finding a way at him. Being around a beautiful woman like Samara day in and day out had just made his need greater. It was nothing more than that.

When this was over, he'd go back home and keep Celeste in bed for days. She always enjoyed his gluttony after a long assignment. Abstaining from sex while on assignment was something he'd trained himself to do years ago. And since Samara wasn't a real operative, his mind refused to see her as such. That was the reason he was so tempted.

His mind resolute, his determination to resist temptation back in place, Noah stood and headed to his computer. It was only a little after ten. Samara might be out for a few more hours, but that didn't mean he couldn't do a little trolling on his own. He was almost positive they'd found their guy . . . Brian Sanders, who'd been one of the first to respond.

After that first message, Noah had sent a couple of his people to the real Brian's home to talk to him and his parents. Brian had denied chatting online. Noah believed him. This had to be the bastard. It was too much of a coincidence not to be, and he wasn't a big believer in coincidences.

So far, Brian's messages had contained nothing more than some heavy flirting and mild sexual innuendos. Though he still didn't want to come on too strong and have the creep run, he was getting tired of this silly crap they'd been playing.

Noah typed in the email address for BS626 and wrote:

Hey Brian, I'm so pissed off I can't see straight. My mom is making me go stay with my grandmother in Arizona while she goes on a cruise. Can you believe how selfish she is? Taking me away from school and all of my friends for two whole weeks? I won't even be able to email you unless I go to the library. Gram doesn't even have a computer.

I'll miss you but hopefully when I get back, we can start chatting again. I'll be leaving in a few days. Hope to talk to you before I go.

Noah signed off. Now it was up to Brian to take the bait.

A key turned in the door and Noah looked up as Samara entered the apartment. His breath caught. She wore the dress she'd worn to Jordan and Eden's wedding. The one he fantasized about taking off every time he'd allowed himself to think about her. Blue silk covered her body with the kind of modesty that entices a man to stare hard to determine the secrets beneath. The dress enhanced every curve, hugged tight to every feminine detail.

All good intentions disintegrated. His cold, logical explanations for wanting this woman crumbled. Self-preservation evaporated. Self-denial took a backseat to raging desire. Without conscious thought, Noah found himself standing in front of her. Glaring down at her, he growled between clenched jaws, "No promises. No future. Just this. Here. Tonight. Your choice." A part of him desperately hoped she'd slap his face and tell him to go to hell. Another part was just as desperate for her to agree to the incredibly unromantic proposal he'd just uttered.

Her eyes, wide and filled with shock, locked with his. She stared hard, as if reading his soul.

Breath held in check, Noah waited for an answer. Desire surged and pulsed through him, strong, potent, and consuming. His breath caught in his chest when a slim, delicate hand touched his arm, giving him the answer he sought.

Taking the hand, he kissed it softly and pulled her to the bedroom.

Samara couldn't believe she was going to be so stupid. Fleeting images of every bad decision she'd ever made flashed through her mind. None of them compared to what she'd just agreed to.

So what if her date with Brad had been unexciting and dull. So what if she'd been unable to take her mind off Noah and his anger at her for not canceling her date. So what if she wanted him like nothing she'd ever wanted in her entire life. Did that mean she had to be so stupid? The door closed behind them.

Evidently so.

"Noah, I . . ."

A hand held both her wrists behind her back as his big body pressed her against the door. "Shh." Moving his mouth softly, slowly, he traced her entire face with his lips. "Every night, I dream about this body. And every morning, I wake up hard and aching for you."

"Then why haven't . . . ?"

"Because this can't be. . . . We can't be." He drew away from her and looked down. Dark, solemn eyes held secrets beyond her imagination and a desire beyond her comprehension. "You know that, right?"

Her mouth moved up in a wry smile. "Yeah . . . I think you've mentioned it a time or two."

"And?"

Her decision had already been made. Leaning forward, she whispered, "Kiss me. Please." She'd been reduced to begging and didn't care in the least.

"Mara." He said her name as if it were a reverent prayer, his mouth moving against hers as soft as a whisper. A ragged groan escaped, and Noah swallowed it as his mouth closed over hers.

Dear God, she'd forgotten how he kissed. Her arms still trapped behind her, Samara pressed up toward him and Noah released her hands, only to pull her harder against him.

As his mouth devoured hers, his hands swept down her body and her dress dropped to the floor. Pulling away slowly, he looked down at her.

Samara knew she was lacking in the chest department. Had once even considered surgery, but could never make herself go through with it. The way Noah stared at her breasts, she got the distinct impression size definitely didn't matter to him.

Pulling farther away from her, he flipped the front clasp of her bra and slipped it off. A dark, calloused hand moved over one breast, then the other. Her breath caught on a gasp of delight as her nipples peaked in anticipation.

"Are your breasts sensitive?"

"Yes."

His hands cupped both breasts, then he ran his thumbs over the distended nipples. Leaning back against the door, Samara closed her eyes as desire thrummed and whipped through her like a live electrical wire. She cried out in delight when he pinched both nipples with just the right amount of pressure.

He lowered his head and licked each nipple, swirling his tongue around them till they hardened into aching peaks. Her body trembled with need and an arousal so vicious and intense, she could barely make a coherent sound. His mouth . . . she needed his mouth on them, not just his tongue. "All . . . Noah . . . please . . ."

Lifting his head, hot breath floated across her chest. "What, baby?"

"More . . . I need more."

Cupping her butt with his hands, he bent his head and set his mouth to her breast. Taking almost the entire mound in his mouth, he sucked hard, then harder. Shock waves of lightning blasting through her, Samara placed the palm of her hand against the door to hold herself up and held Noah's head against her with the other. Tiny little sobs and moans left her mouth as arousal, dark and throbbing, pulled at her.

Lifting his head, Noah stared down, those glittering black eyes almost scaring her. Shuddering, heavy pants escaped her lips. She refused to ask herself why he looked more angry than aroused. He'd said one night, this one time. She fully intended to take advantage of this opportunity.

Reaching for his shirt, she unbuttoned the top button. His hands covered hers. . . . They worked to gether to undress him. With every piece of clothing he dropped, Samara's desire grew. She'd seen him in shorts and a T-shirt, but seeing him like this . . . totally, wholly masculine. Broad shoulders, muscular, defined arms, flat washboard stomach. Her fingers ached to trace the lines of light scarring on his chest and abdomen. Scars she'd noticed before but had never been able to ask about. Those questions rose to mind again . . . things she desperately wanted to know, but might never be able to ask. Anything beyond the physical release he sought would be met with the blank stare he used so well when she asked something he didn't want to answer.

Her thoughts scattered as a calloused hand parted her thighs and caressed boldly as it moved up toward the hot throb beating inside her . . . dying for his touch. A whimper of sound fell from her mouth as reason and thought dissolved. With gentle but purposeful intent, he fondled her curls . . . parted the folds, a finger pressed into her. Gasping cries caught in her throat as she pushed her body toward his hand.

"Mara." Her name was a groan of need. Pulling her hard against him, he slammed his mouth on hers and devoured.

Overwhelming need consumed her as she gave herself up to the glory of his mouth and arms. His tongue plunged, retreated, and plunged again, over and over, building heat, creating tension and even more need. Samara was to the point of trying to climb his body when he stopped, scooped her up, and carried her to the bed. The memory of the last time he did this, but left her lying on the bed, went through her. She soon learned he had no intention of leaving. He placed her on the bed, stripped off her panties, and spread her legs wide.

"Noah!"

Triumphant, glittering eyes gleamed up at her. "Everything, Mara. I want it all." Opening the folds of her sex, he bent his head and licked her as if she were a melting ice-cream cone.

Bucking her hips toward him, she groaned at the thrust and retreat of his tongue, first on her clit, then another lick over her entire sex . . . then a full thrust into her vagina. Release blasted through her with volcanic intensity. . . . Bucking up against him, riding his tongue, she screamed his name.

Before she could recover, Noah lifted himself away from her, slid a condom up his hard length, and plunged. Another scream . . . this time for a completely different reason. "Noah . . . wait . . ."

His penis throbbing, insistent inside her, he held still as his hot mouth, moving with delicate precision over her face and neck, whispered, "Shh. Wait a minute, sweetheart. It'll get easier." The soft, almost tortured words muttered against her neck speared straight to her sex, causing her to throb and spasm, allowing him fully inside her. "Mara, you feel so damned good."

The pain subsided as quickly as it came and with it came a realization of fullness she'd never experienced. Wrapping her legs around his hips, her arms around his shoulders, she enfolded him and gave him everything he asked for and more.

Noah rode her hard, knowing he was going too fast, giving her too much, too soon, and unable to stop himself. Control had been his life for so long and now that control was as close to being shattered as it'd ever been. His eyes locked with hers. They were glazed with passion and heat. . . . He pumped harder. She was going to come. . . . He could see it in her eyes, feel the tension in her body, winding tighter and tighter.

When she let out a little scream and he felt her

pulsing around him, he forced that control, not wanting to give in too soon, not wanting to let go too quickly. God, she felt so good . . . so right. As her gasping sobs quieted down, Noah finally allowed himself the freedom of release. He plunged, retreated, plunged again. . . . Bright, colorful fluorescent lights burst behind his eyes, electricity and heat zipped up his spine as his body exploded.

Burying his face against her shoulder, Noah gasped against her soft, fragrant skin as he fought to control another surge of desire. He could take her all night long with no problem. Going months without sex usually meant full gluttony when his body finally let go. He couldn't do that to Samara. For one thing, she was too small. She'd be tender tomorrow just from this one time. Another, larger reason existed. He'd just made a mistake of monumental proportions. No way in hell did he intend to repeat it.

He gritted his teeth as he withdrew, his cock hard and throbbing again, wanting to drive back into her, relive the tight, hot clasp he'd just experienced. It had been years since he'd done something so incredibly stupid. He wished he could blame it on Samara, but he'd been the one to initiate it. The one to take her. Now he had to live with the consequences of his stupidity.

"Noah."

The way she groaned his name said it all. Deep satisfaction, total satiation, and insatiable hunger. Exactly the way he felt and the very reason he couldn't take this any further.

He pulled himself off her and then from the bed. She raised her head, her expression startled, then confused.

"What's wrong?"

"We need to get back to work."

She wilted like a tender young flower under a blazing sun. He refused to have any guilt feelings about what had just happened. He was a prick and a bastard. She'd known that from the start. He'd warned her. She shouldn't be surprised or shocked. They'd come into the bedroom, both knowing this was sex and nothing more.

Pulling his briefs on, he turned away and dressed quickly, well aware that she still sat on the bed and watched him with wounded eyes. As he walked out of the room, he said, "I'll see if we have any messages." Then shut the door behind him.

Staring in shock at the closed door, fury and hurt waltzed, then stampeded through her. "No good, low-lying, evil son of-a-bitch bastard."

Samara sprang from the bed, ignoring the slight aches in her body. Muttering curses and vile descriptions of what she was going to do to his manhood, she jerked on a pair of jeans and T-shirt and marched to the door. A hand, shaking with temper, but mostly hurt, reached for the knob. She stopped and closed her eyes on a long sigh. Hell, what was she going to say to him? She'd walked into the bedroom with the full knowledge that he wanted to fuck her. That was it. He hadn't put perfume or flowers or anything remotely romantic in the invitation. A fuck and no more.

So stomping out into the living room and demanding an explanation or an apology would achieve what? Absolutely nothing . . . other than embarrass her. He'd only tell her what she already knew. She'd been a warm, more than willing body. Nothing more. If she made a big deal out of it, she would reveal that it meant a lot more to her.

No way in hell was she going to do that. She stripped off her clothes, covered her hair with a towel, and practically threw herself into the shower. The spray of water on her face mingled with the tears. Angry tears, mixed with deep, pain-wrenching tears. She'd be damned if he ever saw them.

Shuddering for control, Samara turned the water off and leaned against the shower stall. The knowledge that she'd been manipulated again hadn't escaped her. Not only had Noah gotten her into bed, he'd maneuvered it so that if she complained at all, she was the one who would look foolish and immature. Damn, the man was good.

Determined to look as though she could have sex with a man one minute and act like it had meant nothing other than a casual conversation the next, Samara dressed again. The fact that the jeans molded her butt quite nicely and the baby-blue T-shirt made her eyes deepen into pools of silver blue didn't escape her notice.

She quickly applied minimal makeup to her face, just a hint of blush and mascara. She didn't want Noah to comment or think she'd gone to a lot of trouble to make herself more attractive, but she also wanted to look as good as possible. Let him see what he had given up.

At that thought, her spirits flagged. What was the point? She meant nothing to him other than one good lay. Her spine straightened. She might mean nothing to him, but it didn't negate her pride, which had been mightily bruised by this man more than once. She'd be damned if she let him realize how he'd hurt her again.

Noah heard the door open and turned. She looked fresh, lovely, and so damned alluring, his body reacted before his mind could control it. Hell, just what she needed to see . . . a fully aroused man who'd just screwed her and would willingly stay inside her for days if he could.

Something else he saw, she worked desperately to hide, was her hurt. Noah was widely known for his charm and diplomacy. He negotiated and manipulated heads of state, local governments, and law enforcement with little effort. His ability to control and use people to the good of LCR had been his main focus and role for several years. He was damn good at it. So why couldn't he handle Samara Lyons with the same finesse? Why did she get under his skin so much that he ended up crushing her spirit and making her feel used?

Noah had no answer and refused to ponder it any further. The best thing he could do for her was to get this project over and done with and get out of her life. His gaze flicked back to the computer screen. The response he'd just received from Brian would no doubt do just that.

Samara offered him a tight smile. "Any responses yet?"

"Yeah, I sent something while you were gone on the chance I'd get a bite. It produced just what we've been looking for."

Her eyes flickered with excitement. "Really." She dashed toward the computer and sat beside him. "Show me."

Refusing to allow the sweet scent of her hair and the alluring warmth of her body to deter him, Noah slid the screen around and showed her the message he'd sent while she was out.

"Wow. That was gutsy."

His shoulders lifted in a shrug. "I was tired of flirting with the bastard." He clicked on the message he'd just received. "Here's his reply."

Carly, parents can be so selfish. . . . I know my mom can be a real bitch too. Do you think we could go out before you go? I can't imagine not talking to you for two whole weeks. Can you meet me somewhere?

She grinned up at Noah. "Cool."

"Yep. Exactly what we want."

"Do you have a place you're going to suggest?"

"Yeah, but I doubt he'll take it. He'll want a place he feels he can control."

Beside him, he felt her slender body shiver . . . nervousness or excitement?

"You'll be okay. You know that, don't you?"

Full lips tilted slightly. "I trust you in this."

She didn't need to expand on that comment. She trusted him to handle this. Anything else, she obviously had serious doubts. Since he didn't want to get into a conversation about what she didn't trust him with, he turned the screen back to him and typed, *I think I can get away. Remember, I'm grounded because of my grades. Can you meet me at the Ice Cream Dream . . . maybe around eleven tomorrow night?*

"Ice Cream Dream? You mean the one on Galantine Road?"

His eyes on the screen, hoping for an immediate reply, he nodded. "If he says yes, that's great. My people have pretty much commandeered the entire restaurant. If he shows up there, LCR will be able to neutralize him fairly quickly."

"But you think he'll suggest somewhere else?"

"He's probably already got a place picked out. But as soon as he gives a location, my people will get there, analyze it, plan the scenario, and we'll be good to go."

They both stared at the screen, waiting for a reply. Tension and nervousness bounced off Samara in waves and Noah could feel each pulse of the emotions as if they were tangible. Desire rose in his body. Everything within him fought against touching her. Just as he didn't think his hands could keep still any longer, an IM popped up.

Carly, meet me at the Mandolin pub on Pinson at 11 tomorrow night. Tell Robert at the door you're with me.

"Bingo. He wants a new spot." Noah typed, *See you there,* and jumped up. Grabbing his keys, he muttered, "Be back later."

Samara watched in shocked amazement as he slammed out of her apartment without any other words. What the hell had she expected? She was a tool to be used. Tomorrow, she'd dress as a teenager, evil, vile men would be captured, and Noah would be gone from her life for good.

It was what she should want. It was definitely what he wanted. He'd come to her for help, he'd gotten that, plus he got laid on the side. What more could a jerk ask for?

Samara stood and winced slightly. It had been well over a year since she'd had sex . . . if that's what one could call the incredible experience she'd had less than an hour ago. She'd always enjoyed sex immensely and was grateful that her lovers . . . all two of them, had been excellent . . . caring, considerate, and very skilled. With Noah . . . of course, one quick screw on the bed didn't really qualify him as her lover. Still, she couldn't help but compare her past experience to this time with him. Unfortunately, it couldn't compare. The heat, intensity, and sheer sexuality of the act had overwhelmed her. Noah, without a doubt, was an excellent sex partner. As a caring, considerate lover, he failed on every level.

Trudging to her bedroom, Samara stripped and slid under the covers. Ignoring the titillating scent of their recent sexual encounter was almost impossible, but she was too tired to change the sheets. She buried her face in her pillow, refusing to admit that the fragrance of hot sex and Noah's masculine musk were deliciously enjoyable. She fell asleep still trying to convince herself of that.

Noah let himself into the quiet apartment. It was a little after three in the morning and thankfully Samara was in bed. He didn't need to see her until he came to terms with this odd weakness. He'd practically run from the apartment, using the ruse that he needed to do something on the op. Which he did, but he could have made the calls from there. No, he left because if he didn't, he was going to do his damnedest to get her in bed again . . . or up against the nearest wall.

He was honest enough with himself to know he was in trouble but had enough self-preservation to know how to get out of it. All he needed was one more day and he'd be gone. Though well acquainted with self-denial, he was more than aware that he'd never been tempted like this.

Samara was pure, unsullied, and innocent. Noah had left those things behind years ago. The best thing he could do for her and himself was get out of her life as soon as possible. In a few days, he'd be just a bad memory . . . with maybe a slight twinge every now and then when she thought about the sex.

Something that surprised the hell out of him was the sex. It'd been about as hot as he'd ever had it and he'd had his share. Samara looked like an innocent angel but she'd been wild, wanton . . . perfect.

Well hell, his body was hard and aching once again. Since he was doing nothing other than torturing himself, Noah stalked to his bedroom and stripped. Pulling on running shoes and shorts, he headed toward the door. He stopped on the way and jotted a quick note to Samara, in case she woke before he returned, to stay off-line. He didn't want Brian canceling on them. This was possibly their only chance to catch the pervert and nothing could get in his way. Not even a too-beautiful woman he knew he'd never forget.

seven

"You nervous?"

Samara nodded. Trying to pretend otherwise would only be a lie. She knew there was nothing to worry about. Noah and his people were the best. That didn't negate the fact that she was bait for some very bad men. A shiver ran up her spine she couldn't hide.

His hand touched her shoulder briefly, but pulled away before she could find any real comfort. "You'll be fine," Noah reassured her. "There will be at least four LCR operatives surrounding you, inside and outside the bar. You'll be safe as you would be in your own home. Okay?"

"I know. It's just knowing that the creep is there for me." Shuddering at the thought, she said, "Turns my stomach."

"You'll barely get a chance to say hi before we get him."

"But what if it's not him? I mean, I know it's not the real Brian Sanders, but what if it's just a kid trying to impress me?"

"Tell him it's nice to meet him, and I'll get you out. Then we come back home and start again."

"You don't think that's going to happen, do you?"

"No, I don't. This is the creep we're looking for." His gaze swept down her body. "You ready to go?"

She looked down at her clothing. Her favorite jeans paired with a multicolored cropped T-shirt that showed a fair amount of gleaming skin. On a whim, she'd glued a fake jewel in her belly button. "Do I look okay . . . like a sixteen-year-old?"

He grinned. "Actually, with your hair pulled back with that clip thing, you look about fourteen."

"It's called a barrette."

"Whatever it's called, it makes you look sweet and innocent." His eyes focused briefly on her mouth and darkened with something hot and raw.

Her body responded to that look with the same need it had the night before. Samara shut down that feeling as soon as she recognized it. He'd given every indication that she might never see him after tonight. No way in hell would she entertain the slightest thought of wanting something she could never have again.

She frowned at his attire. "Why are you in disguise?"

Turning away, he grabbed his car keys from the desk. "I always wear a disguise when I'm on an op." He looked back at her and tilted his head. "What do you think?"

"You look old enough to be my father . . . my very sleazy, greasy father."

Long, oily gray hair was halfway hidden under a dirty baseball cap. A salt-and-pepper mustache covered most of his upper lip. Something had been done to his face to make it seem harder, more menacing. Colored contacts changed his eye color from almost black to an eerie mud green. He wore an old pair of jeans, scuffed snakeskin cowboy boots, and a sweat-stained shirt two sizes too small for him. How in the hell did she still find him attractive?

Samara pulled her eyes away from him. "Let me grab my purse."

Noah jerked as if startled out of a daze. "Right." He handed her a set of keys. "There's a light blue Jeep

Renegade in the parking lot. I'll follow you. One of our guys is already inside the bar. Another two are waiting in the parking lot. You get to a table and sit down. I'll stay as close to you as possible. When Brian or whatever the hell his name is sits down, talk to him. The second you're sure it's our guy, pull on your left ear." He grabbed his left earlobe and tugged. "Like this. We'll grab him and you jump the hell away. Okay?"

She nodded. It sounded simple enough. Noah was right. What could go wrong?

The bar was even nastier on the inside than it looked on the outside. Body odor blended with alcohol, cheap aftershave, and something else her nose refused to even consider. One lone window, several feet from the door, competed with the bar's yellowed tiled floor for filth supremacy. Squinting with one eye, she tried to see the streetlamp outside. The window won.

If she hadn't been sure before, she was sure now. The Brian she'd been chatting with couldn't be just a kid trying to impress her. No way would any guy, no matter how cocky or clueless, entice a young girl here for that purpose. This place was all about getting drunk and getting laid. Totally different from the guy Brian had portrayed himself as.

Robert, the doorman Brian told her to look for, had leered at her as though he'd be glad to take a turn at her. When this was over, her first order of business would be to take a long, hot shower. And then, perhaps something for a queasy stomach.

Noah sat two tables over, nursing a beer and trying to avoid offending the worn-out-looking waitress who kept flirting with him. He'd winked at Samara a couple of times, trying and succeeding in looking even sleazier. They were probably supposed to be as leering as Robert's looks had been, but all she could think was how much she'd like to go over to his table and have him hold her. Samara gave a little shake of her head. God, she was stupid. What did the man have to do to totally turn her off and make her hate him? Kill her?

A few drunk and overamorous couples swayed against each other on the minuscule dance floor. The mournful sounds of a depressed country singer added to the overall gloomy ambience. Samara looked warily around for the man who had been posing as Brian. It was fifteen minutes after their appointed meeting time. Had he changed his mind? Suspected a setup?

She'd ordered a diet drink and had barely taken a sip from the spotted, nasty-looking glass. Her mouth sandstorm dry, Samara lifted her glass for another small amount of moisture. A drunk weaved by just as she brought it to her lips. Stumbling against her chair, he upended the entire glass, saturating her shirt and jeans.

With a gasp, Samara jumped up. The drunk mumbled something and staggered away. She grabbed the one cocktail napkin on the table and sopped up as much of the soda as she could. Noah had told her not to look directly at him, but she was at a loss as to what she should do.

The heavyset waitress who'd served her drink appeared in front of her. Offering Samara an odd, grim smile, she jerked her head toward a door. "There's a bathroom in the back. Go on back there and clean yourself up."

Samara glanced over at Noah. His table was empty. A little disconcerted, her eyes swept the room. Tension mounted when she couldn't find him. He said he wouldn't leave her. Her legs sagged, noodle limp with relief, when she spotted him stalking toward her. A mixture of fury and disgust on his face. What had happened?

Her head jerked around when a hand grabbed her upper arm. The cold eyes of the waitress stared down at her. "Come on, hon. I'll show you the way." She pushed her toward a dark doorway.

Stumbling, Samara jerked away from her. "That's okay . . . I . . . hold it, just a minute. I don't . . ." A hand came up, headed for her face. Samara jerked back and screamed, "Noah!"

She heard him shout, "Mara, don't—"and then the unmistakable sound of a gunshot.

Before she could react, the hand covered her mouth with a noxious cloth. She gasped . . . then gagged. A burst of light streaked through her vision and then nothing.

Pain seared, throbbed, and drilled. Heavy eyelids blinked rapidly to force away the nightmare visions. Noah willed himself awake. Muffled sounds of a woman and man whispering fiercely in both English and French caused him to turn his head toward the voices. He made out blurred images of two people standing a few feet away from him. Swallowing hard, he croaked, "What happened?"

A soft sigh from one . . . a vile curse from the other. The images grew clearer. Eden and Jordan stood over the bed. Eden's expression was a mixture of concern, worry, and anger. Jordan's was all fury.

"Well, the son of a bitch is finally awake." Jordan's furious voice set up a fresh throb of pain in his skull.

"Stop it, Jordan," Eden snapped. "Your anger isn't going to get Samara back."

Samara.

Noah jackknifed from the bed. Pain ripped and

roared through his head and side, nausea washed over him. Gritting his teeth against both, he rasped, "Where is she? What happened?"

"I'd say, by now, she's been raped a few dozen times, you bastard."

Eden whirled around at her husband. "You're not doing anyone any good. The most important thing is to find her."

The room swayed and lurched as he placed his feet on the floor and fought for control. They had Samara. Agony, more vicious and hideous than any physical pain, swept through him.

Sweet Jesus, they had Samara.

To get his bearings . . . to focus, his bleary eyes took in his surroundings. Samara's apartment . . . her guest room. While Jordan and Eden continued to argue, Noah gritted his teeth and pulled himself to his feet.

"Noah, you can't be up. You've got a concussion. A bullet grazed your rib cage, cracked a rib. You're in no shape to do anything."

He glared at Eden, her concern for him unappreciated under the greater need to find Samara. What the hell had gone wrong? Gripping the bedpost to stay upright, he ground out between clenched teeth, "Tell me what happened."

Apparently realizing she wasn't going to convince him to lie back down, Eden gave him a brief account. "We don't know if they realized it was a setup or not. The men you placed in the parking lot, Peter and Eli, were shot. They're both in serious but stable condition. Joseph was knocked unconscious, but he's okay. No one saw them after they got her out of the bar. We found their abandoned car a few blocks away."

"So, we don't even know what kind of vehicle they're in?"

"No."

A fresh wave of pain almost overwhelmed him. What had spooked them? And what did any of this matter while Samara was most likely being brutally tortured?

"How long ago?"

Jordan and Eden exchanged anxious looks. "Over twenty-four hours now."

Noah closed his eyes. *Shit.* Jerking his head up, ignoring the piercing throb of his head, he snapped, "We get any of their people?"

Jordan nodded. "Two. One's in bad shape. The other one won't give us shit."

"Where are they?"

"Stashed in an abandoned warehouse a few miles down the road."

Jaws clenched to keep his spiraling emotions locked inside where they belonged, he headed for the bathroom. "Give me five minutes, then take me to them."

Jordan blew out a sigh. "Hell, Noah. We've done just about everything but kill them. They're not talking. Besides, you don't look as though you could intimidate a rabbit. You look like shit."

Walking with exquisite care to avoid jarring any part of his body, Noah made it to the bathroom and closed the door on Jordan's words. He might look like shit, but he felt worse than shit and nothing and no one could make him feel better. Samara was in the hands of some of the most vicious and evil men he'd ever known. He had to get to her, had to save her.

Knowing what she was going through was made even worse by the knowledge of who had her. A fresh wave of pain had him almost bent double. Precious, innocent, sweet Samara. He had promised she would be safe. Told her she had nothing to worry about, that he would protect her with his life.

God, what had he done?

Her head pounded with vicious intent. Samara thought she might be able to handle the pain if she weren't so incredibly terrified. Only seconds ago, she woke to darkness and the feeling of movement beneath her. Based upon the noxious fumes almost choking her, she assumed she was in the trunk of a car.

Though unable to see, perhaps she could find the taillight and knock it out. She'd read somewhere that if you were ever trapped in the trunk of a car, you should kick the taillight out and stick your arm or hand through it to attract other motorists. She wiggled slightly and blew out a sobbing sigh. The article failed to mention what to do if your hands and feet were tied together. Bowed up like this, there was no way in hell she could kick anything. Agonizing cramps in her shoulders and numbness in her legs told her that when she did get out of the trunk, she'd be unable to run. The lack of circulation in her legs and feet would render her legs powerless.

Memories of what had happened were sketchy and dim, but she remembered two things vividly. Noah had shouted her name and then she'd heard the blast of a gun. Had he been shot? Killed? Dear God, was Noah dead? Grief swamped her, consuming her fear and physical pain. Anguish overwhelmed her for the man he'd been, and what they could have had together, if they'd been different people. Whatever he'd done to her, however he'd hurt her, Noah had done some remarkable things in his life and she knew she'd have a gaping hole inside her forever if he was indeed dead.

The movement beneath her slowed and stopped abruptly. Fear crashed upon her again. Swallowing past the panic, Samara prepared herself to fight and survive any way she had to. Would she be killed? Raped before she was killed? Sold into sexual slavery like other young girls that'd been kidnapped? No matter what they had planned, she set her mind to overcoming and enduring whatever she had to and staying alive.

Bright sunshine flooded the small space when the trunk lid flipped up. Her eyes closed automatically against the painful intrusion.

"Get her out."

The voice, harsh and devoid of emotion, startled her and she blinked up at the giant leering down at her.

"Shit. She's awake."

This voice came from another man standing beside him. Her eyes still adjusting to the brightness, Samara couldn't make out either of their faces. Hard hands grabbed her shoulders and a groan escaped before she could hold it back.

"Cut the rope. I love to see 'em try to run."

A loosening of her wrists and legs was her only warning. Rough hands grabbed her shoulders, lifted her from the trunk, and dropped her on the ground. Slamming down onto the hard surface of the dirt road jarred her but barely penetrated her consciousness. Only aware of stinging needles tearing and ripping through her limbs, Samara gasped against agony, a jagged edge from passing out.

A heavy, muddy boot kicked at her shoulder almost playfully. "Come on, get up and try to make a getaway."

Samara gritted her teeth, refusing to move. First of all, she couldn't. There was no way her legs would hold her. Second, doing anything this vile creature wanted her to do went against every instinct she had. Would she run to get away from him? Hell yes. But only when he least expected it. Her best bet right now was to play weak and dumb, and see what she'd gotten herself into.

"Aw shit. She's just gonna lay there."

Crude laughter sounded above her. "Yeah, but when they're quiet like that, it makes for a easier screw."

Another foot nudged her, even harder. "She's about the skinniest one we've had. Good thing they don't charge us by the pound."

Dread and nausea slammed into her at the words. Frozen on the ground, Samara lay there while panic, fear, and rage twisted within her.

"Come on, little girl."

Yanked up by her hair, Samara screamed with pain and fury. The world lurched as she swayed drunkenly on her feet. Her vision blurred and thick, she made out the outline of two men, one oversized and one average. Before she could comprehend anything about her surroundings, the biggest man pulled her to him and threw her over his shoulder.

Hanging upside down, Samara squirmed and beat against his back as nausea almost overwhelmed her fear.

Hard fingers pinched her butt. "Be still."

As they walked, Samara forced herself to concentrate on their conversation. If she heard something she could use to escape, she had every intention of using it.

"You know what you're going to say?"

"Yeah . . . like we talked about. The bitch screamed out for somebody named Noah. We shot the bastard and two others in the parking lot. KJ and Billy both took hits and they're dead."

So it was true. Noah was dead. As she bounced against her abductor's back, tears poured from her eyes as grief seared her. Samara made a silent vow to avenge Noah's death in some way.

"But we don't know if KJ and Billy are dead. The radio just said several dead. We don't know if that included them."

"They looked dead to me. . . . You gonna tell him we left 'em without checking?"

The large man blew out a ragged sigh. "No, but he's going to want to know what went wrong."

"Hell man, you were there, too. You tell me. One minute the bitch was coming right at us and then she screamed. We didn't have any other choice than to pop the pricks."

The giant holding her rubbed her butt, then pinched it again. "Sure as hell hope she's worth the trouble."

"She's so small, she can't be more than fourteen or fifteen. I heard that the big boss is getting upwards of ten thousand for the real young ones. Bet nobody's even popped her cherry yet." He let out a long-suffering sigh. "Sure wish they'd let us. We're the ones taking all the risks."

The big man holding her stopped abruptly. "Hell man, why didn't you tell me you wanted to do that. I'd let you have her back there."

Her heart stopped. Was it about to happen? Was she about to be brutally raped by these two gorillas?

"Naw, she's too scrawny for me. . . . I like that bitch we got a few weeks ago. . . . You know, Lara something or the other . . . the one with the big tits."

Samara closed her eyes at the small reprieve. The longer she could hold out, the better her chances of surviving and escaping this nightmare. Though upside down and fighting through nausea and terror, she'd been able to look around. They were in a heavily wooded area. Where, she had no idea. Were they still in Alabama? How long had she been unconscious? Hours most likely since she'd been knocked out around midnight. The sun was shining bright in the sky, so the chances of her being even close to Birmingham were slim.

The one holding her froze with tension and came to a grinding halt. "There's the boss. Damn, he looks pissed, too."

"Hell, it ain't our fault. He's the one who set this up."

"You want to tell me what the hell happened?" The deep voice, thick with a southern drawl, sounded strangely familiar. Where had she heard that voice before?

The big man shrugged, almost dislodging Samara from his shoulder. "Hell, boss, we just did what you told us to do. Go get the bitch . . . is what you said. It ain't our fault somebody come with her."

"She brought someone with her?" Funnily enough, he sounded insulted.

"Yeah, some guy named Noah."

"Shit! Noah McCall."

Their boss had evidently heard of Noah. So if he knew about LCR, would he automatically realize she was a plant . . . bait for them? What did that mean for her? Would she be punished . . . treated more severely since she'd double-crossed them?

"Bring her on in here and let's tag her. Then we'll figure out what we need to do." She heard footsteps going away from her, then he stopped. "Where's KJ and Billy?"

"They got kilt, boss."

"And you just left them there?"

"Well, we had to. The police were sure to show up, so we took the bitch and ran."

The man blew out a disgusted sigh. "Did you at least take care of the man with her?"

"Yeah, shot him up good."

"Did you kill him?"

There was a long pause and the man beside her mumbled, "We think so."

"Idiots. Get in here."

Though filled with terror of what was about to happen, Samara knew a brilliant triumph. Noah might not be dead. He could still be alive and if he was, he would do everything he could to rescue her.

She vowed to stay alive, do whatever it took, enduring whatever she had to. Yes, she would try to escape when the opportunity arose, but just knowing Noah would be looking for her too gave her hope. And Samara desperately needed hope.

They entered a building and she felt a slight, quick relief when her captor pulled her off his shoulder and dropped her to the floor. Trying with all her might not to cower, to be brave, courageous, and strong, Samara flipped her long hair out of her face and raised furious eyes to the man responsible for so much misery.

Every muscle, cell, and nerve in her body went still with shock. The man with the familiar voice had the eyes of a cold-blooded killer and a smirk of pure evil. That wasn't what filled her with horror.

The man leering down at her had the face of Noah McCall.

eight

After splashing his face with water and swallowing a handful of aspirin, Noah emerged from the bathroom, filled with the cold, hard determination he was famous for. Jordan and Eden were in the living room, pacing, planning, and arguing.

Gripping the doorjamb, Noah interrupted with a growl, "Tell me what's been done so far."

Though glaring at Noah as if he'd rather beat the hell out of him than talk, Jordan nevertheless knew what the priorities were. "We used our contacts to cover the shooting. Took our injured men to a hospital. The authorities, as usual, are helping us keep it out of the press.

"The two we captured are at a warehouse. One of them was damned close to dying, so we had to bring in one of our doctors. I just got a call that the bastard's escaped into a coma, so we can't get anything from him. The other one sustained a flesh wound in his arm and a concussion, so he's got plenty of life in him. Gabe's working on him, but he can't get squat."

"What's the press reporting?" Noah asked.

"We kept it vague. Bar brawl, several killed."

Noah nodded. "Go on."

"Hell man, that's it. We don't have shit on where they've taken her."

Noah forced his legs to move forward. "Take me to the warehouse."

Noah ignored the look Jordan flashed him as they walked out the door. Jordan thought this was a waste of time. Noah didn't have time to reassure him that his method for extracting information was almost infallible. When he finished, sometimes even before he got started, most people were only too happy to talk.

It took barely ten minutes to get to the warehouse, but it felt like a year by the time he walked into the abandoned building. Two LCR operatives guarded the front of the building. Two more stood in front of a door. Sounds of fists pounding flesh and grunts of pain and rage came from the other room. But no answers.

Nodding at the two operatives, Noah pushed open the door and looked at one of his best men, beating their prisoner to a pulp. "Stop."

Gabriel Maddox jerked around. "Hell, Noah, what are you doing here?"

"Get out. Let me talk to him."

Gabe turned toward the man hanging from the ceiling and spat on him. "My pleasure."

The door behind Noah shut, leaving him alone with one of the bastards responsible for taking Samara, as well as countless other young girls. Standing with a quiet stillness that often unnerved the most unflappable, he took a few seconds to assess their captive.

Blond hair, cut military short, was matted with sweat. The man was muscular and fit . . . definitely military. Gabe had worked him over good. Eyes swollen shut, nose a bloody mess, lips busted and bleeding. He'd been stripped to nothing but his underwear. Bruises covered most of his torso. A bloody bandage covered his left upper arm. He'd been battered heavily and all apparently for nothing. The man wouldn't talk. Why?

Bennett didn't train his people to withstand torture.

If this man was former military, that would make him stronger than most . . . but why loyalty to a scumbag who preyed on children? The people they'd captured in the raids last year sang like a choir when presented with only the slightest bit of coercion. What would make this man hold out like this? What made him different?

Noticing a bottle of water sitting on the floor, Noah picked it up and held it to the man's bloodied mouth. The man gulped it down, but still didn't speak.

Though time was of the essence and he didn't plan on giving the guy much time to change his mind, Noah sensed he would resist to the death what Noah had originally planned to get him to talk. Maybe there was another way.

Pulling a chair up, he sat down in front of him. "Looks like you've been through a lot. Want to tell me why you'd protect such scum?"

No answer.

Narrowing his eyes, Noah studied the man's stoic expression. Though he would have liked nothing more than to beat him within an inch of his life to force the information, the beatings so far had gotten no results. He got the impression nothing would deter him. Which meant something held him back . . . something very important to him.

"You're not part of this, are you?" Noah asked quietly.

No answer.

"You're undercover." It was a calculated guess, but when something flickered across his face, Noah knew he'd hit pay dirt.

"Government or private?"

No answer.

Noah blew out a sigh. The longer this took, the more Samara would suffer. Noah slammed the door on that thought. He had to concentrate on the here and now. Thinking about what Samara might be going through would destroy his concentration. He was the only one who could save her and he needed this man's cooperation to find where they'd taken her.

Leaning forward, Noah laid it on the line. "Here's the deal. These bastards have kidnapped at least thirteen young girls over the past couple of months. I believe they'll take a few more and then gather them together at one meeting place. We plan to find that place, rescue the girls, and take down the organization."

He knew full well he'd just revealed information that could blow their entire operation. That didn't worry him. If this guy wasn't undercover for a good reason, the knowledge he gained from this conversation wouldn't matter. He'd never be set free.

"If there's someone you're trying to help, work with us to find her before it's too late."

A long, jagged breath sawed from the injured man's lungs. He swallowed hard. "My sister, Lara. She was taken six weeks ago in Macon, Georgia. She's fourteen."

Noah sat up. "How'd you find them?"

"I have some contacts. They hooked me up. I've been involved in three of the kidnappings." He closed his eyes and whispered, "Did my best to make sure the girls aren't hurt. They're not raping them. Just storing them until they're ready for transport."

"Do you know where the meeting place will be?"

"An old fishing camp outside of Monarch, Mississippi. We were supposed to head there after we got the girl."

Sliding his hand down his face, Noah breathed out a ragged sigh. He should have known Mitch would go home.

"How many men are involved?"

"Hard to say . . . seen three of them." He glared through swollen eyes. "One of them looks a hell of a lot like you."

Noah stood, pulled a knife from his jacket, and cut the ropes holding the man. He collapsed on the floor. "Take it easy, man. We'll get you some help."

"Gabe, get in here!" Noah shouted.

Gabe stalked into the room. "What the hell did you do?"

"I'll tell you in a minute Let's get . . ." He looked down at the half-conscious man lying on the cold concrete floor. "What's your name?"

"Justin Kelly," he mumbled.

Noah nodded. "Let's get some medical care for Mr. Kelly."

Jordan appeared at the door. "What's going on?"

"Get as many people as you can together. We need to go through some scenarios."

"You know where Samara is?"

"Yes."

"Thank God."

While Jordan pulled out his cellphone and began the task of gathering LCR operatives, Noah helped Gabe carry Justin to a cot in another room.

With barely a glance at the injured man, Eden turned to Noah. "What's going on?"

"I know where Samara is. . . . I'm heading there tonight."

She shook her head. "I know you feel responsible for Samara, but you're in no condition to go after her. Jordan and I will—"

"No, I'm the only one who can carry this off."

Eden looked at him with narrow-eyed suspicion, reading between the lines. "I knew something was going on. I think it's time you told us exactly why you've been so heavily involved in this case, when another operative could have just as easily handled it."

The time had come to reveal all. "Get Jordan and come to Samara's apartment. I need to grab some things. While I get ready, I'll tell you."

"You're sure this is the one?"

Richard nodded, ever eager to seem agreeable. "Oh yeah, boss. She told Robert she was there to meet Brian."

Mitchell Stoddard scratched the stubble on his jaw as he stared down at the unconscious girl. She kind of looked like the picture she'd sent him, but her hair had been shorter and she had more meat on her bones in the picture. He kicked at her shoulder with his boot, knowing she wouldn't wake up for a while. She seemed younger than her picture too . . . and almost too skinny.

Some of the pervs they'd sell her to went for the real young skinny ones, so getting rid of her wouldn't be a problem. If that's what he decided to do. But if she had information on Noah McCall, just how much would his boss rather have the information than another dumb, skinny-assed girl? He was willing to bet a lot.

Thomas Bennett hated Noah McCall and his no-good do-good outfit. With good reason. They'd fucked up everything last year, forcing Thomas to go underground. His boss hadn't been happy. Having his boss unhappy was not a good thing. Mitchell might never admit it to another person, but if there was one man who scared him, it was Thomas Bennett. After watching Bennett de-ball a man with a giant knife, he had a respect for the man and his knife. Mitch's balls shriveled as he remembered the poor bastard's screech of agony.

He'd decided then and there to always be on his boss's good side. Getting the whereabouts of Noah McCall would definitely put him there.

Turning back to Richard, he growled, "Go put her in the supply cabin."

"But there's no bed in there."

"Yeah. So?"

Richard was dumb as a mud ball but had enough sense not to question him any further. Instead, he hefted Carly, or whatever the hell the bitch's name was, over his massive shoulder and stomped out the door.

Mitch lay back into his leather easy chair and gazed around his cabin. He'd fixed it up a little, knowing he'd be here awhile. The place had gone downhill since nobody used the fishing camp anymore, making it the perfect place to store the merchandise until it was ready for shipment. Besides that, this place brought back good memories. Just him and his daddy. Weekends full of hunting, fishing, and fucking. What his daddy always called the three essentials of life. Damn, they'd had some good times.

Those long weekends would begin early Friday morning. Most times his mama and brother would still be sleeping. Even during the school year, his daddy would let him go. His brother never got invited, which made him enjoy himself even more.

After they picked up their supplies, his daddy would go to one of the whorehouses on the east side of town and find two ripe women out to make an extra buck. Course, they never expected some of the rough stuff, but that was half the fun . . . surprising them.

They'd all pile into Daddy's truck and be at the campground just in time for breakfast. Then, their weekend could begin. Damn he missed his daddy.

The old man would have loved to get in on this setup. Good money and all the women he could want.

He'd died before his time. Stupid drunken brawl at his favorite hangout. Mitch had been down in Texas hiding out from the law at the time or he would've come back and killed the sons of bitches responsible.

Ah well, it was over and done with and there wasn't a damn thing he could do other than live the life his daddy would've wanted for him. Last time he'd talked to the boss, he'd indicated that Mitch might be ready for bigger and better things. He kind of liked the idea of settling down in one place, making a name for himself. No law or do-gooder could touch him. He'd be indestructible.

His daddy would be proud.

Nausea soared and roared like tidal waves as consciousness returned. She'd barely had the chance to register the identity of her abductor before a noxious-smelling cloth covered her mouth and darkness swamped her once more.

Raising what felt like a watermelon-sized head from the floor, she searched blearily around. She was in some sort of cabin. A rickety old picnic table and three chairs took up most of a minuscule kitchen that looked like it hadn't been used in a decade. Two ratty-looking easy chairs sat in the middle of what was apparently a small living room. The wooden floor held garbage from fast-food restaurants. A foul odor permeated the room, causing another giant wave of nausea to almost overwhelm her. Swallowing hard, she leaned against the wall and took a moment to get her bearings and gather her composure.

The room might be filthy, vile, and disgusting, but it had one good feature. She was the only person in it.

Teeth clenched together to control the pain in her head, she managed to get to her knees, then to her feet. Swaying like a drunken sailor on a storm-tossed ship, she pressed against the rough-hewn wall behind her for balance. Blowing out a long breath to gather her wits and courage, she took a tentative step forward and grimaced at the creak of the wood floor.

"Going somewhere?"

Samara whirled around and then gasped as the room continued to spin around her. Nausea and dizziness swamped her with a vengeance. Holy hell, there was no way she'd escape feeling as though she could keel over at any time.

Wood screeched against wood as he pulled out a chair and placed it in front of her. "Have a seat and let's get acquainted."

Looking everywhere but into his too familiar face, she eased into the chair. This man had to be Noah's twin brother. There was no other explanation. Why hadn't Noah told her? Would it have mattered? Would it have changed what happened? Probably not. But the worst had happened and now she felt blindsided and so damn disoriented it was hard to think straight.

Did this man know his brother was out to get him?

Taking a deep breath, she raised her head to look at him. Until she knew what she faced, she saw no reason to stop pretending. She was a teenager who'd planned to meet another teen by the name of Brian Sanders. "So were you just pretending to be Brian?"

The smile he flashed her was so much like Noah's, a sob built in her chest she had to bite her lip to suppress.

"Yeah, that's me . . . the jock de jour. Though now that we've met in person, you can call me my preferred name . . . Mitchell."

"Why did you lie?"

A calculating scowl replaced the smile. "Princess, don't play games with me. You know exactly what and who I am. And I ask the questions, not you. Are you part of the operation that Noah McCall put together or was he using you as bait?"

"Who's Noah McCall?"

The back of his hand flew at her face so fast, she had no chance to avoid it. "I said, I ask the questions. You know damn good and well who Noah McCall is, so don't be giving me any of your lying shit."

Tears blurring her eyes from her throbbing cheekbone, Samara pressed her lips together to stop them from trembling. "I don't know what you're talking about. I was supposed to meet a guy named Brian Sanders at that bar. I spilled a drink on me. A waitress was showing me where to clean up and then someone knocked me out."

"And you're telling me you didn't scream the name Noah?"

"I might have screamed 'no.' "

A broad, swarthy hand scratched at his beard stubble, as if trying to determine the validity of her answer. They couldn't prove Noah had anything to do with her. The longer she could put them off, the better the chances of Noah finding her. She refused to ask herself how he would know where to look, if he was even alive.

As his black eyes seared her, Samara worked hard to look like a scared teenager who only wanted to go home. Which wasn't really far from the truth.

A smirk appeared on Mitchell's face. Then he gave a slow, taunting shake of his head. "You can't lie worth shit, darlin'. I know enough about LCR people to know you're not one of them. Which means he hired you for this particular gig. Why?"

Samara remained silent. Since whatever lie she told wouldn't be believed, and she refused to tell him the truth, her only option was silence.

His stare continued for another long minute. Then

Mitchell stood and looked over her shoulder. "Come on in, boys."

Samara's head jerked around. The two men who'd abducted her headed toward her. Their knowing leers giving her a good idea of what was to come.

"Strip her," Mitchell ordered.

Jumping from the chair, Samara took two steps to the door before a hand yanked on her hair, stopping her in midflight. She slammed back into the mountainous man. The other man came at her from the side. Samara whimpered. Agonizing terror took control of any courage she'd been able to gather.

Closing her eyes against the horror ahead of her, a small sane part of her prayed for the guts and fortitude to survive.

She screamed at the first slice of the knife.

nine

The acid stench of defeat and despair grew stronger as Noah made his way toward his boyhood home. Getting within a hundred miles of Monarch, Mississippi, was something he'd gladly travel across the globe to avoid. Avoidance now was impossible. Samara was in that hellhole and the brother he'd planned to bring to justice was with her. What Mitch had done to her, Noah refused to think about.

Samara was strong, a survivor. She would do what she had to do until he could get to her. And she knew full well he would move heaven and earth to save her. He might have treated her badly in many ways, but rescuing people was his job and he knew of no one more important to rescue.

Jordan and Eden had been furious when he told them the full story. Eden felt she'd been betrayed. She had tried to understand his reasons for keeping this to himself, but he'd seen her hurt.

Last year, when Noah had realized his brother was working for Bennett, he'd been stunned. Not by Mitchell's involvement in the sleaze of human trafficking, but how close he was to him. For years, Noah had searched for his brother, always seeming to be just within reach but never catching him. There was little Mitchell hadn't done and Noah knew almost all of it. The only thing he hadn't known was where his brother was hiding.

When Bennett had gone underground, so had Mitch. Since he'd never been so close before, he worked endlessly trying to uncover their location. When this new Internet scam popped up, Noah had paid careful attention. Bennett's stink had been all over it. Wherever Bennett was, Mitch wouldn't be far behind. Evidently Thomas Bennett had become Mitch's replacement for dear old Dad. Made sense. Bennett and Farrell Stoddard had so much in common.

Well before LCR came into existence, Noah had planned for the day he would bring his brother to justice. Raping Rebecca had just been a starting point for Mitchell.

After Noah's release from prison, he'd had but one goal, making Mitchell pay. Fortunately, his friend and mentor, Milo Evans, had helped him see that he possessed much more potential than just a thirst for revenge. Through the long years of creating LCR and developing its people, Noah still had full intentions of finding Mitchell and putting him where he belonged.

With that in mind, he'd kept a tight cover for Michael Stoddard, Mitchell Stoddard's twin. Records indicated that Michael had been in and out of prison for various offenses, including assault, robbery, rape, and attempted rape. The records weren't real, but he was one of the few who knew that. If anyone tried to find Michael Stoddard, they would only find information about a career criminal with a remarkable and impressive rap sheet. Noah had known full well that was the only thing that would ever impress his brother.

The one thing he'd never planned was to involve an innocent. Using Samara to set the trap had made such sense at the time. And it would have worked if he hadn't screwed it up. He'd watched Samara sit at that table, nervously sipping her drink, and he'd been filled with the overwhelming urge to get her out of there. Seeing her in that filthy place, knowing he was responsible for her being there had suddenly been too much. He'd gotten up and said something to Joseph that either they'd been made or something had happened. That's when the men had grabbed Samara. The look of sheer terror on her face would be something he'd remember to his death. He was responsible for that terror and would fight both heaven and hell to make it up to her.

Surviving wasn't even an issue. This battle with Mitchell had been building to a fatal ending for years. Noah was sure of only two things: when this was over, Samara would be alive and Mitchell would be brought to justice. And if that got Noah killed, perhaps there was justice in that, too.

Huddled on her side in a corner, Samara shivered from shock, pain, revulsion, and anger. They'd sliced her clothes off with knives and then tore the rest with their hands. Once nude, she'd been pushed, shoved, and thrown between the three men as if she were a ball. With each pass, they grabbed, pinched, and slapped anything and everything they wanted. And with each toss, they'd screamed obscenities and questions regarding Noah McCall. . . . Who was he, where was he, how did she know him?

At first, she'd been so terrified she had barely managed to do anything but cry and scream. When she realized her tears and terror only amused them, she'd forced herself to stop. Then the anger had emerged. After that, she began to fight. Each time she was thrown to another man, she did her damnedest to inflict some kind of harm. Scratching, punching, and kicking. They seemed to enjoy this too until she'd kicked gorilla man deep in the balls. She saw fury and pain flash in his eyes right before his fist came at her. Then there was only blackness.

Chills shuddering through her, Samara pulled up to a sitting position and wrapped her arms around her legs to keep warm. She was still nude, covered with bruises, cuts, and scratches. Everything hurt. But she had been lucky. They hadn't raped her.

Why, she didn't know. She only knew that though she'd been violated, it hadn't been as bad as it could have been. Now she just needed to figure out how to escape.

Hands pressed against the wall, wincing with every movement, she rose to her feet. Her eyes swept frantically around the small, stark room, hoping to find something to put on. She would escape, clothes or not, but she greatly preferred clothes if she was going to be traipsing through the woods.

Spotting a man's shirt on the back of a chair, she hobbled over to it, her ankle throbbing with every step. That last kick had cost her. Ignoring the disgusting body odor emanating from it, she eased her arms into the shirt, pleased it was large enough to hang almost to her knees. Shoes would be good, but she'd lost hers somewhere between Birmingham and here. Finding a pair of size six narrow lying around this dump seemed doubtful.

Now to escape. Night had fallen, so she'd apparently been unconscious for several hours. She had no idea where anyone was, but hoped and prayed they were asleep and wouldn't come looking for her until daylight. Why they hadn't tied her up was something she couldn't figure out, so she didn't try. This might be her only opportunity to get out and she was going to take it.

Easing the door open, she stuck her head outside for a quick peek. Silence. The entire place was pitch-black. She knew she should be thankful for that since hiding from them would be much easier, but it would be nice if she could see to escape. However, going into a dark, unknown forest was much more desirable than staying here with these lunatics. Samara gingerly hobbled from the porch and took off.

Mitch pulled a beer from his private stash and took a long swallow. The bitch was hiding something. He'd seen it in her eyes, smelled it on her skin. His daddy had taught him lots of useful things, and one of them was how to detect a liar. She was tough, though, he had to give her that. After being stripped and mauled by three men, she hadn't given them anything.

As they'd thrown her around the room, his dick suddenly noticed what his eyes had appreciated all along. The girl might look skinny in her clothes, but naked she had a nice form. Sweet, juicy-looking tits, firm, squeezable ass, and those soft, smooth thighs would make for a long, sweet ride. He'd just been ready to go in for a taste when she'd slammed her foot into Richard's gonads. Idiot had reacted before he thought, which was pretty typical for the moron. He'd knocked the hell out of the girl and then that was that.

Mitch thought about punishing Richard, but seeing the poor bastard's tears, he figured he'd been punished enough. Besides, a man had a right to protect his privates, didn't he?

She'd wake up eventually and then if a good, hard screwing didn't get the truth out of her, he'd see if his other men wanted to give her a try. After five or ten went at her, she'd be singing a whole new tune. Once he got what he wanted, the bitch would die. No way in hell was he leaving her alive to spill her guts. Nor could he take her to Bennett. By the time he got what he was after, she wouldn't be much to look at. If there was one thing Bennett liked, it was to have the girls nice and fresh. This bitch might have looked good when she arrived, but that wouldn't last long.

Samara barely noticed the rocks and sticks poking and cutting her bare feet. Arms extended in front of her, she ran slower than she would have liked. Besides getting caught, or eaten by a wild animal, she also feared running smack into a tree, ending any chance of escape. If she could get at least a couple of miles away before dawn, she'd have a better chance of succeeding.

A muffled sound caused her to stop abruptly and sink to her knees. Rapid thumps of her heart and breath wheezing from her lungs drowned out the sound. Samara forced her breathing to slow as her ears strained to listen. Was someone behind her? Maybe an animal in the brush? Holding her breath, she listened.

A feminine sob. The sound unmistakable and heart wrenching. No matter how desperately she wanted to escape, Samara knew she couldn't leave without trying to help. Standing again, she squinted through the darkness. But where was the girl?

Just as she took a step toward the sound, the moon passed beyond a cloud, illuminating the entire area and highlighting a small cabin hidden almost totally in the trees. Sending up a prayer of thanksgiving, Samara dashed toward the cabin. Within a few yards, she stopped to check her surroundings. She hadn't been guarded, but it didn't mean this girl wasn't. She heard and saw no one.

Tiptoeing up on the porch, wincing with every creak, she eased the door open. Two young girls sat on a cot, holding each other, naked and no doubt terrified. Their heads jerked around when the door opened, fear and horror etched on their faces. Sweet God. Ashley

Mason and Courtney Nixon . . . she recognized them from the pictures Noah had shown her.

Samara raised a finger to her lips, indicating they should keep quiet. Her eyes searched the dimly lit room but found no one else. Ignoring her throbbing and bleeding feet, she tiptoed to their bed and whispered, "Can you run?"

Anxious eyes gleaming with gratitude, they both nodded and stood. Samara's heart twisted and then cracked. They were handcuffed together and then cuffed to the bed. How the hell was she going to free them?

Her eyes searched wildly for anything she could use. The room was devoid of everything but the cot, a small lantern, a bedpan, and some scattered clothing.

She pulled hard on the handcuffs attached to the bed, already knowing they would be secure. Panicked frustration set in and she fought the urge to sit down and have a good cry. Running her fingers through her mass of tangles, her mind desperately searched for an answer. She winced as her hand caught on something, yanking at her scalp. Her fingers pulled it away from her knotted hair, and she looked at what she held. Her heart kicked up with an optimistic beat. Her barrette. Using her teeth, she quickly stripped the rubber from around the stem, sat down, and began to work.

The girls remained quiet and Samara could feel waves of desperation bouncing from them. With shaking hands and absolutely no knowledge of how to pick a lock, she probed and prodded the small opening. With one small poke and a twist, she heard a soft click. They were free!

Though both girls looked too weak and traumatized to do a lot of running, she knew from experience that fear was an excellent motivator.

Pointing to the discarded clothing on the floor, she kept her voice as low and soundless as possible. "Get your clothes on. Quick."

While the girls dressed, Samara kept a lookout at the window. Her heart was racing full speed. The longer they stayed here, the better their chances of getting caught. Something inside her told her they had to leave . . . now! She turned to see that most of the clothing they'd put on was nothing more than rags. Most likely their clothes had been cut off of them, as hers had been.

Forcing the terror and fury back, Samara concentrated on the task ahead of them. Gesturing with her hand, she indicated they should join her at the door. Barefoot and barely clothed, relief and gratitude on their terrified faces, they moved quickly to stand behind her.

With as much stealth as time would allow, Samara eased the door open again. Still clear. And thank God, the moon still glowed. They stepped from the porch and began to run. Earlier she tried to run as quietly as possible, but had been more than aware of the noise she'd made. Her feet had crumpled and shuffled dried leaves with an almost unearthly loudness, at least to her ears. Now, with three of them running, a herd of galloping horses would probably be quieter. Since there was nothing they could do about that, she forced herself to forget about the sounds and run all the faster.

They ran perhaps half a mile when one of the girls cried out. Samara turned in time to see Ashley fall face-first onto the ground. She dropped to her knees beside her. "Are you all right?"

Gasping and wheezing, Ashley nodded and scrambled to her feet. Waves of admiration for these two young girls almost overwhelmed her. What had they suffered from those brutes? Since sympathy would do nothing for them right now, Samara jumped up and took off running again, looking frequently over her shoulder to make sure they were still behind her.

About a mile from the cabin, Samara stopped for a new reason. A cessation of sound. Other than their pounding feet and harsh breathing, silence surrounded them. The creatures of the night, crickets, frogs, and owls, were quiet and still. Why? They'd been happily chirping, croaking, and screeching only seconds before.

"What's wrong? Why did we—"

Samara raised her hand for silence. Something was off. Using her God-given instincts and remembering Noah's and Eden's words, Samara knew someone was out there, watching them. Mitchell and his men?

Nothing moved. No sound was made. Samara knew that even if they were being watched, they still had to make a run for it. If even one of the girls made it out, it was better than nothing. With that thought, she forced her body to move forward.

She took two steps. Mitchell stepped out from behind a tree.

"Well, well, well. Looks like I found me some escapees."

Nails extended like claws, Samara threw herself at Mitchell and screamed, "Run!"

ten

Kicking the door open with his foot, Mitchell threw Samara into the cabin she'd escaped from only hours ago. Landing on the floor with a hard crash, she lay there panting, cursing, and hurting like hell. Still, triumph raged through her. The girls had gotten away. Mitchell had been by himself and her distraction provided exactly what they'd needed. Now she just prayed they were able to find help or else all her efforts would have been wasted.

Mitchell stood at the door and shouted, "Richard, get in here . . . now!"

From her experience yesterday, Samara knew Richard was the largest of the men who'd abducted her . . . and she suspected the dumbest.

The thump-thump of heavy booted feet came closer. "Yeah, boss?" The big man sounded timid and scared. Samara couldn't help but be happy that one of them knew that feeling, too.

"You were supposed to be watching her. What happened?"

Raising her head, Samara was shocked to see tears pooling in Richard's eyes. He was more than just scared, he was terrified.

"I just went for some coffee."

"To Tupelo?" Mitchell bellowed.

"No . . . I . . . uh . . . she was unconscious and I . . ."

Mitchell grabbed Samara's arm and yanked her up from the floor. "This bitch weighs a third of what you do and has three times the brains."

"I'm sorry, boss. I'll be more careful."

"I know you will."

Surprised at Mitchell's soft, almost conciliatory tone, she jerked her head up to look at the two men. Perhaps Mitchell had some kind of humanity in him after all. Neither looked any happier. Richard was literally shaking in his giant boots and Mitchell's cold face had Samara shivering.

Pulling Samara with him, Mitchell growled, "Come on."

He pushed her outside, onto the porch, and then down the steps. The moon now glowed with bright intensity above them, illuminating the small grassy area. Several men stood around, none of them meeting Mitchell's eyes. Richard stood in front of his boss. The fear on his face almost, but not quite, made her feel sorry for him.

"Everybody, listen up," Mitchell's voice boomed. "We got two girls running loose. Find them. I want them alive. If you have to rough 'em up a little, that'll be overlooked. No sampling the merchandise, though. Understood?"

Everyone, including Richard, nodded but remained in place, obviously waiting for their boss to issue further orders.

"Brady, you organize the search. Take everybody but Vince and Stephen."

"You want me to stay here too, boss?"

Mitchell turned to Richard and smiled. Then, as casually as one would scratch an itch, he pulled a gun from his pocket and fired into Richard's face. Blood, bone, and brain matter splattered everything within five feet of the dead man.

Horrified, Samara stared at the man lying on the ground, not two feet from where she stood. A foul odor permeated the area. Her face and body felt wet. A quick glance down at her shirt had her stomach revolting. *Oh God. Oh God. Oh God.* Sobbing . . . gagging, she turned and vomited. Since there was little to throw up, dry heaves attacked. She fell to her knees, her legs no longer able to hold her up.

A distant part of her brain heard Mitchell order his men to remove Richard's carcass. Then he grabbed her arm and pushed her back into the cabin.

Flinging her into a small corner of the room, she watched as he pulled a beer from a cooler on the counter and pulled a chicken leg from a bucket on the table. He sat at the table, took a swig of beer, a giant bite off the leg, and grinned. "Bet you're hungry."

After what she'd just witnessed? She had serious doubts of ever being able to eat again. Samara had never seen a human being killed. Actually, the nearest she'd come to seeing something killed was perhaps a spider and that was probably only because one of her brothers had killed it for her.

She closed her eyes. God, she'd been so protected, so cosseted. Had stupidly believed she could handle herself, defend herself against an attacker. Now she felt furious with her own inadequacies. After this was over, *and by God, she would survive*, never again would she be this helpless and vulnerable. No one would ever get a chance to do this to her again.

Though her shirt was splattered with blood and other things, she had to get Richard's remains off her skin. Twisting the back of the shirt around, she found a relatively clean spot and rubbed her face, almost gagging again when she saw the results. A wave of dizziness washed over her. Leaning her head against the wall, she closed her eyes as consciousness floated away.

A loud belch woke her. Blinking, she looked up to see Mitchell staring at her, and still eating his chicken.

"Bet you're thirsty. It's been almost two days since you had anything to eat and drink. You give me something on Noah McCall and I'll get you some water and food."

Samara tried to swallow and found she couldn't. Her tongue was swollen, her mouth burned and stung. When she put her tongue to her chapped lips, all she could taste was dried blood. She refused to wonder if the blood was hers or Richard's.

Yes, she was thirsty . . . thirstier than she'd ever been in her life. But not enough to betray Noah.

"I don't know Noah McCall, but he evidently scares you shitless." After witnessing the cruel brutality of Mitchell, and knowing firsthand he was a cold-blooded, ruthless killer, she could barely believe those taunting words had come from her mouth.

Black eyes narrowed, glittering with cold finality. A slow smile spread over his face. Sick dread filled her. He'd looked like that right before he blasted Richard's head off.

Mitchell pulled his big body from the chair and unbuckled his belt.

A panicked gasp of air wheezed through her dry mouth. Was this it? Had she enraged him enough that though his men had been warned not to rape the girls, he was willing to break his own rules?

When the belt whisked out of the loops and without warning whipped against her bare skin, Samara squealed in pain and grabbed her stinging leg. The belt whooshed toward her again, licking like fire over her face. She doubled over, her arms covering her head. As the leather ripped into her flesh, she wondered bitterly if this would satisfy him or if he had something more planned for her. That was her last coherent thought.

Again and again Mitchell swung the belt at every angle over her body. Samara curled up into a ball, the thin shirt she wore providing no protection from the biting sting of leather.

Sobs ripped and exploded from her lungs, the pain burning and intense. She tried to force her mind to focus on something besides her agony and had little luck. With one last vicious sting against her shoulder, he stopped.

Almost unconscious from the searing pain, Samara gritted her teeth to keep from passing out. The rasp of a zipper told her he hadn't finished. Biting her lip to keep from screaming, blood filled her mouth. She braced herself for the coming event . . . determined to fight him no matter what. She waited till he reached for her. With the last bit of strength, she sprang to her feet, grabbed a chair, and swung it at him. "Bastard!"

With a surprised laugh, he batted the chair away. Having nothing else to fight with, she jumped at him. One fist glanced his chin. He caught the other one with his hand and bent it back behind her.

Samara squealed with pain and fury . . . helplessness.

An expression of shocked amusement covered his face. "Damn, bitch. For such a little thing, you got spunk." Shoving her onto the floor, he followed her down. Pinning her arms above her head, he spread her legs. Hot, fetid breath washed over her face. "Fight me, baby. It's my favorite kind of fuck."

Screaming, crying, cursing, she bucked and squirmed, trying with all her might to dislodge him. Everything within her screamed denial. This couldn't be happening. . . . She couldn't let it happen.

His erection pressed against the inside of her thigh.

Samara screamed, "No!"

Someone pounded on the door. "Hey, boss."

"I'm busy," Mitchell shouted.

"You might want to put that on hold, boss. We got a situation here."

Breath sloughed through her lungs like an asthmatic marathon runner. His image wavy and surreal above her, and then the heavy, smothering weight of his body lifted off her.

Blowing out a deep sigh, Mitchell stomped to the door and flung it open. "What the hell is it?"

"We got company."

"Who?"

"There's a man at the gate . . . looks just like you . . . says he's your twin brother."

"You don't say? Well, bring him on in here."

While they talked, Samara rolled over and crawled into her corner. She didn't look up when the door slammed shut, but she knew Mitchell hadn't left. She was afraid to look at him. If he saw the excitement and joy in her expression, Noah would never make it past the door alive.

The clomp-clomp of big feet came toward her. He stopped in front of her, pulled her up by her hair, and smirked. "Later, bitch."

A fist slammed into her jaw.

Mitchell leaned against the doorjamb and forced a welcoming smile on his face. "Well, well, well, the prodigal brother returns."

Michael had changed, that was for damn sure. Last time Mitch saw him, tears had streamed down his skinny face as they'd trotted him off to jail. Now the face that looked so much like his was granite hard, his eyes as cold as a January deep freeze. As usual, Daddy had been right. Michael going to prison had been the right thing to do. Nothing like a solid dose of badasses to toughen a guy up. His pansy-assed brother didn't exist anymore.

Funny, but Mitch realized he still hated him. Some things would never change.

He'd heard about all his brother's adventures. Michael Stoddard had a reputation to be envied. Not that Mitchell would ever admit that. Having his brother think he had any kind of admiration for him went against every cell in Mitch's body.

A mean smirk of a smile twisted at Michael's lips. "Heard you were back in town. Thought I'd see what you've been up to."

Mitch jerked upright at that news. He didn't need anybody knowing anything about him. "Who's been talking?"

Michael lifted a careless shoulder. "Stinky Brighton told Pete. Pete told me."

"Where'd you see Pete?"

"He was just coming out of the Farm when I was going in."

"Pete's dead."

A slow grin spread across his brother's face. "Yeah, fortunately I talked to him before that."

Mitch guffawed. "Yeah, he probably wouldn't have much to say after that. What were you in the Farm for this time?"

"Some stupid shit . . . only stayed a few months. I'm running low on funds. Figured I'd check and see if you had anything going."

Mitch stood back, allowing his brother entrance. "Come on in. I might have something for you."

He turned around when he heard Michael stumble behind him and jerk to a stop. "What's wrong?"

His brother nodded toward the bitch lumped in the corner. "She get sleepy?"

Mitch chuckled. "Naw, gave her a little knock when I heard you were coming. She'll wake up eventually."

"Sorry to interrupt."

"No problem. She's not really my type anyway . . . too skinny." He pulled a couple of beers out of a cooler and handed one to Michael. "So tell me, bro, what've you been up to?"

Michael sat at the table, leaned back, and propped his feet on the table as if he owned the damned place. Mitch felt the familiar fury. How he hated this bastard. Almost from birth, he'd been taking what should have been all his.

Eyeing his brother with feigned interest, Mitch took a swig of beer and halfheartedly listened as Michael bragged about his last few years. Like he should give a shit? The only reason he'd never killed the fucker was because his daddy wouldn't let him.

Daddy wasn't around anymore though . . . was he?

Michael had started his fourth story when Mitch just couldn't take it anymore. Standing, he stretched and yawned, making no effort to hide his boredom. "There's an empty cabin three doors down. You can stay there. It's cleaner than most of the others . . . even got running water and clean sheets on the bed." Tucking his shirt into his pants, he headed toward the door. "I gotta go do a few things. When I get back, we'll sit down and talk. I got a proposition for you."

Michael stood and rubbed his crotch. "Got anything around here to take care of an ache?"

"Not right now. I'll try to find one for you on the way back."

"What's wrong with the one in the corner?"

"I'm still trying to break her in. She's got something I need."

"She's got something I need, too. Come on, man. Let me give her a try."

"No, I—"

"You owe me, bro."

Michael's voice was about as hard and mean as he'd ever heard it. Shit, he was still pissed about that prison thing. Better give in to him now, just in case he'd come here for retribution. If he asked for too much, he'd do what he'd wanted to do for years, only sooner. He'd whack his brother's ass and bury him where even buzzards couldn't find him.

Mitch pretended an exasperated sigh. "Okay, but see if you can get any information from her. Specifically on a man named McCall. We've been at her for two days and she won't give us shit."

Ignoring the smug smile Michael flashed him for getting his way, Mitch stomped out the door. Twenty to thirty minutes was about the longest he'd ever been able to stomach his brother's presence.

And if Michael got something out of the bitch? What the hell, it saved him the trouble.

With monumental effort, Noah maintained his sleazy smile as he crossed over to Samara, every ounce of his control almost depleted. Having to sit and brag about his corrupt life while Samara lay on the floor, unconscious and helpless, had him teetering at the edge. He stooped down and only when he heard the door open and close, indicating his brother had left, did he whisper her name.

Moving her hair from her neck, Noah quickly checked her pulse and blew out a long sigh at its strong beat. "Mara . . . sweetheart. Can you hear me?" That control cracked further when he saw the thick welts on her legs. Holding her shoulders gently, he slowly turned her over. Face bruised, bloody and so damned pale, if he hadn't felt her heartbeat, he'd have assumed she was dead.

The shirt she half wore was torn, covered in blood and other matter he could only speculate on. He drew a long, shaky breath. The best thing he could do was get to a place where he could care for her.

Noah scooped her up into his arms and stalked out the door.

Locating the empty cabin, he kicked the door open, slammed it shut with his foot, and lowered her to the cot. Her eyelids flickered but remained closed.

"Mara, can you hear me?"

Still no answer. Going to the adjoining bathroom, Noah ran the water till it was clean. Pulling a T-shirt from his duffel, he wet it and returned to the main room. He stopped abruptly at the door. The bed was empty.

"Shit." Noah ran to the door. Samara had managed to get to the bottom of the steps but had collapsed on the ground. Pulling in a shuddering breath, he scooped her back up and returned to the cabin.

Laying her down again, Noah began the heartbreaking task of washing her body and registering and examining her injuries. Thick red welts stood out against the paleness of her skin. She'd been beaten with something . . . most likely a belt. He remembered the distinct markings from the days his father used his belt. He also remembered they hurt like hell.

He pulled her shirt off and wiped her torso. Two large bruises on her right breast and a wicked-looking red welt on the left one. He washed the rest of her body, noting and grimacing at each cut, scratch, and bruise. Had she been raped? He smelled . . . saw no semen, no bruising or redness on the inside of her thighs. That didn't necessarily mean she hadn't been sexually violated. He would wait until she woke, then deal with the truth.

He rinsed the T-shirt of blood and returned, relieved to see she'd stayed put this time. He didn't know if she was unconscious or awake but in such shock she couldn't speak. As he continued to clean her wounds, Noah talked. It was mostly nonsense and soothing, inarticulate sounds and words, but for some reason she seemed to rest easier. He refused to ask himself if he was just imagining this to ease his conscience. Noah knew full well she'd never forgive him for his betrayal, nor would he ever forgive himself for what she'd been through.

Returning to his duffel, he dumped his clothes on the bed and pulled away the fake bottom. It was filled with various medical supplies and other things he would need. Mitchell's men had searched the bag but thankfully were too lazy to look at it closely. Grabbing medicated ointment and bandages, Noah turned back to Samara. Teeth clenched against pure fury, he covered her body in ointment and bandaged the oozing cuts.

When he got to her feet, vile curses flew from his mouth. They were almost black. Blood crusted over several deep gouges and cuts. Samara had most likely tried to escape in her bare feet. Noah returned to the bathroom and wet another T-shirt down. As he cleaned her feet, his mind returned to last week when he walked into the living room and found a laughing, happy Samara talking on the phone as she painted her toenails a scarlet red. He gently wiped at her toes, where only a small amount of polish remained.

Knowing his torturous thoughts would lead him nowhere, Noah forced his mind back to his task. Continuing his litany of soothing, nonsensical words, he hoped that something was getting through to her traumatized mind.

Peace. She floated in it. Why? Had she died? No, if she were dead, she wouldn't be hurting. Waves of pain ebbed and flowed through her like a never-ending tide. Something was different, though. What?

Should she open her eyes? No, might be a dream. If she woke and the nightmare continued, she didn't want to know. Staying in this semiconscious state of not knowing was much more pleasant.

A gravelly, masculine voice, so much like Noah's, penetrated her numbed mind. Yes, must be a dream. How many times had Noah come to her in her dreams? Soothing her, reassuring her. With Noah, she was safe. Nothing and no one could hurt her.

"Mara, sweetheart, please wake up and flash those pretty eyes at me."

No one but Noah had ever called her Mara. She smiled at the memory.

A wet cloth moistened her mouth, tracing the smile. "That's my girl. Now open those beautiful eyes."

Blinking lids heavy with exhaustion, she barely squinted, so afraid that this really was a dream and she'd wake up from it. Noah sat beside her, his black eyes blazing with more emotion than she'd ever seen in him. A soft sob hitched in her chest. "I thought you might be dead."

"And here I was thinking the same thing about you."

Tears fell from her eyes, stinging the cuts on her face. "Was so afraid."

A warm, wet cloth dabbed at her tears. "I know, baby. . . . God, I'm so sorry. I never meant any of this to happen."

Samara tried to swallow, but her tongue was too swollen and dry for moisture. "Can I have something to drink?"

Noah surged to his feet and returned with a soda can. "This is the only thing I could find. I rinsed it out. . . . The water should be okay."

Samara tried to raise her head and found herself too weak. Noah lifted her head and gently pressed the can to her mouth. She sipped slowly, knowing too much at one time would make her feel worse.

She swallowed gratefully as her eyes took in her new location. "Where's Mitchell?"

"Said he had business to take care of."

She took another sip of water and dropped her head back to the pillow. "He's after two of the girls, Ashley and Courtney. . . . They escaped this morning."

"How do you know?"

"I helped them. They got away. But he caught me and brought me back here."

Samara closed her eyes. The events after that would remain forever in her mind. The grizzly killing of Richard and then her beating and near rape. Water surged back up her throat. She tried to raise her head.

"Stay still. You're too weak to move."

She pressed her hand over her mouth. "Need to throw up."

Noah shot up from the bed, grabbed a small trash can from a corner, and placed it on the floor, beside the bed. While he held her hair back, she heaved until all the water she'd swallowed was gone.

Gasping and feeling even more ill, she lay back down.

Regret, anger, and guilt were etched like granite in his face. "I'm going to get you out, Mara. I promise you."

Her eyes felt heavy in her head, while the rest of her body felt as if it were floating above her. She mumbled, "Sleep," then unconsciousness claimed her.

More than a decade had passed since Noah felt consumed with a killing rage. He'd learned to harness his anger, focus the energy and pain where it would do the most good. Self-discipline and control kept him sane and alive for years. All of that was gone. Mitchell would pay. For what he'd done to Samara. The young girls he'd abducted. For Rebecca. And countless other women over the years.

When Noah had started on this mission, his plans had been very specific. First, he would rescue the victims, and second, he would bring his brother to justice. Justice had meant prison. Lawful, just and right.

Now, despite the knowledge that taking his brother's life might well destroy his remaining humanity, Noah could no longer deny the very real possibility that Mitchell Stoddard would finally meet his maker and that his brother, Michael, would be the perpetrator of that act.

As Samara slept, Noah sat beside her, watching the rise and fall of her chest as she breathed and thanking God that she could. He'd known she was gutsy and strong, but what she'd been through and surviving it with her sanity intact spoke volumes about the steeliness of her backbone. The term *steel magnolia* was a fitting description for this beautiful, gutsy woman.

Though he hated to leave her, he needed to find Mitchell and get more information. The man Justin Kelly, who'd joined Mitchell's band of thugs to find his sister, had told them the truckload of teen girls would arrive here and then be transported for shipping somewhere along the coast.

His people wouldn't move until the truck arrived. If the bastards bringing the girls suspected a problem, there was no telling what they'd do to their victims. Until then, he would play the sleazy, lowlife, perverted man Mitchell expected.

Refusing to acknowledge his exhaustion, Noah pushed himself to his feet. He needed to get going before his brother showed up at this cabin. The last thing he wanted was Mitch to see his hostage sleeping peacefully or that her physical injuries had been treated. He was supposed to be in here raping her, not helping her.

With one last look at Samara, Noah walked out the door. On the porch, he jerked to a halt. Mitchell was just getting out of a truck. Two young girls, bruised, handcuffed, and barely dressed, were lifted from the backseat. Ashley Mason and Courtney Nixon. *Damn!*

eleven

Disgust knotting his stomach, Noah swaggered down the steps and headed toward the group. "Whatcha got there?"

Noah clenched his fist to keep from knocking the sly, evil grin off Mitch's face.

"This here's my new business." He turned toward the two men holding the terrified young girls. "Take 'em inside. Give 'em some water and something to eat. Let 'em clean up a bit, too. We don't want Mr. Bennett to think we've been mistreating his property."

After giving them an expected leering once-over, Noah ignored the girls. There wasn't a damn thing he could do for them right now. Soon, but not yet. He smirked at Mitchell. "Looks like you definitely got something going, man. You going to cut me in?"

"Maybe." Mitchell headed toward his cabin, assuming Noah would follow. Halfway there, he stopped and turned. "How's that little treat I gave you doing?"

Noah snorted with disgust. "I barely got started when she passed out again. When's the last time you fed her."

"I wasn't planning on keeping her around that long. Didn't see the need to waste good food."

"Well, I like them to be at least halfway conscious." Mitch chuckled and started walking to his cabin again. "You sound like Daddy. Come on in and let's have dinner. Maybe I'll even find something for your new play pretty."

Noah had to force his legs to move. Good thing Mitch's back was turned or he would have seen his brother's face and known the truth. To be compared to his father in any way, shape, or form was an anathema.

The cabin wreaked with the stench of old fish, stale sweat, blood, and greasy barbecue. Noah's stomach took another revolting tumble.

Opening a sack, Mitch pulled out a tinfoil-covered pan. "Remember these? Joe Pa's ribs? Member how Daddy would bring them home sometimes on Saturday?"

Noah nodded but didn't bother to mention that the ribs had always been purchased the night before and that dear old Dad would sling the half gnawed-on ribs onto the breakfast table before he staggered to the bedroom to sleep off another drunken night. Mitch always tore into them as if eating cold half-eaten barbecue ribs for breakfast was the ultimate dining experience.

While Mitch devoured his meal, Noah sat at the table, his eyes searching for something he could take back to Samara. Spying some packaged peanut butter and crackers, along with a couple of bottles of apple juice and water, he got up and grabbed them. Mitch was too involved in his feast to notice.

Knowing he'd be questioned if he didn't at least eat something, he pulled a couple of ribs from the rack. Spooning out some potato salad and beans onto his plate, he sat down and forced the food into his mouth.

"Good stuff, huh?"

Noah grunted and ate.

"Bet you're dying to know about those girls."

Lifting a shoulder in a careless shrug, Noah took a

swallow of his warm beer. "Only if it involves money."

Mitch stopped in the middle of licking sauce from his fingers and flashed a greasy grin. "It always involves money, bro."

Unable to swallow anything else, Noah shoved his plate away. "So, tell me about this venture."

Wiping his face and hands on a paper towel, Mitch took a long gulp of beer and belched. "It was actually my idea. . . . That's why I got to be in charge. Those two girls you saw, we lured them from the Internet. Told 'em we were jocks from another school. Used real names and everything. We arranged a meeting place and then, whammo, they're ours."

"Damn." Knowing it was expected, his voice revealed his deep esteem and admiration for such a novel idea. "So what are you going to do with them?"

"That's the beauty. We got fourteen girls already. . . . I'm waiting for number fifteen to come in any day now." He winked. "You know fifteen was always my lucky number."

Blood seeped from the hand Noah pressed into the edge of the table. He could feel it dripping from him and didn't bother to stop it. No one would notice another puddle of blood on the floor. Mitch's sly teasing that Rebecca had been fifteen when Mitch raped her was a taunting reminder to Noah. His brother felt no remorse for the act or for the fact that Noah had gone to prison for the crime.

To discuss Mitch's remark would only invite a discussion that would solve nothing other than the possibility of Noah revealing his real feelings. Just to show that the taunt hadn't gone unnoticed, Noah managed a mocking nod and waited for Mitch to continue.

Though he looked slightly disappointed that Noah hadn't taken the bait, he continued to describe his operation of abducting teen girls. "Anyway, we'll bring 'em all here and load 'em all on one truck. Then we'll take them to a warehouse in Biloxi. My boss, Mr. Bennett, examines the merchandise. If he's pleased— and I plan to make sure he is—we get paid."

"What happens to the girls?"

Mitch blinked, obviously surprised at such an off-the-wall question. "I don't know. . . . They get shipped out somewhere. Most likely to Thailand this time."

"This time?"

"Yeah, this'll be the third group we've gathered." He grinned like a kid who'd just aced his math test. "We've brought in some of the most prime teen ass this country has to offer."

Shit. Shit. Shit. LCR was hell and away behind on this. He'd actually thought this was Bennett's first attempt at this type of abduction. How had he missed so many other young girls disappearing in a similar fashion? Noah and his people had their work cut out for them. Not only would they rescue these girls, but would do their damnedest to find the others.

"Where'd the other ones go?"

"Huh?" Mitch paused in picking his teeth. "Oh, uh. Hell, I don't know . . . Mexico and Brazil, I think."

"That's a really cool idea, but aren't you afraid that after a while the cops are going to catch on. Taking that many girls, using the ruse that you're a high school jock is—"

"Naw, this was the first time we used the school jock thing. Last time we just prowled a couple of websites that kids like to go to. Only got five that way, though. Bastards decided to start asking for more information before they'd let us chat." He said the last part as if insulted he hadn't been trusted.

Nodding as if this was another inventive and brilliant idea, Noah leaned back into his chair and allowed his brother to gloat. Listening to Mitch was much easier when he knew that every ounce of information he gained would be used against him very soon.

"The first time was just kind of an experiment. We went to teen hangouts. Malls . . . shit like that. Ended up with three girls and even a few boys." He grinned at that. "We're an equal opportunity organization."

"Teen boys?" That was a new bit of information.

"Yeah. You'd be amazed what some perverts will pay for a fresh piece of young male ass."

Mitch calling someone else a pervert was pretty damn scary. Few people were more perverted than his brother.

"Stalking the malls got damn dangerous, though. Never know where cameras might be. This way . . . nobody knows."

"You got some major balls, bro."

Mitch flashed another slimy grin at his brother's obvious admiration. "Yeah. Boss is going to shit when he sees how many I got him. Man's going to be mighty pleased with me."

Noah forced another admiring glance.

"And we'd be doing another truckload if it wasn't for that idiot 'do good' group that's after us now."

"Who's that?" Already knowing and relishing the disgust on his brother's face.

"Called Last Chance Rescue. Ever heard of them?"

"Don't think so. What'd they do?"

"Caused a shitload of problems. Last year, they shut down four of the boss's businesses."

"And they're after him again?"

"Yeah. That's why I wanted to get something from that bitch I gave you. She's involved with them."

"How do you know that? Thought you said she wouldn't tell you anything."

"She didn't. But my men heard her call out 'Noah' right before they grabbed her."

"So?"

"Noah McCall's the head of the group. He's somehow tracked us down. Now we're going to have to come up with another plan."

"Got any ideas?"

"Not yet. When I get the merchandise to Mr. Bennett, we'll sit down and have a planning session."

Just like any successful business would. Hell, the freaks probably had a five-year plan and a vision statement, too.

Noah leaned forward with all the eagerness of a lowlife sleazeball. "So, how can I get in on this? Sounds like you already have almost all the girls you're going to get."

"Yeah, but I need another man. One of mine got a real bad headache a few hours ago." Mitch's small, mean smile indicated the headache wasn't one the man would ever recover from.

"Okay, I'll stick around. Then what?"

"We take the shipment to Bennett. I'll introduce you. You got an impressive record. I'm bettin' he'll give you a job."

Noah stood. He was pretty sure he'd gotten all he could out of Mitch for the time being. Now he just wanted to go back to Samara and reassure himself she was truly all right.

He gathered the small amount of food he'd collected for her. "Thanks for the meal, man, but I gotta go feed my new little playmate. She's going to need the strength."

Noah walked out the door on Mitch's guffaw. Not for the first time, Noah wished for a way to withdraw the tainted blood from his body. Having Mitch and his father's genes and blood inside him sickened him to the point of nausea. He'd come to terms years ago with the knowledge that no matter what he did, his DNA was contaminated. No matter what he did. How many he saved. He could never change that.

For the next two days, Samara drifted in and out of consciousness. Exhaustion and trauma had taken a toll. Only able to keep her eyes open for a few minutes at a time, every time they did open, Noah was beside her. She took comfort in the sight. Funny that his brother, identical in looks, could send chills of revulsion down her spine and the only chills Noah gave her were of delight.

Her mind skittered away from thinking about what had happened. Noah was full of questions. She could see them in his eyes. He didn't want to push her into talking. At some point she'd have to tell him. For right now she just wanted to rest and not think about it.

She hoped for the best for the girls who'd escaped. Noah hadn't mentioned them again. He went out several times during the day and night, but always returned quickly. Each time he left, he gave her his gun, his instructions simple but explicit. "Shoot to kill." Then he would give her that searching, concerned look that warmed her and sent alarm through her at the same time.

She knew he was worried about her, for her. At some point, she would come out of this lassitude and talk, but not yet. She closed her eyes and drifted away. It wasn't time.

A gentle hand caressing her hair brought her eyes open. She blinked sleepily and smiled.

"You feel up to talking?"

Her eyes flittered away from the intense stare as her heart rate zoomed. No, she wasn't ready. Wasn't sure she'd ever be ready. Postponing it as long as she could, she grimaced down at the T-shirt and shorts Noah had given her, which she'd been wearing for two days. "What I'd really like is a bath and some fresh clothes."

He stared silently for a few seconds and then nodded. "I'll go run the water for you. I've scrubbed the tub several times . . . so it should be clean enough."

She watched him walk away and sighed. Admittedly, a small reprieve, but perhaps getting cleaned up and refreshed would make her feel more ready.

Noah returned and scooped her into his arms, startling her. "I can walk."

"You're still weak and your feet are too sore." Carrying her into the bathroom, he sat her on the closed lid of the toilet. "Do you need help bathing?"

He'd seen her nude, when they made love and whenever he put the salve on her injuries. Samara knew she had nothing to hide, but right now she didn't want his help. Perhaps it was a control issue. For now, she just wanted solitude.

"I'll be fine." When he looked doubtful, she added, "You can stay by the door and if I need you, I'll call out. Okay?"

Though he nodded and closed the door behind him, she could tell he wasn't convinced. That, more than anything, gave her determination. She'd needed his tender care the last couple of days, but it was time to recover and regroup. Time for strength, and at some point soon, time for action.

Ignoring the dismal surroundings of the decrepit facilities, Samara stripped. She avoided looking at her body as she eased into soothing water. Beside the tub, Noah had set out a towel, along with soap, shampoo, conditioner, and a razor. She leaned back into the tub, closed her eyes, and allowed the hot water to seep into her bones. Cleansing, healing, soothing.

Noah paced back and forth in front of the door. She'd been in there for half an hour. He'd called out several times to make sure she was okay. The last time she'd reassured him, there had been a definite snap in her voice. Hearing her irritation pleased him beyond measure.

The last two days, she'd drifted in and out of consciousness. When she woke, he'd done his best to ply her with liquids and food. Her appetite had been almost nonexistent, but with a bit of coercion he'd gotten some nourishment in her. That she'd let him get away with bullying her was just another indication of how weak and vulnerable she'd been.

He hoped that was about to change. She'd need to be strong to face what lay ahead. He wanted to know what happened, what she'd been through. Part of him felt selfish and evil for making her relive it, another part told him she needed to tell it. Cathartic release a part of the healing process. This wasn't an optimum time for counseling, nor was it the right setting, but he had another reason for needing to know. If she'd heard or seen something, no matter how seemingly insignificant, that information might be vital.

The truck would most likely arrive within the next couple of days. Which was why he needed Samara to talk and needed to assess her condition. What he planned wouldn't be pretty, but it was necessary.

Samara needed to be long gone before the other girls arrived. She'd already been through too much. Putting her through further trauma went against everything within him. Getting her away from these bastards was his first priority.

The bathroom door opened and Samara emerged. The bruises on her face stood out green and blue against creamy, pale skin. The welts on her body were healing and had turned to ugly, narrow bruises. The medicated cream he applied two to three times a day had fought any infection from all the numerous cuts and scrapes she'd sustained, including her feet. Every time he looked at her, rage engulfed him. He had a good idea of how she'd gotten all her injuries, but he still wanted to hear it from her. And he still didn't know if she'd been raped.

"Feel better?"

Lips, still chapped and bruised from abuse, tilted in a reassuring smile. His chest ached. Damned if she should be trying to make him feel better.

"Much better . . . thanks." Wearing the clean T-shirt he'd loaned her, she wobbled to the bed. Despite the knowledge that she was struggling to gain control, his arms reached out automatically to carry her. He checked himself before she saw his mistake. He had to give her space. Time, unfortunately, was no longer something he could give her.

"Mara, we need to talk about what happened."

"I don't know if I can."

Moving carefully, not wanting to have her feel threatened in any way, he approached the bed and sat down. Her body, warm, slight, and delectably made, tempted him. He snarled at the unwanted desire. The time for that had come and gone and would be no more. Hell, after what she'd been through, he didn't know if she'd ever be able to have a sexual relationship with a man again. Though everything within him rebelled at another man touching her, more than anything he wanted Samara to have a normal life. To be safe and happy. The thought that this experience might prohibit that filled him with gut-wrenching guilt.

He should never have involved her in this operation.

But he had. Now he had to figure out a way to help her deal with it.

"Sometimes it helps to talk about it. Get the anger, pain, and humiliation out in the open."

Shuddering violently, she shifted away from him. Noah stilled her with his hand on her arm. "I need to know. . . . You may have inadvertently picked up some information."

"I didn't hear anything. I was too scared. It's all a blur. . . . I barely remember . . ."

"You remember more than you think you do."

Wounded eyes, filled with tears, tortured and seared him. "I can't, Noah. . . . I just can't. You don't understand what's it's like . . . how it feels to be so helpless and vulnerable. All those vile, hideous things they said to me. Not knowing if they were going to rape me. Wanting them to stop, but knowing if they stopped one thing, something even more horrible might take its place."

Easing her into his arms, he pulled her head to his chest. "I promise you, no one will ever hurt you again. I'm sorry this happened and I'd give my life for it never to have happened. But the fact is, it did. Now, we need to deal with it and go on."

She jerked away, glaring in accusation. "Easy for you to say. You're not the one who was violated . . . treated like garbage. Pinched, slapped, stripped, beaten, and . . ." She looked away. "There's no way you could understand what it's like to be so vulnerable, helpless . . . so incredibly powerless."

Noah pulled her into his arms again and rocked her. "It will get better. . . . I promise."

"Rationally, I know it will. It has to. I've counseled women who have been physically and sexually abused. I know what I'm supposed to do . . . what I'm supposed to feel. Knowing and doing . . ." A slow shake of her head. "It's not that easy."

"I know but—"

"But nothing, Noah. You can't know until you've been through it yourself."

Stiff and still, he barely breathed. Then, with a long sigh, ragged with understanding, he spoke in a cool monotone. "I was sixteen years old when Mitch raped a girl from my school." His shoulder lifted in a small shrug. "I had a crush on her and she'd paid attention to me. Mitch never could stand me having something he didn't have. Always wanted what he thought I had or wanted."

As if unable to sit still, Noah stood and turned toward the window. He blew out a snorting laugh. "Back then, I was Michael Stoddard. And believe it or not, considered the bad twin, with the dangerous reputation. Mitch was known as the good one. When Rebecca told her parents, her parents called the sheriff. . . . I was the one they came for.

"Rebecca's parents refused to let her testify. She knew it was Mitch, though he'd done his best to make her believe it was me—even wore my clothes. No one believed her. Said she was too traumatized to know the truth. The sheriff was convinced they had their rapist.

"I was sentenced to two years. My lawyer thought it was a damn good deal." Another pause and then, "My first night, I remember sitting in my cell. . . . I'd always pretended to be tough, while all the time, I was just a scared kid. But I knew it could no longer be an act. I had to be tough for real. My mental pep talk lasted all of five minutes . . . then the cell door opened."

Samara forced herself to stay seated, barely breathing.

"Two of the inmates decided to give me a demonstration of what my victim had gone through. First they beat the hell out of me. The whole time I was thinking that someone would come and save me . . . never happened. When they got tired of that, they slapped tape over my mouth and took turns."

Dead silence followed his tragic statement. Samara hadn't thought she could hurt any more than she already did. . . . She was wrong.

When he turned back toward her, fierce determination blazed in his eyes. "That's why I know you can overcome it, Mara. It won't be anything you'll ever forget, but it will be something that will dim . . . eventually."

"What happened after that?"

A shrug. "They left. I cleaned myself up and the rest of the night, I made plans."

"What kind of plans?"

His mouth lifted with a hint of wry humor. "You name it, I planned it. From killing everyone who'd had anything to do with what happened to me, to getting out and killing my brother and father."

He stayed silent for so long, she was afraid he wouldn't share any more. Finally, his voice rumbled across the room. "Of course, I didn't do any of those things, but I did become the tough guy I needed to be to survive. When there's a new kid on the block and he's already been broken in, they come at you like vultures, thinking they can get an easy piece. I showed them I'd never be that easy again."

Her heart bled for him, because no matter how much he denied it, the hurt inside him still lingered. What would he have been like if he hadn't been forced to be who he was? Was that young man still inside him? The sensitive, unworldly, and kind person he probably was before he'd suffered such a trauma?

"After that, it got easier. Most everybody stayed away from me. I probably would have gotten out in a year or so. . . . I didn't know until I got out that Rebecca finally convinced her family it wasn't me. They worked like hell to prove it'd been Mitchell. Nobody wanted to believe them. My dad had too much clout with the sheriff and the judge, who also happened to be his best drinking buddies."

"Your father wanted you in prison?"

"Mitch was his favorite." He paused. "They had a lot in common."

By that she figured he meant his father had done pretty much the same things Mitchell had done. "What about your mother?"

"She left home when I was a kid. Couldn't take the abuse anymore."

"You said you probably would have stayed in prison a year. What happened?"

A genuine grin kicked up his mouth and despite their topic of conversation, her heart lightened.

"New kid came in. Same thugs decided to break him in. I broke it up. Got more time tacked on for beating the shit out of them. The extra time was worth it."

"What happened to those men? Were they ever punished for what they did?"

He shook his head. "Not by the law, no. One of them was found dead in his cell one morning. Somebody had gutted him in his sleep. The other one died from a burst appendix a few months before I was released."

Samara blew out a ragged sigh. She'd never been happy to hear about anyone's death, but she couldn't help but be glad the bastards who had hurt Noah were in hell, where they belonged.

"How long were you there?"

"One thousand, one hundred, and eighty-two days . . . little over three years."

"How did you finally get out?"

"A minister came by once a week. Of course, I didn't want to hear anything he said, since my father pretty much trained me to hate anything to do with religion. But he was a good man . . . the best I've ever known. We'd just sit and shoot the breeze. I began to trust him . . . told him a few things. He ended up helping me get out and helped me set up LCR."

"What was his name?"

"Milo."

A memory caught her . . . something Eden had mentioned. "He was the man who was killed last year?"

"Yes."

So there was more than one reason for Noah to want Bennett. "How did Milo help?"

He shrugged. "In more ways than I can count, but one of the most important was his advice. He told me I had two choices. I could let what happened ruin my life, or I could make a difference in others."

"So you made a choice to rescue people?"

"I made a choice to help victims instead of being one."

And in that moment, Samara knew she loved him. Probably had from the beginning but had fought almost as viciously as he had to prevent that from happening. Now she knew that with every fiber of her soul, this man was the love of her life. There was a quality inside Noah that had remained unsullied and pure . . . the part he hid from everyone. Noah was a true hero, though he'd deny it to the death.

After the heartrending account of his trauma, hers no longer seemed as scary or horrendous. Scooting back on the bed, she held out her hand for Noah to join her. Crossing the room, he sat beside her, took her hand in his, and kissed it.

She blew out a sigh, determined to stay as factual and unemotional as she could. "I woke up in the trunk of a car. My arms and legs were tied together. I didn't know where I was, or who had me. Finally, they opened the trunk and threw me on the ground. One of them untied me, because the other one said he liked to see them try to get away.

"I lay there for a few minutes while they talked about what they were going to tell Mitch about what happened. One of them—a man named Richard—picked me up and slung me over his shoulder. While they walked, they talked about not being able to taste the goodies. One said I looked so young, that I was probably still a virgin. The other one said he should have said something earlier and he would have let him have me." Samara swallowed thickly. "He said no, I was too skinny, but he wouldn't mind getting the girl with the big breasts they'd picked up a few weeks ago."

"They say her name?"

"Lara." She saw the recognition of the name in his eyes. "You know about her?"

"Met her brother recently."

When he didn't say anything else, Samara continued, "They brought me here and dumped me on the ground. When I heard Mitchell's voice, I knew it sounded familiar . . . but not. Then, when I saw his face . . ." She closed her eyes. "God, I couldn't believe it."

"I didn't think it was something you needed to know, because I never intended for you to get anywhere near Mitch."

"I know, Noah, but seeing him, with your face and the pure evil in his eyes. . . . It was terrifying."

He picked up her hand and kissed it again, apologizing once more.

"Anyway, they brought me in and threw me on the floor. When Mitch asked me about Noah McCall, I told him I didn't know any Noah." She laughed softly. "He said they heard me scream 'Noah.' I told him I said 'no,' not 'Noah.'"

"Smart girl."

"Yeah well, unfortunately, he didn't believe me. He and two of his men sliced my clothes off and then threw me around the room to one another like it was a game. I managed to kick one of them in the groin and got knocked out again."

Noticing her voice was getting so thick she could barely understand herself, she swallowed again and cleared her throat. "When I woke up, it was dark and no one was around. I stole a shirt I found and tried to run away. On the way, I heard someone crying. I went inside a cabin and that's when I saw Ashley and Courtney, handcuffed to a bed. I got them loose and I thought we were going to get away. Mitchell found us. I threw myself at him, told the girls to run."

"They brought both girls back."

Tears flooded her eyes. "So it was all for nothing."

Tilting her face with his finger, he brought her gaze up to his. Gleaming admiration in his eyes healed a small slice of her pain. "That was an incredibly brave thing for you to do. I'm proud of you for thinking so fast. It was just pure bad luck they got caught. You gave them a chance, which was more than they had before you got here."

Samara nodded at his praise, wishing with all her heart it had ended with the girls getting away.

"What happened when Mitch brought you back?"

"I . . ." She reached for a water bottle and took

several long swallows. "He was furious. He called his people together and told them to go after the girls. Then he shot Richard as casually as you please. . . ." Her eyes closed on the image she doubted would ever leave her mind. "It was horrible."

Noah pulled her into his arms and just held her, apparently knowing that nothing he could say or do would erase that experience.

"After that, he dragged me back inside and threw me down on the floor. Then he took his belt off and beat me. Then . . ."

"What, Mara?" he asked softly.

"He spread my legs . . . was about to rape me. . . . He didn't."

"What stopped him?"

"You."

"What?"

"You showed up, and he knocked me out. When I woke up, you were there."

Waves of rage literally pulsed from Noah's body. She petted his arm to comfort him. He'd been right. Talking about it had helped. Intellectually, she'd known it would. She'd counseled plenty of victims of abuse, but when it came to talking about her own experience, it'd been damned hard. Perhaps, if she learned nothing else from this ordeal, she'd be able to identify with and understand her clients better.

A giant yawn attacked her, as exhaustion slammed so quick and hard, her eyes blurred.

Noah pushed her gently back onto the bed. "Get some rest. I need to go back and see Mitchell again."

"But don't we need to talk about what's going to happen?"

"We will later."

Too weary to argue, she allowed Noah to pull back the thin blanket and cover her up. Pressing a chaste kiss to her forehead, he straightened and headed toward the door.

"Noah."

He stopped and turned to look at her.

"Thank you for sharing your experience with me. I didn't think I'd be able to get through talking about what happened."

Emotions flickered over his face before he could mask his feelings. Samara saw them and her heart soared. Compassion and mutual understanding, but most important, tenderness and affection. Before she could say anything, he'd disappeared behind the door.

Closing her eyes, Samara breathed out a long sigh. For the first time since this whole ordeal began, she finally felt safe.

twelve

Noah shut the door behind him, grimly aware he'd let his feelings show. That couldn't happen again. He turned to walk down the stairs and stopped. Mitchell had one foot on the first step, apparently about to make a house call.

Mitch jerked his head toward the door behind Noah. "You broke her yet?"

Pasting on his cockiest, most evil expression, he bragged, "No, but I've broken her in real good."

An evil, leering grin curled up at Mitch's mouth as he took a step up to the cabin. "Good. I've decided I want a taste."

In an instant, Noah was at his brother's side, grasping his arm. "She's mine."

"The bitch was a loan," he snarled. "She's not yours."

"I. Said. She's. Mine."

Mitch looked down at the hand on his arm and then up at Noah's hard stare. "She a virgin?"

He raised an arrogant brow. "Not anymore."

"She good?"

"Good enough till I'm done with her. She won't last more than a couple more days."

Mitch nodded. "I want her before you kill her. She ain't given us shit so far. If you can't get it out of her, I can."

"If she knows anything, I'll get it . . . but she's mine

and nobody else's till she draws her last breath. Got that?"

"Ever fuck and strangle one at the same time? They clamp down like a vice on your dick right before they die." He grinned as if sharing a fun piece of brotherly advice.

Noah studied his brother. This was extreme, even for Mitch. Was he trying to shock him? Or had Noah somehow maintained a small amount of naïveté about his brother? Thinking him evil but still redeemable. No, he'd known for years that Mitchell had nothing left in him that held an ounce of goodness or morality.

Unable to come up with anything better, he just shook his head. "I don't kill and tell."

Laughing hard, Mitch backed down off the steps. Noah breathed out a low, relieved sigh. It would have screwed up everything to show his hand this soon, but if Mitch had taken another step toward Samara, his brother wouldn't have lived another second.

"Come to the cabin. I got some news."

Noah followed Mitch. Anyone looking would see two men who looked as though they were as identical on the inside as the outside. Noah had known almost since he was a toddler that something was wrong with his twin. He hadn't known what it was at the time, but he and Mitch had never played together like brothers do. From the time they were able to walk, his father had catered to his brother and Noah, thank God, had followed his mother around. He always wondered if his mother had seen the evil in Mitch. If so, she'd never treated him any differently, until he refused to have anything to do with her.

They entered the small cabin. A pair of lavender panties lay on the filthy kitchen table. *Shit.* He picked up the delicate lace underwear. "Looks like you've been tasting the merchandise yourself."

"Naw, ripped them off your bitch when she first got here."

Jaw tight, Noah wadded the material and shoved them into his back pocket. "I'll put 'em back on her before I dump her."

Mitch grinned. "It's the least you can do."

Grabbing two beers from the cooler, Mitch handed one to Noah and sat at the table. "Truck's coming day after tomorrow. We pick up the last piece of merchandise tomorrow night in Arkansas."

"What happens when they get here?"

"We'll load 'em up and head to the boss's warehouse."

"He's got a warehouse in Biloxi?"

"Yeah."

"And he'll come and check them out?"

"Oh yeah, he likes to take personal inventory. Once that's over, we'll load up and ship them."

"They're all going to Thailand?"

"Hell if I know. That ain't really my concern. Once we get our money, we'll head out for a little rest. The boss'll call us back in a week or so." Mitch took a long swig of beer. "That's what I wanted to talk to you about. I been working for the boss going on three years. It's 'bout time for a promotion. I called and told him about you. If he approves, he might let you take over for me."

Noah propped his feet upon the table, took a swallow from his can, and belched. "What's it pay?"

"Two thousand per ass, but you have to split that with the help. I'm pretty generous when it comes to that 'cause I want their loyalty. Sometimes, if it's a real sweet prize . . . say a real young one, he'll pay extra. That's mostly profit. I don't share those 'cause they're damned rare and hard as hell to get."

Noah gave an understanding nod.

"So, you interested? Want me to set things up with the boss man?"

"Hell yeah, I'm interested. But what are you going to be doing?"

"Don't know yet. Boss likes to keep all his businesses separate. Once I'm done with this, you probably won't see me again."

"Fine by me." And never had Noah been more sincere or honest.

Mitch grinned, not one bit insulted. Both men knew the hatred still existed and always would. "That's what I figured . . . but I owed you something for taking the heat for me all those years ago. But we're square from here on out. Right?"

Like hell. "Yeah, we're square."

Mitch's eyes skittered briefly away. When he looked back, Noah was shocked to see his eyes filled with tears. "I haven't mentioned this to you, 'cause it's so hard to talk about. You know Daddy's dead, don't you?"

Oh yeah, he'd gotten drunk to celebrate when he'd heard the news. "Yeah, I'd heard."

"Broke my heart. I know he was a tough son of a bitch, but damn, he was fun."

Yeah, a riot a minute. "Yeah, he was." Mitch didn't know he meant he was a son of a bitch and not that he was fun. The only time his daddy ever seemed to have fun was when it involved beating his wife or sons.

Noah knew he shouldn't but said it anyway. "You know Mama's dead, too, don't you?"

"Yeah, the bitch got what was coming to her." He slanted his eyes over to Noah. "Though you were always a mama's boy. Bet you pissed your pants when you heard she died of AIDS. Daddy said she was screwing around on him. Guess he was right."

The fact that Farrell Stoddard screwed everything

he could get his dick in and had given their mother the disease evidently never occurred to his brother. Too bad his father died in a drunken bar fight before he could waste away himself.

The chair Noah sat in screeched across the floor as he moved to get up. If he stayed any longer, he'd kill the bastard and accomplish almost nothing, other than the peace of mind of having one less Stoddard in this world. He had to remember this wasn't about him and his revenge. It was about doing the right thing. When the time was right, Mitch would join Farrell Stoddard in the fiery hell pit they could call home for eternity.

"I'm going to get some shut-eye. Be back later."

Mitch grinned as if he knew exactly what Noah was going to do and it had nothing to do with sleep. And he was right. Noah wasn't going to sleep, he was going to contact his LCR operatives standing by and give the good news that this nightmare was almost over.

Then he would return to Samara and tell her goodbye.

Cozy and pain free for the first time in days, Samara rolled over and felt a hard, warm body beside her. A hand covered her mouth before she could let loose a scream. Noah's calm voice whispered, "Shh. You're fine."

Shivering from shock and fear, Samara did what she'd wanted to do for days: she threw herself at him. Masculine arms, warm and comforting, wrapped around her. Samara closed her eyes in thankfulness. She hadn't been sure she'd ever be able to be close to a man again. She should have known that Noah, a man who could infuriate her faster than anyone she'd ever known, would be the one man she would be able to trust. Even while angry with him for so many things, she'd always felt safe.

"You okay?"

She nodded against his chest. "You just startled me. Sorry."

His arms tightened, his voice fierce. "Don't you dare apologize. If it weren't for me, you wouldn't be in this situation."

"I don't blame you, you know that. You didn't plan for this to happen and it was my decision to get involved." She paused for half a second. "But just how are we going to get out of it?"

"Let me worry about that. You just go back to sleep."

"Don't treat me like a child, Noah."

"The truck is coming tomorrow."

"And?"

He held his body stiff against her and she could almost hear him arguing with himself. There was something he didn't want to tell her. No, she refused to be in the dark again. She had a right to know what was coming. What they both faced.

"What, Noah? Don't try to protect me by not telling me. I deserve to know your plan."

Noah blew out a sigh and began to talk. The more she listened the more terrified she was. Not for her . . . for him.

"Are you serious?"

"Trust me, babe, it doesn't get more serious than this."

"But Noah, how . . . what . . . ?"

A hand smoothed her hair. "That's why I didn't want to tell you, Mara. You'll just worry about it and there's no need for you to worry. You'll be fine."

Furious, she jerked away and sat up. "Hell, Noah. Do you think I'm only worried about me? Don't you think I'm worried about you, too? Do you think I could bear it if something happened to you?"

Noah pulled her back down into his arms again. "I'll be fine. I promise." He pressed a kiss on top of her head. "If you're not going to sleep, let's talk about something else."

"Like what?"

"Are you still in love with Jordan?"

They both jerked at the question. Samara got the idea he was as surprised as she was that he'd asked it. This was one of the few personal things Noah had ever asked.

"I admire him tremendously and care for him, but I never loved him . . . at least not the way I was supposed to."

"Why do you say that?"

"Because I would never have just stood by and let him marry Eden . . . not without fighting for him."

Her head vibrated against his chest as he chuckled. "Yeah, I can see you doing that."

"Can I ask you something?"

She felt him stiffen briefly before he answered, "Sure."

"Can you tell me how LCR got started? I mean, you're only what, early thirties, but from what I can tell, you've got politicians and law enforcement eating out of your hand."

"It's not quite as good as that, but LCR does have some powerful allies." He settled more comfortably in the bed. "Milo was about ten years older than me and a hundred years wiser. We started working together, training, learning what we needed to learn. I happened to be good with languages, he was good with self-defense, so we taught each other."

"How'd you get so good with languages?"

"My mother grew up in France. Her parents moved here when she was just a teenager. She taught me French from the time I could talk. Mitch never wanted to learn, but I picked it up quickly. The small school I attended . . . Not too many kids could speak two languages. My teachers were excited about that, so whenever I wanted to, they'd let me go to one of the foreign language classes. I picked up a couple more."

"Just from listening?" She, who'd struggled with Spanish in high school and college, found this an amazing gift.

He shrugged as if it were no big deal. "Anyway, once I got out of prison, I wanted to get as far from my past as I could. My mother loved Paris, talked about it all the time. To me, it just made sense to go there. Milo's parents had left him a small inheritance, so we used the money to set up shop. We thought we'd just get our feet wet . . . see how good we could be. We figured it'd be years before we could establish ourselves and do some of the things we dreamed about." A dry chuckle grumbled from his chest. "We got lucky and early on, by sheer accident, got involved in the rescue of the wife and daughter of one of the highest-ranking officials in France. He was grateful when we kept it secret, as he asked. He sent us some business. From there, it just snowballed.

"We started getting more and more business, which meant we needed people. And not just any people, but people who could understand our philosophy."

"And what philosophy is that?"

"That our victims are the most important people, and our operatives are second. We do whatever it takes to bring victims home, no matter the cost."

"I would imagine it's hard to find people who agree totally with that philosophy."

"We have a rigorous interview system." His tone grew grim. "We're rarely wrong."

"And that's how Milo was killed? Because you hired a bad person?"

"Yes."

"I'm sorry."

"You would have liked Milo. He was Eden's favorite."

She snorted lightly. "Well, if you're as charming to her as you were to me, no wonder."

"Hey, I'm known worldwide for my charm and communication skills."

"You've never used those skills on me."

Moving quickly, Noah suddenly loomed over her. "You didn't seem to have a problem with my communication skills a few nights ago."

Heat flooded through her . . . amazing and thrilling at the same time. She'd been worried she'd never have these feelings again. With another man, she wouldn't. But this was Noah, who not only made her feel safe and secure, he could also turn her on with a smile.

"That's because you didn't talk . . . with your mouth."

"Oh yeah, what about when I did this?" Lowering his head, his mouth whispered along the edge of her jaw, then up to her ear, hot breath teasing . . . exciting.

Samara inhaled, loving his scent, a mixture of masculine musk and pure male heat. She arched her body toward him. "Kiss me."

With a ragged groan, he pressed a soft kiss to her mouth and moved to get up.

Samara grabbed his shoulders. "No. Really kiss me."

Want and need flared across his face, but his words denied them. "You're not up for that and it'd be dangerous as hell to have sex in this kind of situation."

"Isn't that what everyone thinks you're doing?"

"That doesn't make it smart or right."

"Why is it wrong?"

"Mara, nothing's changed . . . we can't . . ."

She pressed a finger to his mouth. "I'm not asking for promises, Noah. But I need this. I want to feel alive. To forget those men touched me, put their hands on me. I need to replace those memories with your touch."

Black eyes, heated with an intensity she'd never seen before, stared down at her. Whispering what sounded like a tortured curse, Noah lowered his head and placed his mouth on hers.

God, he loved kissing this woman. Full sensuous lips moved under his, opened, taking his tongue, sucking on it. His hands tangled in her hair . . . beautiful, wild, sensuous Mara. How in the hell was he ever going to let her go and what choice did he have?

Going to his knees, he grabbed his shirt to pull it over his head, but her hands were there before his, moving under his shirt, caressing his abdomen, his chest. Her hands, soft silk, blazed a fire that spread everywhere and then shot straight to his groin.

In between kissing her softly groaning lips, he managed to pull his pants and underwear off. Her hands were on his erection before he could take another breath, stroking him from the head to the base. "Mara, baby . . ." When her mouth replaced her hands, Noah's mind went blank, his pulse rocketed, and lightning streaked up his spine.

Taking her face in his hands, he pulled her away gently. She smiled up at him as if she knew exactly what he was thinking . . . doubtful since he hadn't had a coherent thought since he'd kissed her.

Softly kissing and licking her healing bruises, he turned his mind away from the killing rage at the thought of what she'd gone through. This was for her. If he died tomorrow, this was the memory he wanted, his last conscious thought before he left this world. He couldn't ask for more.

Rolling over onto his back, he pulled her on top of him, allowing her to straddle his hips. "Your back's too tender." Her smile as she settled on top caused a tight pain in his chest and his breath to catch in his throat.

Pulling her down to him, he played with her, licking and nipping, caressing every silken curve and soft shadow, building a need neither of them wanted to end. Poised above him, her body glided against his with an earthy sensuality that came so naturally to this beautiful woman. Like the rarest of all treasures, he explored her as if she were a precious, undiscovered jewel. Every soft sigh he cherished, every groan ingrained into his memory. When she took him inside her, it was as if he were coming home. As if in her arms, all the answers in the universe were hers to give and he greedily accepted them. Surging into her heated warmth, Noah found what he'd been searching for his entire life.

Release exploded through him. His thrusts hard and deep, she rode him through the storm and to the fiery conclusion, until peace settled around them. Pressing small kisses all over her face, his lips tasted and absorbed heaven as emotional tears fell from her eyes. Her body shuddering and quivering above him, he rolled her over, pulled from her hot sheath, and cradled her in his arms. She snuggled up against him, warm and trusting.

Noah had been making hard choices for as long as he could remember. This one should have been easier than most because more than anything, he wanted Samara safe. Refusing to ask himself why this was harder than it should be, he reached for the small hypodermic needle he'd placed beside the bed before lying down. Pressing one last tender kiss to her lips,

Noah inserted the needle in her neck, deep into her skin.

"Ow. Noah that hurt. What did you . . . ?" Before her eyes glazed over and she lost consciousness, betrayal and hurt seared him. Holding her delicate body against his, he inhaled her delicious scent, absorbed her precious warmth. No one would ever feel as right in his arms as Samara.

With a regret-filled breath, Noah pulled away and dressed her in the shirt she'd been wearing when he found her and the panties that had been torn from her. Sliding a knife from his boot, he sliced a gash in his forearm. Squeezing the oozing gap, he poured his blood onto Samara, then smeared it over her face, shirt, and bare legs. The results were so authentic looking he shuddered out a breath.

Grim determination speeding him on, he quickly bandaged his arm and dressed. Turning back to the bloody, unconscious woman on his bed, he couldn't resist checking her pulse once more. Steady and slow, as he knew it would be. Car keys in hand, he picked Samara up and put her over his shoulder. Opening the door, he stalked out.

Yesterday he'd parked in front of the cabin in preparation. Best-case scenario, he'd get Samara inside the car and out of the way before anyone saw him. He opened the trunk, just about to deposit Samara inside. The sound of clumping footsteps warned him that best-case scenario wasn't happening today.

"Damn, bro, you already did it? I didn't even hear her scream."

Noah turned and gave him the satisfied smile of a deadly killer. "She hardly put up a fuss . . . about the least satisfying kill I ever had."

Before Noah could stop him, Mitch grabbed a handful of Samara's hair and pulled her head up. With blood smeared all over her face, plus all the green and blue bruises, she looked dead.

"Shit. You did a number on the bitch." Mitch sounded as proud as a father who'd just watched his son pitch a no-hitter. "Didn't know you had it in you."

Noah shrugged and turned, wanting to get Samara in the trunk before Mitch could take a closer look. He placed her as gently as he could inside, then slammed the trunk shut. Turning back to his brother, he smiled. "Killing's easy. It's the keeping them alive till you're done with them that's hard."

"Yeah, I know what you mean." Mitch looked at the car. "She ever tell you anything?"

"Not a lot. You were right, she was hired by a man named Noah . . . didn't know his last name though. She was just supposed to sit in the bar and pretend to be meeting someone . . . Brady or something like that."

"Brian," Mitch supplied.

Noah shrugged. "Anyway . . . that's all she knew."

"Damn, I wish you could have gotten more."

"I told her I'd let her go if she gave me something. Bitch didn't know anything."

Mitch shrugged. "Guess you're right. Where're you taking her?"

"Up the road. There's a spot where some black bears have been spotted. I figured by the time anyone finds her, won't be much left."

Ignoring the almost admiring look on his brother's face, Noah jumped in the car and sped away, hoping some of the gravel from his spinning tires slapped Mitch in the face. He wouldn't take an easy breath until he could get to the drop-off point. He refused to think about the betrayal in Samara's eyes when she realized what he'd done. She would get over hurt feelings, but he was damned sure he'd never get over anything happening to her. With Samara safe, what lay ahead for him would be much easier.

Something soft touched Samara's cheek. She blinked heavy-lidded eyes open, groggy and disoriented. Nothing registered for several seconds other than the gentle touch of a moist cloth moving over her face and neck.

"I think she's coming out of it."

The voice, husky and cultured, brought her eyes open wide. "Eden, what are you doing here?"

Brilliant tears glistening in her eyes, the beautiful blonde smiled down at Samara. Shaking her head at this bizarre dream, Samara tried to lift her head.

"Stay still, sweetie. I don't think Noah gave you enough to have the headache the drug usually causes, but with your injuries, you never know."

Noah. He had drugged her.

A harsh voice grumbled close by. "At least I know I'm not going to have to kill him. . . . Just maiming him will be enough."

Twisting her head, she looked at the man in the front passenger seat. "Jordan?"

His mouth kicked up in a smile that had once caused her heart to pound faster. Now it only made her smile back at him.

"Jordan," Eden said, "we've talked about this. It's as much my fault as it is Noah's for bringing Samara in on this."

"That may be the case, but you know I won't touch one inch of your lovely skin in anger. Noah, on the other hand, I wouldn't mind putting a few dents in his tough hide. Besides, he kept some vital information from you, too."

Samara waved her hand to get their attention. "Excuse me, but I believe you're forgetting something here. I agreed to do this. No one coerced me."

Eden shook her head. "You didn't know what you were getting into. We should never have involved a civilian in—"

Samara pushed herself forward and sat up. A small headache throbbed behind her eyes but she ignored it. With her myriad of other aches, it was inconsequential. Having Noah blamed for all of this was something she refused to allow. "No one could have predicted what was going to happen. Instead of blaming him, we need to figure out how we're going to get him and those girls out of there."

Eden and Jordan shared an amused smile, and Eden remarked, "You've got spunk, you know that?"

Exhausted and feeling not the least bit spunky, she collapsed back onto the seat. "Yeah, it's been mentioned a time or two." She took a deep breath to regain her focus, worry suddenly hammering at her. Noah had gone back to Mitchell's hideout. Taking in both Jordan's and Eden's glances, she asked, "What's our plan?"

Jordan raised a dark brow. "Our plan is to get you to a safe place. Then we'll go back and wait for the truck to arrive."

"I need to help."

Eden shook her head, looking even more arrogant than Jordan. "You've done enough. You need to rest and heal. We'll take care of Mitchell Stoddard and his people and we'll get the girls."

"What about Noah?"

"Noah can take care of himself."

Samara waved a hand in aggravation. "I know he can, Jordan. But what's he going to do to get Bennett?"

Jordan turned to look back out the window. "He's got a plan."

Samara's eyes filled with tears. "What is he planning?"

Eden placed a soothing hand on her shoulder. "There's nothing for you to worry about. You just rest and get well."

"Stop trying to protect me, Eden. I deserve to know what he's going to do."

Eden gave her an assessing stare as if trying to determine if she was strong enough to take the truth. Samara felt as if her stomach and heart crashed against each other as they sped to the ground. The plan was obviously risky or else Eden wouldn't be so reticent.

"Tell me."

Eden nodded. "You're right, you do deserve to know." She began the intricate details of Noah's plan to take down not only Mitchell and his men and rescue the girls, but to also apprehend Bennett, once and for all.

By the time Eden had finished, Samara was in a tailspin of worry. Noah might be the only man who could realistically do this particular job, but if it turned sour, it would be a suicide mission. Noah had known that. He'd made love to her knowing that it was possibly the last time they would ever see each other.

Tears blurring her eyes, she glanced down at her clenched hands. Breath and heart stopped. "Why do I have blood all over me?"

"It's not yours. . . . It's Noah's," Jordan said.

She raised horrified eyes to Eden. "What?"

Shooting an irritated look at her husband, Eden reassured her, "He probably just cut himself a little and put the blood on you to make it look authentic to Mitchell. I promise you, Noah is fine."

She didn't add the words, but they hung in the air . . . *for right now.*

Emotions cracked, split, and then shattered. Everything came tumbling, crumpling in on her . . . all that had happened since the day of her abduction, the

beatings, watching someone's head explode, her near
rape. Now, with the possibility she'd never see Noah
again . . . that he might not survive . . . it was more
than she could assimilate and cope with. With a harsh
sob that came from deep inside, she threw herself into
Eden's arms and crashed.

Noah slammed the car door and headed straight to
his cabin. He didn't want to see or talk to Mitch until he had his head back on straight. Leaving a bruised
and battered Samara under a tree in the designated
drop-off point had been one of the hardest things
he'd ever done. Seeing her lying there, fragile and vulnerable, ate at his gut with single minded acidity. If
he heard one more vile comment or was forced to issue
one more disparaging remark against her to maintain
his cover, he would lose it.

Lying across the bed that only an hour ago he'd
shared with Samara, he inhaled the lingering sweetness of her natural fragrance. Their lovemaking the
first time had been purely sexual, intense and passionate, but without the intensity of deep feelings. Today it had been that . . . purely lovemaking. A wry
grimace tugged at his mouth. He was thirty-two years
old and had just made love for the first time today.

Not only had he made love to her, he'd shared
things he had never shared with another person, other
than his friend and mentor, Milo. Telling her about his
experience in prison just seemed right. She needed to
realize that no matter how badly battered and violated she'd been, she had a choice to be either victim
or survivor. His Mara was a survivor.

Last Chance Rescue had been created with one
primary goal, to rescue the innocent. Saving victims
was his life, his reason for existence. Doing anything
else was unimaginable, even if that precluded having

normal relationships. Sharing his life with anyone had never been a consideration or a temptation, until Samara. Long ago, he'd learned to hold himself back from people. Allowing feelings only invited heartache. Noah had more than enough of that for a lifetime.

The regrets in his life were many and varied, but involving Samara in this project was one of the greatest. Delicate and fragile, she wasn't meant for covert operations or secrecy, and sure as hell didn't need to be exposed to the scum of the earth, which is what happened.

He would do whatever he had to do to protect Samara and that meant staying away from her. She was purity and goodness and destined for a good life . . . something he couldn't offer.

When he returned home, he'd send her some money. She'd be angry at first, but he'd make sure she realized that she'd worked for it, just like any other operative. Maybe she could buy herself some new furniture and go on a long trip. God knew she'd need the recovery time.

The blast of a gun jerked Noah out of his thoughts. He shot out of bed and out of the cabin in seconds. Who the hell had Mitch killed now?

thirteen

Noah skidded to a stop at the bottom of the steps. One of Mitch's men lay lifeless on the ground. Mitch stood over him, gun in hand.

"What the hell's going on?" Noah snapped.

His brother jerked his head up and grinned. "Caught him trying to steal a taste of the merchandise." He waved the gun drunkenly. "That's against the rules."

"You're wasted, Mitch," Noah growled. "You got something big coming down in a few hours. Go sleep it off before you kill someone else."

"You mean, like you?"

"What's that supposed to mean?"

"Didn't you ever think about it, Michael? How, if you'd gotten rid of me all those years ago, there'd be no one you had to share with. If there weren't two of us, you could have it all?"

Noah snorted his disgust. "I never had anything, Mitch. You were jealous of nothing."

A mischievous smile lifted his brother's lips. "You almost had Rebecca."

Determined not to show his fury, Noah kept his hands loose at his sides. Every cell in his body told him to do the deed and get it over with. He couldn't. Revenge for all the wrong his brother had done him didn't even register on the scales of justice. Hatred could not get in the way of the real goal.

Noah forced a nonchalant shrug. "You got her first."

"Yeah, I did, bro. Remember that. I always win."

Noah examined his brother. Was there something behind his statement other than the drunken bragging of a deranged sociopath? Did he suspect something? No, it had to be his imagination. He hadn't been followed. . . . No one saw him leave Samara and they sure as hell hadn't seen her being picked up.

He was tired, exhausted from his concern for Samara, anxious for this operation to be over. That had to be it. If his brother suspected him at all, he'd be dead by now.

"Whatever you say, Mitch. You're in charge." Noah turned back and headed to his cabin.

A gleeful giggle sounded behind him. "You got that right."

The deluge of water from the hot shower flowed down Samara's head. Noah's blood, intermingled with her tears, disappeared down the drain. Small sobs shuddered through her. She took deep breaths, willing herself to calm down. Noah was a professional. He'd put his life on the line innumerable times and would countless more. This would be no different. He would be fine. She had to believe that.

Wincing, she washed over a particularly deep bruise on her upper thigh. She hadn't looked in the mirror yet. Seeing Noah's blood matted in her hair and on her clothes wasn't an image she wanted in her head. The bruises and cuts she could see just by looking down were more than enough to warn her it wouldn't be pleasant.

Her physical injuries would heal. Her heart though . . . she had serious doubts.

The water cooled, forcing her out of the shower. Hair sopping wet, she wrapped it in a towel. A rush of gratitude swept through her as she took in all the toiletries sitting on the counter that Eden had provided. Along with a steaming cup of mint tea and sugar cookies.

Perhaps only another woman would understand the importance of having all the feminine, girlie products to pamper her body with. Twisting the cap from the delightful-smelling lotion, she moisturized her entire body. Her sore, abused skin relished the pampering. Luxuries she'd always taken for granted.

Managing to do all of this without looking in the mirror hadn't been easy. But now the time had come. A deep breath . . . Samara lifted her eyes and stared at the bruised, battered, and changed woman before her.

She looked no different and yet completely different. A giant bruise colored the left side of her forehead, and another large one was on her cheekbone. A narrow, ugly strip of raw flesh marred her right temple. Mitch's belt. Her lips were still a little chapped and dry, but other than the discolorations, she looked like the same woman she'd been staring at all her life. Except her eyes. They held a knowledge that hadn't been there before. She'd seen evil and had experiences she wouldn't wish on anyone. And she had survived.

A small smile lifted her swollen lips as that realization took on solidity. *She had survived.*

With that thought, Samara let her eyes roam down the rest of her body, able to see beyond the memory of how each injury got there. Good heavens. No wonder she was so sore. Covered in bruises and welt marks, her body was a colorful array of green, blue, and brown. Interspersed between the bruises and on top of some of them were knife nicks from having her clothes sliced off and cuts from the various times she'd been thrown on the ground. She twisted around and grimaced. Her back, buttocks, and thighs received most of the vicious whipping and would probably take weeks to look normal again. But the important thing was, they would heal.

Abject weakness attacked as reaction and exhaustion took its toll. Instead of drying her hair, she half-heartedly towel dried it. Since looking her best wasn't really on her list of priorities right now, she left it damp, hanging in curly ringlets. Stifling a jaw-cracking yawn, she pulled on a pair of cotton pajamas Eden had provided and crawled into the soft, clean bed. The lamp on the night table was on, but Samara couldn't bring herself to turn it off. She was safe here. Not only were Jordan and Eden downstairs, three other LCR operatives were also here. No one was going to breach this safe house and get her. . . . Still she couldn't make herself face the darkness.

She closed her eyes and Noah's beautiful face appeared. He felt something for her. It wasn't her imagination or a hopeful fantasy. When this was over, she would make sure they had a chance to explore what they had together. She didn't fool herself. It would be an uphill battle. For some reason, he didn't believe there was a future for them. He'd reminded her just before they made love that they couldn't be. She'd just see about that. Stubbornness ran deep in her family. Her father had always said that since Samara was so small, her stubbornness was more concentrated. She hoped that was true because she had a feeling it would take every ounce of her stubbornness to convince Noah.

With one last check of his gun, Noah headed out the door. The truck was due in an hour. Jordan and Eden and ten other LCR operatives were standing by, close to camp. When it pulled up, Noah would fire a shot—the signal for LCR to storm the campground.

Noah hadn't been able to determine how many men would arrive with the truck. However, Mitch only had five men left here and if he kept killing them, he'd have even less.

The young girls already here were in a small cabin. An LCR operative would handle that cabin, while all others concentrated on Mitchell's men and saving the girls in the truck.

Noah would concentrate on Mitchell.

He spotted his brother talking to two of his men. Unable to hear what he was saying, he did pick up two words that put him on the highest level of alertness. *Brother* and *bastard*. Hand in his pocket, fingers touching his gun, Noah sauntered toward the group. No matter what lay ahead, he had to play this out till the bitter end. From what he could see, it was only Mitch and two men waiting for the delivery. Where was everyone else?

Noah took a cautious survey of the surroundings. Quiet . . . too quiet. The men standing beside Mitch moved a few steps back as Noah neared. "Where is everybody?"

Black eyes, so like his own, glittered with excitement. Because of the shipment or something else? Mitch's nonchalant shrug seemed overexaggerated. "Couple of the guys had an errand to run. They'll be here soon."

"An errand?" The shipment they'd been waiting on for weeks was coming, and he'd sent his men out on an errand? Something was definitely off.

"Yeah, you never can have too much sugar, you know?"

The roar of a transport truck coming up the drive caught his attention. The oversized vehicle pulled to a stop a few feet from where they stood. Mitchell's men moved stealthily and placed themselves strategically around Noah, not the truck.

Hand still in his pocket, Noah eased his hand around the grip and pulled his gun out.

Another vehicle pulled behind the truck. Two men got out. One opened the trunk of the car. Everything went still, quiet, and furious inside. The man lifted a gagged and bound, pajama-clad Samara from the vehicle and dumped her on the ground.

"Surprised, Michael?"

Noah turned his gaze to his brother. "How long have you known?"

"That you're a traitor?" He gave a slow shake of his head. "I never trusted you, but it wasn't until I saw her move yesterday that I knew for sure."

"You saw her move?"

"Well, actually I saw the little tracking device we injected her with move. Best invention ever. We tag the merchandise as soon as we get it. That way if it ever tries to escape, we can pinpoint the location exactly." He looked over at a wild-eyed and furious Samara lying on the ground. "Just as a precaution, I checked the monitor. Sure enough, about five minutes after you came back from dumping her body, it started moving. We tracked her to a house in town. You killed her and now she's resurrected . . . a fucking miracle, don't you think?"

"Let her go, Mitch. There's no reason for her to be involved."

A familiar childlike giggle burst from Mitch's mouth. "Yeah, like that's going to happen. But I am going to give her sort of a test. Depending on her answer after I administer the test, will determine how long she lives."

"What the hell are you talking about?"

"I'm going to fuck her. After I'm finished, she can tell me which brother gave her the best time. If she liked you better—which I highly doubt—she can die with you. If she says she likes me better, well . . . then, she can stay alive for as long as she interests me and I'll keep giving it to her."

Noah assessed his chances of getting to Samara before Mitch's men killed him. Not good. Two men stood over Samara, their guns aimed directly at her head. Three men, including Mitchell, had their guns pointed at him. Two other men sat in the cab of the truck. He could take out two, maybe three before he died. But that wouldn't save Samara.

Noah did the only thing he could do. He dropped his gun. Hands in the air, he faced his brother. "Let's settle this, Mitch . . . like we should have years earlier. You really want to see who's the best? Put your gun down and show me how good you really are."

Mitchell's mouth moved up in a sneer. "Yeah, you'd really like that, wouldn't you?"

"Hey, even if I win, you still have four men with guns who can take me down. If you win, you'll have the satisfaction of knowing you really were the best." Moving closer, Noah taunted softly, "Come on, little brother. Are you afraid to find out I really am better than you?"

With a slow nod, Mitchell dropped his gun. His glance encompassed his men. "No interfering. I'm going to show this bastard once and for all why I was my daddy's favorite." He jerked his head toward Samara. "She does anything other than blink . . . shoot her."

The men backed away, giving them fighting room.

The brothers circled each other. Mitch's face revealed the utter hatred he held for his brother. One he'd often displayed when they were kids. Noah maintained an expression of amused boredom. An act to play on Mitchell's insecurities. And it was working. Mitchell's complexion turned crimson, his eyes flashed furiously.

Noah's amused taunt broke the tense silence. "We just going to circle each other till one of us drops from dizziness?"

"Fuck you!" Mitch lowered his head and threw himself at Noah. With a speed that always surprised people because of his size, Noah sidestepped him. Mitchell flew past him, then thudded to the ground, flat on his face.

Mitch's brutality and temper were no match for Noah's athleticism and skill. Noah had trained for years. Mitch hadn't devoted his entire life to helping anyone but himself, and it showed. There was no way for him to compete with Noah's strength and experience.

His brother evidently realized this the second time he found himself on his ass, with Noah standing over him without a scratch. With a feral roar, Mitchell jumped up and rushed Noah again, managing to get in a glancing blow to Noah's face. Dodging the next one, Noah whirled and kicked. Mitch deflected a direct hit to his temple, catching it on his shoulder instead. The blow knocked him down, but he was back on his feet in seconds, coming at Noah full force.

This time, Noah took him head-on. With an uppercut to his jaw and a punch to his gut, Mitchell doubled over, gagging and spitting blood.

Cool dispassion his only emotion, Noah looked down at his brother. This man had shared a womb with him, but other than their looks, shared nothing else. It was time to end it. Time for justice to be meted out.

Mitchell straightened and rushed toward him again. Noah didn't see the knife until it made a downward slice into his side. Grunting at the sting, Noah nevertheless jerked Mitch around. One arm wrapped around his brother's neck, another against the side of his head. One snap, it would all be over. . . . Mitch would finally be dead.

God, he couldn't do it.

Furious with himself, he applied just the right amount of pressure for unconsciousness. When his brother went limp, he let him drop to the ground.

Hell exploded.

The man closest to Mitchell raised his gun to fire. Noah kicked the gun from his hand and shoved him toward another man who was about to shoot. Instead of hitting Noah, the bullet slammed into the man Noah had pushed, and both men fell to the ground. Whirling, Noah grabbed the gun he'd dropped and fired at the two men next to Samara. One went down. The other grabbed Samara. His hands shaking, eyes wild with panic, he held her in front of him, his gun to her head.

In his peripheral vision, Noah saw Jordan, Eden, and other LCR employees flood the campground. Two operatives took care of the men in the cab of the truck. When the others saw what was happening, they came to a standstill.

Focused on the man holding Samara, Noah opened his palm, dropped his gun to the ground. Holding his hands up, he kept his tone low and gentle. "You're surrounded. You have two choices. Let her go or die."

Noah's eyes narrowed on the man's trembling hand. The slightest pressure and the gun might go off. He locked eyes with Samara. Taking a chance she could read his mind, his gaze dropped to the ground. He looked back to see comprehension. Hands still in the air, he held up one, two, and then three fingers. On the third finger, Samara's knees bent and she dropped as low as she could go. In that instant, Noah pulled his knife from the back pocket of his jeans and threw it, hitting the man in the throat. He released Samara and fell to the ground, clutching the mortal wound.

Eden ran to Samara and untied her. Other LCR operatives spread out, searching for more men.

Jordan sauntered over to Noah. "Hell, Noah, did you leave anything for us to do?"

Noah jerked his head toward the men on the ground. "Handcuff the bastards together, then get the medics over here."

Without another glance at his brother, Noah walked away. Doing what he'd been doing for years, he focused on the needs of the victims as he called out orders. "Check the truck—there may be more men. Then let's get the girls out and looked after." He gestured in the direction of a cabin. "Three girls in the third one on the left. Take a couple of the medics and a counselor with you."

"You're hurt."

Samara stood in front of him, tears pouring from her eyes.

"Just a scratch."

"Scratches don't pour blood, Noah."

Her voice, so thick with tears and emotion, was more painful than the cut in his side. She had been through hell and he was responsible for every bit of it. His fingers touched the hideous bruise on her cheek. "You okay?"

"I'm fine." She shuddered out a sigh. "I woke up and they were standing over me. I never even got a chance to scream. I heard them say they would come back and take care of the others after they brought me back to Mitchell."

Noah wrapped his arms around her and held her

close. "It's over, Mara. I'm sorry for what you've gone through, but I wouldn't have been able to do this without you."

Samara tilted her head back to look up at him, her heart in her eyes. "It'll never be over, Noah. You know that as well as I do."

"What are you talking about?"

"You can't just ignore—"

A shot sounded, then another one. Noah pushed her behind him as his eyes searched for a threat.

"Stay here." He took off running.

Tired of being treated like a fragile creature, Samara ignored him and followed. Her legs weak and wobbly, it took several seconds longer for her to reach the others. She let out a small cry when she saw Jordan lying on the ground, Eden on her knees beside him.

"Let me see it, Jordan." Eden's voice was thick with tears.

"Sweetheart, I'm fine. Remember, I wore my vest. It just knocked the breath out of me."

Noah walked over and extended a hand to Jordan to help him up. Eden continued to run her hands over Jordan frantically, apparently making sure he wasn't hiding an injury from her.

"Eden, stop that or we're going to have to go find a room." The tender amusement in Jordan's voice broke the tension.

Noah looked around. "Tell me what we've got."

An LCR operative Samara knew as Dylan nodded toward the man lying on the ground. "He came from around the corner . . . took us by surprise. We've got medics and a counselor in with the girls in the cabin." He jerked his head toward the truck. "Go over and take a look."

Samara followed the others and stopped on a gasp.

A dozen young girls sat on the floor, all chained to the wall of the truck and to one another. Some were nude; others were clad in panties and bras. Two LCR operatives were working on unlocking the chains. Some of the girls were crying. Many were in shock, just staring into space.

Noah stood at the end of the truck. "Ladies, we're going to get you home to your families as soon as possible." His voice was just loud enough to be heard by the girls and so compassionate and caring that tears pooled in her eyes. Was it any wonder she loved this man?

Unaware of the woman who stood only inches away, dying to be held in his arms, he turned to Dylan. "Get them out and see if you can find a halfway clean cabin to put them in. Take the medics and counselors with you. Get them treated and clothed before anybody else sees them. Also, see if you can find a girl named Lara Kelly. . . . She may be one of the girls in the cabin. When you do, call Gabe's cellphone and tell him to let her speak to her brother Justin."

As Dylan nodded and took off, Noah stood and talked to two other LCR people. Samara turned away, unwilling for him to see the overemotional, exhausted, and lovesick woman standing beside him. She desperately needed to get control of her emotions before she said anything else. The last thing he needed was a silly, weepy woman declaring her love in front of his employees. If she opened her mouth right now, that's exactly what she'd end up doing.

Taking a deep breath, Samara headed to talk with Eden and Jordan. Perhaps Eden's calm rationality would rub off on her.

Out of the corner of his eye, Noah watched Samara walk toward Eden and Jordan. She was barefooted and exhausted—her feet literally dragging as she moved. His jaw clenched. More than anything, he wanted to scoop her up and take her away from all of this. Once again she'd suffered because of him. Once again he'd failed her.

With the iron control he'd forced himself to adapt years ago, he locked his legs together to keep from going after her. No matter what his personal desires, commitment to his cause kept his feet rooted to the ground. He had a job to do.

"Well, I'll be damned. If it ain't Michael Stoddard. All grown up and still causing trouble."

Noah turned toward the man who'd been instrumental in putting him behind bars all those years ago. With a barely raised eyebrow, he acknowledged Luther Prickrel, sheriff of Bolton County, Mississippi. He'd been a mean son of a gun years ago when Noah had been a teenager and Luther, the deputy. Based on the smirk on his lips and the clenched fists on his thick waist, he hadn't gotten any nicer over the years.

Prickrel looked down at Mitch's unconscious body. "Always knew one of you would end up killing the other. Just kind of figured it'd be the other way around."

"You mean you always kind of hoped that's the way it'd be."

Luther grinned, revealing the giant gap between his two front teeth. One of the few times he could remember he and Mitch laughing together was at the way Luther whistled some of his words. Noah slammed the door on those thoughts.

"I've got no time for this, Prick. As far as I know, there's only one dead. . . . You'll recognize him as the man with the knife sticking out of his throat. Everyone else should live out a nice long life behind bars."

Luther glared, clearly not appreciating the nickname

he'd been called most of his life. "I'm the law round here. You don't be tellin' me who's going to jail. That's my job."

"I believe the mayor's already given you the details you need."

"Mayor ain't the law round here, neither." His eyes roamed the myriad of people milling around the campground, including LCR operatives, medical personnel, and the bodies on the ground. "Just like you did years ago, you've caused a passel of trouble for this town. This time, I aim to make sure you don't get out of it." Luther's hand went to his gun.

Three LCR operatives took a step toward him. They knew not to draw their guns unless necessary. Fortunately most of his people could knock the gun out of a hand before the pull of a trigger. Point was . . . he didn't have time for this shit.

Noah whirled around to his closest operative. "Dylan, give me your phone."

Luther's beady eyes narrowed as Dylan reached into his pocket. Pulling out a cellphone, he gave Luther a small, mean smile as he passed it to Noah.

Noah pressed a few buttons and held the phone to his ear. The woman barely got a greeting out before Noah growled, "It's me. He in?"

Within seconds, an affable southern voice drawled, "What's up, Noah?"

"Got a sheriff here that needs to have a word with you."

"Put him on."

Noah offered the phone to Luther, who glared at it as if it would explode in his hand. "Better take it, Prick. Not a good career move to keep certain people waiting."

Luther's bear paw of a hand grasped the phone from Noah and held it to his ear.

Noah stalked away, having more important things to do than listen to Luther Prickrel grovel. Though hearing the stumbling words as he moved away did bring a small lift to his spirits.

"This here's Sheriff Luther Prickrel. Who the hell is— Oh, uh, yes, sir . . . uh, no, sir . . . uh, whatever you say, Governor . . . uh, Mr. Governor, I mean, your honorableness. Yes, sir, uh, goodbye." Luther blew out a loud shaky sigh and then shouted to his deputies, "Okay boys, let's help where we can."

Noah jerked his head at Dylan, barely restraining a grin when one of his best operatives rolled his eyes, knowing and not liking what his orders were. With only a soft growl, Dylan turned and headed back to Prickrel to advise him how he and his people could help.

Mitch woke to a mouthful of dirt and the hangover from hell. Voices surrounded him and for several minutes he lay there, his addled brain unable to comprehend. Spitting out pieces of grass and blood, he lifted his throbbing head and gazed blearily around. People everywhere. He recognized none of them. What the fuck had happened?

Damn, his head hurt. He let his head drop back down to the dirt, unable to hold it up any longer. Footsteps drew closer to him. He lay still, waiting to see what happened.

"Well, I'll be damned. If it ain't Michael Stoddard. All grown up and still causing trouble."

Luther Prickrel. What was the sheriff doing here? And why was he talking to Michael?

As Mitch listened to the conversation going on between Luther and his brother, several facts became clear. He'd known Michael had betrayed him—seeing the tracking device move after he'd dumped the girl

proved that. Never would he have thought he'd bring
the cops in, though. Why the hell would he involve
them? Didn't the law want his brother about as much
as they wanted Mitch?

When Michael moved away, Mitch kept his head
down and whispered harshly, "Luther, what the hell's
going on?"

"Damn, boy," Luther whispered. "You got yourself
into a hell of a pickle."

"You gotta help me get out of it."

"Are you crazy? There's at least fifty people here.
Most of 'em with guns. Hell, the governor hisself just
called me. Ain't no way I'm gonna be able to help
you."

"Dammit, Prick, you owe me. My daddy pulled
your ass out of the fire plenty of times. It's about time
you paid that back."

"Boy, this ain't no piddly fire. You done pissed off
the devil himself. There ain't nothing I can do."

"You better find a way to help me, because when I
do get free, you're the first one I'm coming after. You
hear me?"

"Shit. All right. But for now, you're going to have
to play along. There ain't no way I can help you right
now."

"Who the hell are they?"

"Don't know. Don't care. But your brother seems
to be in charge of 'em."

"Try to find out—"

"Somebody's headed this way. I'll see what I can do
to help."

Continuing to feign unconsciousness, Mitchell began to plan. Michael had betrayed him for the last
time. He cursed his daddy for not letting him kill him
when he could. Years ago, right after his mama left,
he'd brought it up and Daddy had said no, that it

would look too suspicious, having Michael die so soon after his mama left. Instead, his daddy convinced him that having a twin who was considered a bad boy was really a benefit. He could do anything he damned well pleased and Michael would always be blamed for it. Admittedly, that had worked out well when he'd gone after that Rebecca bitch. Now, though, it was coming back to haunt him.

Luther would help. His daddy had gotten Luther Prickrel out of several jams that would have put him behind bars for years. Luther owed him and he aimed to see he got paid back.

After watching Eden hug Jordan for the hundredth time, Samara was no calmer or closer to the rational, unemotional attitude she so desperately needed. A deep urgency inside her told her to find Noah. No matter how much he denied it, the cut on his side was worse than a scratch. There were teams of doctors here. They needed to check him out.

She found him sitting on the tailgate of an SUV, shirtless, while two very attractive women tended his wounds. Her first reaction so startled her, she stopped dead in her tracks. A snarl formed on her lips and vile, accusatory words formed in her head. Every jealous inflammatory cell in her body zoomed toward explosion. She wanted to tell them to back off. To get their hands off her man. Shame flooded her. He needed their help, he was injured. Never in any relationship had she felt the overwhelming need to assert her hold over a man. A clear indication that Noah meant much more to her than any other man in her past. As if she needed more proof.

Acknowledging this only made her feel worse. Noah had been clear. Their relationship ended with this job. But it didn't stop her from wanting to go over and pull the women away. She looked down at herself. She wore cotton pajamas. Her hair . . . Samara touched the ratty mass of curls, wishing now she'd had the energy to dry it before bed last night. She made a mental note to look more presentable the next time she was to be dragged from her bed by a bunch of crazed idiots. She probably looked pale, washed out and exhausted . . . and she was.

Feeling more self-conscious and insecure than at any other time in her life, Samara turned away, needing to regroup once again. Before she took two steps, a hand grasped her shoulder.

"You okay?"

She turned to look up into Noah's grim face. She bit her lip to hold back all the things she wanted to say . . . all the feelings surging inside her she wanted to express. Unfortunately, she couldn't control the tears that flooded her eyes, rolling down her face.

"Come here," he said gruffly.

As his arms folded around her, sobs tore through her. Emotions she'd held in check swamped her. Faced with the fact that as far as Noah was concerned this was over, she felt as if she were dying inside. For Noah, it was mission accomplished. End of project and end of relationship.

"Hush, baby." Noah pressed soft kisses on her head. "It's over. Everything's fine. No one's ever going to hurt you again. I'll make sure of that."

Breath shuddered through her. Wanting nothing more than to stay in Noah's arms forever, she forced herself to pull out of them and back away. A brave smile was beyond her at this point. The best she could hope for was a halfway calm façade. "I'm sorry about your brother."

Sadness flickered in his expression. "Some people

are just born with bad blood. He'll finally be put where he can't harm anyone else."

She brushed a hand lightly down his side where blood stained his shirt. "Are you okay?"

"Yeah. Didn't even need stitches."

Swallowing a giant lump she greatly feared might be a permanent affliction, she asked, "What now?"

An anticipatory gleam glinted his eyes. "Now it's Bennett's turn."

"Eden told me what you're going to do . . . pretending to be Mitch. I . . ." The lump grew even larger, cutting off her ability to speak.

"I'll be fine, sweetheart. Remember, *this* is what I do."

The words were innocuous enough, but his grim expression told her it meant more. He wanted her to realize that this was his job, his life. One she could never be a part of again.

"I—"

A man walked up behind him. "Hey, Noah, you 'bout ready to go?"

His eyes locked with Samara's, he answered, "Yeah. Be there in a minute." With a gentleness she always found surprising in such a masculine man, he tenderly brushed a strand of hair from her face. "Thank you, Samara. For everything."

No. This couldn't be it. She couldn't just let him go. God help her. . . . She couldn't. With a deep breath and a rock-solid belief in her feelings, Samara took the biggest chance of her life.

"I love you, Noah."

Regret and something else flickered in his eyes. "Mara . . . no . . . I . . ."

Standing on her toes, she leaned against him and cupped his face in her hands. "Go. Do what you have to do. Be the hero that you are . . . but come back to me. There's more to Noah McCall than the head of Last Chance Rescue. I see that man. . . . I love them both." She pulled his head down to her and pressed a soft kiss to his mouth. "Return to me, Noah. Please."

Hoping to get away before completely breaking down, Samara turned to walk away. She took half a step before he whirled her around and slammed his mouth down on hers.

Samara wrapped her arms around him as his mouth devoured hers. Passion, heat, and overwhelming desire intermingled with all the love bubbling inside her for this man.

Releasing her, he backed away slowly, his eyes blazing with fierce emotions she knew he fought with every breath. "Goodbye." He turned and walked away.

And that was it. Bare toes curled and dug into the ground to prevent her legs from running after him. Crossing her arms over her chest, her nails pressed into her skin as she literally bit her tongue to keep from screaming for him. This was his choice to make. If he survived apprehending Bennett . . . *please God, let him survive* . . . and chose not to return to her, there was nothing she could do.

"You okay?"

Eden's sympathetic expression told her exactly how she looked. Like a bedraggled, bruised, and broken-hearted waif. She managed a wobbly smile. "Not yet."

Eden jerked her head over to where Noah stood talking to several law enforcement officials. "Give him time to finish this up. This thing with Mitchell has been a long time coming. It was probably one of the hardest things he's ever had to do."

"I know . . . but I don't think time is going to make a difference in his feelings for me."

A smile brightened Eden's face. "No, I don't think time is going to deepen Noah's feelings for you at all."

Samara stiffened at Eden's words. What had happened to her compassionate friend? "That's a cruel thing to say."

Eden laughed softly. "You misunderstand me. I don't think Noah's feelings are going to deepen because I think they're about as deep as a river for you already."

"Really?"

"Yes. Give him time, then go at him again."

Eden was right. She wasn't a quitter. She didn't know the meaning of retreat. But she did know how to back off and come at him from a different direction. If Noah didn't come back to her . . . then she'd damned well go after Noah.

No, this wasn't over by a long shot.

Handcuffed and legs shackled, Mitch snarled as hands shoved him toward a van. Dammit, it was all gone. Every one of his men had been captured. All the girls had been taken away. Thomas Bennett was going to kill him.

"I'm sorry it had to be this way, Mitch."

Whirling around, Mitch glared at the man responsible for all of his bad luck his entire life. "You'll pay for this, you son of a bitch. I'll make sure you do."

"Let it go, Mitch. You've had your fun. Hurt and killed a lot of people in the process. Take your punishment like a man."

Mitch lunged toward his lying, deceitful, bastard brother. Chains around his ankles and hard hands grabbing his shoulders prevented him from moving more than a few inches. "Oh, there will be punishment, Michael, I can promise you that."

His brother shook his head and stared at him with those "holier than thou" eyes. "Goodbye, Mitch."

The hands behind him pushed him into the white van. Mitch didn't bother to fight. Let them think he was resigned to his fate. Let them think they were safe from him. He'd get out. . . . His daddy always said he was the smartest of the Stoddards. . . . He could get out of any kind of jam. He had contacts all over the world. People owed him big-time. They would come through for him. And when he got out, his brother would be the first person he'd kill, followed by that little black-headed bitch.

Before he was through with them, they'd be begging for death.

fourteen

For years, Noah had forced himself to focus on the goals of LCR and ignore his needs. Today, for the first time, he'd come closer to losing focus than ever before. He'd said goodbye to Samara . . . a woman he greatly admired, who filled him with desire and more tender feelings than he'd ever thought he could feel.

It was over. It had to be over. Samara was meant for hearth and home, not the intensely dangerous and often disgusting world he surrounded himself with. She was goodness and light. He had the blood of evil in him. They could never have had a future. No matter how his gut ached at the knowledge, he knew it to be true.

As they headed toward Biloxi, Noah used every skill and trick he'd learned over the years to return to the place he needed to be. Following the large transport truck, three vehicles drove behind Noah and Jordan, all headed to meet up with Bennett.

Grim satisfaction filled him. At last, the man responsible for Milo's death would be stopped. And a large human trafficking ring would be brought down.

This was what he lived for, the reason he created LCR. It was his calling, his destiny, and his repentance. So why didn't he feel the contentment he'd always had when he'd achieved his goals?

Little had gone according to his plan.

He'd killed a man today . . . but not his brother. Mitch was evil, with nothing remotely redeemable inside him, but he hadn't been able to do the job. Killing another human, no matter who it was, wasn't something Noah took lightly. Few people knew that Noah had never killed anyone. He'd once confessed to Milo that he'd broken every other commandment of God and would try his damnedest never to break that one.

When he'd created LCR, avoiding taking lives had been one of his main goals. Rescuing victims was their number-one priority. It rarely including killing, unless absolutely necessary or unavoidable. Killing the man who held a gun to Samara had been an easy choice, but taking his brother's life was a deed he'd been unable to carry out. Let Mitch rot in jail, but Noah refused to have another mark on his soul.

"She's in love with you, you know."

Jerked from his thoughts, Noah looked over at Jordan, who was driving. "What?"

"Samara . . . she's in love with you."

Noah lifted a shoulder and stared blankly out the window. "She thinks she is. Last year she was in love with you and got over that pretty damn quick."

Jordan snorted. "She wasn't in love with me. I recognize when a person's in love . . . maybe because I'm so much in love with my wife . . . I don't know. I do know that Samara might have had affection for me, but it wasn't love. You, however, she loves."

His jaw clenched, Noah remained silent. What the hell was he supposed to say?

"So, what are you going to do about it?"

"Nothing."

"Why?"

"What the hell do you expect me to do? Samara's not meant for this kind of work and I can't do anything else."

"Hell, Noah. I'm not talking about her working for you. I'm talking about spending her life with you."

"My life is LCR. It's all I know . . . what I am. She was meant for a normal life, not one filled with subterfuge and shadows." Noah slid down into his seat and closed his eyes. "Now drop it or stop the car and let me out. I don't need advice on my love life."

Jordan didn't bother to hide his amusement. "No, what you need is a hard kick in the ass. But I think I'll wait and see if someone else will handle that for me."

Noah didn't bother to ask Jordan what he meant. He didn't care. The pain in his side had moved up and set up a dull thud in his chest and head. So what if Samara thought herself in love with him . . . so what if he had strong feelings for her, too. That knowledge only intensified his belief that he needed to stay the hell away from her. He'd determined his course long ago.

Sharing his life with anyone, especially a woman like Samara, was impossible. She'd already suffered because of his stupid mistakes and selfish motives. He'd be damned if he hurt her any more. And if he tried to continue anything with her, she would be hurt. He knew that without a doubt. He just didn't have the necessary emotions to love another human being. Samara deserved all the happiness in the world and staying away from her was his contribution to that happiness, whether she wanted to believe it or not.

"There's something else we need to talk about," Jordan said.

"What?"

"An op went sour yesterday. Cole's dead."

Noah jerked upright in his seat, the ache in his chest intensifying. Cole had been a damn good operative and a good man to boot. "What happened?"

"I won't know all the details till Shea and Ethan come in for a debrief. From what I've pieced together from the others who were there, Cole ignored a direct order from Ethan, went off on his own, and walked into a trap."

"Shea bringing his body to Florida for burial?"

"No."

"Why not?"

"Nothing left. Building exploded . . . demolished. Nothing left to bury."

"Damn." An intense throbbing in his head had him reaching for the aspirin again. "How's Shea doing?"

"I haven't talked to her. Ethan had to sedate her . . . so I'd say not well."

"This has got to be doubly hard on Ethan."

Jordan shot a puzzled look at Noah. "Why?"

"Ethan and Shea had a relationship. I think we all assumed they'd get married someday. Then, the next thing we know, she and Cole are married. Cole was once Ethan's best friend."

"Shit."

"Yeah."

"Ethan was in charge of the op. Why would he choose to work with Shea and Cole?"

Looking out at the flat Mississippi landscape, his mind's eye saw the young, ravaged man Noah had saved all those years ago in prison. "That's Ethan for you. His way to show he's got total control of his emotions. Nothing touches him. Puts himself in the damnedest situations . . . mostly to punish himself."

"The way Eden used to?"

"Yeah . . . until you came along. She's settled down now."

Jordan swallowed a snort. "You'd better not let her hear you say that."

Noah's mouth lifted in a small smile. "I'm not that crazy."

"You want to be there for the debrief or you want me to do it?"

Jump right back into running LCR after leaving a woman like Samara, on top of having finally sent his brother to prison? Even Noah wasn't that emotionless. He needed downtime after this was over. Major downtime. He'd see Ethan and Shea when he got back, but wouldn't be any use to them right now.

"You handle it. I'll be on call in case something comes up."

"Where're you headed?"

"Don't know." Jordan wouldn't be insulted by his lack of sharing. They knew each other too well to worry about that. Besides, Jordan knew how it felt to get your heart ripped out of your chest. Reclining his seat, Noah closed his eyes and wondered how a heart could be ripped out when it never existed in the first place.

He jerked awake when the car stopped. Surprised to have fallen asleep, but immediately alert, he got out of the car and headed toward the operatives gathering out in an open field. Time for a brief scenario meeting and to deal with any remaining concerns and questions. They were about fifteen miles outside of Biloxi. Thanks to Mitch's cellphone, he had Bennett's number and would call to announce their arrival. Adrenaline pumped through him. This was his life, what he lived for. One more person saved, one less bad guy out of business, one less shadow on his soul.

Samara squirmed. Lying still on the couch was killing her, but as weak as she was, if she tried to get up, she'd probably collapse. She'd come home, gone straight to bed, and had slept surprisingly deeply for almost three hours. Then, as if a lightbulb went on inside her brain, she had jumped up, somehow knowing that at this moment, the raid was going down. She'd run out of her bedroom and found Eden sitting in her living room, calmly reading the newspaper. It had been Eden's suggestion that she lie down before she fell.

"Why didn't you go with Jordan on this operation?"

Eden's mouth lifted in a small, wry smile. "He was afraid of how I'd react when I see Bennett again."

The welts on her back still bothering her, Samara wiggled, searching for a more comfortable position. "Why's that?"

"He got away from us last year. . . . He's responsible for Milo's death. Jordan knows I have a tendency to forget myself when someone I love is involved. He just thought it'd be a good idea to spare Bennett."

"Milo was Noah's best friend, his mentor. Will he be able to handle this?"

A flicker of sadness passed over Eden's face. "Noah is the best I've ever seen in shutting down emotions to do what needs to be done."

Samara's breath hitched with a half laugh, half sob. "Why do I feel like you just gave me a warning?"

"Not at all. You already realize how stubborn Noah is. I'm not telling you anything you haven't seen first-hand. You have your work cut out for you."

"Can you tell me more . . . about Noah and LCR, without breaking a confidence?"

Curled up in a chair across from Samara, Eden looked young, carefree, and the total opposite of what she was, a highly skilled mercenary for Last Chance Rescue.

"I met Noah a few days after I was attacked. I was in and out of consciousness those first few days, but I remember seeing this incredibly beautiful man standing over my bed." She laughed softly. "I never told

Noah, but at first I thought I'd gone to heaven and he was an angel."

Both women giggled at that, knowing full well Noah had few angelic qualities.

"When I became more aware, Noah would just come sit in a chair beside my bed and talk."

"About what?"

"Anything . . . nothing."

"But didn't you wonder who he was?"

"He told me he was the hospital psychologist."

"But that's against the law."

Eden raised a brow at that and Samara rolled her eyes. How stupid. Like Noah really paid attention to legalities.

"Anyway, we talked about all sorts of things. He realized my gift for languages. He has an amazing gift as well, so we conversed, sometimes using one language per day. Anyway, I'd been seeing him for a few weeks when he finally revealed who he really was."

"Were you angry?"

"Furious. And do you know what he did?"

"Laughed?"

Eden chuckled. "Ah yes, you do know Noah well. He seemed delighted at my anger. When he told me who he was, what he did, I was immediately intrigued. He asked if I'd like to come to work with him. Of course, I wanted to say yes, but I was so horribly disfigured, I couldn't see what value I would have for LCR."

Her full lips lifted into a small smile. "Even to this day, I still remember those black eyes flashing at me when he told me it was my choice, I could be a victim of my circumstances or become a champion to others. He said my scars were fixable, but it was my attitude that would either make or break me."

"So, you decided to be a champion."

Eden lifted a slender shoulder. "I made a choice. I had but one life, and the way I lived it was up to me. Noah took me to Paris, hired the best plastic surgeons he could find, and . . ." She gestured at her breathtaking face. "This is the result. While I healed, we trained."

"Trained how?"

"You name it, Noah was determined I master it. He brought in a tutor to teach me a couple more languages. He and Milo showed me how to defend myself. Wherever he thought I might have a need, he supplied someone to teach me."

"Why do you think he took such a special interest in you?"

A tiny line appeared on Eden's brow. "What do you mean?"

"Well, he spent so much time and money on you, I just . . ." Samara shrugged, suddenly uncomfortable with Eden's stillness. Had she asked an inappropriate question?

Leaning forward, Eden caught Samara's gaze and answered softly, "Noah does that with every LCR operative."

"That can't be possible. He's got to have at least a hundred people working for him. How could he—"

"Because he's Noah. It's all he knows, all he does. He takes people in and molds them into being the best they can be . . . then he sends them out to save other victims."

"Are you telling me that every LCR operative has the same kind of background as you?"

"Hell, I hope not . . . since mine really sucked. But yes, though I don't know any details and don't want to, I know for a fact that Noah rescued them from some kind of horrific circumstance, and he gave them a choice, just as he did me."

"But what if they said no?"

"I only know of a few who have and he did what you'd expect a man like Noah to do. He helped them start a new life and went on his way."

"But . . . but not every person would be physically able to do what you do. How . . . ?"

"Noah believes everyone has a gift and can make a contribution, if they so choose."

Emotion bubbled inside her, looking for an outlet. This man who acted as though he were so unworthy was the worthiest of all men. Tears spilled from her eyes and she didn't try to stop them. Eden knew how she felt about Noah. Now, knowing even more, made the love even deeper.

She pulled in the careening emotions that would get her nowhere. Instead she focused on Eden's tranquil demeanor, amazed at her serenity. "How do you just sit there, knowing that Jordan is up to his neck taking down some very bad men? Aren't you afraid for him?"

"I don't allow myself to think about that. Jordan is one of the best there is and he has a lot to live for. I know he feels the same way when I'm on a mission, but we don't allow that to eat at us." Beautiful gray eyes took on a faraway look. "Once you've seen hell, you have a much greater appreciation for heaven."

An odd stillness permeated her body at Eden's words. The love Eden and Jordan shared was the kind of love to last beyond death . . . beyond anything the mortal mind could comprehend. Without question, this was the kind of love she had for Noah.

"Do you think I could be an LCR operative?"

Silky white-blond hair brushed Eden's shoulder as she cocked her head and gazed speculatively at Samara. "Do I think you could be an operative? Absolutely. You're smart, savvy, and gutsy. Do I think

Noah, the head of LCR, would ever allow that to happen? Not a chance."

She'd figured that, but she wanted to get Eden's opinion. An idea was beginning to form. . . . It was mushy and gooey, so she didn't mention it yet. But she had been through a hell of a lot the last few days and other than wishing with all her heart she'd been a six-foot, four-inch, three-hundred-pound linebacker so she could kick the shit out of Mitchell and his men, she'd handled herself pretty well. With the proper training, what could she accomplish?

She would wait because despite everything, she still prayed Noah would come to his senses and realize what they could have with each other. If he didn't, then she'd damn well convince him in another way.

Noah pushed the car door open and stepped out. A man of medium height with thinning, brown hair and cool, mean eyes stared at him. Since four men surrounded him with automatic weapons, the small man in the middle would be none other than Thomas Bennett, human trafficker, murderer, and all around evil bastard.

As the truck rolled into place inside the warehouse, Noah plastered on his best Mitch impersonation and held out his hand. "Mr. Bennett . . . good to see you again."

As Bennett shook his hand, his eyes flickered over the bruise on Noah's face. "Looks like you had a little trouble."

A cocky Mitch smile. "One of my employees got a little out of hand. He got in a good shot. I got in the last one."

"Good. So no real trouble?"

"Naw." Noah gestured toward the truck. "We got fifteen of the finest young bitches you ever set eyes on."

A slimy, lascivious look slid over Bennett's broad face. "I'll be the judge of that." He jerked his head to the back of the truck. "Open it."

Jumping up on the rear of the truck, Noah slid the door open. Jordan and ten other armed LCR operatives, with weapons on ready, jumped down. Bennett and the four men with him were completely surrounded.

His face flushed with fury, he whirled toward Noah. "What the hell . . . ?"

"Change of plans, asshole."

"You're making a major mistake, Mitch. One that'll cost you big. Nobody betrays Thomas Bennett and lives to tell about it."

"I guess it's a good thing Mitchell's in jail, isn't it?"

"Whaddaya mean? You're Mitchell."

"Wrong again." Allowing a small smile to lift his lips, he added, "The name's Noah McCall. I think you've heard of me." Without taking his eyes from Bennett's shocked face, he addressed the men beside him. "Get the equipment out and set it up in that small office behind you."

Thomas Bennett huffed and puffed beside him. His arms in restraints, he could do nothing but watch while Noah's people went to work. When the portable heart monitor was rolled from the truck, Bennett's eyes widened. A good setup for what was to come.

"Jordan, why don't you and Dylan escort Mr. Bennett into the office and get him comfortable?"

He looked at the remaining LCR people. "Take these four gentlemen and lock them in the truck. We'll chat with them later."

Bennett locked his body, refusing to walk. Jordan and Dylan each grabbed an arm and carried him inside the small room.

Going over to a small corner in the warehouse,

Noah took a minute to prepare. Gearing himself up for what lay ahead. This was his least favorite part, but it had to be done. There were at least a dozen children, if not more, in Mexico and Brazil, praying for rescue. He was determined to do what he could to bring them home. According to Mitch, Bennett had other side businesses going, too. They would learn about all of them today. By the time they were through, Thomas Bennett would be sharing every secret he'd had since grade school.

Bennett was already tied to a chair and gagged when Noah entered. Jordan had hooked him up to the heart monitor and a blood pressure cuff was wrapped loosely around his arm. A small television set, along with Noah's interrogation tools, sat beside him on a table.

Bennett's nervous eyes flickered back and forth from Noah to the table. He'd probably be cursing if it weren't for the tape over his mouth. They'd tear it off soon enough, but fear of the unknown was an important part of interrogation. By the time he finished with the initial questioning, hopefully Bennett would be in the mood to sing.

Pulling a chair in front of their prisoner, Noah slumped into it and crossed his legs. "Here's the thing, Tommy boy. We've shut down this little operation, but we know about the two similar ones you had before. I'm sure, like any good businessman, you've kept records. So, we're going to want to see those records. And we know you have some other things going. We'll want to know about those, too. If you want to make it easy on yourself and avoid any pain, then cooperate. We'll save a lot of time and you'll save yourself a hell of a lot of hurt."

Bennett's eyes glared hatred as he gave a violent shake of his head.

"Normally, I don't like to hurt people, but I'm more than willing to make an exception with you." Noah leaned forward and locked eyes with him. "Tell us . . . before it's too late."

Bennett mumbled something. Noah stripped the tape from his mouth.

"Go to hell, you son of a bitch. I'm not going to tell you anything. I'll kill you for this, you good-for-nothing piece of slime-sucking—"

Jordan slapped a fresh piece of tape over the screaming mouth.

Noah sighed. "Tommy, gotta say, I'm a bit disappointed in you. I really thought you'd be smart enough to know you don't have a choice." Noah picked up a hypodermic needle and pushed out the air. Jordan held the wild-eyed, squirming man while Noah injected the drug into his vein.

His voice gentle, Noah explained what was about to happen. "The first few seconds, you'll feel a little flush go through your body. Not too unpleasant, but that's just a setup for what's to come in about a minute."

Noah held up another needle. "You say the word. I give you this. The pain stops immediately."

Noah calmly watched while Bennett's face flushed bright crimson red. The beep of the heart monitor sped up well past one hundred. If the tape weren't on, he would be screaming or crying. Putting his face inches from Bennett, he asked quietly, "Where are those children?"

When Bennett looked like he might like to say something, Noah ripped the tape from his mouth again.

"You bloody bastard! I'll cut your fucking heart out, I—"

Noah slapped the tape back on his mouth. "The pain will intensify"—he looked down at his watch—

"in about two minutes." He grimaced sympathetically. "It's going to get bad . . . real bad. Sure you don't want to tell me something helpful?"

Though Bennett's eyes looked as though they were about to pop out of his head, he remained stupidly silent.

Noah blew out a sigh no one could hear as he listened to the rapidly increasing beep of the heart monitor. The drug he'd injected would soon feel as though teams of fire ants had been let loose through Bennett's body. The pain would increase in two-minute increments until severe agony commenced. Then it would get worse.

Bennett didn't yet know that they could do much more ruthless things.

Noah stripped the tape. "Don't make me do something I don't want to do, Tommy. Talk to me."

After sucking in a few gagging sobs, Bennett shook his head. "There's nothing you can do to me that'll make me tell you a damn thing."

"Tommy. Tommy. Tommy. You're beginning to really piss me off." Picking up another needle, he held it in front of Bennett's face. "This one is worse . . . much worse. Tell me where those children are and I'll take all the pain away. We'll get you some water"— he looked down at the puddle underneath Bennett's chair—"and some clean underwear."

Though tears poured from his eyes, the vile curses coming from his mouth told Noah he'd have to ramp up the pain. He stood up and, holding Bennett's arm still, injected the harsher drug. This time he left the tape off so Bennett would have the opportunity to speak immediately. And cruel as he might be, he wasn't cruel enough not to allow Bennett the freedom to scream in pain, which should be coming up right about now. . . .

An unearthly bellow echoed through the room.

Jordan pumped up the blood pressure band, waited, and then gave Noah a nod. Apparently Bennett was healthier than he looked.

Jaw clenched against compassion, Noah watched Bennett's face redden further as the drug zoomed into the man's system.

Screams filled the room. Sobs followed seconds later.

Inches from his face, Noah roared, "Tell me, damn you!"

Shaking his head, Bennett's hoarse voice was resolute. "You fucked me over last year, McCall. . . . You won't do it again. I'm not losing everything I've worked for."

"Kidnapping and selling children is that important to you?"

"I'm a businessman. People pay me to deliver a product."

Children were his product? It took a lot to shock Noah, but this man and his double standards stunned him. Time to see if they really existed . . . if there was an ounce of humanity in him at all.

Leaning back into his chair, Noah crossed his arms. "You know, sometimes people can withstand enormous physical pain, Tommy. You seem to be one of them. But there's always something or someone. . . . I learned that a long time ago." Noah twisted around and flipped on the small television. "You recognize this house?"

His face beet red but still furiously stubborn, Bennett turned his head to the screen. He blinked, then blinked again. His head whirled around to Noah. "That's my daughter's house."

"Yes it is. She's lovely, too, nothing like her scumsucking father . . . but she's not the real joy of your life, is she?"

His eyes flickered nervously back toward the screen. "I don't know what you're talking about."

"I'm talking about your five-year-old grandson, Christopher. What would you do to protect him?"

His body jerking as though he would jump from the chair, Bennett snarled, "You son of a bitch. You leave my family out of this."

"You son of a bitch, you made them a target when you started kidnapping innocent children and selling them. Give me what I want and they'll stay safe and happy."

"No . . . you won't hurt a child. I know about you. You save children."

"You mean, unlike you, I protect children, whereas you sell them. Right?"

Bennett glared at him, mutinously silent.

Noah blew out a harsh sigh. "Sacrificing your grandson's life to save dozens of other children?" He shook his head. "It's not what I want to do. I will if I have to."

Before Bennett could speak, the pain from the drug intensified. His skin grew more crimson, his eyes bugged out farther.

Standing, Noah leaned down and whispered urgently in his ear. "Talk to me, Tommy. I'll make the pain go away. Your grandson will be safe. Everyone will be safe. But the time to talk is now."

Gasping little sobs escaped Bennett and his head jerked in frantic nods. Noah picked up the other syringe and inserted the needle. Within seconds, Bennett's face lost its bright color and now looked almost normal.

Noah seated himself across from Bennett again and asked, "Where are the children?"

Bennett shuddered out a sigh. "All over the place. Once we deliver them to the buyer, we don't know where they go."

"Then you'll tell us where we can find the buyer, won't you?"

"Yes. Yes, I'll tell you."

"Good. Now, those other businesses . . . I'm assuming you have records on them, too?"

Bennett nodded and swallowed hard. "What happens after I tell you everything?"

"You'll be escorted to your residence in Florida, where we'll get your records."

"What about my men?"

"They'll be questioned, too."

"What happens after you get the information?"

"You and your men go to jail. . . . You didn't expect anything else, did you?"

Bennett shrugged. "I thought you might kill me."

"Tempting, but no." Noah looked toward Jordan. "Our jet standing by?"

"Yes."

"Good. You handle it from here." Icy cold rage washed over Noah as he stood. With all the disdain and hatred he felt for the man revealed in his face, he leaned down to the severely sweating and still tied-up Bennett. "Just so you know . . . you were responsible for the death of one of the finest men on this earth. By not taking your life, I honor his."

At the edge of control, Noah stalked out the door, unable to be in Bennett's presence any longer. Everything was finally catching up with him. He needed to get as far away as he could as soon as possible.

"You okay?" Jordan asked quietly behind him.

"Yeah. Fine. You'll handle things from here?"

"Of course."

Noah headed outside.

"Still don't know where you're going?" Jordan called after him.

Without turning, Noah raised a hand, acknowledging he heard but not answering. He had little time before he crashed. Fortunately another plane waited at a small airstrip a few miles down the road ready to take him to a private cabin in Minnesota. Ice-cold lakes . . . pristine air. Once there, alone . . . he would let go. But not until then. He gritted his teeth, *not until then.*

Eden's cellphone rang and it was all Samara could do not to grab it from her. Jordan said he would call as soon as everything was over. As she listened to the one-sided conversation, her adrenaline skyrocketed.

"So, it's all over with."

"And he gave us what we needed?"

"Everyone okay?"

Eden looked up at Samara and gave her a smile and a nod. Her legs wobbling beneath her, Samara sat down as she continued to listen, hoping at some point Eden would mention Noah.

"Did he say where he was going?"

"Yeah, sounds just like him."

"Okay, I love you, too. See you soon."

Eden closed the phone and smiled at Samara. "It's over with . . . no one hurt. Bennett is under guard, on his way to his home to give up all the records he has on the other children and his other businesses."

Swallowing past a pesky developing lump, she asked, "Is that where Noah is . . . with Bennett?"

"No, Jordan said he took off."

"Where?"

Eden perched beside Samara and took her hand. "He does this . . . after an op. He doesn't tell anyone where he's going. He usually shows up in about a week and acts as if he's never been gone."

Samara couldn't move her mouth to say anything. When she'd asked him to come back to her, he hadn't answered. She'd known deep inside he wouldn't come back to her, but that hadn't stopped her from a desperate hope.

Contemplating her next move, she took a deep breath. She wasn't a quitter. Noah McCall was worth fighting for. She'd once told him that she would fight for the man she loved. He had to expect that she would go to battle for him . . . and she would.

Eden's soft laughter caught her attention.

"What's so funny?"

"I was just watching your face. If ever a woman was preparing for a battle, I'd say it was you."

Her spirits somewhat lifted, she managed a trembling smile. Eden was right. She was gearing up for the battle of her life. One she was determined to win.

fifteen

Slumped in his chair, Noah stared at the three screens in front of him. He'd only been home a few days and was still catching up with all the issues that had come up since he last sat at his desk.

Mitch, along with Bennett and his minions, were in jail, awaiting trial. All the abducted young girls were back with their families and the teens from the previous shipments were being hunted down, one by one.

Satisfaction should be zinging through him. He'd put finality to his past and brought to justice some evil people who would never be free again. Everything wrapped up, neat and tidy.

After his usual week of crash and recovery, his normal routine was to get back to work, energized and renewed. Admittedly that usually included a two-to-three-day stint in bed with a beautiful woman. He'd told himself nothing had changed and that's exactly what he should do. Last night, he'd even found himself sitting in front of Celeste's apartment. Something had kept him from getting out of the car.

Absolutely stupid, because he owed her nothing.

Samara was most likely getting on with her life, just as he'd wanted. Eden had stayed with her a few days, ensuring she got the care she needed to get that stupid tracking device out of her arm. Eden's last report indicated she'd been eating and sleeping fine and that the bruises and injuries were almost invisible. She was obviously getting back to her normal routine. Why the hell shouldn't he do the same?

Sure he cared about her. Samara was the type of woman any sane person would care about. But he wasn't in love with her . . . not the kind of love a woman like Samara deserved. He just needed to immerse himself with work and the burning, gut-wrenching ache would go away.

The three monitors in front of him showed detailed reports of lost or missing people from all over the world. Though LCR rarely got involved in cases unless directly asked, he kept abreast of as many as possible. When asked for assistance, he liked to be prepared. It was this type of overseeing that had caught his attention months ago, alerting him to the possibility that Bennett had resurfaced and was back in business.

Noah stared at the face of a young toddler who'd disappeared two weeks ago from her backyard. God, the innocence in their eyes always cut him deep. What horror would this child suffer before she was found . . . if she was found?

So immersed in his world of missing people, he barely registered a slight sound of disturbance. When the door flew open, slamming against the wall, his head jerked up with real surprise. Inhaling a long, deep breath, he prepared for war. He should have known she'd come here. "Hell of a receptionist I have. Remind me to fire Angela."

Hands on her hips and fury in those amazing eyes, Samara Lyons looked like an avenging angel. She also looked healthy, beautiful, and so damned sexy, he hardened at the sight, which forced him to stay seated. "You're a long way from home, sweetheart."

"And it looks as though you took a wrong turn, Noah. I told you to come back to me. Not go to Paris."

Noah arched a brow, trying his damnedest not to grin. Samara in a snit was a sight to behold. Nevertheless, he had to tell her the truth. "Mara, this is my home. There's nothing for you here. Go back to where you belong."

"I belong with you, Noah. I love you. You know I do."

Not allowing his expression to change, Noah gripped the arms of his chair. Every cell in his body wanted to jump up, grab her and run, forgetting all promises he'd made to himself and all responsibilities to LCR. More than anything, Noah wanted to be just a normal man in love with a beautiful woman ... nothing complicated or clandestine. That was never going to happen.

"You think you love me. You loved Jordan last year. My guess, it'll be someone else next year."

Silky black brows arched over flashing eyes. "I knew you'd throw that in my face. Well, I've got news for you, Noah McCall. I don't care what kind of things you throw at me ... or what kind of excuses you give. You know good and damned well I love you ... and it's the everlasting, till-death-do-I-part kind."

"If it is love, it's for a man who doesn't really exist."

"Don't treat me like I'm an imbecile. I know who you are and I love you for that and a thousand other reasons."

He shook his head at her. "You don't know me."

His chest hurt as he watched tears roll down her heartbroken face. Dammit, he'd warned her.

She drew a trembling breath. "I could be pregnant. Have you thought about that?"

Thank God he had an answer for that one. "I can't get you pregnant."

"Why not?"

"I had a vasectomy years ago. I can't get anyone pregnant."

She jerked back as if he'd slapped her. "But . . . But . . . you used a condom the first time we . . ."

Noah shrugged as if it was nothing. As if his flesh didn't feel as though it was being torn from his bones.

"Why, Noah? Why would you not want children?"

"Hell, Samara. You, more than anyone, know what's in my blood. Why would you think I'd want to inflict the world with more garbage?"

A slender, shaking finger pointed at him. The trembling fury in her voice so evident, some of her words were almost unintelligible. "You are not garbage, Noah McCall. How dare you even say such a thing."

Noah gripped the edge of his desk. "Go home, sweetheart. Find that Prince Charming you've always dreamed of, because he sure as hell isn't me."

"You have no idea what I dream, Noah." She turned toward the open door and then whirled to offer one final parting shot. "When you're ready to stop being a coward, you know where to find me." She closed the door behind her, leaving Noah with an all-over body ache he knew he'd never recover from.

Before he knew it, his chair zoomed across his office as he shoved it away and stalked to the door. He couldn't let her leave like that. Seeing her pain, her disappointment. He looked down at his white-knuckled grip on the doorknob. What the hell was he going to say to her? He could offer her nothing.

Feeling like his guts were wrapped around his chest and tightened with every breath, Noah returned to his desk and a world Samara didn't belong in.

Shaking with fury and an ache so deep she felt as if she were bleeding inside, Samara made her wobbly legs move toward the elevator. Damned if she'd let

Noah walk out of his office and see her pressed up against the wall, trying to hold herself together. She'd come here knowing almost exactly what he would say. The shot about Jordan had been low, but he was shooting everything in his arsenal at her.

She thought she was a bit tougher than this, though. He hadn't really said anything terribly cruel and she'd almost crumpled in front of him. It was the vasectomy thing that got her. . . . No, it floored her. How could he think about not having babies? With all the goodness he had inside him, he'd make a wonderful father. A laughing sob caught in her throat. Okay, so he wasn't a saint. Was quite often an asshole, a jerk, and one of the most stubborn people ever put on this earth. But he was a damn good man . . . one of the finest she'd ever known. And she loved him. It was as simple as that.

Pride got her to the first floor without crying a drop. The elevator door opened and she stepped out. Giving a tight, grateful smile and a wave to the beautiful but overtattooed receptionist, she managed a shaky "Thanks, Angela." She wished she could have said more since the woman had been kind enough to let her go up to Noah's office without announcing her presence.

Dashing out the door blindly, she ran smack into Jordan, who stood on the narrow sidewalk, apparently waiting for her. Seeing him was all it took. He barely got out the words, "You okay?" before she threw herself into his arms and burst into tears.

His embrace was comforting, but not the arms she longed for. Nevertheless, they allowed her to cry her heartbreak onto his chest. He made soothing sounds and kissed the top of her head, much as her father would have.

She pulled away and offered him a watery smile. "Sorry, held it in as long as I could."

He nodded toward the door. "Want me to go kick his ass?"

Sniffling, she pulled away completely. "No, thanks. By the time I'm through with him, he'll be kicking his own ass." She reached up and kissed his cheek. "Tell Eden I'll call her . . . but not for a while. I've got some things to do. Bye."

She dashed away from an obviously confused Jordan. She couldn't explain what she was going to do. He'd try to talk her out of it or he'd tell Noah, who'd come to Birmingham and yell at her. She wanted to see Noah again, more than anything . . . but not yet. She had given him his chance. Now, for a while, she was going to step back and redirect her energy. She'd learned too much over the past month to let it go to waste. She had some new skills. She wanted to learn more.

When the check from LCR came to her, she'd been furious. Eden had calmed her down and explained that like any other operative, she'd been paid handsomely. It wasn't an insult from Noah, but payment for a job well done. Looking at it in that light, she'd been able to accept it and began to make plans on how to use it.

Her experience in Mississippi had taught her a valuable lesson, one that couldn't go unchecked. The promise she'd made to herself still existed. Never again would she be vulnerable to the Mitchell Stoddards of the world. Then, she would see where that led her.

And if Noah McCall didn't like it. . . . Well, that was really quite perfect.

Noah stomped around his apartment, unable to find relief from the burning worry inside him. Eden's amused, lackadaisical attitude only egged him on. "Eden, dammit. You've got to have some idea how she's doing."

Leaning back into her favorite easy chair, Eden didn't even bother to hide her smug smile.

"The least you could do is act concerned," Noah snapped.

Her husky laugh grated on his nerves. "I can't help myself. This is just such a reversal, I feel as though I'm in an episode of *The Twilight Zone*."

Noah ran his fingers through his hair. This was getting him nowhere other than more pissed. "When's the last time you talked to her?"

"I called her on her cellphone while she was still at the airport. Remember . . . it was about three months ago? The same day you talked to her, Noah. The day you told her to go home and find her Prince Charming. That there was nothing for her here."

"I can't believe she told you that."

"I can't believe *you* told her that."

"It was the truth."

"Well, if it's the truth, why do you care?"

"Because she's disappeared, dammit! That's why. No one has seen or talked to her in almost three months. I can't believe you're not concerned for her. I thought you were her friend."

"As far as I know, she still lives in the same place . . . doesn't sound like a disappearance to me."

"You know what I mean. She won't talk to any of us. Every message I leave gets ignored, every email I send unanswered."

"You know where she is, go see her."

"I can't."

Noah ignored Eden's exasperated eye roll. She knew full well why he couldn't go see her.

"Noah, you're making this harder than it is. Call her family. Let them tell you how she is."

"I don't do well with family."

"So basically you want to know how she is, as long

as you don't have to go see her yourself, or put yourself out there by introducing yourself to her family? You think they're going to bite you or something?"

Her sarcastic wit was not appreciated. "What do you think they're going to tell a complete stranger? They don't know about me, so I can't . . ." He stopped as Eden shook her head. "What?"

"They do know about you."

"She wouldn't tell them about me. She knows she'd be putting herself and her family at risk if they were linked to me."

"Oh, she didn't tell them you were the famous Noah McCall. Actually, I think she told them your name was Noah Stoddard."

"Why'd she say anything at all?"

"I think that's something Samara will have to explain." A sad little smile played around Eden's mouth, telling Noah there was a lot he didn't know.

"I can't call them. . . . Why can't you?"

Wide-eyed, Eden shrugged. "I'm not the one looking for her."

"Jordan's talked to them and they won't tell him. If they're not telling him . . . they won't tell me."

"Well then, there you have it. They've apparently talked to her. They know where she is and that she's fine. So what's the problem?"

Noah turned away and looked out the window. He needed to know how she was. He didn't need to see her . . . couldn't risk seeing her. Just talking to someone who'd talked to her would be enough. That's all he wanted. Why couldn't anyone understand that?

Before he could snarl a lame reason at her, the phone rang. "What?" Noah snarled into the phone instead.

"Turn to channel eleven," Jordan said.

"I don't have time to watch television."

"Trust me, you'll want to watch this."

Noah picked up the remote on his desk and turned on the plasma TV across the room. Switching to channel eleven, he slumped into a chair and glared at the screen.

An attractive blonde smiled at the camera. "Welcome back. We're talking with a young woman who has put herself in harm's way time and again to catch online predators. Due to her need to remain anonymous, we can't show her face." The interviewer turned toward a petite and distinctly feminine shadow. "Can you tell us how you became interested in this?"

The shadow shrugged with a delicate familiarity. "I had a friend who was involved in catching an online predator. I became intrigued and decided to see if I could do something like this."

Noah shot up in his chair. Breath, heart, and everything in between stopped functioning.

"And you do this with the cooperation of the police department?"

"Yes. Though we're not directly related to the police department, we work closely with them. I make the initial contact. When the men show up, looking for a young girl they've met online, they see me. We chat for a few minutes and then they're arrested."

"Some people might call that entrapment."

"Yeah, well, I call it getting a pervert off the street."

Despite the fury engulfing him, her wry answer had Noah's lips moving up in a grin. Damn, she was a piece of work.

"Have you had any problems with any of these predators, once they come to meet you?"

The slight hesitation caused Noah's blood to go cold.

"A couple of times they were somewhat resistant, but we were able to bring them under control."

"And do you help with this, too?"

Another delicate shrug. "When I have to."

The interviewer thanked her for the interview, turned to the camera, and began to give statistics of predators who lurk online, looking for their prey. Noah had stopped listening. He couldn't believe she had done this.

"Of all the insane, stupid, asinine things," he muttered as he stalked to his bedroom.

"Where are you going?"

Without turning, he snapped, "Where do you think I'm going?"

"So you know who that was?"

"Of course I know." That sweet, husky voice whispered in his dreams nightly.

"So what are you going to do?"

"First I'm going to shake her so hard her teeth rattle, then I'm going to spank her pretty ass until she can't sit down for a week."

Noah closed the door on Eden's burst of laughter.

As he threw his clothes into a suitcase, he couldn't stop shaking his head. Dammit, he'd wanted to keep her safe, away from the scum he worked with every day and what had she done? She'd not only immersed herself in it, she was putting her life at risk.

Did she think that just because they'd worked together, she was trained for this kind of thing? She was too delicate, too fragile. He couldn't allow her to put herself in danger like that.

And if she argued with him? His mouth kicked up in a grin. Well, he still had his ties. Tying her to the kitchen chair had worked once. Why not again?

sixteen

Samara searched the room for her date. He'd sent her a picture showing a nice-looking young man in his late teens. She was willing to bet this creep hadn't seen young skin like that in the mirror in twenty years.

Over the last few weeks, she'd gotten pretty good at being able to spot a real teen who only wanted to hook up and have some fun and a creepy, weasely freak of a sexual predator. The differences were sometimes subtle, but they were there. Most of the time it was a gut feeling and nothing more.

Tonight's meeting place was a coffee shop, a popular teen hangout. A ripple of chills ran down her spine, making her squirm. Why was she so nervous tonight? This would be her seventh sting. The other six resulted in three arrests, two lonely teens who really wanted to meet a nice girl, and a no-show. She had been somewhat nervous on the other jobs. After all, she, more than most, knew what could happen. But tonight's nervousness seemed more acute. She felt as if she was being observed, watched. Her eyes sought out the reason for her uneasiness, but she saw nothing that should cause such alarm.

The last few months hadn't been easy but they had been worthwhile. Not hearing from Noah. Knowing that she'd offered her love to him and he'd rejected her. Knowing that at any time of the day or night, he might be putting his life on the line and she might never see him again. She still held out hope for them . . . for him. Loving him meant understanding him . . . his motives and his beliefs. His rejection of her love had hurt tremendously but hadn't broken her spirit or tarnished her feelings. No matter what he said or did, her love was forever.

But she refused to sit and pine away like some weepy romantic fool. Seeing those young girls so abused and terrified had struck a need in her to do something more. She'd contacted the police and had been directed to the Macklin agency, a small private investigative firm who worked with the sex crimes unit of the police department to catch online predators. She'd been vague about her experience, but they'd seemed to understand and agreed to give her an opportunity to prove herself. She'd been working for them ever since.

Not wanting to dwell on her heartbreak and determined to keep her promise to herself, Samara had also enrolled in a self-defense class and shooting lessons. The self-defense classes were fun and kept her in shape. Shooting a gun not so much. It had taken her almost half an hour to stop shaking before she could shoot the first time. Now it only took about three minutes to settle down and begin shooting. Definite progress. She was now the proud owner of a .38-caliber Smith & Wesson AirLight. Small, light, and the perfect size for her purse or ankle holster.

Last week, she'd purchased a small house in Shelby County. In a few weeks, she'd be moving into it and when she wasn't tracking Internet predators, taking self-defense classes, and learning to shoot, she would enjoy decorating her new home. Staying busy was her panacea. At some point it would begin to work. After all, hadn't she slept almost four hours last night? Definite improvement.

Another chill ran down her spine. What was causing it?

Breathing out a shaky breath, she took a sip of her luke warm latte. Her date, Travis Benson, was late. He'd said nine o'clock and her watch showed eighteen minutes after. Did another one get scared off? Was she giving out vibes without knowing it? Samara tried to relax her body, determined to look like a somewhat nervous teenager looking to hook up.

"Julie?"

A thirty-something ferret-faced man with a potbelly, greasy hair, and desperate, bloodshot eyes grinned down at her.

She allowed her face to show a flicker of uncertainty. "Yes?"

He slid into a chair across from her. "Now don't panic, but it's me . . . Travis."

"But . . . but you're not seventeen." Her eyes widened with shocked wonder.

A sleazy "You've got nothing to be afraid of" smile lifted his thin lips. "That's why I didn't tell you. I knew you wouldn't come." His hand touched hers. "But we made such a connection, I wanted to give us a chance to meet. I don't think age has anything to do with real love. Do you?"

"So you lied to me, told me you were seventeen so we could meet?"

Cold, damp fingers rubbed gently up and down her arm. "I know you're only fifteen, baby, but we've got a connection. Something special. You said you were a virgin. Don't you want a real man to teach you what it's all about? Not some pimple-faced kid?"

Hiding a horrified shudder wasn't easy. "But you're too old for me."

A nauseating blend of cheap aftershave and onions assailed her nostrils as he leaned closer. "I'll make it good for you, baby. I promise. We got something special going on here."

Samara jerked her hand away, scooted her chair back, and stood. "Yeah. I think we've got something real special. Why don't you talk to the nice policeman behind you and tell him how special?"

Travis jumped up with a snarl. "You baited me!" A fist swung toward her. Samara ducked. Two policemen grabbed him, pulled his hands behind his back, and forced him onto the floor.

"You bitch!" He glared up at Samara one more time. Then poor Travis began sobbing his anger and frustration against the floor.

At one time, Samara might have had compassion for someone so obviously sick and desperate. These days, those feelings were much harder to come by. Travis needed help and hopefully he would get it. In the meantime, one less teenage girl traumatized and another sexual predator off the streets.

With a long sigh of gratitude that this had turned out well, she waved at the two plainclothes policewomen sitting at a table close by and walked out the door. The odd feeling had returned, but for some reason it now had an anticipatory edge.

Her head shaking at such an odd sensation, she pressed the button on her key chain to unlock her car. A scream caught in her throat as a masculine arm snaked around her waist. Another arm wrapped around her chest, pulling her against a hard body.

"I can't decide whether I should spank your ass in the parking lot or wait until I get you home."

He had come. Joy infused her and everything within her wanted to melt into him. Samara closed her eyes and offered up her sincere gratitude for a prayer answered. Then, knowing she couldn't let him get away with this, she did what she'd been training to do for the past three months. He'd left one arm free, which was surprising. Not wanting to hurt him but needing to make a point, she swung her arm up and back and punched him in the face. At the same time, she kicked him in the shin.

"Shit!" Noah dropped his arms and moved back.

Samara whirled around to see him rubbing his jaw, admiration and something else gleaming in his eyes.

"Learned a few moves, sweetheart?"

She grinned up at him. "Yeah. Whaddaya think?"

His expression darkened with sensual intent. "I think we need to get to your place."

Needing no further encouragement, Samara jumped into the driver's seat of her car. Noah got in beside her. As she maneuvered out of the parking lot, she cut her eyes over at the gorgeous man beside her and a flush of heat swept through her.

Knowing that once they got to her apartment, talking would be limited, she forced herself to think rationally. Didn't he want to know about her new job? "I guess you're wondering about—"

He pulled her hand from the steering wheel and kissed it. "Tell me later. Let's just get home."

His voice, thick with desire, caused that hot flush of heat to rise toward boiling as it spread through her entire body and then settled deep within her. His voice alone made her nipples go erect and caused a slow throb of need between her legs. With shocking boldness she'd never attempted before, Samara pulled her hand from his and placed it in his lap, caressing the hot, hard length she found there.

"Mara," his voice grated like gravel on velvet, "if you don't want to find your legs straddling me in five seconds, you'd damn well better get your hand back on the steering wheel."

Shudders of excitement rooming through her, Samara did as he suggested. She wanted him with a desperation she'd never felt before, but she would wait. Because more than wanting him inside her, she wanted him to herself, in her apartment, where she could throw herself into his arms and revel in his nearness.

The drive home seemed interminable but was only about fifteen minutes. When she pulled into the parking spot, they were both out of the car and headed toward her apartment before the car fully stopped.

Feeling lighthearted and happy for the first time in months, Samara ran toward her apartment, knowing Noah was only a few feet behind her. She opened the door, Noah slammed it shut, and then she was in his arms.

She tasted delicious. Better than he remembered. God, he'd missed her. Every night, he dreamed about these luscious lips, heard her voice in his head, telling him she loved him, felt her warm and soft under him as he moved inside her wet warmth. Then the cold light of morning sliced him like the blade of a glacier. He was alone. He would always be alone. . . . That's the way it was, the way it had to be.

But for the here and now, his dream was a reality. As he cupped her delectable ass in his hands and pulled her closer, he devoured her mouth. Sucking on her tongue, he gave her his as she moaned into his mouth.

Pulling slightly away, he breathed out his real reason for being here. Once he got her promise, they could devour each other till morning. "Promise me something."

Her eyes dazed with passion, she blinked up at him. "What?"

"Promise you'll stop this . . . that you'll not put yourself at risk like this."

Her eyes widened. "But . . ."

With ruthless intent, he unbuttoned her blouse and unhooked her bra, letting them both drop to the floor. He covered her breasts with his hands and squeezed gently. Their sensitivity would ramp up her passion faster than anything. With his mouth pressed against hers, he breathed the words, "Promise me, Mara."

Her little whimper of arousal and need went straight to his throbbing penis. But he wouldn't take this further until he had her word. His desire for her body was great, his need to keep her safe far greater. Using fingers and thumbs, he pinched her tight nipples with an erotic pleasure/pain.

Arching into him, she groaned his name.

"Promise me, baby." His fingers released the pressure, waited half a second, and applied it again.

Another whimper of arousal and then she breathed the word he needed. "Yes."

Noah wasted no time. He'd gotten what he came for. No further words were necessary. Dropping her skirt to the floor, he groaned at what he revealed. Except for an almost nonexistent thong, she was nude. He bent his head to the breasts he dreamed of tasting. As his tongue curled around a taut nipple, he pulled her legs up to straddle his waist.

Turning, he pressed her against the wall, pulled away, and looked down at her. "I missed you." The words were out of his mouth before he could stop them.

"I missed you too. . . . Kiss me . . . please."

Whatever she asked for in that sweet husky way of hers, if it was his to give, he would give it. Covering her mouth with his, his tongue licked at her lips. When she opened, he plunged over and over, showing her what he wanted, needed.

She dropped her legs and stood before him. With a smile that held secrets he'd die to know, she began to undress him. Pulling his shirt from his trousers, she lifted it off his head and threw it on the floor. He slid his shoes off and they worked together to get his pants down and then off.

Hooking his hands in her thong, he pulled it down as he went to his knees. Her panties holding her captive just below her knees, he set his mouth to her sex, nipping, licking. Ignoring her little cries to do more, Noah did what he dreamed about every night. With his thumbs, he spread the lips of her sex and licked. . . . Nothing tasted as delicious as his Mara. When he heard her squeal, he grabbed her butt and pressed her harder against him, his tongue going deeper and deeper into her vagina. The roaring in his head almost drowned out her sobs of release. As she throbbed around his mouth, he thrust softer, gentler, building heat and need again.

Her hands pulled at his hair. "Noah, please. I need you."

The tears in her voice were almost his undoing. Standing abruptly, he scooped her into his arms and carried her to the bedroom. Laying her gently down, he followed her.

Samara forgot modesty. Inhibitions didn't exist. When Noah followed her down, she spread her legs wide, took his penis in her hands, and led him to her opening. Without giving him time to go slow, wanting him inside her immediately, she grabbed his perfect ass and pushed him deep.

"Slow and easy, babe. . . . We've got all night."

"Can't wait . . . Noah. Please don't make me wait."

He gasped out a half laugh, half groan. "No, sweetheart, no waiting for you." With those words, he went deep, then deeper still. Samara spread her legs wider, wanting him as far as he could go, her need for him unlike anything she'd ever felt before.

Obviously seeing her desperation and sharing it, Noah rose to his knees, hooked his arms under her knees, and plunged. She screamed as heat exploded, then settled deep into her womb, throbbing, pulsing. . . . Explosions of lights went off inside her head.

Noah reared back and plunged again and again. She dimly heard his deep growl as he pulsed inside her. Burying her face against his neck, she held him tight, glorying in his big body over her, inside her. She inhaled deeply, loving the scent of a sweaty, masculine Noah and the musky fragrance of wild, untamed sex.

Pulling from her body, he gathered her to his side and cuddled with her. Tears pooled in her eyes, and she buried her face against his shoulder to hide them. The other two times they'd made love, he'd never held her like this. The first time, he'd left her immediately after he'd gotten his pleasure; the second time he'd knocked her out. Neither one was the kind of memory she wanted to have after having the most incredible sex of her life. This time, however, the sex had been more than incredible and the cuddling all she could have asked for and more.

She snuggled up against him and smiled at the soft sound of a light snore. She'd never slept with him before and treasured this moment, along with all the preceding ones. She had dreamed, hoped, and prayed he'd return to her and he had. Settling her head against his chest, Samara closed her eyes and luxuriated in the bliss.

Noah woke, somewhat startled to find himself still in bed with Samara. He rarely slept with a woman. After finding pleasure, he was usually out of the door or in the shower. Falling asleep meant being vulnerable around another person. That wasn't something he felt comfortable doing. With Samara, oddly enough, it didn't bother him. Sleeping with her felt good . . . right.

Noah jerked his thoughts back to the present. No way in hell did he need to be thinking in those terms. He'd come here for one purpose only . . . to convince her to stop putting herself in danger with this crazy new job of hers. He'd allowed himself to get off track, but anytime he was around Samara, that was bound to happen. She'd tempted him as no other ever had, ever would.

He pulled away to look down at her, still amazed that this petite, angelic-looking creature was filled with so much fire and spirit. Not only did she turn him on like a raging wildfire, he honestly liked her as a person. Liking people wasn't something he knew a lot about. He respected and admired certain people, but there were few he truly liked. Perhaps because he held himself back from people. Most probably because he had so little in common with most of them.

What did he have in common with Samara?

As he gazed down at her, he could only shake his head. Nothing. Another amazing fact. He had nothing in common with this beautiful, fiery woman and yet he liked and admired her beyond measure.

Samara moaned slightly and rolled over to lie on her back, giving Noah an unobstructed view of her delicate, beautiful body. As his eyes roamed, he looked for any remaining signs of her injuries but could see none. Her skin was clear and creamy once more, the dark bruises, cuts, and scratches she'd suffered months ago had disappeared. No outward scars, but what about on the inside? What about her memories? What lingering darkness and horror still lurked because of her experience? How had what happened to her affected her spirit, her confidence?

As he'd made the long flight from Paris to Birmingham, one thought had consumed all others. She never would have involved herself in tracking predators online if he hadn't brought her in on the Bennett case. He'd almost lost her once because of his stupidity and selfishness. . . . He couldn't let her risk her life like this. She'd fight him but he didn't care. The most important thing was to keep Samara safe.

Noah didn't question why he felt so strongly about this. He knew the reason. He was responsible for bringing her into this kind of life, but he'd be damned if he'd let her stay in it.

Unable to resist staring at the lovely creature before him without touching her, Noah pulled away and crawled to the end of the bed. Picking up a slender foot, he began the agonizingly delicious task of nibbling and tasting her tender flesh.

She was having the most incredible erotic dream of her life. Samara knew she was moaning and twisting on the sheets, making all sorts of naughty sounds, but she refused to open her eyes. She couldn't bear it if the dream ended. Big, hard calloused hands tenderly caressed her legs, while male lips nibbled as if she were a delicacy. The stubble of his beard rasped against the inside of her thighs, zinging electricity through her and causing a flood of warm moisture to pool between her legs. Without conscious thought, Samara opened her legs wider and thrust upward. A sexy, laughing growl brought her eyes open wide.

"Good girl. Now that those eyes are open, I can do all sorts of wicked things to this beautiful body and not feel the least bit guilty."

"I thought I was dreaming again."

A tender smile tugged at his mouth. "You dream about this, too?"

"Every single night."

His eyes darkened as he leaned forward. "Let's see if we can make reality better than the dream." Pressing his mouth against her sex, he kissed her. Samara opened her legs wider, held his head to her, and gave herself up to the most glorious oral sex of her life. His tongue licked at her, then went deeper.

Sobbing screams escaped her and Samara put her hand over her mouth to stifle her cries. Noah raised his head and growled, "Take your hand away. I want to hear how good it feels for you. Tell me how it feels . . . if this is what you want, if you want more."

Samara stared into his glittering eyes. "I'll wake the neighbors."

"You let me worry about the neighbors." He pressed a finger on the swollen aroused nerves at the top of her sex. "I want to hear your pleasure. Understand?"

His demanding voice did something to her . . . set free a wildness she didn't know she had. Unable to articulate this strange phenomenon, she could only nod her head in agreement.

Noah lowered his head and started all over again. His tongue licked and plunged, his teeth nibbling at her clit, then his mouth covered her sex and sucked. If he hadn't been holding her hips, Samara would have come off the bed. Orgasm hit her like a bullet and nothing mattered but expressing the experience in the way Noah wanted. She screamed everything, how good it felt, how much she wanted him, and then, when the final shattering release hit her, she screamed her love for him . . . giving him everything he asked for and more.

Shuddering and sobbing, Samara barely realized Noah had pulled her into his arms and held her against him. She'd had orgasms before—he'd been responsible for some spectacular ones—but this went beyond orgasm into a realm she never knew existed.

"Shh." Noah held her tighter and pressed quick kisses all over her face. "Tell me those were cries of delight."

Swallowing one last shuddering sob, she managed a trembling smile. "Delight doesn't even come close. I've never felt anything like that in my life. It was spectacular."

His eyes gleamed with satisfaction and need. "Let's try for beyond spectacular." He pulled her over him to straddle his legs. "Take me inside you."

Her gaze locked with his, Samara pressed down onto his hard length, welcoming him into her body. She took him slowly at first, not wanting this moment over too soon. Noah had other ideas. With a growl, he pulled at her hips and seated her fully.

"Now. Ride."

Samara started a slow, easy rhythm until, with his command to go faster, she picked up speed. Sobbing again in need and hot, wanton desire, she exploded around him. Noah pulled her down and held her as he thrust over and over, finding his release.

The rest of the night passed in a hazy, surreal sexual smorgasbord. For every sexual fantasy she'd ever had, Noah gave her the reality and it was richer, sweeter, and far sexier than anything her imagination could ever dream up.

Finally, at dawn, he released her one last time. Holding her quivering body in his arms, he fell into a deep, exhausted sleep. Samara closed her eyes against the emotional tears. Never would she have guessed herself to be this ravenously sensual being. Noah had given her this . . . freedom to express herself sexually.

Snuggling into his arms, she fell asleep and dreamed about how wonderful their future would be together.

seventeen

Samara sat in a chair at her bedroom window and stared out at the dismal scene of her rain-drenched parking lot. Waking in Noah's arms had been heaven and hell. Heaven, because she wanted a lifetime of mornings like this one. Hell, because it couldn't be. Cold reality had slammed into her just a little after dawn, forcing her to pull out of his arms. She bitterly resented having to leave them, but she needed to think. Last night proved that thinking rationally in Noah's arms was an impossible feat.

He had wrapped her tight in a web of sensuality and eroticism she thought only existed in books and erotic fantasies. Every part of her body tingled and zinged with life and a fierce, bone-deep satisfaction. Out of bed, away from him, things were clearer and coldly stark. Three issues had reared their ugly, truthful heads and she couldn't hide from them.

First, Noah had seduced a promise from her to stop working with the Macklin group. With embarrassingly little coercion, she had agreed to stop something she'd become enormously proud of over the last few weeks. His manipulation incensed her. Her weakness infuriated her.

Second, she screamed her love for him over and over during the night and not once had he even issued anything remotely similar.

Third and most telling, the last time they made

love, right before he fell into a deep sleep, he whispered something. She hadn't understood the significance of the words until she'd woken, but now, their meaning was heartbreakingly clear. "At night, when you're alone, I want you to think about how good it feels to have me inside you." His voice, low and sexy, had caused shivers to cover her body and curl her toes, which was probably the reason she hadn't paid attention to what he'd said.

When you're alone, meaning, he wouldn't be with her. God, she felt so stupid. Of course he wasn't here to declare his love. He hadn't come here to tell her he was wrong and beg her to come to Paris, marry him, and work with him at LCR and share his life. That was one fantasy destined not to be reality and she'd missed it completely.

He'd come to Birmingham with one purpose, to convince her to stop trapping online predators. And, since he was here, why not get in some hot sex? Samara had no doubt he cared for her. . . . Noah might be a jerk, but was actually a very caring person. He didn't want her to get hurt. Yes, he wanted her body and as willing as she was to spread her legs for him whenever he was around, why the hell shouldn't he take advantage of the opportunity? She'd never in her life been an easy lay, but with Noah, that's exactly what she was.

She had started her job with the Macklin Agency because she thought she could make a contribution. There had been another reason, too. She'd wanted to prove herself to Noah. Had wanted to show him that she could take care of herself, that she would be a good LCR operative. That she could share a life with him. Samara closed her eyes in shame. . . . She'd wanted to prove herself worthy of Noah.

For the first time since they'd become lovers all those months ago, Samara realized that her fantasy of

Noah coming to his senses and admitting his love for her was nothing more than a silly dream. One he'd probably laugh at if he knew about it.

"Mara."

The low, husky voice caused an immediate reaction in every erotic nerve in her body. Noah knew them all, where they were and how to turn them on. Gripping the arms of her chair, she forced herself to stay seated, fighting every emotion-filled instinct telling her to forget pride, take any and everything he could give, and be grateful for it. She snarled at those instincts to back off. They'd had their fun last night. Now cold, sane reasoning had to take over.

"Why are you here, Noah?"

Whether it was her cool tone or words, she didn't know, but Noah shot up in bed and stared at her.

"What?"

"You came to see me for a reason." She shrugged slightly. "I'm assuming it wasn't just to screw me. So, what's the real reason?"

Frowning, Noah leaned back against the headboard and stared at the woman who only hours before had been like hot, molten lava in his arms. Now if she got anywhere close to lava, she'd turn it to stone immediately. Never had he seen such a cold, almost mean look in her eyes. What the hell had happened?

"I saw your interview on television. I don't want you involved in this kind of life."

"What right do you have to tell me what I should or shouldn't be involved in?"

"As your friend, I have every—"

"You're not my friend. Where did you get that idea?"

Well hell, so much for his idea of spending the day in bed with her. "Why are you so pissed . . . because I actually care about what happens to you?"

Samara stood. She'd covered herself with a soft, cotton robe, and almost more than he wanted to breathe, he wanted to pull the robe from her body and take her again and again. From the expression on her face, he was destined to be disappointed.

"I don't need you to take care of me."

"Mara, I have to—"

"You don't have to do anything. What I choose to do with my life is my business, not yours. Just because we've had sex gives you no right to—"

"Dammit, we've had more than sex."

Standing in front of him, hands on her hips, she looked arrogant, furious, and so damn beautiful. "What else, Noah? Tell me what else we have."

Shit. Noah dropped his head back onto his pillow and blew out a harsh sigh. She was right. They had nothing else. He could feel her eyes on him, waiting for an answer he couldn't give.

"Go home, Noah." A sad weariness coated her words.

His head shot up again. "You made a promise last night."

"Correction. You seduced a promise out of me."

"Like hell."

"Don't try to deny it. You've manipulated me for the last time. Go home and leave me the hell alone to do my work."

"Mara, you're not equipped to handle these kinds of creeps. You wouldn't even be doing this if it weren't for me."

"I've been doing pretty damned well for almost three months now, and what the hell do you have to do with it?"

"You're putting yourself at risk because of what you went through."

"I won't deny that, but how is it your business?"

"It's my fault. Before I asked for your help, you never would have considered doing anything like this."

She blew out a snort of disgust. "You give yourself way too much credit . . . as always. I'm doing this because I'm good at it and I'm helping people."

"And yourself, too."

"What's that supposed to mean?"

"I've seen it too many times not to recognize it. You were helpless, vulnerable . . . at the mercy of some very bad men. Now you feel powerful and in control."

"Stop psychoanalyzing me. I'm doing this to make a difference and you make it sound like it's a power trip."

"Not a power trip. A need to prove yourself."

"Prove myself to who?"

"Yourself. Me."

"My God, does your ego have no bounds? You think I'm trying to catch Internet predators and pedophiles to impress you?"

"Not to impress me . . . more like to show me you could be an LCR operative."

Flashing eyes narrowed, challenged. "And why couldn't I be one?"

"You're not good enough."

A cold, distant expression crossed her face as her beautiful eyes dimmed. He'd hurt her with his blunt answer. Better for her feelings to be hurt than for her to be dead.

"This may surprise you, Noah, but there are other organizations who do good things other than LCR."

"Dammit, I know that." Shit, this was getting them nowhere. "Mara, you've been through enough. Let someone else—"

"Why? Why should I let someone else? Why am I not equipped to handle a job like this? What makes me so damn special that I shouldn't do this, but other people can? Tell me."

Hell, now she was insulted and he'd only been trying to protect her. "Because, you're too gentle, too good, too pure to . . ." He trailed off at the look of fury and hurt in her eyes.

"Stop trying to protect me. . . . I don't need it."

"It's all I have to offer you."

He saw in her expression that she comprehended the exact meaning of his words. A dull, lifeless look entered her eyes and his chest ached for her.

She turned her back on him and walked into the bathroom. "Leave."

As the door clicked shut, Noah saw an end to something he never could have had. With full knowledge of what he'd done to her, used sex to manipulate her, once again hurting her, he didn't blame her for hating him.

To spare her any more grief, Noah threw his clothes on and was out the door within minutes. He pulled out his cellphone and called a taxi to take him back to his rental car. As he waited, he made another call. She wouldn't like it, but she'd given him no choice. He had to keep her safe.

Ethan Bishop sipped on his fifth cup of coffee for the evening. Since he hadn't slept a full night in years, caffeine was a nonissue for him. As jobs went, this had been his easiest by far, but also his most boring. Not that his mark didn't stay active. If she wasn't taking self-defense classes, going to the shooting range, or tracking down sexual predators, then she was picking out paint, curtains, and other shit for her new house. He'd take hearing the grunt of a body being slammed into a mat or the familiar blast of a Smith & Wesson over decorating crap any old day.

He remembered his orders clearly . . . from the big

man himself. Specific, but agonizingly vague. "She thinks she can protect herself. I don't want to take that self-assuredness away from her. She's fought damn hard for it."

"But?" Ethan had growled, already knowing what was coming.

"She's not as prepared as she thinks she is. She's too trusting, too innocent. Your job is to make sure nothing happens to her. Don't interfere with her life, get in her way, or stop anything she does. Just make sure no harm comes to her." Black eyes had seared him. "No. Matter. What."

Trouble was, nothing ever happened to little Ms. Samara Lyons. Sure she stayed busy. Twice a month, sometimes more, she met up with some freak she'd talked to online and more often than not, the human garbage was apprehended. Admirable for her, boring as all get-out to him. At least five plainclothes cops watched over her. She was as safe as a babe in her mother's arms. No action at all for him.

Not that he wanted anything to happen to her, but hell, even a purse snatching would've mixed up the day a little. Babysitting, even a beautiful woman, was damned boring.

He was on probation, he knew that. After the fuck-up in Bermuda, he was surprised he hadn't been strung up by his balls and fed to the sharks. Of course, since only two people knew what had really happened, and one of them was dead, babysitting the boss's obsession was an easy punishment.

Not that Noah McCall would ever refer to this new job as babysitting or admit he'd put Ethan on probation. He'd just been told that after such a tough assignment, a little R & R in Birmingham, Alabama, would be good for him. And oh, by the way, there's someone you have to protect 24/7, but only because she's a friend of Eden and Jordan's and she did a favor for LCR.

Bullshit. Noah McCall was deep into denial about his feelings for the woman. Other people might not recognize it, but since he'd suffered from the same affliction for years, he had no trouble identifying that kind of sickness. And sickness it was. No way in hell would anyone willingly put themselves through that kind of torture if they could prevent it.

Of course, after what Ethan had done to the woman he was obsessed with, what right did he have to judge other people's ways to deal with their obsessions?

He gulped down the last of his now cold coffee. Getting a man killed, a damn fine one, who'd once been his best friend? Kind of hard to determine a just punishment. The agony and accusation in Shea's eyes, glaring at him with pure burning hatred, screaming how much she despised him.

Yeah, now that was a fitting punishment.

Samara eyed her watchdog out of the corner of her eye. He seemed sadder tonight. Even more than usual. There were a thousand tears in his eyes and Samara felt sure he'd never been able to shed one. His ravaged, scarred face held a deep, dark sadness and though he was a stranger, she ached for him. Whatever this man had gone through continued to tear at his soul.

The first time she saw him, at the little diner where she'd arranged to meet yet another creep from the Internet, she'd been slightly startled by his appearance. He wasn't the kind of man one could ignore. Well over six feet tall, he was built like a tank . . . maybe not as bulky, but definitely as hard as one. His hair was several different shades of blond and hung to his shoulders. She'd never been fond of guys with long hair, but with this man, she couldn't imagine him any other way. The long, shaggy look suited him. A savage, painful-looking scar slashed down the left side of his cheek, marring what had probably been a very handsome face. The scar didn't detract from his looks. Like everything else, it seemed to suit him. His eyes, though . . . those eyes were his most surprising feature. They were a startling shade of peridot and filled with a stark, unending anguish.

After seeing him that first time and registering his presence, she had turned away and continued to look for the man she was there to meet. The second time she saw him had been at the grocery store. That had given her pause. Birmingham wasn't a huge city, but still, seeing him again seemed oddly coincidental. The third time she saw him had been at the paint store.

The realization that she was being followed stunned her only momentarily. She knew that only one man would be responsible for having her followed.

As soon as she'd gotten home, she called Noah's office in Paris. It was five in the morning there. . . . Of course he was at work. He'd picked up the phone and his first words almost broke her heart.

"Mara, you okay?"

She'd taken a breath, determined to tell him what was on her mind. "Call off your watchdog."

He hadn't said anything for the longest time and she'd been at the point of saying something she would have regretted, such as blathering about her love for him. Fortunately, he'd answered, but with a bleak, resolute, "No." Then he'd hung up on her.

"Sam, do you know that guy?"

"What?" She jerked her attention back to Rachel.

"That guy over in the corner. I swear I've seen him before. I think he was at Mama Maria's the other night. And he keeps staring at you."

With a casual "let me see who you're talking about," Samara turned around to stare, point-blank, at her watchdog. And as he did every time they locked eyes, he nodded in acknowledgment. This time he also lifted his cup as if to toast her.

Rachel gasped behind her. "You *do* know him."

She looked back at her friend. "No I don't."

"Then what was that look about?"

"Just a little subtle flirting, Rach . . . nothing more."

Rachel's soft brown eyes searched her face, seeing more than Samara wanted her to see. "I feel as if I don't know you anymore. You disappear for over a month . . . don't even answer your cellphone. When you finally do come back, you have this sad, kind of wistful look on your face as if you're full of secrets. You're hardly ever able to go out anymore and you still don't have a job. And if you're not learning how to kick somebody's ass, then you're learning how to shoot it."

"I just want to be able to protect myself. You should think about doing something like that, too. You never know when it might come in handy."

"Oh no you don't. You're not going to recruit me into becoming G.I. Jane. Next thing I know, you'll be shaving your head and smoking cigars."

Lifting her drink, she snorted a giggle into her soda. "Now that, I promise, will never happen." No better at lying now than before, she took a long sip of her drink to avoid Rachel's searching eyes. "I like being able to defend myself."

"Sweetie, did something happen?"

Samara jerked at the question. She would never tell Rachel about what she'd been through. It would be too complicated and would serve no purpose other than to freak her friend out.

"Of course nothing happened, and I don't intend

for anything to happen, either. Learning how to defend myself has always been something that interested me. My brothers taught me a little, but I wanted to learn more. It's as simple as that." Picking up her fork, she shoveled some of Rachel's fries onto her own plate. "I think that cute waiter gave you more fries than he did me."

Mentioning the waiter was a deliberate ploy, because he had flirted quite openly with Rachel each time he'd come by their table. Since Rachel was just coming out of a bad breakup, having a cute guy flirt with her was a definite mood enhancer. Samara hoped it went further than a little flirting. Even if she didn't get to be happy, there was no reason her best friend couldn't.

While Rachel looked around again for their waiter, Samara twisted around to see if her mysterious stranger was still there. Yes, bless his heart, and now on his sixth or was that his seventh cup of coffee? She hoped it was decaf because the poor guy looked as though he hadn't slept in days.

Most women would probably be upset about being followed. She'd demanded that Noah leave her alone and in his own odd way, that's what he was doing. He'd known she wouldn't stop working for the Macklin firm and instead of trying to convince her again, he was simply making sure she was safe. And sick she might be, but if this was the only way he could show he cared about her, she willingly accepted it.

Mitch glared at his no-account lawyer. The weasel had broken every promise he'd made. First he'd promised to get him a plea deal and that hadn't panned out. Now somehow, without his brother or the bitch he planned to kill testifying, Mitch found himself facing the possibility of a life sentence in a maximum-security prison. There was no way in hell he'd allow that to happen.

Now his bastard lawyer was telling him there wasn't any way he could find out any information on the woman who'd helped put him behind bars. Apparently her identity had been hidden. There were ways around that and the idiot knew it.

"Call Luther Prickrel and tell him what you need."

"I can't do that, Mitch. I'll be disbarred if anyone ever finds out we even talked about this."

Mitch leaned closer so the cameras wouldn't pick up the threat in his expression. "That was a mighty fine-looking woman you were with at Carmine's motel last Friday night."

Bloodshot eyes popped out in dismay. "How did you . . . ?"

His point made, Mitch settled back into his chair. "I have eyes everywhere, Baker. Just remember that. Now, I can almost guarantee that the little honey you took inside that motel room for exactly two hours and ten minutes wasn't Mrs. Baker. Is that correct?"

Baker leaned closer, his voice an urgent whisper. "My wife would kill me."

"She never has to know about it. I can fix it where you can screw to your heart's content as many bimbo bitches as you want or I can fix it where Mrs. Baker learns that her loving husband is loving on other women, too. Which will it be?"

His thin shoulders slumping, Baker gave in so easily, Mitch wanted to pop him for being such a pussy. Maybe later. For now, Baker had some work to do.

"Call Luther. Find out who the dark-haired woman was. Also, find out how my brother got involved with Noah McCall and his people. Does he work for them or what?"

"I'll see what I can do."

"Times up," a CO growled behind him.

Mitch stood and smiled down at his attorney. "I know you'll do your very best, Mr. Baker. It would be such a disappointment if you don't." Mitch sauntered out the door, not looking back to see how his veiled threat had been taken. Baker might be a liar, but he wasn't stupid. Having Mrs. Baker find out about his little honeypot would destroy the man since Mrs. Baker came from money and Mr. Baker wouldn't want to lose it.

Stomping through the narrow hallway back to his cell, Mitch ignored the stench of antiseptic, body odors, and vomit. Some things were easier to get used to than others. He could handle bad smells and shit for food. Even being surrounded by men who'd just as soon tear you a new asshole as look at you didn't bother him.

For months, he'd been working toward finding a way out of this place and for one reason only. To cut out the hearts of the two people who'd put him here. It was what he lived for, his only reason for existence. Once that was done, then he'd think about life after that. Until that happened, nothing else mattered.

eighteen

"Samara, everything okay?"

Adjusting the small hearing device in her ear, Samara fiddled with her hair, her signal that she was fine. No matter what anyone said, the creep she was meeting tonight had weirded everyone out. They'd been tracking him for over a month, much longer than most of the other guys they'd caught. Every time she thought he was about to make the offer to meet, he had backed away. Usually when they were that squirrelly, it meant a setup was suspected, and she eased back from them. With this guy, they couldn't afford to back down.

She'd been working with the police and the Macklin firm for several months now and this was the first guy she could truly say was sicker than even Mitchell Stoddard. The things he said, the way he said them . . . God, if he did even one of the things he said he wanted to do to a girl, her life would be over. This guy went beyond sick into a realm Samara didn't even want to contemplate.

Once they saw this guy was sicker than most, they'd been exceedingly careful in reeling him in. If he weren't caught, there was no telling what he might do. Admittedly it could all be talk, but no one was willing to take that chance.

She was well protected. Not only were the usual plainclothes police surrounding her, but two of Macklin's investigators sat at the next table. Plus, she still had her watchdog. Always in her peripheral vision but never intrusive. She'd had a couple of encounters where she had to handle a furious man and he hadn't interfered. She wondered why. Was his lack of assistance based on Noah's advice or because, unlike Noah, he thought she could handle herself?

Noah. As usual, just the thought of him caused a major tug of her heart. How she missed him. She heard from Eden almost every week and though she never asked, thankfully Eden knew what she needed. So, for at least half an hour each week, Eden gave her an update on the man Samara loved. Nothing detailed or specific—neither of them would dare say his name or anything about the organization—but they had their own little code. Samara treasured every word. Eden understood the pain of loving someone from afar.

"Hey, Pretty Girl."

The young male voice caught her off guard. Samara jerked around, furious at herself for forgetting where she was and why she was there.

"Ruff-ryder?" She blinked innocently up at him, hoping her shock didn't show. The guy was probably no more than sixteen years old.

"Yeah, but you can call me Jeff." He pulled out a chair and sat down. "Sorry I'm late. You been here long?"

"Uh, no . . . I . . ." Crap. She was so disoriented, she couldn't think what to say. The things this guy had said to her, what he wanted to do to her. Where on earth would a young, just-passing-puberty teen get some of the sick things he'd come up with?

"Hi Jeff. . . . This is so cool . . . you and me . . . meeting at last." Hopefully her voice sounded more sincere to him than it did to her.

The Adam's apple in his skinny neck jumped convulsively as he swallowed. Wow, the guy was even more nervous than she was. The way he jerked his head around reminded her of a bird, on the lookout for predators. Why? He was the predator.

"Yeah . . ." He swallowed hard again. "Uh, you want to go somewhere else?"

"No, this is fine. Why?"

"I just thought we could go somewhere more private . . . where we could talk about things."

Samara leaned forward, wanting to make sure her mic picked up his answer. "What kind of things do you want to talk about?"

"You know . . . like we talked about online."

She fluttered her hands nervously, only partially acting. "I told you I don't feel comfortable with those kinds of things. I thought we'd get to know each other."

The way his eyes kept wandering over the crowd at the small restaurant had her worried. "Are you looking for someone?"

"Huh? Uh, no . . . I just thought we could somewhere more . . . like, private."

"Maybe later."

Another convulsive swallow. "Uh . . . okay. I need to go to the bathroom. Be right back."

She watched in astonishment as the sadistic teen weirdo shot out of his chair and practically ran to the back of the restaurant.

"What happened?" a voice whispered in her earphone.

Samara shrugged and shook her head, totally clueless herself. No way would she ever have figured the guy they'd been tracking was really a teenager. She'd agreed to meet him with the understanding that she wouldn't participate in any of the deviant things he wanted to do. She'd told him she just wanted to sit and chat. Everyone had been a bit surprised when he'd agreed, but figured he hoped to be able to convince her to change her mind.

Now, here she sat, waiting and wondering if her teenaged perv would come back.

"You want another soda?"

Samara looked up at her sweet-faced, chubby waitress. "No, thanks. I'm fine."

"Look hon, I'm not one to get involved in other people's business, but I just thought you might want to know that your young man went out the back door."

"He did?"

"Yeah, sorry about that." She waddled away.

Samara looked toward the plainclothes cops at the next table. "I guess that's that."

Linda Knowles, one of the officers, walked over to her table and sat down. "Did you think that was strange?"

"Very. What about you?"

"Yeah. Think he made us?"

"I don't know. I was so stunned that he turned out to be a kid."

"Yeah, well, that is unusual, but all perverts were kids at one time."

Shrugging off her disquiet that something just wasn't right, she nodded. "Guess so."

"We're out of here, then. Want us to walk you to your car?"

"No, that's okay. Think I'll stay a little longer."

Her sharp eyes took one more look around the crowded restaurant. "Okay, see you next Wednesday."

Samara continued to sit at her table, sipping her drink and trying to figure out where they'd gone wrong. First the surprise that the guy was actually a teenager and then the fact that he ran away within seconds of meeting with her.

"Hey Samara, want me to drive you home?"

Kyle Macklin leaned over her. Without meaning to, she immediately backed away. She bit her lip at his grimace. He'd been asking her out for months and she'd run out of excuses. What woman wouldn't want to go out with a tall, gorgeous blond with the smile of an angel and the glint of devil in his green eyes? She could answer that fairly easily. A woman who was so in love with another man she couldn't even begin to think of dating anyone else.

Smiling an apology, she stood. "Thanks. I have my car."

"I'll walk you out then."

Dodging waiters and running preschoolers, they escaped from the busy restaurant. He was going to ask her out again, she knew he was. Her rational mind told her she should go out with him. Nothing was ever going to happen between her and Noah. Her heart said something different. As long as she had breath, she had hope.

The night, dark and clear, held a hint of the rain they'd had earlier. The stars were scarce and the moon cast only a small halo over the parking lot. She'd parked in a well-lit area and immediately headed to her car, hoping she was wrong and Kyle didn't plan to ask for another date.

Just as she flipped the button to unlock the door, he asked, "How about a movie Saturday night?"

She blew out a long, silent sigh as she turned to look up at him. Gosh, she was so bad at this. "I don't think that's a good idea. I . . ." She heard a thud. Breath caught in her throat at the blank look that came over Kyle's face. He fell at her feet.

"Hello, Pretty Girl."

It took barely a second to register the greasy smile of the man in front of her and to make the correct conclusion. This was the real creep she'd been talking with online. The boy had been a decoy, sent by him to check her out.

Holding her hands to her side, she took an easy, calming breath. "Ruff-ryder, I presume?"

"Yeah. And you're Pretty Girl . . . right?"

"Among other names. Why did you send that kid in?"

"Just a little insurance that this wasn't a setup. Good thing I sent him in, wasn't it?"

Not taking her eyes off the man in front of her, Samara relied on her peripheral vision to tell her no one was around. Great, her ever-present watchdog decided for the very first time to take the night off. Just her luck.

A groan from Kyle told her he was waking up, but he wouldn't be much help. She was on her own.

A hand grabbed her arm. "Let's get out of here."

At the touch of his hand, panic disappeared and training kicked in. Twisting away, she pivoted to her left and brought up her right arm, swinging it toward his face. He jumped back, but not before she got in a good blow to his nose.

"Shit!" Holding his nose with one hand, he reached out again.

Samara was ready for him, blocked his arm, then brought her knee up to his groin. His hands went to protect himself, but her knee got there first, jamming hard. He squealed, grabbed his balls with one hand, and lashed out at her with the other. Once again she blocked him. Whirling around, she swept her leg around. The side of her foot caught his chin in a solid hit so hard she heard his teeth clack.

A stunned, blank look replaced the fury as he fell backward against her car and then slid to the ground. Pulling her cellphone from her pocket, she pressed

911. Keeping her eyes on the man, she squatted down and checked Kyle's pulse. Slow and steady. Relaying her request for help, she kept her ear to the phone as her eyes searched for any other threats.

Gravel crunched behind her. Samara jumped to her feet and whirled toward the sound.

Noah's blond watchdog held up his hands. A grin lifted his stern mouth as his eyes gleamed with admiration. "Whoa. Hold on, little warrior. Thought I'd just hog-tie your big bad pervert until the cops get here. Okay with you?"

Adrenaline and fear bouncing like pinballs inside her, Samara jerked a quick nod. She watched as the big man pulled plastic ties from his pocket and looped them around the unconscious man's hands and ankles.

When he finished, he grinned up at her. "You did good."

A feeling, unlike anything she'd ever known, came over her. She had done good. Before she could examine this amazing fact, blue lights flashed into the parking lot.

She turned toward her helper. "I think you should go home now." Would he understand her double meaning?

The man studied her for several seconds. Samara got the idea he was searching for something. Then he nodded as his mouth kicked up in another grin. "You know, I think I can." With those words, he backed away and disappeared into the night.

Samara stooped down to Kyle again as the police made their way toward her.

Her eyes roamed over him. "Are you okay?"

Sitting up, he rubbed the back of his head. "What happened?"

"You got hit in the head with something." Moving

behind him, she touched his hair gently. "Let me see if the skin's broken."

"Samara."

She looked up to see Officer Linda Knowles running toward her. Grinning, she stood and pointed to the hog-tied, now conscious man struggling a few feet from her. "Look what I caught."

Noah stood at the window of his office, looking out at the familiar bright lights of his adopted home. His mother had loved Paris and through her, he'd learned to love the sprawling, exotic city. Making his home here had been his gift to her, the only thing left he could do to honor her.

While in prison, he'd developed a strategy. First, he would find his mother and do what he could to help her. Then, if Rebecca would let him, he would do his damnedest to make up for what had been done to her. He'd failed at both. It had taken months to track his mother down and when he did, he found himself visiting a cemetery in Louisiana. She'd died two years before, while he was still in prison. Records he'd stolen from the hospital had showed she'd died of AIDS. His father's final gift to her. She'd been an indigent and died alone. Days passed before Milo could get a word out of him. Finally, having no other choice, Noah had accepted and moved on.

When he found Rebecca, she'd allowed him to help a little, but not like he'd wanted . . . needed. He realized that more than anything, she wanted to forget and he was bringing it all back to her. He still saw her from time to time, but it was never comfortable and never would be.

Coming to Paris, seeing the sights his mother had talked about, experiencing the beauty that had only existed in his mind, through her words, he'd found a completeness he'd never experienced anywhere else. This was home.

So why now did he feel as though his home had become his refuge, prison, and hiding place? Noah knew the answer but refused to contemplate the solution. Every morning he woke, aching for one woman, and every night he slept in a lonely bed, wanting that body in his arms. He'd told himself it would pass. Several months had gone by since he'd seen Samara. At some point, the obsession had to end.

Twisting his wrist, he checked the time again. Ethan was late. Each day, he received a report on Samara. The information was usually just a brief account . . . giving him only the information he felt he had the right to know. Was she safe for another day?

Sometimes he literally bit his tongue to keep from asking more. Ethan would tell him, but if that happened, he would have become her stalker, not her protector. A fine line he dare not cross.

He couldn't and wouldn't stop her from what she felt she had to do, but he could at least keep her safe.

Checking his watch again, dread filled him. Where was Ethan? Just as he grabbed his cellphone to make the call, it rang. Without looking at the readout, he answered with a growl, "It's about damn time."

"Noah?"

Adrenaline rushed and fear kicked like a mule. "Mara . . . what's wrong?"

"Nothing's wrong. I just wanted to talk to you."

Knowing he shouldn't, knowing it would only increase the useless, unnecessary ache, Noah nevertheless slumped into his chair to listen to the voice he dreamed about nightly.

Sounding unusually tentative, she said, "I hope I'm not disturbing you."

"No, I was just waiting for a call. . . . I'd much rather talk to you, though."

A sound came through the phone . . . a sigh blended with a sob. Noah straightened in his chair. "What happened?"

"Have you talked to your watchdog today?"

There was no point in denying Ethan's existence. "No, he hasn't called me yet."

"I sent him home."

"He answers to me, not you."

"It's time to let me go."

"I don't have you, Mara. But I do want to make sure you stay safe."

"I'm not your responsibility."

"Yes you are, if I hadn't involved you— "

"Don't start that again. You're not responsible for me getting involved in this line of work. It was my decision, my choice."

"Don't be ridiculous. If I hadn't got you involved with Mitchell, you never would've —"

"You may be right about that. . . . I don't know. What I do know is that this is my choice."

"And I need to make sure you're safe."

"No, you need to let me live my life." Her voice turned shaky and thin. "If I can't have what I truly want from you, then at least give me this."

Unable to sit still, Noah stood at the window again. She was asking him to let go of the last connection he had with her. Keeping her safe had always been his number-one goal, but an important secondary one was that he still had a connection with her, no matter how small.

"Has Ethan bothered you? Interfered in your life?"

"No. I didn't even know that was his name. That's not the point. I don't need his protection or yours.

I took down a very bad man last night, all by my-self."

"Where was Ethan?"

"He was there . . . in the background. And he looked pretty damned impressed."

"You shouldn't have—"

"The point is, I did. I can take care of myself. You don't have to worry or feel responsible any longer."

"Mara, I know you feel you can, but I've seen what can happen. I'm not willing to risk your life just because you've taken some self-defense classes. I know you're a strong, capable woman, but these are evil men who could very well kill you. I'm not willing to take that risk."

"It's not your choice. . . . It's mine." The hard swallow that followed told him she was holding back tears with great effort. "I love you. I always will, but it's time to let me live my life and you live yours."

The line went dead.

Dammit, she'd hung up on him. The phone rang again. This time he checked the readout. *Ethan.* Holding his rage by a thin thread, he answered, "Where the hell are you?"

"About five hours away from you."

"Why the hell aren't you watching her?"

"I'll tell you when I see you." The line went dead again.

He had the urge to throw the phone through the window and shout like a four-year-old. His rigid control strained, Noah reined himself in. When Ethan arrived, he would get a full explanation of why Samara was now alone, unprotected. He'd damn well better have a good one.

nineteen

Ethan pressed his fingertips against the security screen. A door slid open, allowing him entrance into the elevator. At this time of night, Noah would be the only one in the building. Hell, as far as he knew, Noah lived here. The man had no life other than LCR. The knowledge that he and Noah had a lot in common brought him no comfort.

The elevator doors slid open and the big man himself stood at the entrance of his office. Fury flashed in his coal-black eyes. The cool, implacable man he'd known for years had been replaced with a man with feelings . . . though Ethan figured Noah would deny those feelings until he died or was forced to acknowledge them. He'd soon find out.

"You want to tell me why the hell you're here instead of doing your job?"

"Hello to you, too."

"Don't push it, Ethan."

Ethan held back a grin that tickled at his mouth. A good way to get a fist down his throat. Not that he wasn't up for a good fight. God knew the last few weeks had been boring. Maybe later. First, he had a few things to tell Noah about his ladylove.

Sauntering past Noah, he sprawled out on the sofa and waited.

"I spoke with Samara," Noah said.

Now that was a surprise. "What'd she say?"

"She told me she sent you home."

"That's true."

"That's not her place. It's mine. You shouldn't have left her. She said she had some trouble last night."

"Did she tell you that she took down a man twice her size?"

"Dammit, that's why you were there . . . so she didn't have to do that. She's not capable—"

Ethan stood and pulled an envelope from the inside of his jacket. "Gotta disagree with you there." Leaning forward, he threw some photos on the desk. "Take a look at her moves, Noah. The woman can definitely defend herself."

Noah barely glanced at them before he turned back to Ethan. "She got lucky."

"No. She's strong. She got herself trained. She'd make a damn good operative."

Turning his back to Ethan, he growled, "I'm not going to argue with you. Go back and do your job."

"No."

When Noah whirled back around, Ethan knew that fight might be coming sooner than he expected.

"What?"

"I said no. The woman doesn't need my protection."

"That's not for you to decide."

"Noah, when I hired on with LCR, you told me my number-one priority was rescuing victims. This woman is no victim and sure as hell doesn't need rescuing."

Noah's next words surprised him.

"I read the file on the Blackburn case."

Ah yes, the op he'd handled two weeks after getting his best friend killed. It had worked out fine, but not to LCR's exacting standards. Trust Noah to come at him from a different direction. "It turned messy . . . still got the job done."

"You almost got yourself killed, too."

"So?"

"So, I've already been to the funeral of one of my operatives this year. I don't want to go to another."

"Like I said . . . I got the job done."

"You truly don't care if you die, do you, Ethan?"

Since Ethan had no answer for that, he didn't bother. He did what he had to do. If he took a bullet someday, big fucking deal.

Noah glared at the one man he probably had more in common with than any other person he knew. Ethan Bishop had experienced hell on earth. Their experiences in prison made them brothers of a sort. They'd survived unspeakable brutality.

Like Noah, Ethan carried a soul riddled with guilt and self-condemnation. In some respects, it had made him one of LCR's best operatives. Most people took one look at Ethan Bishop and quickly changed to his way of thinking. Few people could stand up to that cold, hard stare. But Ethan's guilt also had a negative, self-destructive impact. He had a death wish. No, he wouldn't admit it. For a man of Ethan's Bishop's hardened heart, admitting weakness was synonymous with giving up. Something Bishop would never do.

He'd hoped giving Ethan the job of protecting Samara would give him some thinking time. He should have known the lack of action would be more than he could handle. Not putting his life on the line at least once a week was probably tantamount to a slow death for Ethan.

It didn't, however, negate the fact that Ethan had to be reeled in. The last thing LCR needed was a loose cannon. Too many lives were at risk.

"You want to get killed, do it on your own time. Not LCR's."

Bishop lifted a mountainous shoulder in a careless shrug. "I said I got the job done."

"You almost blew the entire operation. Not only did you almost get killed, you took out three men who could possibly have given us information on Blackburn's whereabouts."

"They wouldn't have talked."

"That wasn't your decision to make. Your job is to rescue. An added benefit is to capture as many people as you can and get information from them. Killing is and always should be a last resort."

"They needed killing. What's your gripe?"

A red haze swamped Noah. After having Samara tell him to let her go, pure adrenaline and strong denial shot like a geyser through his body. The knowledge that the one connection he'd had with her might now be lost had wound him tighter than a drum. This was not a good time to piss Noah McCall off.

He slammed Ethan back against the window, wrapped his hand around the other man's neck and pressed hard. "I told you when I brought you in—egos have no place in LCR. You went against direct orders. Almost got yourself killed. And in the process fucked up an ongoing investigation. That's my fucking gripe."

With absolutely no emotion, Ethan stared at him and in that moment, Noah knew he'd lost him. Ethan no longer cared about anything or anyone. Whatever had happened with Shea and Cole on the op several months back had been the last straw.

No, dammit, I have to try one more time.

Backing away, Noah blew out a long breath. "Take some time off. I'll get someone else to watch Samara. Get your head back on straight. Purge those demons that keep you from being able to do your job. Don't come back until you do."

"No."

"What?"

"You heard me. You don't like the way I handle an op . . . that's just too damn bad."

"You're quitting?"

"Hell no. I don't quit . . . at anything."

Noah could only shake his head. "Ethan, you quit living a long time ago. I thought having Shea in your life would give that back to you. I don't know what happened between you or how she ended up with Cole. I don't need to know."

Noah waited to see if mentioning Shea and Cole would produce some sort of reaction. Other than an infinitesimal flicker in his eyes, there was nothing.

"You're not responsible for Cole's death. I read the report. He got himself killed."

"Tell that to his widow."

"Shea knows the truth, whether she wants to admit it or not." Noah blew out a sigh as he slumped into his chair behind his desk. "The burden you've carried on your shoulder for years has just grown instead of easing. Most people filled with that kind of regret are empowered by helping others and that grief seems to lessen. That hasn't happened for you, has it?"

Still no response.

Noah closed his eyes at Ethan's granite expression. Giving up on this man was not something he took lightly. But he'd been given an ultimatum and both of them knew exactly where it would lead . . . exactly where Ethan wanted it to go. "Fine, Ethan. You got what you wanted. If you're not quitting . . . then you're fired."

A small, humorless smile lifted Ethan's mouth. "Told you years ago, when you hired me, you'd regret it."

"I never, for a second, regretted hiring you. You've

saved a lot of people and done some fine things with your life. The only thing I regret is not being able to help you see your worth."

"Maybe that wasn't your job." With those enigmatic words, Ethan started toward the door. When he stopped and turned, Noah knew a moment of hope. "For what it's worth. Thanks for saving my life . . . and giving me a chance."

"Dammit, man. It doesn't have to end this way."

"Yes it does." Ethan closed the door behind him.

Shit. Shit. Shit. Could this day get any worse? He looked down at the photos Ethan had left. Pride filled him. Though the pictures were still shots, they revealed the precision and grace she'd used to take down the creep. Ethan was right. He didn't give Samara enough credit.

Another photo showed a tall, blond man standing beside her. They were both laughing. Pain speared deep. He knew who he was . . . Kyle Macklin. Smart, successful, and single. Exactly what a woman like Samara needed. The kind of man who would be happy to help her get over a broken heart. The kind of man who could share his life with her, give her a family.

Noah knew he should be happy she was seeing someone. Samara deserved only the best.

The photo crumpled in his hand.

Running his hands up and down his legs, Mitch smoothed the wrinkles in the cheap polyester pants. He'd told the corrections officer helping him to provide something average and common. The idiot had brought in clothes so cheap they'd probably fall apart before he got to Birmingham. No matter. With the money he had stashed away, he'd be looking like a

GQ model soon enough. Just like the wealthy businessman he'd become.

Lifting his foot, Mitch reared back and gave the jerk on the floor a glancing blow to the ribs. "Make it look good" was what Boyd Lemming had told him. Then he'd turned his back so Mitchell could knock him out. Mitch gladly obliged. He'd clubbed the prick with his own nightstick. Damn, that'd felt good. Boyd wasn't dead, but he'd have a nice concussion and a hell of a headache that'd keep him out of it for several days. Who knows, it might even teach him a lesson about helping criminals escape. World was getting too damned dangerous. Couldn't trust anybody anymore. Mitch grinned at the thought.

Rubbing the smudges from his visitor's card, he clipped it to his shirt pocket. Yep, just another slub visiting one of the misguided and unfortunate residents of the Blount County Jail. Slicking his hair back, he checked the wall mirror in the small bathroom once more. The beard stubble gave him a somewhat rakish appearance. With his looks, he'd never had a problem attracting women, but he had to admit, the beard made him even sexier. Once his business was taken care of, first thing he'd do was get him some nice duds, then he'd go find a couple of high-priced whores who could appreciate a well-hung and handsome stud.

The husky laugh he heard in his head was his daddy's, who was probably somewhere cheering him on. Easing the door open, he listened . . . heard nothing. He turned the lock and closed the door, locking poor Boyd inside. By the time he was found, Mitch would be long gone and several hours would have passed before he was discovered missing. They'd been planning this for weeks. No way in hell would there be a screwup. He had important business to handle. One Michael Stoddard to be executed and one Samara Lyons to be screwed until she too begged for death. Damned if he knew which one he looked forward to the most.

"Go!" On Noah's command, five LCR operatives slammed through the doors of André Morley and Associates. Sadistic bastards, who for the last two years had been grabbing kids off the streets of Paris and selling them across Europe.

Noah kicked a door open and then whirled to the side. *Bam . . . bam . . .* Bullets slammed into the wall behind him. One man squealed. Another man shouted a curse. Three more shots rang out and then silence.

Doors opened and closed. Footsteps stomped around him. Holding his gun at the ready, Noah inched his head around and then jerked back out again as another bullet came flying at him.

He pressed back against the wall and calculated. In that split second, he'd seen two men stooped behind a large desk. Both had guns and though he'd only seen the tops of their heads, he was pretty damn sure they weren't likely to give up anytime soon. Shit. He didn't want a standoff. He wanted to get these creeps out of here as peacefully and painlessly as possible.

Barging in on them wasn't really LCR's way. However, since the children were being held at a different facility and even now were being rescued by another LCR team, Noah had wanted to go in with a bang and scare the shit out of them. Unfortunately, he'd overestimated his shit-scaring tactics. Was he getting too old for this? Was his mind so distracted by his personal life, his instincts were off? He gave himself a mental kick in the ass. Great. Now he was having a philosophic contemplation while two thugs a few feet away would love to put a bullet in his head. Next thing he knew, he'd be consulting an astrologer before he planned a rescue.

"Noah, you okay?" Jordan's low growl came into his earphone.

"Yeah, got two holed up in the office. You?"

"Eden and I took care of one up here. There's another running loose. Dylan's after him."

"Tell Eden to stay put and come on down and help me coax these assholes out before I shoot them just for fun."

Jordan chuckled. "On my way."

For the hell of it, Noah yelled out, "Hey, assholes, you're outnumbered! Throw your guns out now before you get hurt!"

"Go to hell!" one man shouted. Another shot fired.

Blowing out a half sigh, half laugh, Noah muttered, "That's what I thought."

Jordan came loping toward him. "They changed their tune yet?"

"Nope, still singing the 'Come in and get me' song."

Jordan's mouth kicked up in a grin. "Hate that song. Much rather hear the 'I'm coming out and throwing myself at your mercy' operetta."

"Don't think they know that one."

"Okay. So what do you want to do?"

"Well, we could talk about what you and Eden are getting Angela for her birthday."

Jordan sank against the wall next to him as if in deep thought. "Yeah. That's a conundrum. We're thinking maybe a gift card to that new tattoo parlor on Chavez."

"Damn. That's what I was thinking, too."

"What are you guys doing?" Eden stalked toward them, exasperation and amusement glinting her eyes.

"Talking about Angela's birthday present."

"Oh, did you tell him our idea, Jordan?"

Jordan pulled his wife to his side and gave her a quick kiss on her nose. "Yes, but that's what he was planning, too."

"Too bad. I bought it before we came over."

Noah grinned, his gun at high ready. "Gabe, you ready?"

"Yep."

"Go."

Glass shattered behind the men as Gabe crashed through the window. Noah, Jordan, and Eden stormed through the door. Noah flew over the desk and landed on top of a man. He only saw a flash of pale flabby skin underneath the giant sweatshirt. He wasn't sure, but he thought this one was Morley's favorite henchman. He hoped so. Pressing harder, guttural sobs came from the man beneath him. Eden held a gun on the other man while Jordan wrenched his arms behind his back and cuffed him.

Noah twisted to look up at Gabe. "Dylan get the other guy?"

"Yeah. Had to shoot a little hole in his leg. Other than that, he's fine."

"Good." Noah lifted himself off his too-soft, sobbing prisoner. "Take them down to the warehouse. A few people want to have a chat with them before they go to jail."

Pulling the man's hands behind him, Gabe cuffed him and then looked over at Noah. "You talk to Angela yet?"

"No. Why? Everything went off okay at the house, didn't it?"

"Yeah. Went fine. Six kids rescued. Four people in

custody. She's been trying to reach you for another reason. Some politician from Mississippi called."

Noah was out the door and headed to his car before Gabe finished his sentence. There was only one reason anyone from Mississippi would be calling. *Mitchell*.

twenty

Wet sand dented under her pounding feet. Hot sun seared her skin. A light breeze floated through the air, cooling her. To the right, waves ebbed and flowed in a lazy, never-ending tide. On the left, hotels, condominiums, and private homes created a mishmash of subtle colors and daring heights. The white sandy beaches of the Alabama Gulf Coast were lovely, but the contrast was almost as breathtaking as her surroundings. Paradise around her, as hell erupted within her. Running toward the sun, Samara picked up speed toward a punishing pace, at some point hoping to outrun a broken heart.

Telling Noah goodbye had to be the single most difficult thing she'd ever had to do. Knowing she'd done the right thing didn't make it any easier to bear.

After saying goodbye to him, she'd grabbed some clothes and headed to the beach. She needed major quiet time and privacy. To mourn, grieve, and then, hopefully, to accept.

The hurt in his voice when she told him to let her go lingered in her head. He'd told her his protection was all he could offer. To Noah, this was a rejection of the only thing he felt he could give of himself. He cared deeply for her, she knew that. . . . Even Noah knew that, but he wouldn't do anything about it and she couldn't bear to be in limbo like this any longer.

She would always love him. Didn't doubt that for

an instant. Unfortunately loving someone didn't always ensure you were loved back. Or that you were meant to be together.

She'd always known that one of the reasons she had allowed Noah to protect her was that she didn't want to let him go. Now she realized another reason. Even after all the training she'd put herself through over the past few months, she still hadn't trusted she could take care of herself. The experience with Mitchell Stoddard and his men had left her weak and vulnerable, her self-confidence shattered. The training had restored some of that confidence, but she'd still been shaky. A bodyguard, no matter how much she protested, gave her a safety net she hadn't even been aware she wanted. Could she protect herself if need be? She hadn't been sure. Until she'd been tested.

The man had been average-sized, with few fighting skills, but bringing him down had shown her something. She hadn't panicked, hadn't run, and hadn't flinched. Was she Wonder Woman? Hell no, but she was a damned sight stronger than she'd been months ago. Not just physically but emotionally.

She'd regained what Mitchell had taken from her and pushed it even further. Moving past that trauma felt freeing and exciting. That realization led her to the next. It was time to move on. She needed a job; she needed a life. In a few days, she'd return to Birmingham and pursue a social work position. She was good at what she did and she made a difference, which is why she'd gone into the field in the first place. If possible, she'd liked to continue her work with the Macklin Agency but more than anything, she wanted to get on with her life.

Without Noah. God, it hurt to hear those words in her head. She couldn't say them yet. Wasn't sure she ever could. But neither could she keep alive a dream that would never be a reality. She'd told Noah to let her go. It was time for her to let Noah go, too.

Mitch held the cellphone to his ear as he maneuvered the SUV around a tractor. He was taking a lot of back roads on the way to Birmingham. The highway patrol had probably been alerted an hour or so ago of his escape. Not that they'd be looking for an escaped prisoner in a dark green Ford Explorer, looking for all the world like a regular person on a business trip.

Luther answered on the third ring. "You get everything, boy?"

"Yeah, I did. You done good. Real good."

"Explorer should be clear for a while. Some boys got it for me in Memphis. Tags changed and I got it painted for you, too. Gun's clean, too. Wish I could've got a passport for you, but just don't have those kinds of connections."

"I'll get out of the country just fine. Appreciate the help."

"You found the money and the file on the girl I put under the seat?"

"Yeah."

"I know you're disappointed I couldn't find out anything on your brother. But nothing ever came up on him."

"That's okay. I'm betting the girl knows."

"What're you going to do?"

"If I told you that . . . I'd have to kill you."

Mitch heard the man swallow a load of spit. The tense silence that followed told Mitch that Luther Prickrel was terrified of him. Suited him just fine. The more you feared someone, the less likely you were to screw them over.

"Just kidding, man. You know I'm grateful."

"I owed your papa. We're even now, you hear? You get caught again, I ain't comin' to your aid."

"Won't be a need. I aim to take care of business and get the hell out of here before they barely know I was gone."

"Report came in about your escape about ten minutes ago."

Smug pride filled him. Damn. He was good at this. He'd been gone from the jail for almost four hours and they were just now finding out.

"That's good to know. Thanks for everything."

"Take care, son."

Mitch disconnected the call and wiggled more comfortably into his leather seat. Poor Prick sounded as though he was about to cry. He'd have to send him some money or something. No, better not. No telling who might be watching Luther's house. Besides, he'd owed him. Prick was right. Their debt was settled.

Flipping the top of the cooler on the seat beside him, Mitch pulled out an ice-cold Pepsi and popped the top. Luther had thought of everything. Hell, there were even rubbers in the glove compartment.

His dick hardened. A few more hours and he'd be putting those babies to good use.

Fists clenched and jaw held tight, Noah forced himself to sit still. Hard as hell to yell at his pilot to go any faster. The man was doing everything he could to break the airspeed record and yet it wasn't enough. A ten-hour flight. Nine hours to go. *Shit.*

Where the hell was she? As soon as he'd talked to the governor, he'd called Samara's home and cellphone and got no answer. Police had been dispatched to her house within minutes of discovering Mitch's escape. They'd reported no one at home. Since the very real possibility existed that she was in imminent danger, they'd entered the residence. No signs of foul play and no signs of Samara.

Noah looked out into the pitch-black night and saw only the blinking of the jet's lights and his own ravaged expression. Mitch wouldn't leave her alive this time. He had a score to settle.

The only good news in his sea of bad was that apparently Samara had been gone for several days. The mail in her mailbox was two days old. Mitch had escaped only hours ago, so he wasn't personally responsible for her disappearance. Even that good news had a dark tinge to it. Just because Mitch hadn't snatched her didn't mean he hadn't paid someone to grab her and bring her to him.

Mitch would use her as bait. Michael was the real person he was after. Problem was, he'd have no compunction in killing anyone who got in his way of revenge. Samara and God knew how many other people might die because of Noah's cowardice. He hadn't killed Mitch when he had the chance.

His cellphone rang, pulling him from recriminations that couldn't be resolved.

"Jordan?"

"Yeah. Called her family. They haven't heard from her. And before you ask, I didn't let on about any trouble."

"How about her friends?"

"She hasn't talked to her Virginia friends in a couple of weeks. Rachel, her friend in Birmingham, is out of town on a business trip and hasn't talked to Samara since last Sunday."

"What about—"

"Called the Macklin people, too. They were our biggest help. Said she called and advised them she wouldn't be in for a week or so."

"When was that?"

"Thursday."

"The day after I talked with her."

"Yeah."

"What're your thoughts, Jordan? You know her better than I do."

"Not hardly. But I'm thinking what you've already surmised. She went away for a few days. Maybe to the beach or the mountains. They're both easily accessible from Birmingham."

"No flights that we know of?"

"No, wherever she went, she drove."

"The police have an alert out on her car. Dammit, if she only had her cellphone on, we could track her."

"What's Mitch planning?"

Noah snorted. "Revenge. Pure and simple. And he knows exactly who to use to lure me."

"You're sure he knows who she is?"

"Yeah. As soon as I found out Mitch had escaped, I knew who'd helped. Luther Prickrel sang like the proverbial bird."

"Sure you don't want Eden and me there with you?"

"No. The police will concentrate on Mitch. My only concern is Samara. If I get to Mitch before they do, I'll take care of him. This thing ends with us, one way or the other."

"You'll keep her safe?"

"With my life."

"Anything you need me to do?"

Noah heard the message behind the words. "You and Eden know LCR better than anyone. No matter what happens, I trust you both to keep it going."

"What about Samara?"

"My will is intact."

"That's not what I'm asking. Is there anything you'd like me to tell her?"

A laugh cracked through frozen pain. "Mara knows

everything there is to know about me. She had me figured out long ago. There's nothing you could tell her she doesn't know."

"How about that you love her?"

When he didn't answer, Jordan said quietly, "Be safe, Noah."

Noah closed his cellphone and then his eyes. *Where the hell are you, Mara?*

Standing behind a tree in the backyard, Mitch watched the white SUV back out of the driveway. A quick glance at his watch . . . wait a couple more minutes. Make sure no one else is coming out. Since the trees came so close to the house, he used their cover. With one more look around, he dashed to the back door, jimmied the lock, and was inside in seconds. One of the many valuable lessons his daddy had taught him.

The back door opened into the kitchen. The scent of garlic wafted through the air. Looks like spaghetti had been on the menu tonight. A stomach grumble reminded him he hadn't had anything to eat in hours. First he'd have a little look around and then maybe grab something out of the fridge before he headed back out.

He wandered through the small rooms, his ears listening for any sound other than the tick of a clock or the distant sounds of the police radio from the car up the street. Nothing. Not even a dog. Good. He'd have had to let it outside and that might have caused a neighbor to wonder. He didn't kill dogs.

Returning to the kitchen, he opened the fridge, pleased to see a plastic bowl filled with pasta. He pulled the tub out, along with a couple of beers. Grabbing a fork from a drawer, he shoveled in mouthfuls of pasta, washing it down with the beer.

His stomach satisfied, he threw the bowl in the sink

and the cans in the garbage. Opening and closing cabinets, in a hurry to get this over and done with, he found what he was looking for. A large bottle of cooking oil. After soaking dishcloths in it, he pitched them around on the counters, threw some oil on the kitchen curtains, and then pulled out a match.

It took a few minutes, but finally a nice, smoky haze covered the kitchen. Pulling newspaper and plastic bags from the garbage can, he added to the small flame and then backed out the door. Going low, he ran back into the cover of trees and bushes and waited.

Yep, there was a nice plume of smoke now coming from under the door. Ten more minutes ought to do it.

Mitch backed farther away and headed to his real destination three doors down. Finding a nice big oak in the yard next to it, he squatted, waited, and watched.

Sirens clanged and screamed. The two policemen in the patrol car in front of Samara Lyons's house jumped out and hauled ass toward the smoking building down the street.

Within seconds, Mitch was at the edge of Samara's backyard. He stayed low as he ran through the yard to the back of the house. Stopping at the door, he grimaced at the locks. He'd been lucky with the house down the street. Should've known the bitch wouldn't make it easy for him. Damn dead bolts ought to be outlawed. He didn't have the time or tools to get in without making a hell of a mess.

Mitch stepped back to assess the house and spotted the small window to the right. Most likely the kitchen window. Even from a distance, his experienced eyes noted the old, cheap lock. Grinning, he pulled out another tool from the bag Luther had supplied. A little slide and jerk—he jimmied the lock and slid the window open. Throwing his tool bag in first, Mitch then lifted himself up, slipping his head and shoulders through the narrow window. Soft curses blew through his lips when he realized he'd have to crawl into the sink. His mind on what he had planned for his bastard brother and his bitch, he climbed into the sink and then dropped to the floor.

He stood and surveyed the kitchen, listened intently. No sound. Keeping low, his steps soft, he searched the first and second floors. No one here. Good. He'd have time to set things up before she got here. It would be dusk soon. He needed to get a good feel for the house and find a nice little hidey-hole before it got dark. Then the part he hated the most. Waiting. His jaw popped with a giant yawn. Maybe he'd have time to take a nap before the party started.

She'd been nice enough to pull the blinds before she left. Now he could just walk around at his leisure and not worry about anyone seeing him. He had his essentials, but it never hurt to have some backup.

It took less than ten minutes to do a thorough search. In that time, he discovered several things about Samara Lyons. First, she was freakishly neat and clean. That went right up there with fucking weirdo in his book. Second, she lived alone. No men's clothing lying around and no other women's clothes other than her size twos and fours. He'd forgotten how skinny the bitch was. Third and final, the girl had a hell of a lot of family. Framed photographs covered several walls and almost every available flat space.

Looked like the girl would be seriously missed. A smile kicked up at his mouth.

"You're sure the place is secure?"

While both officers nodded and explained how they'd arrived at Samara's house late last night, relieving a patrol from the evening shift, Noah's eyes searched the small, quiet neighborhood. Small, older homes with nicely cropped large lawns. Giant trees overshadowed the houses, providing shade and elegance. Also providing a perfect cover for an escaped prisoner.

"And there's been no word on the home owner?"

"No sir. We're still looking."

He held up a key Eden had handed him before he left Paris yesterday. "Mind if we all take another look together?"

Barely seeing their nod, Noah stepped up on the porch and turned the key. Even though he'd never been here, memories assailed him the moment he walked in the door. Samara's living room furniture was the same. He remembered the times she'd dropped onto the sofa and then, seemingly unable to sit still, would pop back up to do something. Every piece of furniture was stamped with a memory of Samara.

Noah took a breath and straightened his spine. No amount of sentimentality or emotion would help save Samara or find Mitch. Cold, hard reason had been his mainstay for years. That couldn't change.

"Sir, do you want us to walk around with you?"

The young cop eyed him warily. No wonder. Not only did he look exactly like the escaped lunatic they were looking for, he stood in the middle of a room as if dazed.

"Why don't we split up? I'll look upstairs while you guys look down here."

Both men nodded. Noah waited for a few seconds to satisfy himself that they were looking around not only for evidence that someone had been here, but also that someone could be hiding in unobvious places. Seeing them look into closets and under furniture, he took off upstairs.

His guts churning, he returned downstairs several minutes later. No sign of Mitch or any kind of foul play. Samara had left the house in the same shape as she had her apartment, immaculate and full of her sweet personality. The door slammed shut on that thought.

"Nothing out of order down here?" Noah addressed both policemen.

"No, sir. We came in last night, before the other patrol left. It's the same."

Rubbing the center of his forehead against the small headache pounding, Noah closed his eyes and tried to be in Mitch's mind. They'd never had the twin bond thing that so many twins swore by. As a kid, he'd been grateful. Last thing he wanted was to be inside Mitch's sick, twisted brain. Now he'd give ten years of his life to know what he was thinking.

Mitch was mean, there was no denying that, but he was also smart. Would he lie low for a while before going after Samara? Would he just try to skip the country and cut his losses? Would he waste valuable time trying to find Michael Stoddard?

Mitch still didn't know he was Noah McCall. Only the governor and his closest advisors knew that. The story they'd circulated was that Michael had turned his life around and was helping the police bring down his twin brother in exchange for immunity. Mitch wouldn't doubt that. If there was one thing Mitchell understood, it was screwing others to save your own ass.

Trying to find Michael without using Samara didn't make sense. Mitch's thirst for revenge would include them both. There was no way his brother would just cut and run, without trying to take out the two people he believed had brought him down.

He couldn't read Mitch's mind, but he knew him well enough to figure out his motives. Revenge, then escape. Mitch had too much evil in him to just let this go. And he was cocky enough to believe he wouldn't get caught.

Noah had to be ready when his brother struck. His

mind speeding with possibilities and scenarios, he turned toward the policemen again. "What are your orders from here?"

"We were told to stay till you got here."

These men were too busy to sit around on the off chance Mitch might show up here. "You guys are probably anxious to get home."

"We're off duty in half an hour."

He headed toward the front door, eager to get them on their way. "Chances are, Mitchell's headed in another direction. I just wanted to make sure Samara was safe. When she gets here, I'll notify the station."

Noah closed the door and turned around. He drew in a deep breath. Just being in Samara's house gave him a sense of peace. Knowing it was useless, since he'd called every fifteen minutes since he'd learned of his brother's escape, Noah nevertheless pulled out his cellphone and tried once more. And got the same sweet-voice message that she'd call him back.

Pocketing his phone again, he headed for the kitchen. The dull tap dance behind his eyes was headed for a full-fledged clog. He needed caffeine and something on his stomach.

Knowing Samara and being familiar with her kitchen in her apartment, he easily located the coffee and filters. Scooping in double doses, since he didn't anticipate sleep within the next twenty-four hours at least, he clicked the brewer on and turned.

"Hey, bro." Noah caught a glimpse of his brother's grinning face before pain speared through his head and then there was nothing.

twenty-one

Mitch put his hands under his brother's arms and dragged his body from the kitchen into the living room. Dropping him in the middle of the room, his booted foot kicked hard into Michael's ribs. No movement. Definitely out for the count. A good-sized purple knot was already forming on his temple. Since he didn't want this over too soon, he felt for a pulse at his neck. Slow and steady. Good.

Pleased in a way only his daddy might understand, since they'd both hated the freak, Mitch whistled soundlessly as he wrapped rope around Michael's arms and then his legs. He'd never mastered the art of hog-tying an animal, but he was damned good at doing it to a human. In his line of work, that had come in much handier.

Finding that little cubbyhole in the pantry had been an act of genius. The girl probably didn't even know it existed, but he'd had all night to find a good hiding place. He'd been somewhat uncomfortable fitting his long frame into the small space, but damn, it'd been worth it. Just seeing the shock of surprise in Michael's eyes right before he'd clocked him. . . . He'd just lived out one of his favorite fantasies.

A stomach rumble reminded him that his stolen spaghetti had been hours ago. Figuring that wherever Samara Lyons was, she wouldn't come home so early in the morning, he sauntered to the kitchen. The smell of coffee greeted him and for the first time in a while, Mitch felt true happiness. His brother would soon get what he deserved, a pretty young woman would be home soon, his for the taking, for as long as he wanted to take and however he wanted to give it to her, and fresh coffee. Who said dreams don't come true?

Opening the fridge, he found bacon, eggs, and even a little roll of canned biscuits. Mitch set to work. Being on his own for so long had made him self-sufficient. He'd rarely had a woman around for more than a few days. Even when he did, most of them could barely boil water. Women were only good for a couple of things. Once he fucked them dry and they couldn't cook, wasn't much use of keeping them around. Of course, by the time he got through with them, they barely knew their own name, much less what to do in a kitchen.

Holding a plate of scrambled eggs, crisp bacon, and fluffy biscuits in one hand and a mug of coffee in the other, Mitch headed back to the living room. Eating a delicious breakfast while looking at his unconscious brother tied up on the floor. Things don't get much better than that.

As he buttered his third biscuit, a memory kicked at him that he hadn't had in years. His mother had always buttered his biscuit before she put it on his plate. He'd never really had anything against his mother. In fact, had kind of liked her until the day she'd found him putting a baby rattlesnake in his brother's underwear drawer and had smacked him on the ass.

He'd never forgiven her for that. It'd just been a prank. No, the smack hadn't hurt. It was the principle of the thing. Hell, he'd told his daddy what he was going to do and his daddy had laughed.

Mitch came to a hard conclusion that day. His mother favored Michael over him. Though he was only seven at the time, he never forgot the incident and never forgave his mother for loving his stupid brother more than him.

A growling moan pulled Mitchell back to the present. Little brother was waking up.

The second Noah opened his eyes, full realization hit him almost as hard as the board Mitch had used on his head. He had screwed up royally. The numbness in his hands and feet, along with a severe cramp in his shoulders, told him he was so far up shit creek that a paddle and seventeen-foot boat with a propeller wouldn't even help.

The knowledge of his stupidity didn't bother him. It was the realization that if he didn't get out of this soon, Samara would pay the price for his idiocy.

A foot kicked at his shoulder. "Come on, Michael. Wake up so we can talk about old times."

"Fuck off."

"Bro, I'm crushed. It's been almost six months since we've seen each other."

"Yeah and sixty years wouldn't be enough."

His brother let out a harsh chuckle, followed by a loud belch. "Yep, feel the same way."

"Then why are you here?"

"You know better than to ask me that question. You screwed me over. Nobody does that to Mitchell Stoddard and lives to tell about it."

"Kind of chickenshit of you to tie me up, isn't it?"

The grim set to Mitch's mouth and the tense silence that followed told him he'd scored a blow. More of that was needed.

"You've always been a little afraid of me, haven't you, Mitch."

The knife pressed against his neck told him his brother was even more pissed than what he thought.

"I could just gut you right here, right now, and get it over with. Wouldn't that be a pretty sight for your little whore to see?"

"Yeah, that'd be just like you. Kill me while I'm tied up, can't defend myself. Then go after a woman who's a third your weight. Good thing Daddy's dead. He'd probably puke shit on you."

A low feral howl was Noah's only warning before something cracked against his head and darkness descended once more.

The garage door opened in a grinding squeak. Samara fought a yawn as she pulled her car inside. Three days at a beautiful beach and she was exhausted. Going away had done nothing but allow her to cry and grieve in a different part of the state. Heartache went with you, no matter where you went. Noah would be there forever.

She grabbed her cellphone from the seat beside her and pulled her duffel from the back. First priority would be to get her cellphone charged. She couldn't believe she'd gone off without her charger. Another indication of how upset she'd been. Her family had teased her for years about her meticulous habits. She had a routine and she rarely deviated. Her cellphone charger should have gone into her little electrical case she always carried around with her. She'd left both the case and charger at home.

Pushing open the door, she entered her kitchen and then skidded to a halt as alarm roared through her. Someone had been in her house. A half pot of coffee sat in the glass carafe, a used frying pan was on the stove. Two things she never would have left.

With slow, easy movements, she dropped her duffel soundlessly onto the floor and pulled her purse around in front of her. Easing her hand into the bag, she pulled out her gun. Backing out slowly, a soft, distant noise from the back of the house sounded. Stay and fight or go for help? Making the easy and right choice, she continued to back toward the door. Her eye caught sight of something in the living room before she could close the door. A man, tied up on the floor. Furious black eyes flared in warning. *Noah.*

All thoughts of leaving vanished. Her gun in front of her, she dashed into the living room. "Noah . . . my God."

"Get out of here. Run, Mara. Mitch is in the bathroom. Run. Dammit."

Tugging on the tightly knotted ropes, she shook her head. "I'm not leaving—"

"There's no time to argue. Run, baby. Please."

Realizing she'd never get him loose without something to cut the rope, she said, "I'll go get—"

"Well. Well. Well. Looks like we got ourselves a little reunion."

Jerking back, she looked up into the eyes of a monster she still had nightmares about. Mitchell Stoddard stood at the entrance of her living room. Wearing the evil grin she remembered all too well, he held a wicked-looking gun in his hand, one that looked eerily similar to the gun he'd used months ago to blast one of his men's head off.

Scooting around to hide Noah as much as she could, she glared up at what she could honestly call "the evil twin." "What the hell are you doing here?"

"Now is that any way to greet an old friend? After all, we almost bumped uglies a few months back."

"You mean, you almost raped me."

The grin grew larger. "Tomato, to-mah-to."

She'd laid her gun in front of Noah when she'd tried to untie him. It was behind her. Where? Her eyes on Mitchell, she moved her hand behind her, searching.

"To your left."

Noah's almost soundless whisper directing her, she moved left. Her heartbeat zoomed as her fingers touched the cool steel. Needing to move just a couple of inches over, she tried to cover her actions by getting him to talk.

"How did you get out?"

"Does it really matter?"

"Mara . . . Shoot. To. Kill." Another whisper reached her ears.

"Just wondering who we need to go after once we get rid of your fat ass." She scooted closer to the gun.

A guffaw sputtered from him. "Damn, girl. I'm really going to enjoy shutting that pretty mouth up."

Wrapping her hand firmly around the gun, she pulled it in front of her and pointed it directly at Mitchell's face. "How about I shut yours up first?"

If he lived to be a hundred or died in the next minute, Noah knew he'd take those words with him, said in the calmest, coldest tone he'd ever heard from her. He'd never been more proud of anyone. Now if she could just go through with it.

The long silence that followed her statement told Noah that his brother was shocked to have a gun pointing at him. He stretched his neck, trying to see around Samara.

"By the time you shoot me with that little peashooter, I'll have ten holes into Michael."

"Why should that bother me?"

Mitch answered with a blast of a gun. Agony seared Noah's right thigh. He heard Mara's soft sob. Then another gunshot.

"Bitch! You shot me!"

Noah heard a hard thud—Mitch was down. But for how long?

"Mara, are you all right?"

"Am I all right? Are you all right? You're the one who's been shot."

"I'm fine. Listen, sweetheart. There's a knife strapped to my left ankle. Can you get it?"

Noah felt her lift the material of his pants and pull the knife from its sheath. Within seconds, she was applying it to the rope. He felt the loosening and then heard her gasp.

"Fucking. Bitch!"

Suddenly she was gone. Noah watched her small body fly through the air. Crashing against the wall, she dropped to the floor and didn't move.

"Mitch . . . dammit. I'm the one you hate. The one you want to kill. Why the hell are you torturing her?"

"Because, brother, she cares about you. You think I didn't see through her act?"

Wiggling and straining as unobtrusively as possible, Noah fought against the loosening rope. Just a couple more inches and he'd be free.

"You know you'll never get away with this. People are looking everywhere for you."

"I won't have to worry about that, bro. That's the one advantage of looking like you. After I kill you, I'll just assume the role of Michael Stoddard. There's not a person in this world who can tell the difference between us."

Despite the dire circumstances, Noah couldn't help but laugh. "You stupid idiot. You really think you could pass yourself off as me?"

"Damn straight," came the cocky answer.

In flawless French, Noah asked, "You don't get it, do you, fuck-face?"

"What the hell are you saying?"

"You stupid prick. You have no idea what I'm saying. How the hell do you think you're going to pass as me?"

"Shut up!"

Noah reverted back to English. "You have no idea who I am, do you?"

Mitch stood over him and aimed the gun at his head. "You're my soon-to-be-dead brother."

"I'm also Noah McCall. Founder and head of Last Chance Rescue. I live in Paris, France . . . where, unfortunately for you, most people speak French."

Shock reverberated through Mitch. *No. Fucking. Way.* His muttered words, "You're lying," sounded weak even to him.

"Think so?" A smug smile curled up Noah's mouth.

He was tired of this shit. It didn't matter who Michael Stoddard had become. In a second, he'd be just another dead bastard. Raising his arm, Mitch pointed his gun at his brother's head. "You're fucked, whoever the hell—" A screeching cry was his only warning. A small body jumped at him and latched on to his back. With a roar, Mitch swung at the woman hanging on to him, beating at her with his gun. With a soft whimper, she slumped from his shoulder and thudded to the floor. He barely registered that before he felt a whoosh of air and Michael slammed into him.

Whirling around, Mitch threw Michael off and raised his gun. The woman came at him again, and this time he felt something sharp jab into his side. *Dammit, she'd stabbed him.* With a roar, he swung his arm and batted at her, knocking her back against a table. This time she didn't move.

His arm and side screaming from a bullet and a

knife wound, Mitch turned back to his brother. One down, another one to go. Raising his gun once more, he . . . *bam!* Agony seared his gut. He caught the determined look in Michael's eyes right before another quick flash of agony pierced his head and then nothing . . .

Between Mitch's last breath and Noah's next gasp, he began to pray. Crawling, scrambling on the floor, Noah rushed toward Samara. He'd heard the crack when she fell. *God . . . Oh God* repeated over and over again. Prayerful words he hadn't said since before his mother left scattered through his mind like fragmented pieces of silver.

Halfway there, the front door burst open. A masculine voice yelled, "Stop!"

Noah ignored the command. The sheer need to get to Samara overrode everything.

"Down on the floor!"

A foot slammed into his back, forcing him down. "I said stop!"

His face flat against the hardwood, he strained to see what was happening. Two people ran toward the small, still body in the corner.

Agony and anger exploded. He had to get to her. Had to save her. "Don't touch her!" he roared. "Don't. Fucking. Touch. Her."

The foot pressed hard on his back. "Shut up."

"Let him up," another voice ordered.

The foot eased and Noah looked at no one other than Samara. He scrambled toward her again, ignoring everything around him.

Paramedics were checking her vital signs. Black silky hair covered her face, preventing him from seeing her.

Finally, he reached her feet and touched her. "Mara." The groan sounded inhuman and tortured.

"She's breathing." The words, said by one paramedic to the other, were the most precious ones he'd ever heard.

"Noah?"

"Lie still, miss. You might have a fracture or concussion."

"Need to see Noah." The husky voice, thick with tears, repeated, "Noah."

Due to the lump the size of Alabama in Noah's throat, swallowing was almost impossible. He managed to croak, "I'm here, baby."

Despite the paramedic's warnings, she raised her head and actually grinned. "You're alive."

Control shattered. Crawling toward her, ignoring the soft cursing of the paramedics he pushed out of the way, Noah gathered her in his arms and held her to his chest. Shuddering with emotions he didn't know existed, he closed his eyes and rocked her in his arms.

How long they sat there, he had no idea. When a hand settled on his shoulder, he looked up into the eyes of the young officer he'd met earlier. The compassion and sympathy on the man's face might have bothered him at one time, but no longer. Samara was alive. There was nothing more important to him than that.

"Sir, we need to take both you and Ms. Lyons to the hospital."

Unable to let go of the woman clinging so tightly to him, he jerked his head over to the people gathered around his brother. "He's dead." It wasn't a question. The second shot he made . . . right between his brother's eyes . . . had done the job.

"Yeah, he's dead. Let's get you and Ms. Lyons to a hospital. Then we'll need a statement from you both."

His arms still tight around her, Samara was the one

to pull away. Tears pooled in her eyes, dripped down her cheeks, but a tremulous smile lifted her mouth. "You rescued me again."

A breath hitched and gasped in his throat as he tried to pull himself from the emotional whirlpool sucking him down. How like Samara to miss the true facts. "No, this time . . . you rescued me."

twenty-two

Groggy and confused, Samara reached out to Noah and felt a cool, bare place. A soft sob built in her chest, escaped and echoed in the empty room. Her heart once more crashed and burned. This time, the heartbreak wasn't for her, but for Noah. The pain on his face, the agony in his eyes . . . those were images she would never forget.

After being checked out at the hospital and giving their statement to the police, they'd come to a hotel. Her house was a crime scene. Not that either one of them had wanted to go back to it anytime soon.

They should have stayed at the hospital. Noah had a bullet wound in his thigh and a concussion. The bullet was removed and only a few stitches were required. The concussion was more serious, but once Noah learned that her injuries consisted of only a few bruises and a lump on her head, he insisted they leave.

They'd checked into a hotel, hung up a do-not-disturb sign, and fallen into each other's arms. They hadn't kissed, hadn't even talked. After visiting the bathroom, she'd stripped naked and gotten into bed. Noah had come into the room wearing only his underwear. He'd slid under the covers with her, opened his arms, and she'd slipped into them. He'd held her through the night. And then left her sometime this morning, without a word.

Another sob built in her chest that she swallowed

back. God, how stupid she'd been. Ms. Invincible. Ms. Independent. Railing against him for wanting to protect her, to keep her safe. She'd called him manipulative and arrogant, and he'd taken it all . . . as if he'd deserved the condemnation.

Now, with eyes wide open and filled with the knowledge of what she'd done, she could only wonder why he hadn't just told her to go to hell and walked away from her. Of course, he wouldn't do that for one very important reason—he was in love with her.

Never had she seen love more clearly than she'd seen it last night. When he thought she was hurt, Noah would have fought hell's own demons to save her. Yes, because he was that heroic, but also because no matter how much he denied it, he really and truly loved her.

Only after the horror had passed, and he'd saved her from Mitchell once again, did he show his true self. Noah McCall, her hero, with the heart of a lion, had a meltdown in her arms. The shudders and convulsions she felt had come from him, not her. Soft words, prayers, and curses . . . all from his mouth. The strongest and bravest man she'd ever known had fallen apart because of his fear for her. She would never doubt his love again.

Samara rolled out of bed and sat on the edge, wincing only slightly at the aches and bruises of yesterday. Her toes curled into the plush carpet as she contemplated her future. More than anything, she wanted to go to Noah. Wanted to tell him she knew he loved her and to not be afraid. But he would have to come to that decision and realization on his own. She'd told him of her love time and again. He knew her feelings and her heart . . . now he needed to come to terms with his own.

Please God, let him do it. And please, let it be soon.

Noah dialed the number, alternately looking forward to and dreading the call. The phone was answered on the first ring. "Hey squirt, where's your mama?"

"Hey, Uncle Michael, Mom's out back with Daddy and Matt. I'll go get her."

"Before you go, anything in particular you want for your birthday?"

She giggled, as only a little girl can. "Surprise me."

Seconds later, another female voice answered. Older, but as familiar to him now as it was sixteen years ago when he'd heard it the first time. "Michael?"

"He's dead, Becca."

Though thousands of miles away, he could hear the small soft sob as if she were right next to him.

"I knew something had happened. Kevin has kept me away from the television and radio with all sorts of excuses."

"I'm glad you didn't hear about it that way."

"So it's finally over."

"Yes."

"I'll tell Mom and Dad. They'll want to know."

"Are you all right?"

"Yes. When he went to jail, I always wondered if that would be the end of it."

"It should have been, but Mitch had other plans. He escaped a few days ago."

"You killed him."

"Yes."

"I'm sorry it had to be you."

He wished he had done it sooner. He wished . . . God, he wished it had never needed to happen.

"Matt doing okay?"

"Yes. Looking more like a Stoddard every day."

"I'm sorry."

"Don't be. He looks just like a boy I once had a crush on years ago."

He had to smile. Rebecca had adjusted much better than he had. "I have to go, Becca."

"Thank you, Michael. For everything."

Noah hung up before he told her again how sorry he was. Rebecca wouldn't want to hear another apology. Only after he'd been released from prison had he learned about the pregnancy that had resulted from the rape. Despite Rebecca's insistence that he didn't owe her anything and her parents' disdain, he'd done what he could to help her.

Still a teenager, she'd had a three-year-old son to raise and support. She lived with her parents and her mother kept the baby while Rebecca worked and went to college. Noah had very little money back then, but what he did have, he sent to Rebecca. At first, she'd sent it back, but after a while, he convinced her to keep it. Telling her, if nothing else, she could use it for her son's future education.

As the years went by, his income increased and he was able to help her more. Despite the fact that Rebecca had convinced her parents Noah hadn't committed the rape, they had understandably hated his entire family, including him. He'd respected their wishes and never tried to visit Rebecca or his nephew while she was living with them. After Rebecca was able to afford her own place, he made a special trip to go see them.

Matthew, Rebecca's son, thought his father had died in a car wreck when he was an infant. He knew Noah as Uncle Michael, his father's twin brother. When Matthew was seven, Rebecca met and fell in love with Kevin Patterson, an insurance agent from

San Francisco. Loving, hardworking, and steady as a rock. That had been the first time Noah had felt the slightest loosening of his interminable guilt. To know that Rebecca had moved on with her life was a great comfort.

Rebecca and Kevin now had three children: Matthew, Emily, and Tyler. And now that Mitchell Stoddard was finally dead, hopefully Rebecca would be able to put all of her grief behind her, once and for all.

Would he ever be able to do the same?

How stupid and pompous he'd been. It had been his problem all along. Standing, Noah turned toward the window of his office. Paris blazed with light and life, but he saw only the darkness in his soul. He'd convinced himself Samara wasn't cut out for this kind of work, that she was too weak, too delicate. He'd derided her efforts and stymied them when he could. Arrogance blinded him to the truth. It had been his weakness not to see her strength. She *could* handle this kind of life. She was strong, gutsy, brave, and resilient. Everything he looked for in an LCR operative.

So now he had a choice to make. He'd wanted to keep her safe, away from any kind of danger. But he owed her this opportunity, if she wanted it. She'd asked him before and he refused, believing her too inexperienced and innocent. Those reasons didn't apply now . . . probably never had.

The way she'd fought Mitchell, not just for herself but for him. She had saved his life.

But how would he handle her working as an LCR operative, putting her life at risk? Could he give her a choice? A life with him or an operative? No, he wanted a life with her and if she chose to work with LCR, that had to be her decision. One he'd have to live with, because God knew—and now so did Noah—he couldn't live without Samara in his life. No matter

what choice she made, he had to offer it to her. She'd
earned it.

"You look like crap."

Noah looked up from his desk as Eden stalked into
his office, determination stamped on her face. Two
weeks of frozen indecision had done nothing but
make him more miserable. Now, if he wasn't mis-
taken, Eden had come to administer a lecture.

"Thank you, Eden. Is there another reason for your
presence in my office other than to give me an update
on my looks?"

"I talked to Samara last night."

"How is she?"

She crossed the room at such a leisurely pace, he
knew she was doing it only to irritate him. He held
his temper. When she sat in the chair in front of his
desk, crossed her legs, and examined her manicure,
he lost it. "Dammit, how is she?"

An arrogantly arched brow was her only acknowledgment of his anger. "Hurt. Lonely. Confused. You
know, the typical things one feels with a broken heart."

He ignored the jab. "She say anything about nightmares? Is she sleeping okay? Are her bruises bothering—" He broke off when she waved her hand at
him. "What?"

"Why don't you ask her yourself?"

"Drop it, Eden."

"You know, Noah, I don't know about your past,
other than what you've told me, but I figure it was as
bad as mine. Maybe worse."

When he didn't reply, she blew out an exasperated
sigh and continued, "You forced me to face my past,
and I'm profoundly grateful you did, since I wouldn't
have Jordan."

"Is there a point to this?"

"I know you believe there's an afterlife and I truly hope there is, because this one can suck for a lot of people, but just because you believe there's a better one waiting, does that preclude being happy in this one?"

"What the hell are you talking about?"

"You know exactly what I'm talking about, Noah. There's a woman in Birmingham, Alabama, who loves you with every fiber of her being. She's beautiful, smart, talented, and so damned sweet, she makes my teeth hurt, but I can't help but like her. Why don't you—"

Dammit, he didn't need this. "Drop it or get out."

"No, I won't drop it. You've interfered in every person's life at LCR and it's about damn time someone interfered in yours. Why can't you have a future with Samara?"

"She wants to be an operative."

"So?"

"Her life would be in danger."

"So basically you're making the decision for her? Have you even asked her?"

"No."

"Noah, I think you're seeing a very narrowed view of LCR. Samara is a trained counselor. Almost every operative you bring in requires some sort of counseling. . . . God knows I did. Why couldn't you ask her to work with LCR in that capacity?"

He stared hard at her. "Do you think she'd be happy with that?"

"Don't you think you owe her an opportunity to make a choice?"

That's what he'd been agonizing over for days. Give her a choice. What if she chose to be an operative? He wouldn't know until he asked. Whatever she chose, he had to give her the opportunity. And he had to live with the consequences.

Another agony throbbed at him, less dangerous, but still an important issue. "She wants children."

Eden's arched brows told him he'd shocked her. "And that's a problem . . . why?"

"I had a vasectomy years ago."

"So? Those things are reversible."

"You've seen what's in my blood . . . what I came from. What if—"

The woman in front of him jumped to her feet and Noah knew he was in for the lecture of his life. Rarely had he seen the cool, composed Eden as furious as she appeared to be now.

"You know my mother, know what kind of person she is. . . . Do you think I'm like her, at all?"

"Of course not."

"Then why in the hell would you assume your children would be bad?" Eden wrapped her arms around herself and Noah felt lower than a slug when he saw the tears sparkling in her eyes. He knew what she was going to say and she had every right to be furious with him.

"I would love to be able to give life to a child. Having Jordan's baby would be the fulfillment of all my dreams, but that will never happen. But if it were possible, my child would have the best of Jordan and me. My mother would have no impact. For you to assume your child would be tainted is stupid, arrogant, and excuse me, downright backward."

Something loosened inside him as her words dented, then penetrated, his long-held beliefs. His father had had two sons. The one he'd favored, he trained to be just like him. Noah knew he was more like his mother, a woman who'd been everything good. Though he was far from perfect, he also knew he had a lot more in common with his mother than with his father.

"I'm sorry, Eden. I didn't mean to remind you of your pain."

Tears still glistened in her eyes, but her smile was one of pure happiness. "Having Jordan is more than I ever thought I'd have. I'm not angry about my past, I'm angry at you for being so stupid."

Swallowing a snort of surprised laughter, Noah nodded. "You're right." He took a deep, cleansing breath and nodded at the thin file she'd put on his desk. "Tell me about the Mallory case."

Her eyes narrowed into a hard glare, but she did as he asked.

Noah listened with one ear, as his mind thrummed and processed questions and possibilities.

A hand waved in front of Noah's face. "All this rescue stuff boring you?"

Noah shook his head. "I heard every word you said. David Mallory believes his mother was forced to go to this, what did he call it . . . hedonistic island . . . and wants LCR to find her and rescue her, if need be."

"Yes. Jordan and I believe Mrs. Mallory went willingly."

"The son know that?"

"Yes. He says if that's so, then okay, he'll try to accept it." She laughed. "I think his biggest problem is knowing his mother is having sex at what he called her advanced age."

"How old is she?"

"Fifty-five." Eden rolled her eyes. "Anyway, we'll go in, play the married couple, which we do really well anyway. If Mrs. Mallory seems distressed at all, we'll act, if not, we'll have a few fun days and come back home."

"Samara's good at reading people, isn't she?"

"Yes, why—" A delighted smile spread across her

face. "She's excellent at figuring out nuances and reading between the lines."

Noah stood and walked toward the door. "Have Angela change your information over to mine and Samara's."

"It's a married-only island. You'll have to show your marriage license as proof."

"That won't be a problem." Knowledge and acceptance spread through him like warm, silken honey.

Eden gave a whoop of delighted laughter as he closed the door on her.

He headed back to his desk to clear up some loose ends while his mind wrangled with his weighty problem. How did one convince a woman to marry him without revealing how desperate he was for that to take place?

twenty-three

"Sam, you've barely eaten anything. Don't you like Mexican anymore?"

Samara swirled a chip into the salsa in front of her without any intention of eating it. "Just not in the mood for it tonight."

"This is the first time you've been at Mama's in forever. I even told Allie and Julie we weren't meeting because I thought we could do a girl chat thing like we used to. You've been out of touch for so long, I don't feel I know you and now that we're together, I can't get two words out of you."

"I'm sorry, Rach. I haven't been much of a friend lately."

Rachel touched her arm. "You'll always be my friend, Sam. You know that. But there's something going on with you. It's like there's no light in you anymore."

Samara looked down at her plate of nachos. Rachel's words rang so true. She did feel as though the light was gone from her life and she hated that feeling. She wasn't a weepy, woe-is-me kind of person. If something bothered her, she either fixed it or said to hell with it. She didn't dwell on it and mope. Since Noah had left, that's exactly what she'd done.

She'd even gone to her parents right after Noah left. She couldn't return to her house for another week and didn't want to stay in a hotel. She could have stayed with Rachel, but since her friend didn't know what had happened, needing a place to stay would have been hard to explain.

Besides, as vulnerable and emotional as she'd been, she had hoped some TLC from her family would help. It had a little. Being the baby of the family always brought out everyone's protective instincts and though she usually resisted their smothering, she had needed it for a few days.

Though none of them knew what she had gone through and never would, they all seemed to sense her need. They knew about her relationship with Noah Stoddard, rather the lack of a relationship. Last Christmas, she'd spilled her guts to her mother . . . giving only select information, of course. Her entire family knew she'd fallen in love with a man and for some reason it hadn't worked out.

Going back home this time, she hadn't mentioned Noah and neither had they. Which was fortunate, since she was pretty sure she'd turn into a sobbing mess. Having her family worry about her more than they already did wasn't something she wanted. Just having their love and support was enough.

After a few days, she realized it was time to go home. No matter how much babying her family gave her, she wasn't a baby. It was time for her to go home and be strong. . . . She hoped to hell that strength hit her soon.

She kept thinking Noah would come back or at least call her. Nothing. No calls, no messages . . . not even an email. Though today, she'd received an incredibly odd email from Eden.

Rachel's voice penetrated her painful musings. "Sam, talk to me. Tell me what's wrong."

Samara blurted out the truth. "I found the man I want to marry."

"Oh heavens, not again. What commercial did you see this time?"

"No commercial."

"Well then, a book, movie . . . what?"

"Nope."

"Okay, I'll play along. What wonderful qualities does he have?"

Swallowing a laughing sob, Samara described the love of her life. "He's stubborn, rude, quite often a jerk, arrogant, frustrating, heroic, incredibly gorgeous . . . the most amazing man . . . and he's . . ." Samara's eyes widened, her body froze with shock. "Oh my . . ."

"What?"

"He's staring straight at me."

Rachel looked around. "Who?"

"The man I want to marry."

"You mean he's real?"

Unable to take her eyes off the man walking slowly toward her, Samara answered, "As real as they get."

Noah stood before her, looking more wonderful, more handsome, than she remembered. Why he was here suddenly didn't matter. What mattered was that he was here.

Black eyes gleamed down at her with a mixture of tenderness, possessiveness, and perhaps a hint of nervousness. "Mind if I sit down?"

"Not at all," Rachel said.

He held his hand out to Rachel. "Noah Stoddard and you're Rachel Enders. Mara's told me a lot about you."

Rachel grinned at them both. "Well, I think she was just about to tell me about you. But I've got a feeling she wants to have a little chat with you." Rachel stood and kissed Samara on the cheek. "Call me." She turned to Noah. "It was nice to meet you, Noah. I hope to see you again soon."

Samara couldn't take her eyes from Noah. He looked different. Younger somehow. Her heartbeat picked up. "What are you doing here?"

"I need your help."

Optimism and her heart raced together to splatter on the floor. *Not again.* "For what?"

"I need you for a job."

Fighting a hurt so large she could barely breathe, Samara grabbed her purse and stood. "Thanks, but I'm no longer in that line of work."

"Mara . . . please."

His voice, more than his words, stopped her. He sounded shaky and almost desperate. Eden's strange, obscure email flashed into her mind and began to make sense. *Don't let pride blind you to what's in front of you.*

She dropped back to her seat. "What's the job?"

A tiny flicker of what looked like relief flashed across his face. "We've been hired to find a woman at a resort. Her son thinks she was coerced into going. We're to locate her and determine if she needs help. If she does, we'll get her out. If not, we'll let her son know she's okay."

"And that's it?"

Noah nodded.

"Why can't another LCR operative do this?"

"It requires certain qualifications."

"Such as . . . ?"

"It's a resort for married people only."

Emotions whipped like small whirling tornadoes inside her. She bit her trembling lips. "No one else wanted to pretend to be married to you?"

His eyes locked with hers, he shook his head slowly. "Can't be a pretend marriage. They check the records."

LCR could produce a fake marriage license within

minutes. Noah knew she knew this and she could see he was waiting for her to call his bluff. She wouldn't. This man, in his own oddly incredible, wonderful way, was asking her to marry him and she was going to do it.

"Well, I guess that doesn't leave us much choice, does it?"

"No. Are you ready to go?"

"To my house?"

"The airport. I've got a plane waiting to take us to the island."

"What about my clothes . . . and don't we have to get married before we get there?"

"I've got clothes for you already and we'll get married on the plane."

"On the plane?"

"Yes." His eyes gleamed. "Every second counts."

Samara grabbed her purse and held out her hand. "Then what are we waiting for?"

Things had gone better than he could have expected. The smile playing around Samara's beautiful mouth and the brightness and joy in her eyes told him more than any words. Though spontaneity hadn't been part of his life since he was a kid, he had to admit he was enjoying it, too. Was it the most romantic way to get a woman to marry him? No, but romance would have to wait. The most important thing was to get them married, then he'd work on the other. A desperate man often resorted to desperate measures and Noah had realized that when it came to Samara, he had passed the desperation point.

The moment they stepped onto the plane and the door slammed shut, Noah let go of the massive tension he'd been holding inside. At any moment on the drive over, he'd expected her to tell him to stop and demand an explanation. He wasn't prepared for that yet. At some point, he would explain his actions. After they exchanged vows and he knew she was his, then they'd talk.

He held her hand tight as he pulled her down the narrow aisleway of the plane. "Come with me. I have something for you."

Twisting and turning to check out the jet, she followed him into the small bedroom. "Uh, don't you think we should get married first?"

Noah swallowed a laugh. "As cute as you look in your jeans and T-shirt, I thought you might want to wear something else." He opened a closet and withdrew a sequined white satin dress. The moment he had seen it, he knew it was made for Samara.

"Oh, Noah."

Her sighing words told him she agreed.

"There are things in the bathroom you might need . . . girlie things Eden said a bride would want."

She peeked inside and gave an excited laugh. A smiling Eden stood in the small room, dressed in a short silver dress, holding a bouquet of flowers for the bride. Turning, her face beaming with delight, Samara whispered, "Give me half an hour and I'll be beautiful for you."

Pulling her to him, he growled against her mouth, "You're beautiful just the way you are." He kissed her hard and then pulled away. "Eden said you'd want this . . ."

Standing on her tiptoes, she kissed him softly. "She was right."

Forty-five minutes later, Noah, dressed in a black tuxedo, stood beside the most breathtaking woman in the world. The dress fit perfectly, molding and caressing every curve. She'd left her hair down, and the contrast between her midnight fall of hair and the stark white brilliance of her dress stunned him into speechlessness.

Thankfully the minister he'd brought with him spoke English. Having to translate, when he could barely remember his name, would have been impossible.

Jordan stood beside Noah, beaming at them both as if he were a proud parent. Eden stood beside Samara and surreptitiously dabbed at her wet eyes.

Reverend Jerome Gardner stood before them. "Dearly beloved, we are gathered in the sight of God to join this man and woman in holy—"

Samara raised her hand to stop him. Noah's heart stuttered.

"You know we're going to have to do this again in front of my family, don't you?"

Noah sighed. "Yeah, I know."

She smiled and then nodded to the minister to continue.

Looking a little bemused, he began again. He'd gotten to the point of "Do you, Samara Lyons" when she raised her hand again. This time a frown furrowed her brow as though she was uncomfortable.

"What's wrong?"

She leaned forward and whispered, "I want babies . . . your babies."

It was all he could do not to grab her and run straight to the bedroom. Instead he whispered, "Okay."

She still didn't look satisfied.

"What's wrong?"

"You're going to have to do something about fixing that."

"I've already made arrangements, sweetheart."

She straightened. "Really?" She looked down at his crotch. "Will it hurt?"

Reverend Gardner sputtered and blushed a purple red. Both Eden and Jordan choked back laughter.

Swallowing his own laughter, Noah said, "We'll talk about it tonight."

"Okay." She turned back to the minister and said, "Sorry . . . you were saying?"

"Yes, uh . . ." The poor man swallowed and began again, "Do you, Samara Lyons, take Noah McCall to be your—"

"You've already said that." She blew out a sigh and looked at Noah. "I take this man, the most amazing, stubborn, and wonderful man in the world to be my husband forever and ever."

Noah kissed her hand. "And I take this beautiful, exasperating, and incredibly brave woman to be my wife, forever and ever."

Reverend Gardner spit out the remaining words, most likely in an effort to get them said before he was interrupted again. "I now pronounce you man and wife."

Noah leaned down and covered Samara's mouth with his, stifling her laughter. The good reverend, flanked by Eden and Jordan, disappeared to a corner of the plane, leaving the newlyweds to continue their passionate kiss in private.

Breathless, Samara pulled away. "I love you, Noah."

Noah smiled down at his new wife. "I know."

After a brief landing to refuel and drop off their wedding guests and minister, they took off immediately. Two hours later, the plane landed on the island of Sulan. Within twenty minutes of arriving, Samara and Noah had located their client's mother and had a brief but informative conversation. They learned that she was not only now married to a younger man, but very much in love. And by all accounts, her new husband felt the same way.

As LCR cases went, it was probably the shortest on record and that was fine with Samara. She and Noah had other things on their minds.

While Samara went to their bungalow to shower, Noah stayed behind for a few minutes to chat with the newlyweds and to call their client to reassure him that his mother was fine.

Samara slid naked between the sheets just as the door clicked open and Noah stood at the entrance of their room. The naked desire in his eyes stunned her. At last he was allowing her to see everything of him. The love she felt for this man almost overwhelmed her.

"Everything okay?"

"Yep. Finally convinced David Mallory that his mother is indeed a woman in love."

"She's not the only one."

Noah leaned over her. "Give me five minutes."

Trailing a finger down the side of his face, she whispered, "I'll give you forever."

Desire flared, dark and sensuous, in his black eyes. "I'll hold you to that promise.

"Good."

Kissing her tenderly, he turned away and began to strip on his way to the bathroom. "Make that three minutes."

Exactly three minutes later, Noah returned, naked and aroused, and slid into bed. Taking her in his arms, he said softly, "Hello, wife."

"Hello, husband."

A tight, almost nervous smile played around his mouth. "This is new territory for me."

She could feel the tension in his body. "Why?"

"I have no problem talking to presidents, political leaders . . . the most powerful people in the world. With you . . ." His finger tenderly traced her brow, the bridge of her nose . . . her bottom lip. His voice thickened. "Ah Mara, with you, I'm speechless."

Tears welled in her eyes and she blinked them away, determined to help him understand that his love was safe with her. Her hand rested on his chest, right above his heart. "This was all I ever wanted from you."

"Funny . . . until you, I didn't even know I had one."

"Make love to me, Noah. Show me what you feel."

Lowering his head, his mouth trailed over her face, barely touching as he whispered, "I can express myself better in French."

Gasping at the fire igniting her blood, she arched her body toward him. "I don't know how to speak French."

His mouth grazed over hers. "I'll translate."

"Okay . . ."

With a solemnity she'd never seen in him before, he gravely gave her the words in French and then the English translation. With each phrase, her heart pounded faster.

"You are the most beautiful creature in the universe."

He punctuated each translation with a kiss.

"You returned joy to my life."

"Humanity to my soul."

"Your courage amazes me."

"Your love humbles me."

Pulling her under him, he locked his gaze with hers as he pushed inside her. "With my body, I thee worship."

Her legs wrapped around his waist, she took him inside her body, glorying in the rightness and sheer beauty of the moment. With a fierce tenderness, Noah made love to her as if this were the first time he'd touched her. His hands glided over her body, tenderly caressing, trailing fire wherever he touched.

Arching to meet every thrust, her groans of desire and need turned to gasping cries of fulfillment.

As he gazed down at his exhausted but smiling wife, Noah knew he'd never been given a greater gift. Samara was more than he ever could have asked for, could ever deserve. Cradling her to his newly discovered heart, for the first time in his life, he knew true peace.

Closing his eyes, he drew in a breath. There was one last issue he faced. He'd made a promise to himself and he intended to keep it. He, who'd risked his life on almost a daily basis for years, was suddenly terrified. But she'd given him so much and he had to give her this. She deserved to live as she wanted. She'd earned the opportunity and he loved her enough to make the offer. No matter what, if Samara was happy, he would be happy. And no matter what, he would keep her safe. He would never fail her again.

"Mara"—he winced at how his voice shook—"if you'd like to be an LCR operative, I think you'd make a damn good one."

When her eyes brightened, the knots in his stomach twisted harder. He'd made the offer, fully intended to keep his word. That didn't mean he had to like it.

Pulling his head down, she kissed him softly on the lips. "Thank you for that, darling, but putting myself in danger was never a turn-on for me. What I wanted more than anything was the ability to see that I made a difference."

"What are you saying?"

"I'm saying that I'm glad you realize I could be a 'damn good' operative, and I would have considered it at one time . . . but that's not really something I want anymore."

Profound relief didn't come close to the emotion zooming through him. "Would you consider working for LCR in a different capacity?"

"Like what?"

"As a counselor? I usually bring in outside people but having an in-house counselor would make more sense."

"I would love to do counseling work for LCR."

Noah gazed down at the beautiful, courageous woman in his arms. Samara had not only returned his humanity to him, she'd returned his heart. He blew out a harsh breath and offered one more phrase in French. One that he'd never offered to anyone, in any language. *"Je t'aime."* And then the English translation. "I love you."

Offering a smile, bright enough to lighten the darkest of hearts, she whispered, "I know."

Acknowledgments

I would like to thank the following people:

The Romance Writers of America's Kiss of Death chapter, who were so generous in answering numerous email questions on the Clues-and-News loop, and Southern Magic, my home chapter, for their friendship and continued support.

Danny Agan, who patiently answered my endless questions.

Darah Lace, friend and favorite brainstormer, who asked one critical question that made all the difference.

And thanks to fellow writers and friends Jennifer Echols, Kelly St. John, Carla Swafford, Marie Campbell, and Erin McClune for always being there when I needed them most.

My sister Denise, my first reader for every book, and my sister Debra and my mom, who are always ready to lend a willing ear. And my husband, Jim, for the plotting suggestions that gave me much-needed comic relief.

My fantastic editor, Kate Collins, and the entire Ballantine team, for their excitement and support of this project. And Kimberly Whalen, my incredible agent, who made me cry when she called and told me how much she loved this book.

Turn the page to catch an
exclusive sneak peek at

RUN TO ME

the third novel in Christy Reece's romantic
suspense trilogy!

**Coming in June 2009 from Ballantine Books.
Available wherever books are sold.**

Three Months Later
Last Chance Rescue Headquarters
Paris, France

"You're sure it's her?"

"Yeah. She doesn't even bother to disguise her appearance."

Noah McCall shot from his chair and faced the window behind his desk. "I can't believe she'd betray LCR. Nothing in her profile indicated this thread of evil inside her."

Gabriel Maddox stayed seated as he watched the head of LCR flounder for an answer. Seeing Noah show emotion no longer surprised him, but the changes in his boss were still fascinating. Before McCall met and married his wife, Samara, Gabe would have sworn that nothing other than God himself could have forced an honest emotion from the man. But in the months since he'd been married, Noah had done a complete about-face. Oh, he could still be a coldhearted bastard and no one dared cross him, but Gabe had heard him laugh on more than one occasion, and last month, when he announced that Samara was pregnant, damned if the man hadn't blushed.

"How many abductions has she been involved in?"

"We're sure of two," Gabe said.

"I could have sworn she was about the straightest arrow LCR ever hired."

Not a patient man by nature, Gabe knew better than to rush his boss in making a decision. Especially as hard as this one would likely be. Didn't take a genius to know that the former LCR operative known as Shea Monroe would have to be dealt with, possibly taken out.

This decision wouldn't be easy for McCall. He'd hired and trained every LCR operative since its beginning. Some of the younger ones called him Pop behind his back, though it was always said with an enormous amount of respect and even affection. Noah McCall had saved every one of their worthless hides and turned them into something. They might sometimes resent the tough restrictions he placed on them, but not one of them would speak against him.

Still, when an LCR operative went rogue, it affected everyone. Taking Shea down wouldn't be enjoyable, but it might well be necessary.

McCall dropped back into his chair. "Anyone talked to Ethan lately?"

It sounded like a casual question. Gabe knew differently. Noah McCall didn't ask casual questions. Ethan Bishop had left LCR under a dark cloud. Few people knew the full reason for his dismissal, but speculation that he'd become a loose cannon was the number-one theory. Gabe knew this speculation was correct.

"I talked to him a few months back," Gabe said.

"So he doesn't know about Shea?"

Gabe felt a slight nudge of guilt. "Didn't see the need to tell him. When she went missing, we assumed she disappeared on purpose. Since Cole's death, Shea's not been at her best. Telling Ethan wouldn't have accomplished anything other than making him feel more like shit than he already does."

Noah turned his dark eyes on him and Gabe suddenly felt like an insect about to be skewered.

"And now that we know she's working for the organization that killed her husband, you don't think that's something he'd be interested in learning?"

The answer Gabe gave was so lame, he inwardly winced as he said it. "Ethan doesn't work for LCR any longer."

McCall continued that black-eyed stare. "You want me to tell him?" His voice softened, which meant only one thing—he was about to lose his temper.

Drawing a deep breath, Gabe gave the answer he didn't want to give. "No, I'll tell him." He shot his boss a narrow-eyed glare. "You know he'll go after her, don't you?"

"Of course."

"Then why?"

"Because despite the evidence, I think Shea's worth saving. There's no one in the world better able to see Shea for what she is. If she's turned, Ethan'll know what he has to do. If she's in trouble, he'll bring her home."

"And if she's turned, she might just end up killing him."

An odd light flickered in McCall's eyes. "Or she might end up saving them both."

Gabe stood, knowing his boss wouldn't change his mind, no matter what objections he gave. Noah McCall was of the opinion that almost everyone had something good in them. Since he'd turned around a lot of lives, Gabe wasn't going to argue with him. But he'd seen what Shea had done to his friend. Loving a woman that much was damned dangerous. Shea had taken advantage of that love, and Ethan would never be the same man again.

Gabe stalked out the door. Bypassing the elevator, he stomped down ten floors. Ethan didn't even own a phone. The only way to reach him was to fly there. His gut plummeted. Few people knew about his problem with enclosed places . . . the fewer, the better. By the time he made it to the podunk town in the Tennessee hills where Ethan had buried himself, Gabe would be in a lousy mood. Ethan wouldn't be happy to see him and would most likely try to throw him off his property.

On the other hand, a good fight never hurt anyone. His mood lightened. Damned if he wasn't suddenly looking forward to the trip after all.

East Tennessee

The sun blasted a welcome searing heat. Sweat poured off Ethan, splattering and dimpling the dirt like slow, fat raindrops. Wiping his hand across his brow, eyes squinted against the brightness, he gazed around at the progress he'd made. After months of doing nothing but chopping down dead trees and clearing brush, he was beginning to see a small amount of progress. Yes, it would have been simpler to hire people to do this but not nearly as satisfying. This was his land. No one would care about this property as much as he did. It was his blood and sweat that would create something out of nothing. Besides, what the hell else did he have to do?

After throwing another tree limb onto the already full truck bed, Ethan jumped into the cab and started it up. One last load—then he'd shower and head to town for supplies. Once a month, he forced himself into town. He'd put it off three days longer than he should have. Out of coffee for the last day and a half, he felt like a rabid dog, on top of having a hell of a headache. The fast-food place a few miles from town would be his first stop. A giant cup of their strong brew would ease the pain. Hopefully, by the time he made it to the store he wouldn't want to kill anyone.

Under the rumble of timber slamming to the ground, he heard the quiet purr of an expensive car headed up his hill. Mercedes, maybe? Not a Jag. Whoever it was, they were lost. He was the only one who lived on this road.

His jaw clenched. He hated that he'd have to see another person on his property, even for the short amount of time it would take to get them off. His fingers combed through a week's worth of growth on his face, pushed through his shoulder-length hair, soaked with sweat. Nice thing about looking like a serial killer—most people who saw him turned around and ran the other way. Whoever was headed this way would soon do the same.

A sleek silver Mercedes rounded a corner and hit the top of the hill. The sun's glare against the windshield couldn't disguise the identity of the dark-haired man behind the wheel.

"Shit." The dull pounding in Ethan's head blasted toward jackhammer status. *Gabe Maddox.* Last time he'd talked to Gabe, he'd told him to go to hell. Looked as though he hadn't taken the advice. Figured . . . bastard was stubborn like that.

Ethan glowered at the other man, letting him know up front that he still didn't want him around. "Don't believe you were invited."

Unfolding his long body from the leather seat, Gabe flashed an arrogant grin that was so popular with the ladies and pissed most men off because of it.

"If I waited for an invitation, I'd never see you again."

"That's the idea."

"Sorry . . . I'm on orders."

"Noah sent you?" Now, that was a surprise. Last time he saw Noah McCall, the man had damned near choked him to death. Not that he hadn't deserved it, but he figured McCall would just as soon pretend that Ethan had never existed.

"Yeah." Gabe jerked his head toward the house. "Mind if we talk inside?"

"Why?"

His eyes searching the hills warily, Gabe shrugged and headed toward the log house without Ethan's consent. "Don't like being out in the open like this."

"Damned stupid, coming from a claustrophobic."

Gabe turned to glare at him but kept walking.

Ethan threw his gloves down and stalked past Gabe into the house. His home was only a few months old, but his furniture was almost as ancient as the surrounding hills. His things served their purpose, and that was all he cared about.

He tugged open the refrigerator and pulled out two beers. Tossing a bottle to Gabe, Ethan leaned against the counter, unscrewed the cap, and took a long swallow.

Easing down into a rickety chair at the scarred, aged table, Gabe swallowed a mouthful of beer and gazed around. "Nice place you got here, man."

"Thanks. I'll tell the decorator you said so. Now, what the hell do you want?"

Gabe took another swig of beer, set the bottle on the table, and blew out a long sigh.

A strange tension zipped up Ethan's spine. "Must be something major for you to take so long in answering."

"It's Shea."

The words were quietly spoken, but the impact to his heart and mind were like bombs exploding. He turned toward the kitchen window, unwilling to allow his former friend to see the naked pain. "She dead?"

"No. If only it were that simple."

Ethan turned sharply and growled. "What the hell does that mean?"

"She's gone sour."

Ethan snorted his disbelief. "Shea wouldn't turn south. I'd believe you turned before her."

"Gee, thanks for the vote of confidence." Gabe waited a beat, allowing Ethan to absorb his statement. "We've got positive intel."

"I don't give a flying fuck what you've got. Shea Monroe would never betray LCR. Not for money . . ." He shrugged. "Not for anything."

"Noah feels the same way."

"But you don't."

Gabe didn't flinch from Ethan's direct gaze. "You know Shea was never my favorite person after she and Cole married."

"Shea did the right thing by marrying Cole. But that's beside the point. Give me what you know."

"First I have to have your agreement on something."

"What?"

"Noah wants you to find her. If she's turned, you're to bring her in. If she's in trouble, he wants her rescued."

"Why me?"

"Says you're the only one who'd be able to determine if Shea has truly turned."

Crossing the room, Ethan slumped into a chair across from Gabe. Noah McCall had fired his ass for very valid reasons. He didn't blame him. Besides, he owed Noah his sanity and his life. The man knew he'd do almost anything for him. But this was Shea. And Noah knew Ethan would slay dragons and fight an army for the woman he'd once loved and lost. Yeah, McCall was right on the money to ask him to go in. No one had more to lose than Ethan if something happened to Shea.

He owed Shea Monroe a whole lot . . . more than he could ever repay. After all, not only had he broken her heart and crushed her spirit, he'd also gotten her husband killed.